Raves for
RICK RIORDAN

"In Rick Riordan's case, believe the hype.
He really is that good."
—Dennis Lehane

"Riordan writes so well about the people and
topography of his Texas hometown that he quickly
marks the territory as his own."
—*Chicago Tribune*

"Rick Riordan has a Texas-size talent for
spinning a great story."
—Tami Hoag

"There's a reason why this guy keeps
winning awards. . . . Rick Riordan is a master
stylist. I can't wait for his next."
—Harlan Coben

and for
THE DEVIL WENT DOWN
TO AUSTIN

"A blast . . . A thrilling and intelligent
detective novel—and a giant leap forward for
the Tres Navarre series."
—*The Austin Chronicle*

THE

DEVIL

WENT DOWN TO AUSTIN

RICK RIORDAN

BANTAM BOOKS
New York   Toronto   London   Sydney   Auckland

This edition contains the complete text
of the original hardcover edition.
NOT ONE WORD HAS BEEN OMITTED.

THE DEVIL WENT DOWN TO AUSTIN
A Bantam Book

PUBLISHING HISTORY

Bantam hardcover edition published June 2001
Bantam mass market edition / July 2002

Library of Congress Catalog Card Number: 00-069665

ISBN: 0-553-57994-0

Published simultaneously in the United States and Canada

PRINTED IN THE UNITED STATES OF AMERICA

OPM   10   9   8   7   6   5   4   3

To Patrick John Riordan

ACKNOWLEDGMENTS

Many thanks to Mike Hames, who taught me about Garrett; Mario Renteria, from the Austin Police Department Office of Public Education; Bill McCann, APD multimedia lab manager; Arney Carbary, APD evidence room; Curtis Weeks, public information officer for the Travis County Sheriff's Department; Travis County Deputy II Scott Schroeder, an excellent host; Lieutenant Keith Dzierzanowski, Travis County Jail; Detective Stan Roper, Travis County Homicide; Rod McCutcheon, chief toxicologist for the Travis County Medical Examiner's Office; Dennis Loockerman, director of the CODIS program for the Texas Department of Public Safety; Alan Tillman, master gunsmith; Russell Johnson, ballistics and firearms expert for the Texas DPS crime lab; Sergeant Tony Kobryn, Bexar County Sheriff's Department underwater search and recovery team; Dale Smith and Rees Haley, computer programmers extraordinaire; Claudia Huntington for investment and stock information; Jay Brandon for information on criminal law; Ken Bennett and the fine folks at Tom's Dive & Ski in Austin for the underwater research; and the online Parrot Heads who shared stories with me: Alex, Kevin Axt, Andrea Biggs, Ty Baker, Cathie, Evan Chesler, and Lisa Hagenow. Ongoing thanks to Kate Miciak and Gina Maccoby, and especially Becky, Haley, and Patrick, who make it all possible.

THE

DEVIL

WENT DOWN TO AUSTIN

Date: Wed 07 June 2000 19:53:16 -0500
From: <host@ashield.com>
X-Mailer: Mozilla 3.01 Gold (Macintosh; I; PPC)
To: <host@ashield.com>
Subject: drowning

The first time I knew I would kill? I was six years old.

I'd snuck some things from the kitchen—vials of food coloring, Dixie cups, a pitcher of water. I was in my bedroom mixing potions, watching how the dyes curl in the water.

That doesn't sound like much, I know. But I'd spilled a few cupfuls onto the carpet. My fingers were stained purple. It was enough to give the Old Man an excuse.

He came in so quietly I didn't hear him, didn't know he was standing over me until I caught his smell, like sweet smoked beef.

He said something like, "Is this what we clean the house for? We clean the house so you can do this?"

Then I realized water was running in the bathroom. I remembered what my friend had said.

I tried to apologize, but the Old Man caught my

wrists, dragged me backward, using my arms as a harness.

I kicked at the carpet and walls as he pulled me down the hallway. When we passed the bathroom door-jamb, I got one hand loose and grabbed at it, but the Old Man just yanked harder, ripping a nail off my finger.

The ceiling sparkled white. I remember bare avocado rings on the shower rod, plastic star-rivets holding up the mirror.

The Old Man lifted me, squeezed me against his chest. I was clawing, grabbing at his clothes. Then he dumped me in.

The cold stopped my blood. I floated, wet to my armpits, my clothes grafted to my chest, heavy.

I knew better than to try standing. I lay low, crying, the water nipping the backs of my ears. My mouth tasted salt.

There was a comma of blood from my ripped nail on the Old Man's shirt pocket, purple smudges from my dyed fingers on his chest.

He said, "What did you do wrong? Tell me what you were doing."

His voice sounded kindly in the tiled acoustics of the bathroom, rich and deep.

I couldn't answer. I cried.

"I don't want to hear that," he scolded. "Until you can tell me what you did, I don't want any sound from you."

I kept crying—knowing it was the wrong thing to do, but crying more because of that. So he leaned over me, pushed my chest, and the water closed over my head.

Sound turned to aluminum. I could hear my own struggling and splashing. Water lapped into the overflow drain, rushed through pipes in the walls like underground machinery.

The Old Man shimmered above me, his hand

keeping a warm, constant clamp on the middle of my chest. I clawed at his wrist, but it might as well have been a mesquite branch.

I held my breath, which is hard when you're facing up, the water flooding your nostrils, gagging you.

I tried to be still. I thought maybe if I were still, the Old Man would let go.

I studied the hazy balls of light above the sink.

My lungs burned.

And finally—the first clear decision I ever remember making—I gave up. I breathed in the water.

At that moment, as if he knew, the bastard lifted me out, rolled me onto the tiled floor.

I curled, cold and trembling, belching water, my throat on fire.

"Be grateful," he said. "Be grateful for what you have."

That was only the first time.

Over the years, he taught me that drowning a thing you hate—drowning it well and drowning it completely—is a slow process. It is an art only the patient can master.

And I learned to be patient. I'll always credit the Old Man for that.

CHAPTER 1

Lars Elder looks like a banker the way I look like a private eye, which is to say, not much.

He was waiting on the porch of my family ranch house, flicking a switchblade open and closed, a computer disk and a can of Budweiser next to him on the railing.

Lars' hairline had receded since I'd seen him last, but he still sported the earring, the Willie Nelson beard. His shirt, vest, and jeans were faded to the colors of a dust storm, and his eyes gave the same impression—dry and turbulent.

"Tres," he said. "Thanks for coming."

"*No problema.*"

What I was thinking: The Navarre family banker drinking beer at ten in the morning is not a good sign.

Lars closed his knife, looked out toward the wheat fields.

Fifty yards away, past the tomato garden, the ranch caretaker was putting hay into the cattle feeder. Harold Diliberto stopped to watch us, his pitchfork suspended, dripping straw.

"Harold showed me the work you've been doing inside," Lars said. "You've been spending a lot of time out here."

"Some," I admitted.

I tried not to feel irritated, like Harold had betrayed a confidence.

Truth was, I'd been out at the ranch every weekend since the end of April—scraping old paint, filling in the spreading cracks in the original section of the house that had been my great-grandfather's homestead in the 1880s. I'd neglected both my jobs in San Antonio, ditched the cell phone, dropped out of my social life with little explanation to my friends.

"Place was overdue for some maintenance," I told Lars. "You ask me out here for the Home Beautiful tour?"

He didn't smile. "Talked to Garrett recently?"

"Maybe four, five months ago."

"But you'll see him soon. You're teaching that summer class in Austin, aren't you?"

Another surge of irritation. "British lit, for six weeks. May I ask how the hell you know about it?"

Lars brought the switchblade up like a conductor's baton. "Look, I'm sorry. I had to talk to you before you left. You know what Garrett's been up to?"

"You mean like Buffett concerts? Smoking pot?"

"His programming project."

"Must've missed it. I tend to phase out when Garrett talks about RNI."

Lars winced, like I'd just told him the price of an expensive gift. "Tres, Garrett isn't working at RNI anymore. He quit over a year ago."

I stared at him. My brother had worked at the same software company for sixteen years. He practically ran the place, took all the days off he wanted, had a retirement package.

"Got himself involved in a start-up company," Lars told me. "That was two years ago—spring of '98. Then last year, May of '99, he decided he couldn't keep working both jobs anymore. Garrett just left RNI—no severance, no benefits."

"Not possible."

"He's working the start-up with Jimmy Doebler."

I studied Lars' eyes, tried to tell if he was joking. Apparently, he wasn't, and beer for breakfast started sounding like a good idea.

Last I'd heard—maybe three years ago—Jimmy Doebler and Garrett hadn't even been speaking to each other. When they *were* speaking, they got along about as well as electricity and gunpowder.

"You're sure?" I asked him.

Lars picked up the computer disk, handed it to me. "Some files—things I was able to find on the Internet. They're calling themselves Techsan Security Software. Three principals in the company—Jimmy, his wife Ruby, and Garrett. They've been designing an encryption product. The beta-testing started in January."

I wagged the floppy. "It's news to me. Why the dossier, Lars? What's your interest?"

He rubbed his beard with his knuckles.

"I've known Jimmy and Garrett for a long time. I was around when Garrett—" He faltered. "Well, you know. I was around for the bad times. But when I called Garrett last week, I'd never heard him sound so bad. He and Jimmy are fighting again. Jimmy and his wife have separated—all because of this company they've started. I asked Garrett how they were holding up financially. He just laughed. The last few days, he won't even return my calls. I thought maybe you could talk to him."

I looked over the split rail fence, down the pasture toward the woods. The Charolais were grazing in the dry bed of Apache Creek. The water tower glistened gray.

I thought about the hundreds of times I'd watched the sun come up over the Balcones Escarpment from here, the topography like an onion, layer upon translucent layer—my first hunting trip with my dad, a dozen Thanksgiving dinners, my first night with a woman, three hurricanes, two fires, even a snowstorm. I remembered my grandfather, over there by the northern property line, digging holes for fence posts.

And even after six weeks of manual labor, rebuilding my relationship with the ranch, I could still feel that Sunday afternoon last April, down in the clearing, when I'd almost died at the hands of an old friend.

All I wanted was a few more weekends, time to scrape paint.

"Look, Lars, I won't say I'm not worried. But Garrett and Jimmy—what you're describing. Unfortunately, it sounds pretty typical. I appreciate your concern . . ."

"You don't understand," Lars said. "Garrett needed capital for his share in the Techsan start-up. A *lot* of capital. With his financial record, nobody else would help him. I hate even talking to you about this, Tres. I know you don't have a lot of money."

I tried to hand back the computer disk. "If you made my brother a loan, I'm sorry, Lars. I don't see how I can help you."

"I couldn't talk him out of it," he said. "The deed is in his name. He made me promise not to worry you, but when he signed the papers he still had a steady job. Now . . . He hasn't made a payment in over a year. It's just—I don't know what I can promise, come July first. My boss is breathing down my neck."

My heart twisted into a sailor's knot. "July first?"

Lars pinched the blade of his knife, threw it toward an old live oak stump, where it stuck straight up.

"Garrett mortgaged this ranch, Tres. And unless I see something—a sign of good faith by the end of this month, I'm going to have to foreclose."

CHAPTER 2

San Antonio and Austin are like estranged siblings.

San Antonio would be the sister who stayed home, took care of the elderly parents, made tortillas by hand in the kitchen, wore cotton dresses until the colors faded. She's the big-boned one—handsome but unadorned, given to long afternoon siestas.

Austin is the sister who went away to college, discovered rock 'n' roll, and dyed her hair purple. She's the one my mother would've warned me about, if my mother hadn't been an ex-hippie.

That afternoon I figured out why God put the two sisters seventy-five miles apart. It was to give irate siblings like me a cooling-off period—an hour on the road to reconsider fratricide.

Around two o'clock, I finally tracked down my brother. A friend of a Hell's Angel of a friend told me he was staying at Jimmy Doebler's place on Lake Travis.

Sure enough, they were down by the water, building something that looked like the third little pig's house. It was a kiln—pottery being Jimmy's second oldest hobby, next to getting Garrett in trouble.

From fifteen feet away, Jimmy and Garrett hadn't noticed me.

Jimmy was hunched over, tapping down a line of bricks.

Garrett was up on a scaffold, five feet above, doing

the chimney. His ponytail had flipped over the shoulder and gotten stuck in a splot of wet mortar. Sweat glistened in his beard. He made an odd sight up there, with no legs, like some sort of tie-dyed polyp grown out of the board.

The afternoon heat was cooking the air into soup. In the crook of a smoke tree, a jam box was cranking out Lucinda Williams' latest.

"Garrett," I called.

He looked down as if he'd known I was there all along, his expression as friendly as Rasputin's.

"Well," he said. "My little brother."

Jimmy wiped his hands on his tattered polo shirt, straightened.

He hadn't aged well. His face had weathered, his mop of sandcastle hair faded a dirty gray. He had the sun-blasted look of a frat boy who'd gotten lost on Spring Break thirty years ago and never found his way out of the dunes.

"Hey, man." He cut his eyes to either side, wiped his nose. "Garrett said you wouldn't be up until your class started."

"Wasn't planning to be," I said. "Then I talked to the family banker. That kind of changed things."

Garrett stabbed his trowel between two scaffold planks. "This ain't the time, Tres."

"When would be the time, Garrett? Next month—when they stick the FOR SALE sign on the front gate of the ranch?"

Lucinda Williams kept singing about her mamma. The bottleneck flew across her guitar.

"What do you want?" Garrett asked. "You want to take a punch at me?"

"I don't know. Are you filled with money?"

Garrett climbed down from the scaffold—one hundred percent upper body strength. He settled into his Quickie wheelchair—the deluxe model with the Holstein hide cover and the Persian seat cushion. He pushed himself toward me. "Come on. You've driven all this way pissed off at me. Take a swing."

He looked terrible. His skin was pasty, his eyes jaundiced. He'd lost weight—Christ, a lot of weight. Maybe fifteen pounds. He hardly had a gut anymore.

I said, "I want an explanation."

"It's *my* ranch."

"It's *our* ranch, Garrett. I don't care what it said in the will."

He puffed a laugh. "Yeah, you do. You care a whole *shitload*."

He jerked the macramé pouch off the side of his wheelchair, started rummaging through it—looking for his marijuana, his rolling papers.

"Would you not do that?" I asked.

"Do what?"

I grabbed the bag.

He tried to take it away from me, but I stepped back, felt how heavy the thing was, looked inside. "What is this?"

I came out with a handgun, a Lorcin .380.

"What did you do—buy this on the street?" I protested. "I took one of these away from a fourteen-year-old drug dealer last week. Since when do you carry something like this?"

Complete stillness. Even Lucinda Williams paused between songs.

"Look, Tres," Jimmy said. "Back off a little."

I checked the Lorcin. It was fully loaded. "Yeah, you're right, Jimmy. Garrett's got you on his side now. Everything's under control."

It was a cheap shot.

Jimmy shifted his weight from one foot to the other. His face turned the color of guava juice.

"We're working things out," Garrett told me.

"With a gun?"

"Jimmy and I made a pact for the day, man. No arguing. You want to stay here, abide by that rule."

His tone made me remember trips to Rockport when I was in middle school, Jimmy and Garrett college kids, forced to baby-sit me while my dad got drunk down on the jetties. Garrett had resented me tagging along, told me to shut up so they could meet some girls. The memory brought back that irrational anger, shaped in the mind of an eleven-year-old, that this was all Jimmy Doebler's fault—that he had always inserted himself into our lives at the wrong time.

I shoved the Lorcin back into the bag, tossed it to Garrett. "Lars Elder passed along some headlines you've been making in the high-tech magazines. Beta-testing problems. Glitches in the software. I didn't understand half of it, but I understood *several million in debt. Millions,* Garrett, with six zeroes. And your friend here wants me to *back off?*"

Jimmy said nothing.

Garrett rummaged in the bag, found a prerolled joint, stuck it in his mouth. "If we thought it was your business—"

"You pawned the ranch."

"And Jimmy got divorced today," he yelled. The joint fell out of his mouth, into his lap. "Okay, Tres? So shut the fuck up."

His voice wavered, was closer to breaking than I'd ever heard.

Jimmy Doebler stared down at his unfinished brick-work.

I remembered years ago, seeing heat tester cones in Jimmy's old portable kiln—how they turned to pools of liquid rock in the fire. Right now, Jimmy's eyes looked a little hotter than those cones.

"All we want to do," Garrett told me, "is build this damn kiln. You want to help, fine. You want to criticize, get your sorry ass home."

I looked at the half-built little pig house.

I looked at my brother's fingers, scarred and bleeding and crusted with mortar.

My anger drained away, left a taste in my mouth not unlike a TV dinner tray.

I said, "Hand me a trowel."

CHAPTER 3

By seven o'clock, we'd built the exterior walls four feet high around the cook box. The chimney and the doorway arch were finished.

The sun was sinking behind the hills on the far side of the lake. My skin itched from sweat and lime dust, my shoulders felt like sandbags, and I was thinking warm thoughts about cold margaritas.

I can't say I felt any better about being around Jimmy and Garrett, but I'd managed to keep my mouth shut and coexist with them for an afternoon.

Jimmy surveyed our masonry.

"Good," he decided. "Got to place the kiln goddess."

He ambled to his pickup and came back with a ceramic statuette—a misshapen female gargoyle glazed a nasty shade of Kool-Aid red. With great reverence, Jimmy placed her over the doorway, readjusted her a few times to get the angle right.

Garrett said, "What the hell is that?"

"Kiln goddess. You know—keep my pots from breaking. Keep them from turning out ugly. I'm naming her Ruby."

Garrett grunted. "You're a masochist."

I wasn't sure Jimmy knew what that word meant, but he grinned slowly. "Stayed friends with *you,* haven't I?"

Garrett let him have the point.

We left Garrett's van and Jimmy's pickup at the kiln

site, piled into my Ford F-150, and drove back up the gravel road to Jimmy's house.

The white dome was visible from just about anywhere on the lake—an upside-down radar dish Jimmy had gotten cheap from a military salvager when Bergstrom Air Force Base closed down. He'd hauled the thing up here piece by piece, reassembled it at the top of his six acres, insulated it, wired it for electricity, and bingo: a two-thousand-square-foot fiberglass igloo.

We stayed long enough to use the outhouse, grab barbecue supplies, stock the ice chest. Jimmy loaned me a fresh shirt that said RACAfest '98. We loaded my Ford and rumbled back down to the waterfront, where we proceeded to use Jimmy's new kiln as our cooking pit.

The summer sun had just set. A line of clouds was thickening on the horizon, charging the air with the metallic smell of storm. Around the curve of Jimmy's cove, the wind blew black lines across the water, dipping the buoys in the boating channel. In the distance, I could make out the edge of Mansfield Dam—a concrete monolith turning blue in its own shadow.

Garrett made the fire. Jimmy marinated fajitas in Shiner Bock and jalapeño juice, snapped a branch off the nearest wild sage plant to use as a basting brush. I mixed high-octane margaritas and poured them into Jimmy's handmade ceramic goblets.

We watched the sunset fade to purple and the storm clouds roll in. Nobody said a word about anything important.

After dinner, lightning traced veins in the clouds. The *chirr* of crickets replaced the daytime hum of cicadas. Flames glowed in the doorway of the kiln, washing the ugly little goddess in orange light.

Leave it to me to ruin a perfectly good cease-fire.

"Techsan," I said. "Give me the full story."

Jimmy reclined against a mesquite, putting himself back into the shadows.

Garrett looked toward the kiln—the shelves of unfired pots, their plastic cover ballooning in the breeze.

"You ever make yourself a promise, little bro? Tell yourself someday, you'll do such-and-such?"

"Play pro ball," I answered. "Be a Fellow at Christ College. Neither happened."

Garrett nodded. "I told myself years ago I was going to make a quick fortune, get out of programming, spend the rest of my life hitting Buffett concerts and Caribbean islands. Jimmy, he wanted to settle down making ceramics right here. Am I right, Jimmy?"

"You're right," Jimmy murmured from the shadows.

"Then we turned thirty-five, little bro. Then we turned forty."

"You quit your job," I said. "Sixteen years, and you quit."

In the firelight, Garrett's face looked as red as the kiln goddess'.

"Maybe you can't understand. We've been in Austin, Jimmy and me, way before the high-tech boom. We go back to the Apple IIe days—working our little grunt jobs in the big companies, making peanuts. Then suddenly we start seeing twenty-year-olds getting sign-up bonuses for four times our yearly salaries, zit-faced kids at UT writing programs for their undergrad theses and retiring multimillionaires the next year, bought out by venture capitalists. It's fucking unreal. Jimmy and me—we realize we've missed the Gold Rush. We were born too early. You have any idea how that feels?"

"So you decided to risk a start-up company," I said. "And you screwed up."

His eyes had a look of vacant anger, like an old soldier struggling to remember the details of a battle. "Mr. Sympathy. All right, yes. We screwed up. Lady named Ruby McBride—somebody Jimmy and I knew from way back. She invited us for drinks at this bar she owns down at Point Lone Star—she owns a whole fucking marina, okay? Ruby said she had some money to invest. She'd done some programming, had some ideas for a new encryption product. She wanted our help. The three of us agreed we could do something big together—something we could control all the way from the planning stages to the IPO. Ruby and Jimmy . . ."

Garrett paused. "Well, you know about Doebler Oil."

It took Jimmy a moment to react.

Then he leaned forward into the light, frowned, and swiped the margarita thermos. "Goddamn it, Garrett. You know Doebler Oil didn't cut me a cent."

"Whatever, man," Garrett said. "You had money. So did Ruby. I didn't, and I wanted to be an equal partner."

"So you mortgaged the ranch," I said.

"We expected a quick profit," Jimmy put in. "Our product kicked ass. Tech companies with programs a lot less solid than ours were seeing their public stock offerings quadruple the first hour of trading. All we figured we had to do was keep alive that long—finance the product through beta-test phase, keep the investors excited. It's like a poker game, Tres. The longer you stay in, the bigger the pot."

I looked at Jimmy Doebler, then at Garrett. I felt like I'd been dropped into a camp of defective mountain men, trying to figure out how to get beaver pelts traded on Wall Street. I said, "No wonder things went bad."

Garrett glared at me. "As of January, smart-ass, we were flying high. Mr. Doebler here even convinced himself he was in love—went off and got himself married to our lovely third partner."

Jimmy shoved the thermos back into the dirt, took a slug of his second drink. "Leave her alone, Garrett."

Garrett waved the comment aside. "We convinced half a dozen companies to do a six-month beta-test—meaning they'd try our product for free, we'd monitor how it went. Things went well, we could market the program commercially. Man, we rented offices, hired staff, did installation."

"You spent more money you didn't have," I translated.

"Three months in, things were going so well we were

turning down buyout offers, little bro. *Turning them down.*"

"And then?" I asked.

"We were sabotaged."

Jimmy shifted his back uneasily against the mesquite. "We don't know that, Garrett."

"The hell we don't. Fucking Matthew Peña."

I made the time-out sign. "Who?"

"Back in April," Garrett said, "we got this buyout offer from an investment banker in Cupertino, guy named Peña. Reminded me of a fucking vampire. He got along great with Ruby, which figures, but me and Jimmy said no way. Right after we turned Peña down, things started to go wrong with our beta-testing. The program is supposed to protect traffic on our clients' computers, okay? E-mail, Internet commerce, important shit."

"That's one of those high-tech terms, right? 'Important shit.'"

Garrett ignored me. He'd had a lot of practice at that over the years.

"All of a sudden," he said, "it was like our program sprung leaks. Our clients start reporting documents showing up in weird places—employees getting termination notices in their e-mail before they were officially fired, salary schedules getting posted on the company Web site, business plans e-mailed to competitors. Worst scenarios you can imagine. We've been busting our asses trying to figure it out, tell the clients the program can't be at fault. The leaks are too malicious, too . . . intelligent. It's got to be somebody—Peña for instance—bribing people to leak files directly from the test sites."

"Yeah," Jimmy mumbled. "Couldn't be Garrett's perfect algorithms."

"Oh, fuck you, man. And what do the beta-testers do? They blame us. We're supposed to protect them and we can't, so it's our fault. Three of the six companies have stopped testing and filed lawsuits, and we don't have the money to fight them. The other companies are threatening to do the same. If they do, we lose everything—two years of work, our IPO, any chance at investors. And now the bastard that sabotaged us—fucking Matthew Peña—comes back to us with a last-ditch buyout offer, a fifth of what he offered us three months ago. And *his* goddamn wife—" Shaking his finger at Jimmy. "His goddamn *ex-*wife is telling us we should feel grateful about it."

Jimmy got to his feet. "Maybe she's just smarter than you, Garrett. You ever think of that?"

I didn't like the looks Garrett and Jimmy were giving each other. I'd been in enough bar fights to recognize the prelude music.

"How much money?" I broke in.

"About four million total in the stock," Garrett growled. "Peanuts. Enough to break even, get out of debt. Nothing more."

I tried to visualize an equals sign between the words *four million* and *peanuts*. I couldn't do it.

"You're hesitating?" I asked. "Sell."

Garrett pitched his margarita cup into the grass, pushed his wheelchair back from the fire. "Two years of my life, little bro. You walk in here, not knowing shit, and you tell me, 'Sell.' "

"It's the same Ruby's telling us," Jimmy said. "You're just too stubborn—"

Garrett broke down in a miniature seizure—cursing and spitting and patting his arms around his chair looking for something else to throw. He grabbed his bag, and before I knew what was happening he had the gun in his hand.

"Ruby!" he yelled. "All I hear about is damn Ruby. What the hell was your fucking divorce for? Here, Ruby. I got something for you."

The round he fired at the kiln goddess blasted her left arm clean off, sending shards of brick and ceramics out into the night.

After that, things got very quiet.

When the ringing in my ears subsided, I said, "Please put the gun away, Garrett. Okay?"

To my relief, he shoved the Lorcin into his pot bag,

then turned his chair toward the road. "Jimmy Doebler wants to ride on *my* hard work, marry the girl, then bail out in the end, what the hell did I invite him along for?"

I said, "Garrett—"

"Forget it, little bro. You and he finally agree on something, you can both go to hell."

Garrett wheeled across the gravel—popping and tilting over the rocks, trying not to keel over.

We watched him hoist himself into his safari van, fold and stash the chair, roll the side door shut with a *SLAM.* Brake lights came on. A mushroom of yellow dust blossomed under the back wheels as he peeled out.

Jimmy drained his margarita, stared into the empty goblet.

"Happy Divorce Day," I told him.

"Your brother's upset."

I kept my mouth shut. I looked down at my own mug—wondered how Jimmy had managed such an intricate fish-scale pattern in the glaze, deep blues and greens, perfect symmetry. I wondered if he managed the complexities of programming the same way. I'd always thought of Jimmy as, if not an idiot savant, at least an idiot honorable mention.

"Garrett really didn't talk to you about the ranch?" Jimmy asked.

"No."

"He kept telling me he would. I know that isn't right, Tres. Somebody tried to sell this place without telling me . . ."

"Difference," I said. "This place legally belongs to you."

Jimmy's face squinched up, like I'd hit him with an invisible pie. "All right. But the last two years have been hell, Tres. You got to understand that. Garrett didn't want you to know how dicey things were."

"I know you're drowning in debt, you have a bail-out offer, and my brother doesn't want to take it."

"Pride—"

"He can swallow it."

Jimmy set his goblet on his knee. "Just back off for a few days, okay? Let me work on Garrett."

"Back off," I repeated. "Like you used to tell me down in Rockport: 'Stay out of my way, kid.' "

Jimmy stared at me with that look of hazy consternation, as if he was still wandering among the sand dunes. But he got the message. And I felt petty.

"If it makes you feel any better," he said, "I spent years resenting you, too. At least you and Garrett have each other. Maybe not much of a family, but it's more than nothing."

My third margarita had started seeping into my bloodstream. A flash lit the sky and a peal of thunder rolled one way across the lake, then the other. God testing the balance on his speakers.

"This was your mom's place," I said.

Jimmy nodded.

"Is it ever hard, living here?" I was thinking about the months after my father had died, when I'd been living alone in his house.

Jimmy cracked a twig, sent one half spinning into the dark. "Getting divorced, watching my career fall apart. I start wondering—what have I got left, you know? In the end, there's just family and friends, and for me the family part has always been . . . difficult. I've got a lot of time to make up for."

He paused uncomfortably.

"What?" I asked.

"I was thinking. You could do a favor for me. You can do background checks, right?"

Most of my nightmares start with those words.

I immediately thought: Divorce. Jimmy's family money, the settlement with Ruby final, but maybe not on terms Jimmy wanted. Knowing him, he'd allowed himself to get bled dry. He'd want detective work in order to appeal the court decision, maybe make his ex look bad.

I said, "Jimmy . . ."

"Forget it."

"It's just, it's not a good idea working for a friend."

He looked at me strangely, maybe because I'd used the word *friend*.

"You're right," he said. "Forget it."

I wanted to say something else, something that didn't sound like an excuse, but nothing came.

We watched the storm roll above us, the air get heavier, and finally break with a sigh, the first few splatters of warm rain hissing at the edge of the fire.

Jimmy stood. "It's too late to drive back to S.A. Take a couch in the dome. I got plenty of spare clothes and whatever."

Staying overnight hadn't been part of my game plan, but when I tried to stand, I realized how the tequila had turned my legs and my anger into putty. I accepted Jimmy's offer.

"Go on, then," he said. "I'll take care of the fire and the dinner stuff."

"I don't mind helping."

"No. Go on." More of a command now. "I want to stay down here a little longer."

"Fix your kiln goddess?"

He gave me an empty smile, picked up his Tupperware fajita bowl. "Thanks for your help today, Tres."

He headed toward the lake to wash his bowl.

I drove up the gravel road in the rain, parked behind Garrett's van, then got fairly well soaked running from the truck to Jimmy's front door.

Inside, the dome smelled like copal incense. One large room—a small kitchenette to the right, sleeping loft in the back, four high skylights like the slits of a sand dollar. The curve of the south wall was sheered perpendicular at the bottom to accommodate a fireplace and Jimmy's pottery display shelves.

Despite Jimmy's years as a programmer, there was no computer. No television. With Jimmy's jam box down at the lake, the most high-tech appliance in the dome was probably his refrigerator.

Garrett's sleeping bag was spread out on one of the

canvas sofas by the fireplace, but Garrett wasn't there. Probably in the outhouse.

I crashed on the opposite couch and listened to the thunder, watched the rain make milky starbursts on the windows above. Lightning flashed across Jimmy's pottery, turned the photos on his mantel into squares of gold. One of those photos showed Garrett before the accident that had made him a bilateral amputee. He was standing next to Jimmy on the Corpus Christi seawall. Another photo showed Jimmy's mother, Clara, a sad-eyed woman I remembered vaguely, dead now for something like five years. Next to her was a picture of Jimmy with a red-headed woman I assumed was Ruby, his newly ex-wife. And in the middle of the mantel, taking the place of honor, was a signed publicity shot of Jimmy Buffett and the Coral Reefers.

I don't remember falling asleep at all.

I dreamt about the ranch. I was lying out in the wheat fields, rain falling on my face. Standing over me was Luis, a drug dealer who'd once stabbed me in San Francisco. We were having a pleasant conversation about property values until Luis drew the Balinese knife on me again and plunged it into my kidney. I heard paramedics, heard my old mentor, Maia Lee, chastising me for my carelessness.

Then a single, sharp report snapped me awake.

My eyes stared into darkness for several lifetimes before I realized I was out of the dream. My side still ached from the knife wound.

I sat up on the couch.

No light came in the windows. The rain seemed to have stopped. The room was lit only by the glow of a stovetop fluorescent.

Garrett's sleeping bag was mussed up but unoccupied. Open facedown on the pillow was his well-worn copy of Richard Fariña—*Been Down So Long It Looks Like Up to Me*. His wheelchair was nowhere in sight.

I climbed the stairs to the sleeping loft. Jimmy's bed hadn't been slept in. The red digital numbers on his alarm clock glowed 2:56 A.M.

Then I heard a car engine—Garrett's van.

I stumbled downstairs, pulled on my boots, and came out the door in time to see Garrett's taillights disappearing below the rise in the woods, heading toward the kiln.

Dry ice started burning in my stomach.

The sky above was a solid gray sheet of clouds, tinted orange in the east from the perpetual glow of Austin. I ran, every rain-soaked branch thwapping into me on my way downhill.

The VW safari van had been parked with its front wheel on the cement slab of Jimmy's future studio, slammed into the side of the kiln. The driver's door was open, the engine idling with its steady, tubercular cough.

The headlights cut a yellow oval in the woods, illuminating wet trees hung with Spanish moss, silver streaks of gnats, the back bumper of Jimmy Doebler's Chevy pickup.

The truck had rolled from where I'd last seen it—down the slope of the bank, over a few young saplings, and straight into the lake. Its nose was completely submerged, the cab just at the waterline.

Garrett's wheelchair was overturned in the mud about twelve feet away. Garrett was on the ground and something metal gleamed in the mud nearby.

When he saw me, Garrett tried to speak. In the dark, his eyes wild, his bearded face glazed with sweat, he looked like some sort of cornered night animal. He lifted one muddy hand and pointed toward the truck.

"I couldn't get down there. I couldn't—"

I focused on the Lorcin—Garrett's .380—in the mud about three feet from him.

I ran past him, toward the truck.

The odor of gun discharge hit me. Then a fainter smell, like a breeze through a butcher's apron. I sank boot-deep into silty water, put my hand on the passenger's side door handle and looked in the open window.

My vision telescoped. It refused to register anything but the smallest details—the gurgle of lake water springing from the cracks at the bottom of the driver's door, glossing the parchment-colored boots a shiny brown. An upturned palm, callused fingers curled inward.

"Tres?" Garrett called, his voice brittle.

The driver's-side window was shattered, the frame and remaining shards painted burgundy and gray.

"Is he in there?" Garrett called. "Please to fucking Christ, tell me he's not in there."

I tried to step back from the truck, but my boots wouldn't come free of the silt.

I want to stay down here a little longer.

Garrett called again. *"Tres?"*

I wasn't seeing this.

I've got a lot of time to make up for.

I grasped at that sentence like a burning rope, but it wouldn't pull me out. It couldn't change what my eyes were showing me.

Jimmy Doebler had been shot in the head, and my brother was the one with the gun.

Date: Fri 09 Jun 00 04:18:05 Pacific Daylight Time
From: faqs@1pal_mail.com
To: <recipient list suppressed>
Subject: the tracks
X-MSMailPriority: Normal

I've spent years imagining what that night must've been like.

His good buddy taught him the trick, didn't he? It was so easy from where they lived, down in the Olmos Basin. The Union Pacific line went straight through, two times a night, always slowing for the crossings.

He was fighting with his father again—about the length of his hair, maybe. Or drugs. Maybe his father didn't like his plans to drop out of business school, become a mathematician. That was his plan back then, wasn't it? Straight math. Pure numbers.

So he stormed out of the house on Contour around eleven o'clock, midnight. He'd already made plans to meet his buddy down at the tracks, and his anger must've given way to excitement.

He made his way down to the crossing—to the far side, the signal box where they always meet. He knelt in a clump of marigolds and waited. It might've been cold, that late in October. Or maybe it was one of those unseasonable Texas fall nights—steamy and mild, moths and gnats everywhere, the smell of river mud and garbage from Olmos Creek.

He waited, and his buddy didn't show.

He knew the train schedule. He was a little late. His friend could've caught the last train, could already be on his way north, to the junction of the MKT line— that underpass where they'd stashed a lifetime supply of stolen beer. His friend could be there right now, hanging out in the broken sidecar where, on a good night, they could find the transients with the Mexican hash.

He gets a sudden thrill, because he's never tried to hitch alone, but he knows he can do it. And when he catches those rungs, he'll be Jack Kerouac. He'll be Jimmie Rodgers. And he knows his friend will be there at the junction to hear him brag about it—because it's a shared dream. His friend gave him the itch, reassured him, that first scary time—*Look how slow it moves. It's beautiful, man. Just waiting for you. Let's get the rhythm. Count to three—*

So he makes his decision, waits for the rumble of the second train, the glare of the headlamp. He smells diesel, feels the strange, steady rhythm of a million tons of steel in motion.

How could he know that his good buddy has forgotten all about him—that he is already in Austin, tending to his poor mamma, who has called out of the blue, after years of fuck-you good-riddance *nothing* parenting? And his buddy went running to her.

He doesn't know that, so waits for a good car—
one of the old-fashioned flatbeds. All he has to do is
jump on. When he targets one, his friend could've told
him—*not that one. Look at the ladder.* But there's no
one to warn him.

He times it, then runs, catches the metal side
rails. His boot hits the bottom rung and slips. His sole
drags in the gravel. He should be able to hoist himself
back up, but he hasn't planned on the rungs being so
wet—cold metal, newly painted. His heel snags a rail
tie and his fingers betray him. The last thing he feels is
gravel and cold steel as he's pulled underneath, and
the slow rhythm is not so slow after all—the giant
metal wheel, a smooth disk, covering what—thirty
inches?—in the space of a second.

Whatever noise he makes can't be heard above
the rumble of the train. There's no pain. No blood
loss—every artery sealed perfectly against the tracks.

He lies there in shock, staring at the stars. How
long—an hour? Two?

How long before this little brother got nervous,
decided to give away the secret of where Big Brother
goes when he's angry?

And what did he think about as he lay there?

I hope he thought about his good buddy who'd
abandoned him, made him fall in love with trains, gave
him a few months of freedom that he would now pay
for by being immobile, bound to metal wheels—
forever. I hope, somewhere inside, he wished his friend
had been the one on the tracks.

Because he's waited twenty years for this train. I
want him to enjoy the ride.

CHAPTER 4

Coffee and stale garlic bagels at the Travis County Sheriff's Department didn't improve my frame of mind. Neither did twelve hours of waiting rooms, shoe prints, fingerprints, atomic swab absorption tests, and questions from the lead investigator, Victor Lopez, who was convinced he had a sense of humor.

I saw my brother once, from across the homicide office. The betrayed look he gave me made me glad the deputies had separated us.

If Jimmy's ex-wife made an appearance, I didn't notice her.

The only member of the Doebler clan I spotted was one of Jimmy's cousins from the wealthy branch of the family—Wesley or Waylon, I couldn't remember his name. Jimmy had introduced us once at a Christmas party, maybe a decade ago. He wore a gray silk suit and three gold rings and a look of professional concern he probably saved for family tragedies and stock devaluations. He spent a few minutes at the opposite end of the room, talking to the sheriff, then gave me a cold glance on his way out.

At 4:30 in the afternoon, I was finally trundled into the backseat of a patrol car next to Detective Lopez and chauffeured toward Garrett's apartment.

We cruised up Lavaca, through West Campus neighborhoods of white antebellum sorority houses and high-rent condominiums. The post-rain air steamed with sumac.

Every front yard was strewn with pink and white from blooming crape myrtles.

On Guadalupe across from UT, a cute Asian girl in plaid pants and a tank top was reading a Henry James novel outside Quackenbush's Intergalactic Coffeehouse. Street vendors were selling glass beads and incense in the Renaissance Market. Construction workers were drilling a crater in the middle of 24th Street.

Jimmy's death was expanding inside my rib cage like a nitrogen bubble, but the rest of the world kept right on going. It was enough to make me resent a sunny afternoon in a beautiful city.

The patrol car turned on San Gabriel.

Garrett's apartment building is a three-story redwood box with exterior walkways like a motel. On one side is a $40,000 steel-frame handicapped-access elevator that the landlord recently installed after three years in court. The landlord loves Garrett. Below and on both sides of Garrett's unit are college kids who put up with my brother playing Jimmy Buffett CDs at full volume night and day. The college kids love Garrett. The rest of the building is populated by small-time drug dealers, angst-ridden artists and drunks, all of whom spend their time fighting and throwing each other's furniture off the balconies and loving Garrett. The name of the apartment complex is *The Friends*.

The Carmen Miranda—Garrett's VW safari van with the Caribbean dancing women airbrushed along the sides and the plastic tropical fruit hot-glued to the roof—had been returned from the crime scene, special delivery. I guess if I were the Travis County sheriff, I would want to get it away from my crime scene as fast as possible, too. Parked next to it was my black Ford F-150.

"I'll only be a second," Lopez told our driver. "You hang tight."

The deputy glanced in the rearview mirror—shot me a not-so-veiled *fuck you* look. "Whatever you say, sir."

Lopez and I walked toward the apartment complex.

Lopez stopped in front of the Carmen Miranda, shook his head in admiration.

"I dig the pineapples," he said.

Lopez's features were satanically pleasant, tea-and-milk-complexioned, framed by a square jaw and a severe, greasy buzz cut. He had a halfback's build and the eyes of a chess player.

"When does Garrett get released?" I asked.

Lopez feigned surprise. "Should be upstairs right now. Why? You thought we would hold him?"

That was a hook I decided not to bite.

"Don't look so down," Lopez said. "Y'all cooperated beautifully. Now we just got to find who whacked your friend, right?"

I leaned against the back of the van, hating how leaden my eyes felt, hating the odor of smoke in my clothes from last night's fire. "Garrett wouldn't kill Jimmy. Even if he wanted to, his wheelchair . . ."

Lopez's eyes glittered. "Sure, Mr. Navarre. According to your statement, there's no way. We're just asking questions, you know? Got to explain those nagging details, like why your brother's gun had been fired. Why there was powder residue on his hand."

"I told you—"

"He shot a statue. Happens every day. And we'll have to explain the fact there was no shell casing at the scene. You know. Just some little details like that."

Lopez was watching me the way a fisherman watches the tide, moving across it with a skeining net.

I said, "He's disabled, Lopez."

"I prefer to think of him as *differently* abled, don't you? But don't worry—I'm sure we'll find the casing sooner or later. Ballistics has the projectile now—probably find out it was from a completely different gun. Some anonymous killer in the night, I imagine."

"Garrett needs a lawyer."

Lopez bopped his fists together, hot-potato style. " 'Course not, Mr. Navarre. I appreciate y'all's candor. And I promise you: I will nail Jimmy Doebler's killer."

"You treat every case with this much enthusiasm?"

"I knew Jimmy. I liked Jimmy. I used to work patrol out at the lake, knew all the folks out that way."

"And his family has a few gazillion dollars," I added. "Jimmy's cousin was talking to the sheriff today."

A safety valve clicked shut in Lopez's eyes.

"W.B. Doebler isn't my concern." Lopez gave the initials their proper Texas pronunciation, *dub-ya-bee*. "You know Jimmy, you know he had a pretty shitty life—that family of his, the stuff with his mom, the clinical depression. Seemed like he was finally coming out of it when he got roped into this business deal with your brother."

He let his smile creep back to full intensity. "But hey, that doesn't matter. Jimmy and Garrett were quarreling, your brother was mad enough to discharge a weapon, I'm sure that's not important."

I looked back at our driver, who was staring at me through the windshield—giving me the look of death.

"Don't mind him," Lopez said. "Some of the guys, they heard about that little accident down in Bexar County, you shooting that deputy. Doesn't play well with the uniforms. You understand."

"And with you?"

Lopez made a *pish* sound. "I got no sympathy for bad cops. That asshole was corrupt: you took him down. Good for you. I believe in weeding out the bad, Navarre. Don't care if it's a friend or a relative or what. I hope we're on the same page with that."

I looked up toward Garrett's apartment door.

"I'm on your side, man," Lopez assured me. "I wouldn't want this to get around, but the people I know in San Antonio—they say you're all right. They say when it comes down to a fight, you're a guy who can be counted on to choose the right team."

"I see your point," I said. "We wouldn't want that to get around."

"You got my card." Lopez turned to go, then looked back, as if he'd forgotten something. I hate it when cops do that. "And Navarre? The discrepancies in those statements you and your brother gave us? I'm not thinking much of them. For instance—were you with your brother when you heard the shot or not?"

I didn't answer.

"I don't know why your brother failed to mention that he and Jimmy were arguing at dinner, like you told me. It's probably nothing. Just—bad form when the statements don't agree, isn't it? I hate going back later, using Wite-Out."

"I know my brother."

Lopez smiled. "Of course you do. Where does he work again—RNI? Oh, no. That's right. He quit that job over a year ago."

Up on the second-floor walkway, one of the apartment residents waddled out in his jockey shorts and a tattered Waterloo T-shirt. He yelled down to us that his neighbor was throwing his sofa off the back balcony and we should stop him.

Lopez grinned. He told the guy he would have to phone it in to the APD dispatcher. The guy began cursing at us.

Lopez gave me a wink. "My point is—an okay guy like you, you could help me out a lot, maybe help your brother, too. We could be straight with each other and get this thing resolved. You could give Garrett some advice on how to play it. If there were hard choices to make, I trust you would make them."

"You want my brother in jail, Lopez?"

He laughed. "They told me you had a sense of humor. That's great. See you around, Mr. Navarre."

Then he climbed into the patrol car.

I watched it back up, disappear around the corner of 24th.

The guy on the second floor kept yelling at me to come stop his neighbor from pitching his furniture off the balcony.

Every day is a love fest when you live at *The Friends*.

CHAPTER 5

Garrett hadn't hired a maid since my last visit, five months ago.

Fast-food containers littered the kitchen counter. The living room was a tornado zone of paperback novels, electronics parts, CDs, laundry. A dead tequila bottle stuck out from the seat of our father's old leather recliner and the carpet was fuzzy with birdseed from Dickhead the parrot, who scuttled back and forth on the window ledge at the top of the vaulted ceiling.

Garrett sat in the far corner of the room, staring at his twenty-one-inch computer monitor.

"Computers get static?" I asked.

The gray fuzzy light made Garrett's face crawl, his eyes hollow.

"Not usually." He slammed the monitor's off button. "I need a drink."

I waited for him to explain the computer problem. Not that I would've understood the explanation, but that was something Garrett always did. This time, he didn't.

I went to the bar, got down his bottle of Herradura Añejo and a couple of moderately clean glasses. "Detective Lopez just got through telling how much you're *not* a suspect in Jimmy's murder. He was very agreeable about it. I got the feeling he'd let you plea just about any degree of homicide you wanted."

Garrett took the tequila. "Lopez has had a hard-on for me for years."

"Really."

"Don't give me that tone—like you assume I'm stoned. Back when Lopez was on patrol, he made a lot of calls to Jimmy's place, had to chew us out for drunk-and-disorderly crap. We got into some name-calling. But you know I didn't kill Jimmy. I couldn't."

I drank my Herradura, found it made a pretty bad chaser for garlic bagels. "Lopez gives you credit for mobility—a lot more credit than he's giving our statements."

Garrett shoved his keyboard drawer closed. "Somebody finally believes in me, and it's a homicide cop."

I ran my finger across the kitchen counter, making a cross with a dustless shadow where a picture frame had stood for a long time. I remembered the photograph. It had been the twin of the one in Jimmy's house—Garrett and Jimmy at the seawall in Corpus, a year or so before Garrett's accident.

"W.B. Doebler was at the sheriff's office," I told him. "If the Doeblers start throwing their weight around, demanding action—"

"Fuck W.B. It's a little late for the Doeblers to decide they care about Jimmy."

"You need help, Garrett."

"And I don't recall asking you for any, little bro. I'll make the calls. I'll take care of things."

"What—you're going to buy a bigger gun?"

"Forget it, man. You didn't like the ranch being mortgaged. You ain't going to like the rest of this."

"I didn't drive up here to build a kiln, Garrett. I sure as hell didn't drive up here to sit on the sidelines while they charge you with murder."

Garrett dug out his wallet, pulled a twenty and wadded it up, threw it at me. "Gas money. Sorry I wasted your time."

I counted silently to ten. Every second was one more

I succeeded in not putting my fist through my brother's wall.

The downstairs neighbors cranked up their stereo. Nine Inch Nails throbbed through the carpet. Up on the windowsill, the parrot ruffled his feathers.

"Let's try to cooperate," I said. "For Jimmy's sake. You told them you were with me when that shot was fired. Your book was facedown on the sleeping bag when I woke up. You were already gone. Where the hell were you?"

Garrett wore last night's cutoffs, and when he shifted, the stub of his right leg peeked through at the end—a pointed nub of flesh like a mole's nose.

"I was sleeping in my van. With the doors locked."

"Why?"

He rubbed his thumb against his forefingers, rolling an imaginary joint. "In Jimmy's house, I woke up in a cold sweat. I have phantom pains and I get these weird dreams—like somebody has been standing over me in my sleep. I would've felt stupid waking you up. I thought Jimmy was sleeping upstairs. So I went to the one place I feel safe and mobile—behind the wheel of my van. I locked myself in, put my gun on the seat next to me, went to sleep. The shot by the water woke me up. What was I going to tell the police? I was afraid of ghosts so I locked myself in my car?"

"It would've been better than lying, Garrett. I'm going to need an explanation for Detective Lopez."

His eyes flared. "*You* need an explanation. Well, let's just stop the goddamn world. Let's drop everything and make sure Tres is okay, because my little brother needs an explanation. He needs the ranch. He needs to know where Garrett is twenty-four hours a day. Well, maybe for once, little brother, you ain't going to get everything you need."

The counting wasn't helping anymore. Downstairs, Nine Inch Nails went into their next song, the bass line massaging the soles of my boots.

"Did you see anyone last night?" I asked.

"No."

"You must suspect someone. The banker guy."

"Matthew Peña," Garrett murmured.

There was something in his voice I hadn't heard often—pure hate.

"You think he's capable of murder," I said. "An investment banker?"

Garrett pressed his palms against his eyes. "I don't know."

"What about Jimmy's ex? Ruby McBride?"

He hesitated. "No. No way."

"But?"

Garrett stared at his monitor. "There are reasons I didn't talk to you sooner, little bro. Not just because I wanted you in the dark."

"I snoop for a living, Garrett. Let me help."

"In all the years Dad was sheriff, do you ever recall me asking him for help?"

"Maybe you should have. He would've done damn near anything if you'd ever called."

"Here it comes, the guilt trip from the good son. Forget it. I don't want you in my problems because I don't want you hurt, man. And believe me, you would get hurt."

I looked at Garrett's clock—Dad's clock. I'd been in Austin twenty-five hours. The ranch was still mortgaged. Jimmy Doebler was dead. My brother's life was falling apart. And he didn't want me involved because I might get hurt.

I set my shot glass on Dad's army locker, which served as Garrett's makeshift coffee table. I stared at Dad's recliner, thought about Dad's old saddle that hung on Garrett's bedroom wall.

Not for the first time, I had to swallow back a comment about hypocrisy. Garrett always insisted I'd been Dad's favorite, the model son, and yet I owned almost nothing of the Sheriff's. Garrett, who had always railed that he wanted nothing to do with our father, lived surrounded by his things.

"You don't want my help," I said, "at least get a lawyer. You want some names?"

He gave me an uneasy look. "I told you, man. I'll handle it."

"Fine," I said. "Just primo."

I was halfway out the front door when he called, "Tres."

The sun through the skylights made his beard glow almost blond.

"You're right about cooperating for Jimmy's sake," he told me. "But you've got to trust me, little bro. I've got to handle this without you. I just can't—"

He looked at me as if he was trying to explain a smashed vase. "Do you understand?"

"I'm trying, Garrett. I am."

He held my eyes, searching for some stronger commitment. When he didn't find it, he turned and wheeled himself into the bedroom.

I pulled his front door locked behind me.

The afternoon sun was heating the walls of *The Friends* into a cooking surface. I walked toward the stairwell, listening to industrial rock and the neighbors arguing behind every door.

CHAPTER 6

I managed to stay home a whole twenty-four hours, but San Antonio felt like a ghost town.

My colleague George Bertón was in L.A., spending his life savings on the Spurs playoff games. My boss, Erainya, and her son, Jem, were vacationing in the Greek Isles. Even my mom was gone—off fishing with her new beau at a mountain cabin in Colorado.

I spent Saturday alone in the offices of the Erainya Manos Detective Agency, eating Erainya's week-old dolmades and trying to gather information. I e-mailed a friend at the Bexar County ME, asked if he could finagle Jimmy Doebler's autopsy report from Travis County. I tried the Bexar County Sheriff's Department and SAPD, hoping somebody knew somebody in Austin who could give me an inside read on Vic Lopez's investigation. Nobody got back to me.

The Doebler family proved to be a brick wall.

Most of the clan lived in Austin. I'd even met some of them. But nobody wanted to talk to me on the phone. Yes, they remembered me—Garrett Navarre's brother, Jimmy's friend. Yes, they'd heard about Jimmy's death. Could I please refer all further questions to the family's law firm?

I couldn't tell which name they spoke with more coolness—Garrett's or Jimmy's.

W.B. Doebler, Jimmy's cousin and present chairman of the board of Doebler Oil, was in a meeting. Could I please call back? I did, six times over the course of the day. W.B. Doebler was still in a meeting.

I almost thought I'd struck gold when I discovered that Jimmy had an aunt, Clara's younger sister, also living in Austin, but even Faye Doebler-Ingram turned me down.

"Oh, Mr. Navarre." Her voice was small and plaintive, snagging on every word—a silk handkerchief brushed over bricks. "I'm very sorry, but there's nothing I can do."

"If you'd spoken to Jimmy recently, if you knew anyone the police should talk—"

"I'm afraid I couldn't help."

"This is your sister's son, ma'am. As the closest relative—"

"Oh, no. No." A new snag in her voice—fear? "You must realize how sad this is for my family. They felt so much pain over Clara's whole life, her death, and now Jimmy . . . puts himself in a position like that."

"A position like what?"

"The family wants to put this behind them, move on as quickly as possible, you see."

"And you agree?"

Ninety miles of silence over the phone line. "Jimmy was a sweet boy. I'll miss him terribly."

"Will I see you at the memorial service, then?"

The softest sound I ever heard was Faye Doebler-Ingram laying the receiver of her phone in the cradle.

I sat at my desk, staring out the Venetian blinds at the traffic on Blanco.

I turned to the computer, logged on to a news database, and started digging for dirt on the banker Garrett had mentioned—Matthew Peña.

According to *Silicon News,* Peña was a Texan by birth, Californian by choice. BS in computer science from UT Austin. MBA from Stanford. He'd spent the past few years as an investment banker, orchestrating buyouts and providing venture capital for high-tech start-ups. His clientele read like a who's who list of Silicon Valley. Peña's only noted hobby was scuba diving, which he was so zealous about that his business adversaries had started calling him the Terror of the Deep.

He was, by all accounts, the most vicious set of free-lance teeth a company could hire.

August 1998. Peña's first major conquest—a promising start-up company in San Jose. In the course of one month, Peña sabotaged their prospective deals with venture capitalists, hired their best talent away, and set the principals of the company at each other's throats. One of the principals filed a complaint with the San Jose police. She claimed Matthew Peña was harassing her with phone calls, visits, e-mail. When asked for specifics, the woman backed away from her allegations. The complaint fizzled. A month later, the start-up agreed to sell. Once Peña bought them out at a fire-sale price, their product became the backbone of Peña's client's virus-protection software—a cash cow.

February 1999. Similar story. Peña strong-armed a Menlo Park start-up into selling to a major tech company for six million in stock—little more than glass beads and trinkets compared to what other computer businesses were trading for then. Opposition to the sale collapsed when the most vocal of the principals was found dead in his garage—apparently a suicide, shotgun to the mouth. The other principals turned the police investigation toward Matthew Peña—claimed Peña had been calling them up, e-mailing them, threatening their lives. Police investigated Peña, but he came away clean. Peña's quote on the matter to the press: "If the guy killed himself because I was about to make him a millionaire, he's so stupid he deserves to die." Mr. Peña: big warm fuzzy.

January of this year. A glimpse into Peña's private life. His girlfriend of six months, Adrienne Selak, disappeared off a privately chartered dinner cruise boat in San Francisco Bay. Selak had been seen arguing with Peña earlier in the evening. The couple had gone off alone toward the back of the ship. Thirty minutes later, Peña called for help, claiming that Ms. Selak had fallen into the Bay. A search was launched, but her body was never recovered. Selak had been a competent swimmer. In fact, she and Peña had met because of their shared interest in scuba. After her disappearance, one of Selak's girlfriends informed the police that Selak had complained about Matthew "getting creepy" on several occasions, threatening to kill her.

One of Peña's employees, Dwight Hayes, gave a witness statement supporting Peña's assertion that the fall had been accidental. Peña hired the best legal counsel money could buy. As near as I could tell from follow-up articles, the investigation was still open, but no formal charges had been filed against Peña.

In March of this year, Matthew Peña's services had been contracted by AccuShield, Inc., a Cupertino-based company that made security software—virus protection, encryption, network firewalls. Peña had apparently sold AccuShield on the idea of expanding into the Austin market, and one of Peña's first buyout targets was Techsan Security Software: Garrett, Ruby, and Jimmy's start-up.

The *American-Statesman* chronicled Techsan's beta-test problems, which began shortly after Techsan rejected Peña's first buyout offer of twenty million. I tried to get my mind around the kind of optimism, hubris, stubbornness, whatever, that had made my brother and his two partners turn down twenty million dollars. What were they thinking?

Then I thought about the guy from Menlo Park who had been offered millions by Matthew Peña, then went into his garage and ate his shotgun.

The latest article I could find, dated last week, talked about Peña's second offer—a rescue buyout proposal to the now-beleaguered Techsan for four million in stock of the client company, AccuShield. Techsan had been wavering on whether or not to accept it.

And now Jimmy Doebler was dead.

There were no available pictures of Matthew Peña. I had no luck finding solid information on his background except for what the business articles told me secondhand— nothing that made Matthew Peña human for me. I liked that just fine. It made it all the easier for me to hate the bastard.

That evening, I wanted to go out to the ranch. I wanted to honor Garrett's wishes to butt out of his problems. Instead, I packed and unpacked my bags for Austin three times.

Sunday morning, after forty-five minutes on the road, I was still reconsidering. I pulled over on the side of I-35 at the Onion Creek rise, just inside the Travis county line.

I looked down the valley, up the opposite hill from which I'd first be able to see the silhouette of downtown. Last chance. Once up that hill, the gravity of Austin would pull me in. There was no avoiding it.

I could call UT, cancel the damn extension course. My department head at UTSA had pushed me to take the job, to get some more upper-division teaching experience under my belt, but he could live with the disappointment.

I let the engine idle. Next to me, Robert Johnson meowed complaints in his carrying cage. My Ford shuddered as a semi rig barreled past.

I opened my backpack and pulled out the page and a half of notes I'd gleaned from my search on the agency computer. I read through them again, hoping I might be able to interpret them differently.

Unfortunately, Matthew Peña wasn't the thing that bothered me most. The real worry was down there at the bottom of my notes—the name of the law firm that had represented Peña in the Menlo Park shotgun suicide, and then successfully shielded him from charges in the Adrienne Selak drowning.

Peña had good taste. His legal firm was Terrence & Goldman of San Francisco.

Unless things had changed at Terrence & Goldman, they had only one criminal lawyer, a junior partner whose sole job was to defend their less socially upright corporate clients from their own vices, shield them against criminal inconveniences so they could continue to make millions. That lawyer was, unfortunately, the person I would have to call if I wanted more information on Matthew Peña.

I looked down the highway. Another big rig plowed past and all the metal on my pickup truck rattled.

Robert Johnson said, "Roww?"

There would be nights, later, when I'd lie awake wondering how my life would've been different had I turned around that morning on I-35—later, after I'd seen things that made my previous repertoire of nightmares look like the Charlie Brown Halloween Special.

But I couldn't turn around, and I suspected that Garrett, damn him, had known I wouldn't all along.

I put the Ford into drive and started rolling north, heading into Austin.

Date: Sun 11 Jun 2000 16:59:07 -0000
From: TGLaw@TGLaw.net
To: TGLaw@TGLaw.net
Subject: magic thinking

That was a good Christmas. Nineteen eighty-seven.

You remember? It was the last time it snowed in Austin.

Pickup trucks were sliding down that big hill at Lamar and 24th—nobody had a clue how to drive on ice. Old women were breaking their hips, slipping on sidewalks. Classes at UT closed down. All because of half an inch of snow.

Autumn had been rough for me, but I'd ended it feeling euphoric. I'd gotten through a bleak period, vented my anger on a few experiments—no one important, no one who would be missed.

Now I was feeling like the snow, like I could do the smallest thing, make the least effort, and I could shut down the whole town.

I decided to give myself an early Christmas present.

I remember it was a hard ride into the Hill Country. The roads were pitch black, glazed with ice that gleamed in the headlights of the little car I'd stolen. The barbed wire sparkled like Christmas garland. There was nothing except dark and mist and the scraggly outlines of bare trees.

I finally found the house where they were attending their party. Excuse me—*gala*. It was always a *gala*, with them. Huge ranch villa, the lawn crusted white, the driveway outlined with glowing *luminarias*. Real holly in the windows. A dozen top-of-the-line pickup trucks and BMWs in front. Their car was there, too— the old green Mercedes.

I watched from the road until I saw them through the window. The woman with a gray helmet of hair, a sequined black gown. The man in a rumpled brown suit, always the humble escort.

I smiled, watching them. I drove from the party all the way to the old couple's house, five miles away, then back again. There was only one route, and I knew the point where they would turn off, come around the hill, speed up in anticipation of home. It was a road nobody much used.

I parked my car on the shoulder, hugging the side of the hill.

I got out and waited, knowing I would see their headlights on the tree branches before I saw the car round the bend. It was perfect.

I wasn't wearing gloves. Or a hat. The wind ripped through my coat, stung my eyes and skin like jalapeño juice. I looked up at the snow, swirling like gnats out of complete darkness, and I thought about being underwater—cold and black, visibility nil, the sparkle of small bubble trails, everything colorless. I thought about how I had started to master that fear. How good it felt. How much I wanted to be underwater right then, scared as hell but loving the taste. The thought warmed me.

When the trees illuminated, I slid the rough paper

cylinder out of my coat pocket. The thrill was not knowing whether the plan would work, whether I would have to use the little gun I had in my other pocket.

Headlights appeared and I knew it was the right car. It could be no other—not at this time of night, on this little country road.

The rest happened fast.

I snapped the end of the flare and stepped into the glare of their headlights, waving the orange fire frantically, making a huge arc to my left—toward the drop-off.

And they were going too fast. In driving class, they always tell you—don't look at the lights in the opposite lane, because you will drift toward them. You instinctively want to look at the light, and you will drift toward what you see. That's what happened with the wave of the flare, in those three seconds.

That old fart could have run me down. He could have swerved the other way, into my car, into the side of the hill, and caused me to use a much more difficult plan, but instead he turned the car toward the wave of the flare and swerved into nothing—a short *BUMP-BUMP* of wheels leaving the road, the cracking of brittle tree branches and crunch of metal, rolling, insanely large sounds of a dump-yard compactor, and then quiet.

No fire. No headlights. Just darkness. Two large wet marks at my feet where the old green Mercedes had taken flight.

I knew the cliff. I'd seen it in daylight, many times. I estimated a fifty-foot drop, forty-five degrees, until they hit the creek bed.

I smiled, thinking about that—the place where water touches your life. You have to confront it, sooner or later.

I knew there was an outside chance they hadn't

died. But I also knew they would get no help. At least not soon. No one would think to look for them until morning, maybe longer.

Part of Providence is trust, isn't it? Magic thinking. Words said over and over again, "I wish they were dead." And now I trusted.

The snow helped cover my traces—what few there were.

I watched for media coverage. The police were anxious to dispel rumors of foul play. Too much work for a sleepy county sheriff's department to construct a murder scenario when it was so obvious what had happened—an elderly couple drinking, unused to the icy roads, bad eyes and reflexes. Perhaps a deer had run in front of them. Or a dog. It had happened before.

Call it Providence.

Sometimes all you have to do is wave that arc of orange fire in the wrong direction, and the ones you love will follow it.

CHAPTER 7

The police tape made a satisfying sound as I ripped it off the railing on Jimmy's front steps.

I found his spare key behind the ceramic angel on the wall, unlocked the door.

The dome was dark. In the stale air of the closed-up house, one smell hit me as completely wrong—a woman's perfume. Halston, maybe. A faint trace.

"Gas company," I called. "Ma'am?"

No answer.

There'd been no other cars on the property. Maybe the scent had been trapped here since Travis County did the crime scene, two days ago. A reporter or detective could've brushed against the door frame. Still—the place had a presence, like it was holding its breath.

I put Robert Johnson's cage down and let him out. He padded his way up to the canvas sofas, sniffed the fringed edge of the Oriental rug, looked at me.

"Just for a few weeks," I said. "We can do anything for a few weeks, right?"

He did not give me a rousing huzzah.

Morning sun filtered down from the skylights, making stripes across the railing of the sleeping loft above. The stove-hood fluorescent flickered. I went around the ground floor and turned on every light I could find.

On the fireplace mantel, some of Jimmy's photos were missing. His rolltop desk was open. Bills and receipts were scattered across the coffee table—the work of deputies not worried about leaving a mess.

I put my suitcase on the kitchen counter and brought out the high-tech artillery—cell phone, caller ID unit, Macintosh laptop, VOX-activated audio recorder, shotgun mic, digital camera. None of it was mine, of course. It was agency equipment. But when one's boss is in Greece for a month, one gets lax about sign-out procedures.

Last I pulled out Erainya's Taurus PT-99.

It was a Brazilian 9 mm. parabellum, about eight inches long, thirty-five ounces, Erainya's least favorite backup piece. The size made it too unwieldy for her, but it fit well in my hand. All blued steel—match grade barrel, checkered grip. A nice reliable gun, as guns go.

Erainya had offered it to me a dozen times. Each time I'd refused. I don't believe in guns for PI work. You carry a gun, you will eventually convince yourself you have to use it.

Which did not explain why I'd brought it.

Probably the same muse that told me staying in a dead man's house would be an insightful experience.

I put the Taurus on the kitchen counter, next to Jimmy's blender. I told myself the gun would stay there—unloaded, unused.

Robert Johnson was amusing himself under the sofa. Garrett had never come to claim his sleeping bag, and Robert Johnson was on his back, pawing the down and nylon folds that were slipping off the edge. He clawed and chewed at the enemy until the bag came down on top of him and he had to do a 180-degree flip-and-run maneuver to get away. He leapt up onto the opposite couch, gave me a nonchalant stare. *I meant to do that.*

"You're the king," I told him. "Hold down the fort for a minute, will you?"

I went outside to get a second load from the truck—my other suitcase, some groceries, the cat dish.

When I came back inside with a dozen plastic H.E.B. bags hanging off my arms, I found that Robert Johnson had failed in his duties. He was now on the kitchen counter, ecstatically purring and mewing for the woman who was pointing Erainya's gun at me.

She was a tall redhead—elegantly cut white cotton pantsuit, hair swept back so it made a St. Louis Arch around her face. One of her eyebrows curved slightly higher than the other, giving her a quizzical look.

The smell of Halston was much stronger now.

She raised the muzzle of my Taurus. "This was extremely obliging of you."

"I have some apples in the bag. I can put one on my head, if you want."

She glanced up toward the sleeping loft. "Oh, Clyde?"

At the railing, a Viking appeared. He was about three hundred pounds' worth of Aryan—long hair and beard the color of lemon sours, black leather pants, beefy arms and belly stuffed into a T-shirt emblazoned with the words JAP BIKES SUCK. He was holding a Bizon-2, quaint little pistol–machine gun, just right for hunting rhinos.

"Great," I said, upbeat, friendly. "We can set up a crossfire. Mind if I put down my groceries?"

The redhead's eyes were set at a diagonal, mirroring the V of her nose and chin. The faint dusting of red-brown freckles matched her hair.

"I do mind," she decided. "I like your arms full, until you explain what you're doing in my husband's house."

"You're Ruby."

"And you're Garrett's little brother, obviously. You still owe me an answer."

"Obviously?"

To my knowledge, no one had ever pegged Garrett and me as brothers simply by looking at us. It was a point of pride.

The corner of Ruby's mouth crept up. "You've got the same eyes. Don't you think so, Clyde? Same eyes?"

The ladder creaked under Clyde's weight. He got halfway down, jumped the last five rungs. He pointed his gun lazily in my direction.

"Pictured him younger," he mused. "More like a snot-nosed kid."

"You've been spending time with Garrett," I guessed. "Bandidos MC?"

"Fuck no, man. Diablos."

"Your last name's Simms. Went on that Florida trip with Garrett last year."

Clyde grunted.

"Well," Ruby said. "Now that we've all made cordial, how about you tell us why you're here, Tres?"

"I'm moving in for a few weeks."

She arched the eyebrow a centimeter higher. "On whose invitation?"

I set my groceries on the floor.

"I told you—" she started.

I stepped in, grabbed her wrist, spun her so she was facing Clyde. Clyde raised his Bizon-2 just in time to point it at Ruby's throat.

I applied a little pressure to her wrist. She dropped the Taurus.

"Bastard," she murmured.

Clyde shifted his weight.

"We're all friends," I suggested. "Lose the bazooka."

He hesitated.

"Come on. You want to explain to Garrett why you had to shoot his little brother?"

The line was a gamble. Clyde might've thought he could earn brownie points by shooting me. But he tossed the machine pistol onto the sofa.

I let Ruby go.

She smoothed her white pantsuit, glared at me. "You think I wouldn't have shot you?"

I picked up the Taurus, ejected the empty clip.

I'd known it wasn't loaded, but I checked the chamber anyway. There was a bullet in it.

I looked at Ruby.

She smiled.

The master detective accepts the Golden *Oops* Award.

I emptied the chamber, put the bullet and the gun next to Robert Johnson. "Where's your car?"

"We're on a lake," Clyde said. "There's a boat dock. Figure it out."

"You've been searching the house. What for?"

"How about we call 911?" Ruby suggested. "I can explain it to the police."

"Mr. Simms have that weapon registered?" I asked. "Be a toss-up which of us the cops kick out."

Her face acquired a new hardness, a one-millimeter-thick mask. "Clyde, why don't you wait outside?"

"Should've killed the bastard months ago," Clyde complained. "You and Garrett listened to me—"

Ruby put a finger lightly to his lips. "That's enough, Clyde. Thanks."

He flexed his paws impotently, snatched his Bizon-2 from the sofa, and lumbered toward the front door—the frustrated berserker, going home to Mama.

On the counter, Robert Johnson nudged the Taurus lovingly. "Mrr?"

Ruby reached over, stroked his fur. Typical. I get guns pointed at me. The cat gets petted.

A gold and diamond wedding set sparkled on Ruby's ring finger. I tried to imagine Jimmy Doebler picking it out—standing in some chic jewelry salon in his blue jeans and tattered polo shirt, his face speckled with dried red clay. I tried to imagine him married to this woman, her designer ensembles hung up in the same closet with Jimmy's work clothes.

"Clyde's a bit overprotective," Ruby apologized. "He runs the marina repair shop for me. He's quite good with boat engines."

"I bet. They break, he shoots them."

"Which brings us back to the point," she said. "You shouldn't be here."

"You have claim to the property?"

"I—No. This was always Jimmy's place. I live on my boat."

"Then what were you looking for?"

Her eyes traced the curve of the ceiling. "Now that Jimmy's dead, your brother and I have to make some

decisions. I wanted to get the company paperwork—
documents we might need."

Her voice was as thin as drum skin. She was lying.

"Matthew Peña," I said. "He's been pressuring you to
sell?"

"If Matthew Peña were harassing me, it would be
bullshit. I'd ignore it."

"I didn't say *harassing*."

I could almost see her mental effort—reinforcing the
facade, like a wall of loose blocks. "There's nothing to tell.
Nothing . . . provable."

"Peña offered to buy you out once before. You refused."

"You can thank your brother and Jimmy for that."

"The security problems started shortly thereafter.
Your potential worth took a nosedive. Peña's made a second offer—a substantially reduced offer—and when you
hesitated, Jimmy died."

"It isn't like that," she insisted. "What you're
implying—Look, I know Matthew Peña. I've had dinner
with him. I've gone diving with him. He isn't a monster."

I told her about the shotgun case in Menlo Park a year
ago. I told her about Peña's girlfriend Adrienne, who'd
also gone diving with him.

Ruby's complexion looked like she'd suddenly developed the flu. She stared at the empty gun on the kitchen
counter. "That's got to be other people, misconstruing the
facts. Matthew would have no reason to kill anyone, especially not Jimmy."

Matthew, I thought. First-name basis.

"You talked to the police?" I asked.

"Of course."

"They ask where you were the night Jimmy was
killed?"

"I was working late at the marina. Lots of people saw
me."

"You mention Peña?"

"The detective, Lopez, told me not to worry about

that. He told me something else, Tres—they've already matched Garrett's gun to the bullet that killed Jimmy."

It was my turn to look sick. "When was this?"

"Yesterday evening."

After I'd talked with Lopez. I wondered if he really had a ballistics match, or if he had just been trying to press Ruby into making a statement that would hurt Garrett. I tried not to get angry, to remind myself that all homicide detectives played games like that. "You believe Garrett shot Jimmy?"

"Of course not." She was a good liar, I'll give her that.

"Your friend Clyde Simms," I said. "Clyde said there was a bastard he wanted to kill months ago. I assume he was talking about Peña?"

Her composure was just about reassembled now—all the blocks in place. She sat back, let the cat rub his face on her diamond ring. "You should leave now, Tres. I have a lot to do."

"Unless you've got legal right to kick me out," I said, "you're the one who should go."

She studied me, apparently decided the battle wasn't worth it. "Let me get a few things upstairs."

"Leave them," I said. "I like you empty-handed."

She managed a sour smile. "You are related to Garrett, aren't you? A real Southern gentleman."

"See you all at the funeral service?"

"Wouldn't miss it."

Once she'd left, I loaded a full clip into the Taurus, so it would be more of a challenge the next time somebody tried to use it on me. Then I set the gun back on the counter and climbed upstairs to the loft.

Out the window, through the tree branches, I could see Ruby and Clyde walking down toward the lake. Clyde was speaking emphatically, offering Ruby his open palm, like he really wanted to give her a gift.

I thought about what Garrett had said Friday night: *Ruby McBride—somebody Jimmy and I knew from way back.*

I wondered how a woman like Ruby got involved with guys like Jimmy and Garrett, and how she got the loyalty of someone like Clyde Simms. I wondered what Clyde was capable of in the *overprotective* department.

On Jimmy's bed was a pink cardboard cake box, the lid open, the contents spilling out. It contained various memorabilia—love letters signed *Ruby;* postcards from Jimmy's friends; dog-eared photos, many of which included Garrett. The missing photos from the mantel were here, too—Jimmy and Garrett at the seawall; Jimmy's mom, Clara Doebler. Why Ruby would've wanted these I had no idea, but divorce makes you weird. You get proprietary about odd things.

There were no company records for Techsan.

I dug to the bottom of the cake box, came up with an old denim-covered journal. I flipped through the entries quickly—all addressed to Jimmy, each signed by his mother.

After reading a few lines, I realized the book was a lost-child diary.

I sometimes advised my own clients to start such diaries, to keep their hopes up when children had been taken away in custody cases, or kidnapped by ex-spouses. You chronicle your daily life for your child, as a way of keeping them with you, keeping faith that one day they will be able to read your words. The first entry in Clara's journal was dated 1963, about the time she'd lost custody of Jimmy to the Doebler family trustees.

I didn't remember the specifics of the court battle—only that she'd had mental health problems. Jimmy had rarely talked about the custody case, at least to me, and the diary told me nothing. The entries seemed mundane—what Clara had done during the day, where she'd eaten, what the weather was like, what birds she'd seen in her backyard. The entries ended in mid-1967, when Jimmy would've been about ten.

The rest of the journal was blank. Somehow all those empty lined pages, yellowed with age, made a more pathetic statement than the five years Clara had managed to chronicle. I wondered how Jimmy had felt about the journal, and why Ruby would stick it in her *take* box.

I went downstairs, rummaged through the rolltop desk—standard bills, paperwork on the incorporation of Techsan, one folder neatly labeled *Family*.

I checked Jimmy's phone bills first. The police had apparently taken the most recent one, but April's statement was full of calls to other members of the Doebler clan—a lot of the same numbers I'd called myself on Saturday. I recognized Faye Doebler-Ingram's number. Garrett's number a dozen times.

I folded the list, set it aside.

I skimmed through the *Family* folder and found photocopied requests for county records, listings from the Social Security death index, deeds, marriage certificates, birth certificates. Jimmy had been looking into his own family's past, but apparently hadn't been at it very long. Most of the requests were dated only a month ago, barely enough time for any bureaucracy to respond.

I thought about what Jimmy had told me the night he died, about wanting to make amends with his family. Maybe the background search he'd wanted me to do was simply that—family history. Still, something about the folder bothered me. I put it aside for later.

Robert Johnson was circling my ankles, purring, no doubt asking where his new friends with the weapons had gone.

Jimmy's memorial was tonight. Garrett would be there. Ruby McBride would probably talk to him sometime today, let him know I was staying at the dome. Better to face him now, let him know I wasn't going to stay out of his problems.

Either that, or I could make the call I was dreading to San Francisco.

Robert Johnson looked up at me smugly, his eyes half closed.

"You're lucky," I told him. "You never have to visit your siblings."

CHAPTER 8

Sunday at lunchtime, there shouldn't have been any rush hour heading into Austin from the lake, but I hit one anyway.

It was forty-five minutes before I pulled in front of Garrett's apartment.

The Carmen Miranda was parked by the stairs, which may or may not have meant Garrett was home. If ballistics had come back positive, that might've been enough for Lopez to get an arrest warrant, start the indictment process, after which things would happen fast. I ran down all the possibilities I didn't like—all the things that could've gone wrong since I'd left Garrett on Friday afternoon. I hoped he'd gotten himself a lawyer.

I parked in the shade, sat with the engine idling, and thought about what to say if Garrett were home. *Just checking in. Been indicted yet? Still in debt a few million? Want to grab a beer?*

I walked up the steps of *The Friends.*

When I knocked at Garrett's door, a woman's muffled voice said, "Just a minute."

Even then, I didn't see it coming.

I stood there stupidly as the door opened, the woman looking down at a fistful of bills, saying, "I don't have correct change."

And then she looked up.

She was barefoot, dressed in khaki walking shorts, an

army green tank top. Her skin was a rich honey color, her hair long and glossy black.

Some vestigial gland in my body started to work, dumping a few cc's of acid into my bloodstream—just enough to make every vein burn.

"Hello, Tres," Maia Lee said. "You're not the pizza man."

She wore no makeup, no jewelry. Her eyes glowed with that internal heat which makes her a formidable enemy, or friend. If she was at all ruffled to see me again, after nearly two years, she hid it superbly.

"Okay, I'll bite," I managed. "Why are you in my brother's apartment?"

"Nice to see you, too."

"Let me rephrase that. Where the hell is Garrett?"

She stepped back, out of the doorway, motioned me inside.

I brushed past her. Acid kept coursing around my circulatory system. My hands were sweating like an adolescent's.

Nobody was in the living room, just Dickhead the parrot up on his window-ledge perch. Music was playing—Buffett's greatest hits, but set to Maia's volume level, so soft, intimate, for Garrett's place that it struck me as insulting.

I walked through the kitchen, into the bedroom. No suitcase on the bed. No unpacked Maia clothes.

Out on the shoebox-sized deck, Garrett was sitting in a patio chair, the tails of an XXL Hawaiian shirt melting around his waist, a John Deere gimme cap shading his eyes. Papers littered the deck around him. He had an open beer at his side, a laptop set up on a TV tray, a joint hanging off the corner of his mouth. Hunter S. Thompson does South Texas.

"I see you made your calls," I told him.

He missed a stroke on the keyboard, glared up at me. He spoke with the joint still in his mouth. "I'm busy. Wait a minute."

He went back to typing—the way Garrett always types, with a vengeance, as if the keys needed to learn their lesson.

I stepped to the railing, tried to put aside the appealing idea of throwing Garrett's laptop off the balcony.

Of course, I wouldn't have been the first to have that thought at *The Friends*. The alley below was littered with broken couches, smashed TVs, mounds of clothes still on hangers.

Floorboards creaked behind me.

Maia stood in the doorway, her arms crossed, pizza money still crumpled in one hand. The sunlight through the canopy of branches made her face and shoulders look like camouflage. I resented the fact that she looked even better than I'd remembered.

She met my eyes—daring me to speak first.

"Where did we leave off?" I mused. "That's right—you were just telling me how much you hated visiting Texas."

"Garrett called *me,* Tres—months ago, when Matthew Peña first approached them."

"You represented Peña twice—got him off the hook twice."

She nodded. "And when Garrett asked my advice, I told him as much as I could without breaking attorney-client privilege. I told him that under no circumstances, ever, should his company deal with Matthew Peña."

"That worked real well."

Anger flickered in her eyes. "Garrett kept me posted. When Jimmy Doebler—With what happened Thursday night, I felt responsible. I came down."

"From San Francisco."

"Yes, Tres. Modern conveniences, like airplanes, make that possible."

Her expression gave me nothing to feed on. It was calm, irritatingly professional.

"You could've at least—"

"What, Tres? Called? Garrett made it clear he did not want you involved. Frankly, I agreed with him."

Garrett kept clacking on the keyboard, pretending to ignore us.

Across the alley, on the second-story deck of the frat

house, a bare-chested Greek was drinking a beer. Perfect contentment—a lazy Sunday afternoon, one more party day before summer school started. I wondered if I could bean him from here with a rock.

Instead I reached down, scooped up some of the papers around Garrett's seat.

There was a list of the companies who were beta-testing Techsan's security software. Co_op.com, Austin's online health food store. Ticket Time, the local event promoter. Four others I'd never heard of—a West Texas petroleum company, two Internet financial service groups, a boating supply retailer—no doubt Ruby McBride's contribution to their client list. There was a list of reported security leaks, about a dozen in all, most from the petroleum company and the two financial service groups, the companies with the biggest budgets and the most to lose. One letter from the CEO of the oil company formally canceled the contract with Techsan and warned of a suit. The letter cited three different confidential in-house reports that had been posted anonymously to a Usenet group—a leak that could cost the company millions. There were more letters like that—horror stories from the beta-testers, irate e-mails, threats to sue Techsan out of existence. There was also one fax to Garrett, on Matthew Peña's letterhead, dated April 1, just before all hell broke loose. The fax read, *Look forward to doing business with you.* —M. An Austin number was written underneath.

I stared at the M. for a long time.

Garrett finally slammed the top of the keyboard shut. He took the joint out of his mouth, smushed it against the back of the monitor.

Maia said, "I guess that means no luck."

"There's nothing else I can try from here. I need to get to the office."

"You go through a lot of laptops?" I asked.

Garrett glowered at me. "Ruby insists on a meeting tonight. She's scared—wants to sell out. I've got one afternoon to find something—some proof that we can isolate the problem."

"Can you trace the leaked documents?" I asked. "Figure out where they came from?"

"You don't think I've thought of that, little bro? I'd have to have permission from the beta-test companies—get full access to their servers. The ones that were most affected are suing our asses. They aren't letting me anywhere near their machines."

"Can you get somebody to help you look? Ruby?"

"No."

"The police?"

"*Hell* no."

I held up the fax from Matthew Peña. "Any more love notes lying around?"

Garrett looked at the fax like he wanted to set it on fire. "You're starting your class tomorrow. I hope that's the only reason you're here—you need a place to stay."

"But you've already got company."

Maia stared at me stonily.

Garrett set aside his computer, brushed the ashes off the cover. "She's staying at the Driskill, little bro. Don't be rude."

"Let me guess," I said. "Matthew Peña's staying there, too."

Maia raised her eyebrows. "What makes you so sure?"

"You'll crowd him. Give him no room to breathe. Try to redirect the police investigation toward him. That's your plan, isn't it?"

"You assume a lot."

"You wouldn't come down here to defend Garrett. You're an offensive player. Something turned you against Peña. It's Peña you're after."

Three seconds of silence. "Tres, do us both a favor. Leave now."

It was the first break in her coldness—when she said the word *favor*. It wasn't much, nothing I would've caught had I not known her for a decade. Just the slightest indication that she wanted me gone for more reasons than one.

I folded Peña's fax. "I can't sit this out, Garrett."

"You and the goddamn ranch."

"It's more than that."

He stared past the balcony railing, like he was taking aim at something a long way off. He didn't reply.

After a moment, Maia pointed at me, then pointed inside.

Reluctantly, I followed.

In the living room, Buffett was still singing his greatest hits. The parrot was bobbing his head, crooning the only words he knew—"dickhead," "noisy bastard," a few other cute obscenities.

"It would've been more helpful if you were the pizza guy," Maia told me. "I had nothing but peanuts on the plane, went straight from the airport to the homicide office."

"Peña," I said. "Is he as bad as he looks on paper?"

She made a boat out of her money. "Worse."

There were pale Vs on the tops of her feet, remnants of a suntan through flip-flops. I wondered if she still spent Saturday afternoons in the Mission, seeking out the only oasis of sunshine in San Francisco.

"I have to turn the investigation away from Garrett," she said. "If the case goes to the DA the way it is . . ."

She didn't finish. She didn't have to. We both understood why she couldn't wait for an indictment, why no defense lawyer would ever want to defend a friend in court. If the police felt confident enough to arrest Garrett, if the case went to trial without a plea bargain—the odds for acquittal got very long indeed.

"And you still don't want my help," I said.

"That's Garrett's call."

"Is it?" I picked up Garrett's phone.

Maia frowned. "What are you—".

I hadn't really been expecting any luck—not on a Sunday afternoon—but on the third ring a cheery receptionist's voice said, "Mr. Peña's offices. This is Krystal."

I knew she spelled it with a K. She sounded like the K variety of Krystal.

I told her I was the personal assistant to one of Matthew's venture capitalist friends. I knew it was last-minute, but my boss was going to be *super*-pissed if I couldn't squeeze him in for an appointment with Matthew sometime today.

Maia made an emphatic *cut* gesture across her throat.

"Oh, man," Krystal sympathized. "This is such a bummer, but Mr. Peña is out the rest of the afternoon."

"Out?" I tried to sound devastated.

"Yeah. I'm *really* sorry. He took some prospective clients to Windy Point."

Maia was glaring at me.

"Windy Point," I said. "Isn't that on the lake somewhere?"

"Yeah," Krystal agreed. "The scuba place. Mr. Peña is big on that, you know? Likes to impress clients by taking them under, bonding with the fish. Ha, ha."

"Yeah," I agreed. "Ha, ha."

"So, like, he's out there teaching these guys to scuba dive. I'm really sorry."

I winked at Maia. "That's okay, Krystal. In fact, that's just about perfect. Thanks."

I hung up, told Maia where Matthew Peña was, what he was doing.

Her reaction was just what I expected.

She looked nauseated, swallowed deeply. "I'll catch him tomorrow."

"Sure," I agreed. "Me, I think I'll go out to Windy Point. I'll try not to mess things up for you too bad."

She glared at the floor, called me several unflattering names in Mandarin. I knew the names well enough. She'd called me them before. "You insist on wedging your way into this, don't you?"

I gestured toward the door. "After you?"

The pizza man was just coming up the stairs.

Maia told him to go upstairs, give the pizza to the guy with no legs.

She said she didn't anticipate being hungry again for a very long time.

CHAPTER 9

The man in the wet suit had just finished getting sick.

He was hunched over on a picnic bench, elbows on his knees, the purged contents of his stomach speckling the grass between his feet. His face glistened with sweat and lake water, the sclerae of his eyes an unhealthy shade of egg yolk yellow.

As Maia and I walked toward him, his expression turned from misery to embarrassment. The message was clear: *Please let me suffer in privacy.*

"You okay?" I asked.

He had pinched features, a Mediterranean tan. He was probably in his late twenties, though he looked older from the sun lines scoring his eyes and mouth. Handsome, in a small, tight way. His hair was a close-cropped skullcap of chocolate brown, water trickling off behind his ears. He had eyes like an old lady's poodle—big and dark, filled with mournful self-consciousness, anxiety over the fact that he wasn't a bulldog.

"Guess I need a little more practice," he said.

We were at the last picnic table on Windy Point, next to the metal stairs that led down a twenty-foot limestone cliff to the water. Dragonflies zagged in drunken orbits over the grass. A strong, steady breeze blew off the headlands— the kind of wind that would hide a sunburn on a day like this, not let you know you'd become fried and dehydrated until it was too late.

Behind us, in the woods, several dozen scuba campers had set up their tents, equipment trailers, barbecue pits. I could smell hamburgers cooking. Red and white dive flags decorated everything. Swimsuits and dive skins were draped over lawn chairs. The black rubbery hoses of regulators hung in live oak branches like trophy-kill octopi.

The little gravel road ended at our feet. There was nothing farther but the drop-off and the lake.

Maia Lee didn't look much better than the scuba diver. She'd looked progressively worse the closer we'd gotten to the lake. Apparently, though, she remembered scuba training better than I did. She noticed the sick man's air tank standing upright on the table—a big no-no in the world of diving. She picked up the tank and laid it on the ground sideways, where it couldn't fall over and cause mischief.

"Thanks," the man murmured. "Forgot."

And then he took another look at her, squinting to make out her face in the sun. "Don't I—Miss Lee?"

"Hello, Dwight."

If it was possible for Dwight to look any more nauseated, he did. "Oh my God. Matthew called you out here?"

I placed the name. Dwight Hayes—the AccuShield employee who had supported Matthew Peña's statement about his girlfriend falling off the dinner yacht.

"Dwight," Maia said, "this is a friend of mine, Tres Navarre."

He looked surprised by my proffered hand, reached for it, then almost immediately pulled back. "Navarre?"

"As in Garrett Navarre of Techsan Software," Maia said. "That's right."

Maia had slipped into her professional tone, the one she used for reluctant witnesses—putting them at ease, reassuring them, letting them know she was a friend.

Her tone didn't seem to work too well on Dwight.

"Not again," he moaned. "You're here about—"

"About Jimmy Doebler's murder," Maia supplied. "Yes."

"Then Matthew *did* call you."

"No. I'm afraid Mr. Peña will need different representation this time. How's he been treating you, Dwight?"

Hayes looked miserable. He unzipped his wet suit to the waist, peeled his arms out of the sleeves. The warm neoprene let off its unmistakable smell. If car tires had armpits, they would smell like that.

"I couldn't—" He faltered. He made a claw over his nose and mouth, pantomiming an oxygen mask. "I have no control down there. I panic. He asks me to clear my mask, twenty feet down, and the water rushes into my nose—I forget how to breathe."

I could tell Maia was fighting to keep the professional demeanor intact, trying not to betray her own phobia.

"It takes a few tries," she sympathized.

Hayes shook his head dejectedly. "You don't get it. This is the third time. He makes me keep trying—embarrassing myself in front of clients. Matthew enjoys seeing me panic. He enjoys it."

"Sounds like the conversations we had in San Francisco, Dwight. Do you remember?"

He blushed. "Maia, I shouldn't even talk to you. I could get fired."

"Then maybe we should talk to Peña directly," I suggested.

Hayes gave me the apprehensive poodle eyes, then he pointed over the edge of the cliff, down toward the water. "Blue flag."

The lake was calm—no speedboats in the channel. A hundred feet out, buoys marked off the diving area. Bubbles of submerged divers made glassy scars on the water. About twenty feet from the shore, three bubble marks were stationary, right next to a blue donut-shaped marker.

"How long have they been down there?" I asked.

"Not long," Hayes said. "I panicked right away on this dive. They'll be down another forty minutes, at least."

"Tres . . ." Maia started. Her *fair warning* tone.

"We're about the same size," I told Dwight. "Mind if I borrow your gear?"

"No, Tres," Maia said. "We can wait."

"I'll pay the rental for it. You'll recoup your losses. Think how glad Matthew will be to see me."

Dwight looked stunned. Then he surprised me, maybe surprised himself, with a faint, queasy smile. His eyes glimmered with a kind of mischief he probably didn't get to practice much. "I'm going to regret this. Take the stuff."

"You are *not* going into the water," Maia insisted.

I checked the pressure gauge on Dwight Hayes' tank, found that it was just below max at 3,000 psi. "You want to come, Maia? By all means. We're a team, right?"

Her face turned livid. "You haven't become less of a bastard the last two years, Tres Navarre."

She turned and stormed off, realized she was heading toward a dead-end cliff, strode the other way, down the road.

It isn't often I get to discombobulate her so thoroughly. I had to smile.

"Oh, Christ," Dwight said. "I shouldn't have—"

"Don't worry," I told him. "She just hates it when I get to have all the fun."

Then I stripped to my Texas-flag jockey shorts right there in front of God and everybody.

Five minutes and thirty pounds later, I was suited up. Dwight's buoyancy compensator—the inflatable vest divers call the BC—was a little tight on me, but everything else fit tolerably well. The lead weights on the belt thudded against my hipbone on the way down the ladder.

It was a relief to hit the water and go weightless, feel the coolness work its way under the wet suit. I floated away from the ladder, the BC inflated to keep me up, and struggled to get the fins on over the neoprene booties. The water smelled of soil and fish spawn and oily slicks of the baby shampoo divers use to defog their masks.

From the top of the cliff, Dwight Hayes watched me as I kicked toward the blue floating marker.

I put in the regulator mouthpiece, sucked in a first dry, cold breath, then raised the deflator hose of the BC and let out the air.

I had a moment of disorientation as the world flickered white, melted in a soup of green bubbles. Then I was
underwater, sinking slowly.

Sound became a physical force—an insect doing circles around my head, making kamikaze runs into my ears.
Every exhale set off a minor earthquake of bubbles. I
heard pings and clicks and whines and had no idea where
any of them were coming from.

I pinched the nose pocket of my mask to equalize
pressure. I remembered to breathe, to swallow the pow-
dery coldness of the regulator air out of my throat. The
skills came back to me—but Dwight Hayes was right. It
was unsettling. My breakfast had been mercifully light,
but even the yogurt and fruit was threatening to retreat up
my throat.

I sank through green and yellow light, following the
frayed nylon rope of the marker into the murk below.
There was about five feet of visibility.

I saw bubble streams below me first, then the figures
from which they came. Three streaks of oil resolved into
human forms. A silver sheen became a floating underwater
platform—a railed grid of metal maybe fifteen feet square.
Two divers were on their knees on the platform, feeding
hot dogs to a frenzy of Guadalupe river bass and catfish.
The third diver was floating effortlessly above them, observing. The water around them was cloudy with fish poop,
and pieces of hot dog that would soon be converted to fish
poop.

I turned horizontal, aimed my fins, and kicked toward
the floating guy. Anybody who could float must be the instructor.

He was dressed in a Farmer John style wet suit—
sleeveless, U-neck. The highlight stripes on the suit were
blue, as was his mask frame and the middle of each fin.
Even his tank was blue. His arms and neck were smoothly
muscled, the rest of his body lean, athletic. His hair was
a short black cloud that moved in the water the way
smoke boils over a petroleum fire. His hands were clasped

lightly over his weight belt and his legs pigeoned, scissoring gently whenever he needed to correct buoyancy.

When he noticed me he raised his hand—either as a greeting or a sign to stop, I couldn't tell which.

I looked at the blue man's two companions, gave them the okay sign. Each returned it. I pointed at them, then at the platform, telling them to stay put.

I looked at the blue man.

Behind the mouthpiece of his regulator, I could see he had a mustache and goatee. His skin looked extraordinarily sallow, but that may have been a trick of the water. His eyes were preternaturally clear in the mask's pocket of air—milk-white corneas, pupils the color of burnt wood, calm to the point of being scary.

He pointed at my chest, then pointed away.

I gestured for the message slate hanging on his belt.

After a moment's hesitation, he handed it over. I put the black grease pen to the white surface and wrote, *Maia sez hello*.

He took the board, read it, then hesitated, the tip of the pen over it, as if he was considering his next move in tic-tac-toe. He crossed out my sentence, wrote, handed it back.

CLASS—GO AWAY!

My knee bounced lightly against the platform. I tilted off balance like a Ferris wheel basket. I groped for the inflate button on the BC hose, sent a burst of air from the tank into the vest until I neutralized. Matthew Peña just floated there, analyzing me.

I regained enough control to use the message board, then wrote, *5 minutes—Jimmy D insists*.

Matthew Peña read, wiped the board clean, clipped it back in his belt. He pointed at his two students, tapped his pressure gauge console. Both checked their own gauges. Each made finger numbers to indicate they had about 2,000 psi left. Peña gestured, *Okay. Wait here*.

Then he pointed to me and pointed over his shoulder.

He kicked off into the green murk.

I followed.

Distance was hard to measure, but we sank down to about thirty feet, headed what I judged to be north, along the shore. I had to equalize my ears again. A catfish the size of my forearm flicked by. Giant boulders made a wall to our right. The bottom was furry with tan sediment—nature's shag carpeting.

After about twelve kick cycles, a new shape resolved on the lake bottom—a welded metal sculpture of a diver, canted down at forty-five degrees. His limbs and body were six-inch pipes, his mask and fins 2D sheets of steel. Apparently he was a major attraction at Windy Point. He'd been decorated with three different sets of sexy lingerie. A lacy purple bra floated off one of his fins.

It was as good a place as any for a conference with Matthew Peña. Then I looked over and realized I didn't know where Matthew Peña was. He'd disappeared—a ridiculously easy task underwater, where peripheral vision is nil.

I turned my head the other way, then heard a *squeak-squeak-squeak* that seemed to come from inside my skull. It wasn't until my next inhale proved hard to pull that I realized Matthew Peña had come up behind me and turned off my air.

I rotated face-up. Sure enough, Peña was floating above me. His burnt eyes weren't gloating, weren't smiling. They were just observing, the way a fish observes—impartially looking for something smaller to devour.

My next inhale was a wall—nothing came into my lungs.

Matthew Peña tapped his fingers to his palm in a little bye-bye wave.

The first rule of diving: Don't panic. I knew that. But rules take on a new dimension when you're thirty feet under with no air. A more experienced diver might've gambled on getting to the valve of his tank without panicking, without getting tangled in his own equipment. I knew I needed a simpler alternative.

I kept exhaling—kept the little trail of bubbles coming out of my mouth, even though I knew there was nothing to replace them with.

Then I reached over, grabbed Matthew Peña's mask and ripped it off his face. The snorkel came with it.

Peña protested with an explosion of white bubbles, grabbed after the mask.

I left him blinking in the green, his vision reduced to smudges. Then I kicked for the surface, holding the BC hose up and keeping my other hand on the weight belt, one finger still hooked on Peña's mask and snorkel.

I tried to avoid kicking up too fast, even though my lungs told me I was dying. The pain was unbearable when the water turned silver and the top shimmered like sun on aluminum foil, but I still wasn't to the surface. A thousand decades later, I broke through and gasped, then found my head underwater again. I used my exhale to manually inflate the BC, kicked to the surface again, got another gasp, went under, repeated the inflation process until I was buoyant.

I floated on the surface, breathing hard.

No problem. Just a little thirty-foot-under chat with a suspect. A little near-death experience.

Great plan, Navarre.

I put my snorkel in, went down headfirst, and started fumbling around behind me for the K-valve. I soon realized I'd have to free up both hands to accomplish the task. I pitched Matthew Peña's mask and snorkel out toward the boating channel, then put my face back underwater, found the K-valve, turned on the air.

I saw Peña below me, making a casual ascent, his eyes dark and open and completely blind. I put my head above water as he surfaced ten feet away.

He used the automatic inflate on his BC, rose a few more inches out of the water.

His eyes were bloodshot, his face crawling with irritation.

The paleness of his skin had not been a trick of the

water. Now that the regulator was out of his mouth, I could see cruel thin lips, outlined by neatly trimmed, coarse black whiskers.

He said, "Where's my mask?"

I pointed toward the middle of the lake.

He started to say something, stopped himself. "That was $400 worth of equipment."

"And I'm charging $200 per breath of air, which makes us even."

He brought up his hand console, read the computer, let it float back under. "I'll get the mask later. Which way did you throw it?"

I showed him.

"That's about a hundred and twenty feet deep, the way the shore drops off into the river channel. Thanks a lot."

I smiled. "I'm Garrett Navarre's brother. It was no problem, really."

Peña's eyes got small. "I don't have time for this."

"You shouldn't have time to screw with people's lives, either. But you seem to manage."

Peña put his mouth and nose underwater, seemed to whisper something to the fish, then raised up again. "Maia warned me about you. She was quite irrational on the subject—claimed you could be an annoyance."

"I'm flattered."

"Annoy me, and you'll get hurt."

"I read about your girlfriend," I said. "She must've annoyed you pretty bad."

The scariest thing was the millisecond delay in his face, the processing time during which Matthew Peña seemed to make a conscious choice which emotions to show me. He decided on a combination of hurt and anger.

"You have no right to speak about Adrienne. You know nothing about it."

"I know this, Peña: Maia's not protecting you this time."

"And you're doing your best to jeopardize your brother's only chance at a buyout, aren't you?"

I hated that he made me hesitate.

"Techsan isn't my concern," I said.

Traces of a smile flickered across his mouth. "Really."

"I'm just here to tell you, Peña—if you had anything to do with Jimmy's murder, you will be nailed. If you decide to harass my brother with any more faxes, e-mails, or mess-with-your-mind presents, I'll become a regular at your scuba classes. I'll follow you to work every day. I will introduce myself to all your prospective clients. You will get to know me very well."

He looked toward the shore where Maia and Dwight were both now standing—little six-inch dolls from this distance.

"Maia Lee in the flesh," Peña said appreciatively. "A shame she couldn't take a friendly warning, stick with a winning team."

"You're the one who's been warned, Matthew."

"Yes," he agreed easily. "I was sorry to hear Doebler and your brother had a falling-out. Sorry your brother went off the deep end. But this is a high-stakes business, Mr. Navarre. Those things happen. I'll attend the service tonight to pay my respects."

I started to kick back toward shore. "I can hardly wait."

"And Mr. Navarre? If I really was the sort of person you think I am, you realize I would now make it my personal hobby to destroy you."

"Be an expensive hobby, Matthew. Stick to scuba."

He put the regulator back in his mouth. He raised his BC hose and hissed out the air from his vest, sunk below the surface, still without a mask.

What he would do down there with limited vision, I had no idea, but something told me Matthew Peña was a lot more vicious than anything else he might encounter under Lake Travis. He'd find his way.

I got to the ladder.

At the top of the cliff, Maia Lee was waiting, looking furious. "What were you saying earlier, Tres, about not messing up?"

I dismantled my gear at the picnic table.

Dwight Hayes held the air tank while I detached it from my back.

"He didn't recognize the suit," Dwight asked anxiously, "did he?"

I stripped off the wet suit, left two twenties under the weight belt to pay for the rental, then put my T-shirt and jeans back on over damp jockey shorts.

"I'm not going back in there," Dwight decided. "I don't care what Matthew says."

Maia put her hand on his shoulder. "Dwight—think about what I said, okay?"

He shook his head. "I can't, Maia. He's already going to be mad enough. You don't blame me, do you?"

Maia gave me a cold stare, and I realized I really had screwed up. I'd completely misread Maia's reasons for coming out here.

"Of course I don't blame you," she told Dwight. "Take care of yourself. You have my number if you change your mind."

As we walked back up the gravel path, Maia muttered a few choice curses in Mandarin.

"You came out to work on Dwight Hayes," I said. "He's the weak link in Peña's armor. You didn't want to pressure Peña at all."

"And by hardballing Peña, you just made Dwight more apprehensive about talking to me. Nice job, genius."

"You could've told me."

She muttered some more curses, then trudged ahead, apparently determined to get out of scuba country as fast as she could.

I took one last look back at Dwight Hayes, but he was paying us no attention. He was staring out over the edge of the cliff, watching the smooth scars on the water below, waiting for his boss to emerge.

X-eChats-Return: sentto-355226-181-959416158
Mailing-List: list MyFriends@echats.com; contact
MyFriends-owner@ echats.com
Delivered-To: mailing list MyFriends@echats.com
Date: Sun 11 Jun 2000 8:29:18 -0000
From: watcher@echats.com
Reply-To: noone@echats.com
To: list@echats.com
Subject: women

She's intriguing.

Reminds me of Adrienne.

This one's apartment rises from the top of
Potrero Hill, above the wine shop, between an Italian
restaurant and an antiques store, on that cold stucco
and asphalt hill that always smells of roasting coffee.

White inside—stark white. Huge windows.
Hardwood floors. Not much else. You can stand at
her windows at night—watch the fog pour into the
valleys, the lights of downtown, the pearl necklace of
the Bay Bridge. You can stand there in a thousand
square feet of air and almost believe she's as cold as
she lets on.

You have to look deep to find anything softer,
anything interesting.

Her closet is a row of beige and white. Good
brands, expensive fabrics—raw silk, pure linen.
Running fingers through her wardrobe, you can just
catch her scent—a perfume she wears too lightly to
be perceptible on a single outfit.

In the back of her closet is a shoebox, fastened
with rubber bands. Inside are her naturalization papers
from 1969. She was ten years old, a cute kid, judging
from the picture—but sad, looking like she was just hit
and is trying real hard not to cry. There are five or six
other photos—not enough for me to take one, unfortunately. Yellowing black and white shots—an old man

in a traditional Asian robe. The writing on the back is in Chinese—at least I suppose that's what it was. A few other pictures of old people.

Then there's the photo of the house. I guess you could call it a house. It looks like something from Tijuana or Zaire—a box put together from old doors and corrugated tin, clinging to the side of a rubble mound as if it had just slid there from the top. No grass, just dirt—chickens pecking at rocks. A huge mulberry tree on a hill in the back—the only thing that looks healthy.

I memorized that photo. The old Chinese people didn't interest me. But places. Places are important.

I looked at the photo, then I looked at the apartment—the clean white walls, the glass. I understood why it had to be perfect, how she must wake up at night and imagine she is six or seven years old—rocks under her straw mat, rain dripping through cracks in the tin roof. I felt close to her, thinking about that.

In her nightstand drawer, on the left-hand side, she keeps a gun—a Sig Sauer. I toyed with the idea of using that information, but no. The right path for her is too obvious, if it comes to that.

I remember sitting on her bed and thinking about Adrienne. This wasn't long after the night on the boat. I still had that small electric current inside, that sense that I'd played it close. Too close. And it had been wonderful.

I attract women like her—the ones who don't know when to stop.

"Yes," I wanted to tell her. "I remember what it was like. I remember what happens when a woman steps into your life. And I will step into yours, instead."

CHAPTER 10

I've never shared a quieter forty-minute drive.

We stopped by the Driskill long enough for Maia to change. I waited in the lobby, tried not to look too stunned when Maia appeared in black—a color she never wore, and one that looked damn good on her.

Jimmy Doebler's memorial service was on Airport Boulevard at a small Unitarian church—a prefab Box-o-God wedged between a Taco Bell and a While-U-Wait key shop.

I looked for the drive-thru window on the church, didn't find one, and decided we'd have to park.

Inside, pews made a C around the altar. About forty people sat listening to the organist play her prelude—a mournful, highly spiritual rendition of "Cheeseburger in Paradise."

The crowd looked like what you'd expect at a funeral for a Parrot Head, as Buffett fans called themselves. There were scruffy men in jeans and Hawaiian shirts, ladies in tube tops and Indian-print skirts—people who knew their way around a margarita machine.

One notable exception in the front row was W.B. Doebler—a blue pin-striped island in a sea of tropical prints. At the opposite end of the pew sat Ruby McBride in black pants and V-neck blouse, white linen jacket, pearl necklace.

Behind her sat her biker bodyguard, Clyde Simms.

Clyde had forgotten his Bizon-2 this evening, but his fashion statement still qualified as lethal force—a scarlet silk suit, black dress shirt, silver bola. His blond hair fanned out around his shoulders. The World Wrestling Federation goes to a wake.

Garrett sat beside a pew in the back, where his wheelchair wouldn't get in the way. He was holding note cards for his eulogy. I tried to remember the last time I'd seen him in a coat and tie.

Next to him, at the end of the pew, sat Detective Victor Lopez. Something told me that Garrett had not been the one to pick this seating arrangement.

Maia made a short hissing sound when she spotted Lopez.

"Detective," she said. "Would you mind moving—perhaps to a different sanctuary?"

Lopez grinned, scooted over. "That's okay, counselor. Plenty of room."

We slipped into the pew—Maia next to Lopez, me next to Garrett. Four friendly mourners.

The lines in Garrett's face were deep, his eyes watery.

"You okay?" I asked.

He looked at me, bent his index cards. "Not the first adjective I'd pick. No."

Lopez reached across Maia's lap and tapped my knee. "Say hey, Mr. Navarre. We need to talk."

He wore jeans and a dress shirt and a beige summer-weight jacket. His eyes were bloodshot, his chin shadowed in stubble. Either he hadn't been to sleep last night or he was trying to blend in with the Jimmy Doebler crowd. "You got somebody to call the medical examiner's office for you," he said. "That's a big naughty."

An older, well-dressed woman in the pew in front of us glanced back, frowning.

Maia said, "You did *what*, Tres?"

I whispered to Lopez, "Did it work?"

Lopez sighed. *What's a cop to do?* "I don't know how many other friends you've got who can pull favors for you in Austin, Mr. Navarre—"

"Tres," I insisted. "You're going to chew me out, call me Tres."

"—but this is not your home turf. You try your normal crap here—I shouldn't even bother warning you. You want something, you *ask* me."

"Ha," said Maia.

"Shhh," said the woman in front of us.

Lopez handed across a manila folder, which Maia intercepted. She pulled out the papers, stared at Lopez. I could see the letterhead—Travis County Medical Examiner. Jimmy Doebler's autopsy report.

"You're letting us read this?" Maia asked.

"Counselor, you hurt me. You underestimate how much I would do to allay your suspicions. The things you and your friends could accomplish if you only asked."

We both stared at him.

He cracked a grin.

Maia shook her head in disgust, began to read.

The minister began his introductory spiel. He directed most of his comforting comments to Ruby, the grieving ex-widow. At the other end of the pew, W.B. Doebler shifted uncomfortably, checking his fat gold watch.

Maia finished reading the autopsy report, slipped it to me.

"Lethal levels of amitriptyline?" she asked Lopez.

"It's Elavil," Lopez said. "An antidepressant. Doebler had been hospitalized for clinical depression about a year ago. He must've had some stash left."

Garrett was clutching his note cards, glaring intently ahead, trying not to look at the report in my hands.

A guy in a red Aloha shirt and black Levi's came to the podium with a guitar. He said he wanted to play "A Pirate Looks at 40," Jimmy's favorite song. We could all sing along.

I finished scanning the report, offered it to Garrett, who shook his head adamantly. I returned it to Lopez. "Why would Jimmy poison himself?"

Lopez gave me a look I couldn't quite read, but it was obvious the tox report bothered him.

"The levels in Doebler's blood," he said, "the amount he took, combined with the alcohol, would've sent him into a coma within thirty minutes. Another thing, there were no undigested pill casings in Doebler's stomach. Could mean he's a fast digester. Could mean he didn't take the medicine in pill form."

The guy in the Aloha shirt kept murdering Jimmy's favorite song. The lady in the next pew kept giving us evil glances for talking.

"It was Doebler's medication," Maia said. "He was depressed."

"Sure," Lopez conceded. "On the other hand—now this is my sergeant talking, you understand, just speculation—if you wanted to kill somebody, what better way to make them docile than to OD them with their own medication? Especially, say, if you couldn't normally overpower this person."

Lopez glanced at Garrett, gave him a friendly smile. "What's your take on it?"

Maia said, "Ballistics."

Lopez snapped his fingers. "Yeah. Knew there was something else. The projectile was pretty mangled—soft bullet, a .380. It was, sorry to say, definitely a .380. Lands and grooves were pretty messed up, but ballistics couldn't rule out that it was fired from Mr. Navarre's gun."

"And couldn't say for certain that it was," Maia pointed out.

Lopez paused. "You know, you're right, counselor. I guess you could look at this as good news." He gave Garrett a thumbs-up sign. "Good news, Mr. Navarre. Now all we have to do is find the other guy who was roaming the lake at 2:00 A.M. with a .380, and we got this case cracked."

"The shell casing," I said. "You recover it?"

Lopez looked irritated. "You should see the grass stains on the knees of my slacks. All us diligent deputies, rooting around in the dirt. Several acres later, we still have no casing."

"You know that's wrong," Maia said. "You claimed

the shot was close range—someone inside the truck cab. And the casing is missing?"

"We looked hard, counselor. Even sent a diver in the water. If it was anywhere, we would've found it."

"It's like the drugs," Maia said. "You're working this as a crime of passion, argument between friends—it doesn't fit. Somebody picked up that casing. That's the mark of a professional."

"Yeah, well. You or your—what should I say, client or friend? How does this work, you being an attorney from out of state, and all?"

Maia didn't deign to answer. We both knew Lopez would've researched exactly how it worked.

I knew from past interstate cases with Maia, she would be able to handle one case in Texas as a professional courtesy from the state bar—*pro hac vice*—if it came to formal charges. Before charges, however, Maia's professional status in Texas, and thus the professional courtesy the police had to extend her, was questionable, at best.

"Whether it's client or friend," Maia told Lopez, "depends on your department."

He smiled. "Your friend, then. Mr. Navarre wants to explain things to me, maybe throw a little hard evidence my way, I'd be more than obliged."

The song ended. The Wicked Witch of the Tenth Pew gave Lopez a scowl. Probably she didn't even know Jimmy Doebler. Probably she came to all the Unitarian funerals just to get her dourness fix.

Lopez sat back, spread his fingers out on his knees. The back of his right hand was dimpled with pockmarks, the skin slightly puffy—like he'd been bitten by a snake, numerous times, many years ago. I hoped it had been an unpleasant experience.

The preacher came to the podium, fixed his glasses, and said it was time for a eulogy by one of Jimmy's oldest friends.

He called my brother's name and complete stillness fell over the room. Some of the mourners glanced back in our direction with cold stares. In the front row, W.B. Doebler cleared his throat.

Lopez whispered, "Go on, Mr. Navarre. Your moment to shine."

Garrett didn't move.

More heads started to turn.

Finally Maia said, "Come on. I'll go with you."

She scooted past me, took the back of Garrett's chair, began pushing him toward the front. I'd never seen Garrett allow anyone to push his chair. He considered it an egregious insult. Nevertheless, he sat still, intent, as Maia wheeled him toward the microphone.

In the pew behind me, someone murmured a question to a friend, something that ended with the word *murder*.

The friend's response was audible: "I were Garrett, I sure as hell wouldn't get up there and give no speech."

I turned. The guys behind me were a couple of innocuous-looking Parrot Heads—standard flowery shirts, day-old beards. I'd probably met them before at one of Garrett's parties.

"If you were Garrett," I told them, "you wouldn't have kneecaps I could shoot off if you don't shut up."

I turned back around.

Lopez muttered, "Somebody without a sense of humor might take what you just said the wrong way, Navarre."

Garrett started his eulogy. Maia stood to one side for moral support.

"I know a guy at state ballistics," I told Lopez. "Department of Public Safety. Let me call him—get a second opinion on the projectile."

Lopez laughed quietly. "A second opinion. DPS has a six-month turnaround, and you want to use them for a second opinion. Tell you what, you find me some reason to justify that—some damn good reason—then maybe. We go to court—and please God, if you have any leverage with Ms. Lee, assure her that would be a bad thing—then you can hire all the experts you want. As it stands—for the purposes of presenting this case to the DA? I'm afraid not."

Presenting the case to the DA.

"Matthew Peña," I said. "You investigate him?"

"We are not stupid, Tres. We have already been scolded by your friend Ms. Lee on that very point. Yes, Mr. Peña seems to be slightly less docile than your average man-eating tiger. Yes, he is the subject of an open homicide investigation in San Francisco. He also has a solid alibi for the night in question. He was on the Internet."

I stared at him. "You're joking."

"He was in a video conference with clients, some of the AccuShield execs, back in Cupertino. Lasted into the wee hours. I've made calls. I've seen the computer logs. It checks out."

"This guy's a high-tech mogul. You're going to accept the Internet as an alibi?"

"Welcome to the millennium, Navarre."

"There have to be ways logs could be faked, timed, dubbed, something."

Lopez smiled. "You're suggesting that AccuShield, a multibillion-dollar corporation, is an accessory to the murder of a *programmer*? You think I should arrest the CEO, maybe? The entire board?"

"Wouldn't want to do that," I said. "That would mean bringing in the Feds. And you don't want to give up this murder investigation for anything, do you?"

His reaction wasn't much, just a little tightness in his jaw, but I'd succeeded in hitting a nerve.

Garrett kept talking about his parties with Jimmy, their road trips. Nothing about Techsan. Nothing about their many past arguments. Maia stood behind him, the silent sentinel. Ruby McBride was watching her with curiosity.

Then Garrett's voice stopped mid-eulogy. Another sudden hush fell over the chapel.

Garrett was staring at the front entrance, his note cards forgotten in his hands.

Matthew Peña and Dwight Hayes stood at the back of the aisle, looking for a place to sit.

Dwight Hayes didn't look much better than he had two hours ago. His off-green tie was knotted so the skinny end was longer than the fat end.

Peña was dressed like an on-the-rise businessman, and I knew what the crowd would be thinking— Here's another of Jimmy's rich relatives. Then I glanced at W.B. Doebler, who was studying Matthew Peña with more than a little apprehension.

I wasn't sure what W.B.'s expression meant, but one thing was clear. He knew Peña.

Garrett's hesitation in the eulogy probably wasn't as long as I imagined.

Peña and Hayes found seats and sank out of sight behind some Parrot Heads.

Garrett continued talking.

I looked at Detective Lopez, but Lopez was no longer there. He was squeezing over the legs of five or six people to get out the far side of the pew. When he got to the exit he paused, glanced in Peña's direction, then at me.

I gave him a questioning look. He winked, then was gone. Probably gone to change into his Batman suit.

I tried to listen to the rest of Garrett's eulogy, but my eyes kept drifting to Maia Lee—the black shoulder straps of her dress, the way her hair curved around her ear. I looked away and happened to lock eyes with Ruby McBride, who smiled.

I refocused on Garrett.

When I looked back at Ruby a second later, she was still studying me—not in an unfriendly way. More like amused.

She turned back toward Garrett and kept that little smile on her face the whole time my brother was describing what a great fellow her murdered ex-husband had been.

CHAPTER 11

"W.B.," I called.

He was three steps away from his white Infiniti, his Nokia in one hand, his alarm deactivator in the other.

Another ninety seconds—if I'd waited for Maia and Garrett, or pushed my way out of the chapel a little less rudely—W.B. would've been gone.

"I'm Tres Navarre," I said. "Garrett's—"

"I remember."

W.B.'s eyes reminded me of Jimmy's. They had the same look of distant anger, like he was gazing past me, impatient for something to happen on the horizon.

Otherwise, W.B. bore little resemblance to his cousin. He was dark-complexioned, perfectly groomed, with features one would value in a catalogue model—handsome yet inconspicuous, completely uninteresting, so that you'd notice the clothes rather than the man. He was in his midforties, and radiated a sort of old energy that suggested he was born to be this age. It was impossible to imagine him as a child, or wearing anything but a suit.

"Glad you could make the service," I told him. "I wasn't sure any of the Doeblers would show."

"Criticism?"

"Observation."

He beeped the Infiniti's remote control. The car responded with a perky chirping noise, and the door unlatched itself.

"You saw the crowd," W.B. said. "Jimmy's people. He would've wanted them here more than he wanted his family. He got his wish."

"So Jimmy disowned the Doeblers. Not the other way around."

"I have to go, Mr. Navarre."

W.B. got into the Infiniti, selected the ignition key.

I leaned over him, one elbow on the open door. "I called your Aunt Faye. She seemed to think the family wants Jimmy's murder swept under the rug as soon as possible."

"Would you mind stepping back?"

"What'd you talk to the sheriff about, W.B.?"

He stared at me, evaluating. There wasn't a hair out of place in his part. The interior of his car smelled like Jordan almonds.

"You needn't worry," he told me. "If your brother killed Jimmy, that wouldn't surprise me. Especially not with that woman involved. But neither would I go out of my way to seek justice."

"That woman," I said. "You know Ruby?"

W.B. jammed the key in the ignition. A glowing green circle illuminated around it.

"Mr. Navarre, I came here tonight to set aside my resentment. To say goodbye to my cousin. And I'm leaving here even angrier than before. It hardly matters who killed him. Jimmy wasted his life. Now you and his self-proclaimed real friends can go have a beer in his honor. It's a damned shame."

"And if the wrong person takes the blame for his murder? That doesn't matter either?"

"Get your arm off my car, Mr. Navarre."

"You know Matthew Peña, don't you? You know what he's capable of."

W.B. picked up his Nokia, dialed a single number with his thumb.

"Deputy Engels," he said into the phone. "Would you call city police for me, please. I'm at the Unitarian church on Airport, having some trouble with an irate man from the memorial. I'd call it harassment, yes."

I stepped away, slammed Doebler's door closed for him.

Without looking at me, W.B. Doebler dropped his phone onto the passenger's seat. The door locks clicked.

His lights came on in the glare of the setting sun, and the white Infiniti pulled out onto Airport Boulevard.

CHAPTER 12

"I hate crowds," Garrett told me.

We were sitting at a window table in Scholz Bier Garten, drinking German beer that tasted like antifreeze.

A socialite wedding reception had taken over the back patio of Austin's oldest watering hole, leaving attendees of Jimmy Doebler's memorial beer bust to fight it out with the regular customers for the dozen tables and booths that were left in front.

The wedding reception guys drifted around in tuxes, the women in designer dresses. They didn't coordinate well with the neon beer signs and baseball trophies and the green vinyl booths. I thought they had a disk jockey playing Kinky Friedman tunes on the patio until somebody sneaked a look and told me nope, it was Kinky Friedman playing Kinky Friedman tunes.

At the bar, Maia was having a heated discussion with Matthew Peña—a discussion she'd insisted I stay out of. Sitting on the stool beside her, Dwight Hayes was trying to peel the label off his beer bottle.

"Shouldn't leave without your date," I told Garrett. "Looks like she's still having fun."

Garrett grumbled.

Being down so low in the wheelchair, Garrett creates the illusion of an open space in a crowd. People swarm toward him, see him only at the last second, usually spill beer on his head. One of the tuxedoed gentlemen had almost made that mistake a few minutes ago.

"You're enjoying this," Garrett told me. "You want me punished."

"Just trying to figure out why your brother, who lives seventy-five miles away, can't help, and your brother's ex-girlfriend, who lives two thousand miles away, can."

"She's better than you," he said.

Leave it to my sibling to craft the most diplomatic response possible.

"She's prettier," he added. "And she *knows* Peña. She's dealt with him."

"And like you, she's already convinced Peña's the problem."

He glared at me. "You met him today. You don't think so?"

"The guy just tried to kill me once. That doesn't exactly set him apart."

Garrett grunted. "You wonder why I don't invite you up much."

Out on the back patio, Kinky launched into "Asshole from El Paso." Wedding guests and bar patrons milled around, jostling us. Ceiling fans circled lazily, kicking around the smells of chewing tobacco and sausage.

"How did you meet Ruby?" I asked.

Garrett turned his beer in a slow circle. "What does it matter?"

"Just wondering," I said. "If Peña was going to kill somebody at Techsan, if he was trying to force a deal, why kill Jimmy? Why not Ruby or you?"

"Thanks."

"I mean Jimmy seemed . . . harmless."

Garrett's face turned as bitter as the German beer. "Write that on his fucking gravestone, why don't you?"

He ripped his cork drink coaster in two, threw the halves on the table.

"I guess I didn't mean that," I said.

His eyes were our dad's eyes—steady, scolding, a

slow-burning fire that said, *You best not lie to me, 'cause I know better.*

I watched the soccer game playing in triplicate on the TVs above the bar.

Maia's conversation with Matthew Peña didn't appear to be getting any friendlier. The bartender put two margaritas on the rocks in front of her. I wondered if she planned on drinking them both.

"You were going to have to square things with her eventually," Garrett told me. "You know that, little bro."

"My brother the shrink."

"Tell me you're over Maia," he insisted. "Tell me there's been one time since you moved back to Texas you were really convinced. If you listened to me once in a while, dumbass—"

He stopped abruptly. Maia Lee was standing by us now, a margarita in each hand. "Don't stop insulting him on my account."

She plopped into a chair, shoved the margaritas forward, spilling most of them. Her face was bright red from her encounter with Peña.

"Went that well, huh?" I asked.

Maia crossed her legs at the knee, tugged at the hem of her black linen funeral dress. Her calves below the hemline were lean and smooth. I didn't notice them at all.

"You can't sell out to Peña," she told Garrett. "You can't give the bastard the pleasure."

The margarita wasn't bad. Cointreau. Probably Cuervo Gold. Maia had called it well. Then again, I'd taught her.

I took another sip. "What did Peña do to you, Maia?"

Her eyes managed to look ferocious and serene at the same time. Predator cat eyes. "He didn't *do* anything."

"Used to be, you had two rules. You didn't defend pedophiles, and you didn't defend anyone you knew in your heart was guilty of murder. Now you're telling me this guy—a guy you defended twice—could be a murderer."

Over at the bar, Dwight Hayes was now arguing with Peña. Peña looked amused—as if he was not used to hearing anything but yes from Dwight Hayes.

Maia spread her fingers on the table, waited long enough to count them. "Ronald Terrence, my wonderful boss. He gave me the job of representing Matthew Peña last year."

"The Menlo Park case," I said. "The guy who ate his shotgun."

She nodded. "It wasn't a hard assignment. There was evidence Peña had harassed the victim, but absolutely nothing to suggest foul play in the shooting itself."

"Harassing like how?"

"Peña sent the victim e-mail threats, spiked them with a virus so they'd crash the victim's system. He made some taunting phone calls. But the shooting *was* a suicide. In the end, the police couldn't touch Peña for it. I came away with the feeling that my client was a creep, but not a murderer. I could live with that. Most of my clients are creeps. Then in January, Terrence sent me down to see Peña again. This time it was a little tougher."

"Adrienne Selak."

Maia pressed her fingers on the table, made a silent piano chord. "One of Adrienne's friends came forward. She gave a statement that Peña was violent, that he had threatened Adrienne several times. Adrienne's family pushed the police hard, demanding he be charged. They told the press their daughter's death was no accident, she was a good swimmer, she never drank to excess. Plenty of witnesses on the boat saw Matthew and Adrienne arguing. There was no physical evidence, but the circumstantial case looked bad. Peña's attitude when I interviewed him—he seemed stunned, maybe even grief-stricken. But I didn't know. I had my doubts."

"You defended him anyway," I reminded her.

"That was my job. Dwight Hayes' statement was solid. I rounded up other statements from people on the boat who'd seen Adrienne inebriated, clearly not in full control of her faculties. I found some . . . less reputable acquaintances of Adrienne's, people from her past. I got statements about her unstable personality, her drug use, some other things . . . things that would've been embarrassing for her family to hear in court. I made it clear that I would destroy Adrienne Selak's character in a trial, make it seem highly plausible she'd fallen off that boat, maybe even committed suicide. I would trash the prosecution's lack of physical evidence. Adrienne's family backed off. The police wavered. That's where we left it, as of January. They never filed charges."

"All in a good day's work," I said.

Maia didn't respond.

Garrett nursed his margarita. He was watching Peña and Hayes, who were still having words at the bar. Despite the crowd, the seat Maia had vacated there was still empty. None of Jimmy Doebler's friends was rushing to fill it.

"Most of what I learned about Matthew Peña," Maia said, "I learned afterward. He tries to destroy people, Tres. It doesn't stop when he gets what he wants. He follows up, pays visits, twists the dagger as much as he can. He toys with people's minds."

"And you found this out . . ."

"Because he tried to do it to me."

Before I could respond, Ruby McBride was there, her large friend Clyde Simms in tow.

"Well!" she said. "This must be the happy people's table."

Ruby had shed her white jacket since the memorial service. Her blouse was sleeveless and sheer. She'd wrapped a Cleopatra-style silver snake armband around her biceps. Versatile outfit—perfect for the woman who needs to hit the singles scene right after her ex-husband's funeral and doesn't want the hassle of changing.

There were no seats for our guests. Clyde folded his arms, seemed content to root there and let the crowd navigate around him.

Ruby knelt next to Garrett, draped one arm around his neck, then slipped a tiny silver camera out of her pants pocket.

She smiled at Maia and me. "*Got* to get this for the scrapbook."

The flash left me blinking black amoebas.

"We are *so* indebted to you for coming, Miss Lee," Ruby said. "Your advice so far—well, we wouldn't be here today, would we?"

"You want to blame somebody—" Garrett started.

"No blame," Ruby protested. "Of course, I hope Miss Lee won't mind—just this once—if we don't invite her to our meeting tonight. I really think it should be just the company's principals. Those of us who are still left."

Maia started to get up. "I'll see you later, Garrett. Tres."

"Oh, Miss Lee. Don't leave on my account!"

"I've got to go to the little girls' room," Maia said. "Repair my hairspray and stuff. You understand, Miss McBride."

Once she was gone, Ruby said, "I love that woman."

"She's good looking," Clyde grumbled. "You made her leave."

Ruby waved her camera like she was dispelling smoke. "You have bad taste, Clyde."

"You make me talk to Peña and Hayes again," Clyde warned, "I'll show you taste. I'll murder them."

Ruby rolled her eyes. She slid into Maia's chair, aimed the camera at me diagonally. I held my hand in front of the lens until she gave up. "Spoilsport. I'm not excluding *you* from tonight's meeting, Tres, honey. After all, you have some direct interest in the capital at stake, don't you?"

"You mean he's likely to side with you," Garrett complained.

Ruby said cheerfully, "That too."

Over at the bar, the argument between Peña and Hayes was escalating, some of the words even cutting through the bar noise. *She. Sell. No.*

From the back patio, Kinky Friedman let out a loud *aiyy-aiyy-aiyy!* There was a spattering of applause, then

Kinky launched into "Waitress, Please Waitress." The perfect romantic wedding song.

Clyde was glaring at the fight between Peña and Dwight Hayes, which was now beginning to stop the conversations around them.

"Somebody should kill that guy," Clyde groused.

"Now, now," Ruby said. "That guy is our next paycheck, dear."

Then Dwight Hayes pushed his boss. Maybe Dwight didn't mean to push as forcefully as he did. Maybe he caught Peña off balance. But Peña toppled backward, right off his barstool, flat on his ass.

There were two seconds of frozen surprise at the bar, then bemused looks, then catcalls. Somebody started clapping.

Matthew Peña got slowly to his feet.

Dwight was apologizing, his arms raised, and Peña nodded reassuringly that everything was okay, then picked up a beer bottle and slammed it into the side of Dwight Hayes' face. It was Dwight's turn to go down.

A woman shrieked. The crowd surged back.

Clyde Simms said, "That's fucking *it*."

Ruby tried to call after him, but Clyde was hearing none of it. He plowed through the crowd, toward the bar.

There were two Travis County deputies working the wedding party's security by the back door, but they weren't moving yet—probably trying to decide if their duties included breaking up a non-wedding-party bar fight.

Clyde tapped Matthew Peña's shoulder, got his attention, and decked him.

Another surge backward from the crowd.

I stood, but it was still hard to see.

Dwight Hayes had just gotten up, and some misguided sense of loyalty or guilt prompted him to grab another beer bottle, which he brought down in a ship-christening maneuver on top of Clyde Simms' skull with a loud, hollow *POCK*.

That just made the big man mad. Clyde swung around,

bellowing "Fucking motherfucker!" and slashing three or four drinks off the bar.

He tried to lift Dwight by his shirt, but that only works in the movies. All Clyde managed to do was yank fabric into Dwight's armpits, showing us all his skinny, tan midriff. Clyde slammed Dwight against the bar, slipped on something, and both men went over onto the floor, crushing Matthew Peña, who'd just been trying to get up.

Garrett was cursing at me to wheel him the hell out of there before he got trampled. Ruby had her hand over her mouth. Whether she was amused or mortified, I couldn't tell.

Across the room, the two deputies were finally trying to push toward the fight, but the crowd kept pushing them back. Maia Lee had come out of the bathroom; she wasn't having much luck moving, either.

Clyde came up for air like a breaching whale, holding Dwight sideways by one leg and his neck. Dwight had found another bottle on the floor and was swinging it desperately, occasionally hitting Clyde, more often swiping somebody in the crowd. Someone yelped. Clyde started wading across the room, toward the bathrooms. People scrambled to get out of his way.

Kinky Friedman was playing "We Reserve the Right to Refuse Service to You." The tux-and-dress folks were pressing their faces against the patio windows, watching us lower classes partake in our quaint amusements.

It was now an easier matter for me to get close to Clyde, although the deputies still had the bulk of the crowd in their way. One of the guys at a nearby table yelled, "Hey, that's Dwight! Fuck that!" and tried to jump Clyde. The guy missed and slid out of sight. Another guy picked up a chair. Dwight kept swinging the bottle and hitting people, causing a chain reaction of pissed-off drunks.

I'm not sure where Clyde thought he was taking Dwight, but when he got to the booths on the opposite side of the room, between the *Damen* and *Herren* rest room doors, he decided the trophy case of German biersteins on the wall was as good a spot as any. He stepped onto the platform of the first booth, the people at the table cringing away from him, and he heaved Dwight into the glass. It broke with a mighty crash. Dwight didn't fit in the cabinet, so he fell onto the booth table, his knees straddling a woman's blond hairdo, glass and broken biersteins showering on his back and into the diners' plates of sausage and sauerkraut.

The deputies yelled for people to get out of their way. The music on the back patio was finally unraveling to a stop.

Clyde Simms swung around and started scanning the crowd—no doubt looking for his original target, Matthew Peña. He seemed surprised to find me blocking his way. "What the faaaaaah—"

The last sound because of the knuckle-strike I jabbed into his larynx.

I shoved my palm into his nose hard enough to spout blood. Then I grabbed his wrist, twisted myself under his arm and came up behind him, putting Clyde's arm in a double joint lock—his arm twisted at the elbow and wrist so he was forced to make a capital letter C between his shoulder blades.

He said, "Aaaadddd!"

I suggested, "Let's go outside."

Fistfights were breaking out here and there like brushfires, slowing down the deputies who were wading toward me.

I walked Clyde toward the door. The crowd parted for us. Ruby got a great shot of us with her camera.

Over by the back patio, I caught a glimpse of a swarthy guy in black Western clothes—pencil mustache, cigar, white Stetson pulled down over his eyes. He was watching the proceedings calmly.

Kinky Friedman, collecting lyrics for his next song, no doubt.

I got Clyde outside and was trying to figure out where best to deposit him when a voice said, "Freeze!"

Just like that. *Freeze.* Like he'd been watching *Real Cops.*

Without turning around, I said, "Just trying to help calm things down here, sir."

The next sound I knew—the dry *swish-click* of a metal asp being extended. The deputy said, "Let him go."

"I'll fucking kill you," Clyde murmured to me.

"My friend here just got a little upset, Deputy," I called back to the cop. "I was just trying to cool him down a little bit. No harm done. Right, buddy?"

Clyde stopped cursing. I think the word *Deputy* sobered him up. I could feel the tension seep out of his shoulders.

"Yeah," he agreed. "This fucker's right."

I tightened the joint lock.

"Aadd! Yeah my good buddy's right, officer. No problem. No problem."

I let Clyde go, stepped quickly out of his way. We both turned and smiled at the deputy. He looked familiar— probably one of the guys who'd been giving me dirty looks at the station on Saturday.

Clyde did a good job looking friendly, even though he had a line of blood leaking from his left nostril. The blood matched his suit beautifully.

The deputy didn't smile back. His collapsible baton was a black television-antenna-looking thing with a handle on the thick end—the only difference being that a television antenna could not break your thighbone.

A second deputy burst out the door, dragging poor Dwight Hayes by the elbow. They were followed by Ruby McBride and Matthew Peña. The latter sported a beautiful contusion on his left cheek.

The first deputy looked at Dwight. "This your good buddy, too, Mr. Navarre?"

It bothered me that he remembered my name.

"Misunderstanding," I promised. "Everything's fine."

"Be even finer in the city jail," he said. "You like assaults, you'll love it there."

Matthew Peña said, "No."

The cops looked at him.

Peña's eyes were remarkably serene—that same burnt black look that had unnerved me thirty feet under Lake Travis. Blood traced his cheekbone, there was beer drool on his designer jacket, but the attack had not ruffled his composure for long. He seemed the same untouchable, patiently dangerous man he'd been that afternoon.

"I don't want to file charges," Peña said. "Mr. Hayes and Mr. Simms don't want any more trouble. Am I correct, gentlemen?"

Dwight stared at the asphalt, muttered something in the affirmative.

Clyde said, "Goddamn—"

I elbowed him. He said, "Yeah. Uh-huh."

The cops exchanged glances, silently conferred with each other. I'm sure they could've worked up enough justification for an arrest, called APD and had us all hauled away. But then the music started up in the back, Kinky Friedman started singing, and I guess the deputies remembered who was paying their tab.

The first one pointed at me.

"I see you again . . ." He let the threat hang in the air.

Peña turned and headed inside.

Ruby smiled at me, mouthed the words, *See you later, honey,* then followed.

Clyde gave me a look that was slightly less friendly. He wiped a string of blood off his lip, then stomped down the street toward the parking garage.

Dwight Hayes didn't look too bad for a guy who'd just decorated a display case. He had some superficial lacerations on his arms, a more respectable gash in the leg of his jeans, specks of broken bierstein in the brown fuzz of his hair.

I said, "Peña offer good health benefits?"

His features were pinched with anger. He reached into his pocket, pulled out part of a bierstein handle.

"Need a goddamn taxi," he mumbled.

"I'll give you a lift," I said. "Black truck across the street."

I got out my keys and pressed the remote, beeped off the car alarm and unlocked the doors.

Dwight muttered something. Maybe it was "thank you." Maybe it was just something stuck in his teeth. He stumbled across the street and climbed into the passenger seat of my F-150, slamming the door behind him.

Finally, Maia and Garrett appeared in the doorway of the club. Maia helped Garrett pop a wheelie, then bump his way down the front steps to the sidewalk.

I told them I was taking Dwight home.

Maia took the news about as well as I had expected. She looked like she wanted to kill me, then like she wanted to throw up, then she gave in.

"I'm going to my hotel," said Maia. "I'm going to eat, take the longest bath in history, and then sleep. And Tres—just take Dwight home. All right? No weapons. No interrogations. No humorous excursions. Please?"

"Trust me," I said.

She closed her eyes, muttered some bitter ancient curse, and then walked toward the taxi stand.

I looked at Garrett, who seemed in a somewhat better mood now, no doubt thanks to the drubbing recently inflicted on Matthew Peña, Inc. "What's your plan?"

"My plan," he said, "is tequila shots on Sixth Street. The Iron Cactus. Pick me up on your way back."

"And then?"

"And then, just maybe, I'll be ready for Ruby."

Approved-By: hunt.guide@INFO.COM
X-MSMail-Priority: Normal
X-Mailer: Microsoft Outlook IMO, Build 9.0.2416
(9.0.2910.0)
Date: Sun 11 Jun 2000 17:14:20 -0012
Reply-To: hunt.guide@info.com

Sender: "A free newsletter from info.com"
From: <hunter-@info.com>
Subject: whitetail season
To: gn1@rni.com

I can only go by what she's told me, but she's told me so
much—more than she realizes.

I imagine a girl of fourteen.

She's too tall for the boys, developed, impossible
to miss with her long hair, her brilliant eyes, her tem-
per. She is so physical, so sexual, that she intimidates
her peers, and yet she tries to imitate them as best
she can. She studies fashion the way she studies calcu-
lus. She wears the right jeans, the right designer tops
and shoes. This just sets her apart even more. She has
never had a date, or a best friend. Since she turned
twelve, she has learned to endure the looks grown
men give her—comments from her father's workers
at the dock, bits of Spanish they think she doesn't
understand.

She understands.

Her discomfort makes her more stubborn, more
determined to look mature and feign confidence.

I imagine this girl on a November afternoon at
the top of a hill, in the woods, the lake spread out below her, glittering in the long winter light. Today she is
not fashionable. She is wearing a pair of boys'
Wranglers, a long-sleeve T-shirt, hiking boots, an orange down vest. She is not worried about how she
looks now. She is with the one man she is not
afraid of.

The air is cold enough to let steam escape from
the cavity of the whitetail deer she and her father are
field dressing.

She thinks of it as a joint effort. In fact, she does
all the work, while her father stands nearby, drinking
from a thermos, watching the lake.

He has green eyes, like hers, but they are cloudy, troubled. His hair has thinned over the years to a weak shade of pumpkin. His features are angular, like the eroded ridges of a chewed cuttlebone. She thinks of him as tall and strong, but he has already started his decline. The smoking and drinking, the bouts of depression—all this has begun to take its toll.

She cuts the connecting tissue from the liver of the deer, holds the organ in her gloved hands—a heavy thing, milky black like petroleum, quivering as if it still held life. She checks for disease spots. Finding none, she sets the liver on ice along with the heart. Her father always insists on this—save the heart. Save the liver.

She tells him that the liver is healthy, hoping this will please him, but he just stares at the lake. She wishes his thermos held coffee, but she knows it is whiskey with lemon and sugar.

Her job done—the entrails scooped out, the carcass cleaned with fresh water—she wedges a stick into the deer's empty chest to keep the rib cage apart.

Her gloves are sticky with blood, but she doesn't mind the work—the cutting, the cleaning. There is something satisfying about seeing the mess, the chaos of organs—and slowly cleaning it out, tying off the tubes, avoiding spills that could spoil the meat, sorting the innards, leaving a clean and empty shell, neatly framed by the symmetry of ribs.

"Would you like me to clean your doe?" she volunteers.

Her smile is sincere. She hopes for a smile in return. She has been so efficient—learned everything he taught her, done everything to make him proud.

She recalls the time when she was about eight, going with her father to Crumley's Store. He had ruffled her hair, told his friends that he needed no son, that he had his best hunting buddy right here. She protects that memory—drinks from it when she's thirsty, keeps her hands cupped around it like an exposed pilot light.

Now, her father is not five feet away from her—wearing the hunting parka she bought him for his birthday, tattered jeans, the deer rifle he has had as long as she can remember, even before her mother died.

It takes him several minutes just to remember she is there. He has been watching the waterline, as if suspecting that even now, so many years later, the lake is rising, eroding what is left of his inheritance. Only recently, a third business failed on his property—another lessee defaulting on their contract. What little money he has invested in stocks is doing poorly. He doesn't share the worst of this with his daughter—not yet—but she knows something is wrong. She knows the lake is sapping his life.

At last he says, "I'm sorry, sweetheart."

And he looks as if he wishes to say something more, but his voice dissipates as quickly as the steam from his mouth.

She remembers that brief moment of clarity in his eyes, twenty minutes before, when he aimed the gun, brought down the doe with a single well-placed shot. She wishes there were another whitetail deer to kill.

Her buck is a much greater trophy, but she is willing to field dress his doe as well. She wants to be shoulder to shoulder with her father in the work, touch his hands, smell his breath, even if it reeks of whiskey.

Instead, he sets his gun against the tree. He kneels, grasps a handful of dry leaves and cedar nettles, lets them slip through his fingers. There, at the highest point of their property, at a place where the flood can never touch, he seems to be praying, and she knows instinctively that whatever his prayer, it will not be answered. Fourteen years on the lake have taught her to expect that.

So she cleans her knife blade—the sharp steel, four inches, well weighted. She goes to the doe and turns it belly up, feels along the white fur until she finds the point for incision below the sternum.

She makes the cut as her father once showed her—inserting her fingers under the skin, making a V, cutting with the blade up, being careful not to puncture the intestines.

She can tell the doe was nursing, and she knows she must remove the mammary organs right away. Milk goes bad quickly. Nothing will spoil the taste of the meat worse than that.

She works with the knife, trying to be hopeful, trying to believe that she is drawing closer to her father, that he is not slipping away, becoming less and less present the more deer tissue she slices through.

She ignores the smell and the blood. She cuts away the mess—lets the offal spill out, prepares her father's doe lovingly.

And the less he pays attention, the more meticulous she is, the more she needs the knife and the well-made incision, the liver without spots, the heart cut away and drained of blood.

Imagine her on that hill, and you will realize why she treats men as she does. Her affections were cut away long ago, examined for impurities and set on ice, claimed at the point of a hunting knife.

CHAPTER 13

"I can't talk to you," Dwight Hayes said.

He'd already helped himself to one lukewarm bottle of beer from the six-pack on the floor of my truck, and was starting on his second.

"Of course you can't," I said. "Which way on I-35?"

"North."

We did a U on San Gabriel, went under the highway, took the entrance ramp. I said, "What was your little disagreement with Peña?"

One street lamp went by. Two. We passed the UT campus on the left, the Longhorn stadium lit up for an event.

"Bastard hit me," he said. "He *hit* me."

"Relax. You're in better company now."

Dwight was silent for a few hundred street lamps. "Is it true what Miss Lee said about—you and her?"

"I don't know. What did Miss Lee say?"

"Never mind," he decided.

We kept driving. Dwight directed me east on Highway 290.

"How long have you worked for Peña?" I asked.

His eyes were heavy-lidded from all the beer, irritated, as if I'd just woken him up. "Forever. I'm his technical adviser."

"I take it you're not talking about scuba gear."

"I sniff out the most promising software start-ups. I

look for market potential, point him in the right direction."

"Like the start-up in Menlo Park. Like Techsan."

He looked at me, miserable. If guilt had a smell, it was permeating the truck.

"You've seen what happens to the people Peña attacks," I guessed. "The people you sicced him on. Over and over."

"You want to kick me out?" he asked. "It's okay."

Unlit subdivisions went by, closed-up malls, empty fields.

"Maia Lee is right," I suggested. "She's a good person. You should think about talking with her, Dwight."

It was too dark to see his face.

"I thought Techsan would be different," he said. "There was no reason . . . Ruby and Matthew got along so well at first."

"Got along how, exactly?"

"Ruby was the one Matthew approached, back in March. She took him diving out on the lake. They seemed to like each other, came to some kind of agreement in principle. I thought—the program was solid. The algorithms were excellent. I thought Matthew would make them a fair offer, make an easy buy."

"But your employer doesn't enjoy easy buys."

Another mile of darkness. Dwight pointed ahead to a blinking yellow light, told me to take that exit.

"You were with Peña the night Adrienne Selak drowned," I said. "I suppose you can't talk about that either."

"She was nice. She was good for Matthew. I don't think— He wouldn't have killed her. No way."

"You don't think. I thought you saw Adrienne Selak fall. You made a statement on Peña's behalf."

"I meant— He never would have hurt her."

"You sure that's what you meant?"

Dwight let my question die in the air.

We ended up in an aging subdivision of northeast Austin, just south of 290. The houses were 1970s prefab, the lawns all gone to crabgrass. It was the kind of neighborhood that looked best at night, which is exactly the time the local police would tell you not to go there.

Dwight drank his lukewarm beer, told me where to turn.

"The police talk to you about Jimmy Doebler?" I asked.

"A detective came to Peña's suite at the Driskill. That Lopez guy. Matthew was working late the night of Jimmy's murder—video conference."

"And you?"

"I was home. Too many goddamn witnesses."

Before I could ask what he meant, he directed me into the driveway of a green-trimmed two-story. Television light glowed behind curtained windows. A strip of duct tape ran up one cracked pane like a lightning bolt. The yard was dirt with a few sad clumps of dandelions and one sickly pecan tree filled with webworms, a tipped-over tricycle on the sidewalk. A banged-up gray Honda sat next to the curb.

I'm not sure what I'd been expecting as a drop-off point, but this wasn't it.

"You've got a family?" I asked.

Dwight scowled. "You don't need to come in."

Then he opened the truck door and fell into the driveway.

I got out my side and came around to help.

Dwight was cursing the pavement.

"Should've warned you about that first step," I apologized.

"I'm fine," he snapped.

He pushed my hand away, stumbled to his feet. I followed him to the front door.

I heard children before we even got to the porch. A girl and a boy were yelling. Feet stomped. Porcelain crashed and a woman's limp voice escalated over the noise: "No, no, no."

Dwight turned toward me. "I'm okay now."

Then the door opened and a grinning Latino boy about eight said, "Mr. Hayes, tell her to stop hitting me!"

A younger African-American girl pounced on the boy in a flurry of small fists. Both children yelled, did a one-eighty, and raced up the green shag-carpeted stairwell that faced the front door. Their thumping feet on the poorly constructed steps sounded like mallets on a cardboard box.

Dwight took a deep breath. Then he plunged into the house like he was entering the first circle of hell. He followed the children up the stairs.

"Dwight?" a woman's voice called after him. "Are you hurt, son?"

Dwight got to the top and turned the corner. He yelled, "Get the hell out!"

The Latino boy and his nemesis, the little girl, came rushing down the stairs, grinning, and disappeared into a room on the right.

The woman's voice said, "Chris, Amanda, no, no, no."

Despite everything I'd ever been warned about high-risk entries, I stepped inside.

The place smelled of long-ago meals—fried chicken, oranges, grilled cheese sandwiches. A wall unit AC was humming and whining somewhere in back, but it made no difference. The house was hotter than the summer night outside.

To the left was a den, illuminated only by a television. Half a dozen school-aged children reclined on sofas, eating Chee-tos and watching *The Magic School Bus*.

To the right, where Chris and Amanda had run, a woman dominated a blue couch in the living room. A portrait of Jesus hung on the wall above her. At her feet, two toddlers sat V-legged on the carpet amidst a Gettysburg of Legos and blocks. The last child—not counting however many might be packed into the closets—was an Anglo boy of about ten. He stood next to the woman, fanning her face with a piece of cardboard.

The woman smiled pleasantly at me. "I'm Mrs. Hayes. Are you Dwight's friend?"

She looked in her late fifties, pale-skinned, not merely

fat but big in every respect, from wrists to ankles to fingers. She wore a pink tent-dress and gaudy makeup that struggled to create contours on her otherwise shapeless face. Her hair was the color of diet cola, and looked like it had been cut and combed by a barber who usually did men.

I introduced myself, told her I'd given Dwight a ride after he'd had a minor accident at Scholz Garten.

Her pleasant smile didn't change. "Is my boy all right?"

"Yes, ma'am. Just a little scraped up. Dwight'll be fine."

She nodded contentedly.

I couldn't help thinking about a white lab mouse I'd once seen at A&M—a psychology maze graduate who'd figured out how to push the reward button. The mouse was allowed to sit there all day long, punching, gorging, punching, gorging, until it became an enormous, fuzzy mound of rodent complacency, its pink eyes glazed and disconnected with the world beyond that quarter-inch-diameter red circle which gave him bliss.

Mrs. Hayes looked like a woman who had found the reward button.

Chris and Amanda did another lap through the living room.

Mrs. Hayes called after them halfheartedly, "Chris!"

The boy leapt over a toddler thumping blocks on the floor, knocked down a vase, kept running with the girl close behind. Mrs. Hayes blinked, mildly annoyed, like the food button was stuck.

"Chris!" she called again.

The next lap through the living room, Chris stopped. The girl ran into him. She pummeled his back while he waited for instructions.

"Chris," Mrs. Hayes said pleasantly, "what video will keep the children quiet for a while?"

"*Star Wars!*" he shouted.

"*Austin Powers!*" protested the girl, whapping him.

The two of them started arguing. Mrs. Hayes looked

ever so slightly pained. "I don't approve of those choices, but I must have it quiet for a while. I'm getting my headache again."

Chris widened his eyes, as if Mrs. Hayes' headache was a thing to be avoided.

"We'll figure it out, Mrs. H.," he promised.

Chris and Amanda herded the two littler children out of the room, leaving us only the boy with the cardboard fan. Soon the sounds of screaming and chasing were replaced by roaring ships and blasting lasers.

I sat in the chair by the window. Mrs. Hayes smiled at me from her couch, the boy with the cardboard making her hair flicker with every sweep. My scalp started to itch from the heat. I wondered how much the kid charged.

"Well," Mrs. Hayes said, starting over. "You work for Matthew's company?"

She said *Matthew* with lazy familiarity—two warm, fluffy syllables.

"No, ma'am," I said. "You know Mr. Peña?"

"Oh, goodness, yes. Matthew's been wonderful to my Dwight. They went to college together, you know. Would you like some iced tea?"

"Don't go to any trouble, ma'am."

"No, it's no trouble." She waved toward the kitchen. "I believe I'd like some, too."

We sat there beaming at each other for a few seconds before I realized I'd received my marching orders.

The kitchen was all Formica and particleboard, the wood-grain veneer peeling away from the cabinets in large strips. The sink was piled with dishes. A Cheerios box was overturned on the counter.

It took me a minute to find two clean glasses, then to find a pitcher in the refrigerator that held anything resembling iced tea. I opened the freezer for ice. On the bottom, swirling in mist, were little strips of notebook paper, each one with a name in cursive: Marcy, Deborah, Chris, Amanda, John, Clement. There were others in the back, stuck there so long they were grafted to the frost. I scraped away one. It said "Dwight."

The kids in the den kept eating Chee-tos, happily watching space ships detonate on TV. I filled two glasses and brought my spoils back into the living room.

I gave one glass to Mrs. Hayes, then sat across from her on a wicker rocker.

The kid with the fan said, "Are you cool enough yet, Mrs. H.?"

"You keep going, Clem."

The boy switched the cardboard to his other hand.

Mrs. Hayes smiled at me. "Clem stole money from my wallet last week. Now he's paying me back."

"Really."

"They all try it when they first come here. 'Do not despise a thief, if he steal to satisfy his soul when he is hungry.' "

Clem kept fanning her, his face weary and bitter.

"Proverbs," I said.

Mrs. Hayes beamed approval. "Yes, dear. Very good."

"Clem's name is in the freezer."

"Oh, they're all in the freezer. All the ones I pray for. Children are forced to grow up too fast, nowadays. Don't you think?"

I sipped some tea. It had absorbed a residual taste of something else from the refrigerator—ham or bologna, something decidedly nonkosher. I sat my glass on the end table. "These are . . . neighborhood children you take care of?"

"Mostly," Mrs. Hayes said. "Their parents work late and can't afford child care. This is my ministry to them. The house was so lonely after Dwight graduated. That's what started me taking in children. It was good of Matthew to arrange for Dwight to stay here."

"Matthew did that?"

More smiling. The reward button was working fine, now.

"He called me even before he'd arranged it with Dwight. Said it seemed a shame, getting an expensive hotel room or an apartment, when Dwight could spend a few months here with me. Especially after all those years in California. Naturally, I agreed."

"Naturally. And when Dwight didn't want to impose?"

"Oh, Matthew insisted. Such a polite young man."

Above Mrs. Hayes' head, the framed portrait of Jesus had his hands clasped, his eyes heavenward. If I stayed with Mrs. Hayes all day, I imagined I'd look like that, too.

I thought about Dwight upstairs, probably in his boyhood room, Matthew Peña having a good laugh about it every night when he went to sleep in his luxury hotel. I wondered if Dwight had his head buried under a pillow right now.

"It isn't Dwight's fault," Mrs. Hayes mused. "I don't expect him to do as well as Matthew has done, but I do tell him to pay attention, learn from Matthew. Matthew is so good at what he does."

"Yes, ma'am," I agreed. "Very good."

There was a crash in the den. A boy said something too soft to interpret; a girl giggled.

Mrs. Hayes took a deep breath. "No, no, no!"

When the giggling didn't stop, Mrs. Hayes seemed to sniff the air for a scent, then called, "Marcy and John. I know that was you. You come in here this minute."

Another crash.

Mrs. Hayes sighed. Clem the fan boy started to smile, but quickly stifled it when he caught me looking at him. I gave him a wink.

"I should go," I said. "Thanks for your hospitality, ma'am."

"I'll keep you in my prayers, Tres." And then she gave me her empty bologna-flavored tea glass to take to the kitchen on my way out.

As I left, Mrs. Hayes was still calling from her couch for the children to behave. Clem was fanning her hair into a cowlick with his piece of cardboard.

I stepped out into the cooler summer night and said a silent prayer to Our Savior of the Sofa Painting that my name would not be going into Mrs. Hayes' freezer.

CHAPTER 14

"Now tell me this wasn't worth it."

Ruby McBride set Garrett's folded wheelchair on the deck and waved her hand toward the horizon.

Garrett unclamped his arms from around my neck, transferring himself to the bench that ran around the railing. I tried not to wheeze too hard. Nothing like carrying your brother up three flights of stairs to burst your illusions of being in good shape.

Ruby's house-in-progress was a square tower, built on the slope of a hill overlooking Point Lone Star—a roughly triangular piece of land that jutted into Lake Travis.

The business part of her property was at the shoreline, about a hundred yards downhill—a well-illuminated marina, a small floating restaurant, a drive-down boat launch. She even had a warehouse for dry-stacking and a giant forklift with padded teeth for retrieving the boats. A glowing pier stuck into the water and Y-ed about ten yards out, making two rows of wet slips for yachts. There were maybe a dozen boats docked—from twenty-footers all the way up to sixty-footers.

The lake was scored with moonlight. Lights from other palatial homes sprinkled the hills on the far shore. The Milky Way shimmered above us.

All in all, not a bad view.

"The plumbing works," Ruby announced. She waved toward a sliding glass door that led into an unfinished kitchen/breakfast area. The room was starkly lit, glowing in the night like an empty fish tank. "So if you need the john, gentlemen, please don't whiz off my balcony."

Garrett popped his wheelchair open, shoved the Velcro cushion in, then eased himself onto it. He'd taken off his tie. The untucked flaps of his dress shirt hung from the edge of the seat like elf shoes.

Ruby produced two Shiner longnecks from an ice chest and passed them to us. The light from the empty kitchen silhouetted her hair like red-hot filaments.

"Hell of a step up from a houseboat." She leaned against the railing, rested her fingertips lightly on Garrett's shoulder. "Next winter I'll be able to shoot deer from here. I swear to God, they walk right up my driveway."

"Sportsmanlike," Garrett mumbled.

She drank from her Sprite can. "It's either shoot them or wait for them to run in front of my Miata, dear heart. The gun is more humane."

We watched a meteor streak across the western sky, fade and die.

Crickets and owls were sounding off. The air smelled of piñon smoke from the dried cedar deadfall collected and burned daily in the Hill Country.

Down below, I watched the small form of Clyde Simms emerge from the dry-stack warehouse, stand in a pool of light by the forklift. He was smoking a cigarette, maybe looking up at the moon. Maybe watching us.

"We can't sell Techsan," Garrett told Ruby. "You know that."

She smiled frailly. "I know we don't have much choice."

"We can hold out. We prove the bastard sabotaged us."

Ruby looked much sadder now than she had at her ex-husband's funeral.

She ran a finger along Garrett's beard. Garrett stayed stone still, as if her touch was an icepick.

"There was a time, Tres," Ruby said, "when your brother and I actually got along. Before Jimmy— Well,

Jimmy was a sweet man. He had a talent for GUI, graphic interfaces. But Garrett is the genius. If he'd applied himself to the job ten, fifteen years ago, he could've written industry standards. I've never seen anybody better."

Garrett didn't look happy with the compliment. He took Ruby's finger, pushed it gently away.

"What's your specialty, Ruby?" I asked. "Public relations?"

"I'm the QA person."

I looked at Garrett.

"Quality assurance," he translated. "She breaks things. We write a program, Ruby figures out how to screw it up. That way we find the glitches and fix them before the product goes to market. And yeah, she's pretty fucking awesome at breaking things."

Ruby nodded her thanks.

"We were a good team," Garrett said. "We could prove Peña sabotaged us, pull things out of the hole. We could still do it."

Ruby moved away from the railing. "With you under investigation for murder? It's only a matter of time before they charge you."

A meteor streaked past the tail of Canis Major. Garrett kept his eyes on the sky long after the trail was gone. "You think I killed Jimmy. Don't you?"

"Of course not," Ruby said.

He looked at me. "You *both* think I killed him."

I wanted to speak up for him, say something optimistic, but the truth was, I didn't understand why Lopez hadn't already filed charges. Garrett looked guilty as hell. Most likely, with Maia's appearance, her reputation as a defense attorney, Lopez had simply decided to take his time building an airtight case.

"I'm sorry, Garrett," Ruby said. "With Jimmy's murder. With the beta-testers suing us. With investors treating us like the Black Plague. I don't see it, Garrett. I don't see how we can stay in business."

"Peña screwed us," he said, "and you still want to deal with him."

"If we'd taken his first offer, dear heart—"

"He killed Jimmy. Do you *care* about that?"

Her expression turned brittle. "I can't believe Matthew would go that far."

Again, the first name. The way she spoke it, I couldn't help thinking of Mrs. Hayes, sitting obliviously on her couch, extolling young Matthew's virtues.

"He stands for everything Jimmy and I hate," Garrett told Ruby. "He's a vulture capitalist. He feeds off other people's talent."

Ruby pursed her lips. "Unfortunately, dear heart, he's also our only hope—he's doing us a favor. Either sell Techsan or go under."

Down at the lake, a small motorboat came toward the marina, its forward light cutting an arc across the water. The prow was shiny white, pin-striped blue. From here it looked like a bathtub toy. The night air carried up the sounds of its outboard motor, laughter, a radio playing the Dixie Chicks.

Clyde Simms flicked his cigarette into the dark, went to meet the newcomers.

From a nearby deck chair, Ruby picked up a sheaf of paperwork, tossed it into Garrett's lap.

"I won't sign it," he said.

The motorboat veered to port. The engine cut out and the boat glided silently toward home. Passengers kept laughing. Music kept playing.

"You have to sign it," I told him. "You have no choice."

Garrett glared at me. "Your idea of help, little bro?"

"I don't like it. But she's right. Peña has backed you into a corner. You don't have time to find the problem in the software. Especially if you insist that the program isn't at fault, if you don't let anyone help you look."

"The code is solid. I can do one thing well—I can program. I will *not* let Peña steal that from me."

Clyde Simms was at the dock now, one foot on the prow of the boat, tying up the line. I wondered what the boaters thought of him as they strolled off deck for a last drink of the evening—if they even paid attention to the big Viking with the bloodied nose.

"You need to cut your losses," I told my brother. "You're in a bad place with the police. You put yourself into debt. You have to take responsibility."

"Responsibility. My little brother's lecturing me on responsibility. Despite your awesome credentials in that department, man, I am *not* selling."

Ruby sat down on the edge of her hot tub, laced her arms around her knees. "Here's the thing, dear heart. You don't really have a choice."

Garrett pivoted his chair toward her. "And why would that be?"

"Because, as per our incorporation agreement, I'm buying out Jimmy's share in the company. Unless, of course, you are in a position to make a counteroffer. In the event one of us died, that's how it was supposed to work, remember?"

Garrett was silent long enough to replay her words several times. "You're buying control."

"I'm sorry, Garrett. I've already called my lawyer."

"You cold-blooded—with Jimmy not even in the ground two hours?"

"By tomorrow, I expect to control two thirds of Techsan. You can sign the sellout agreement or not, dear, but I'm afraid you're outvoted. We are selling Techsan to Matthew Peña's client, AccuShield."

Garrett made a fist around his beer bottle, then drained it.

He chunked the empty Shiner off the deck. It spun in the light, a brown pinwheel, landing somewhere below with a metallic CLANK-CLANK.

"That better not have been my convertible," Ruby told him.

"I should be so lucky."

Garrett produced a pen from his wheelchair pouch, clicked it, signed the papers.

I looked down at my untouched beer. Condensation had soaked a cold ring through my jeans.

When Garrett finished the signatures, he tossed the papers at Ruby's feet.

"Another divorce, Ruby. That's what this is. Pay me off. Then leave me the fuck alone."

The night air between them was radioactive—glowing with grief and rage and recrimination so intimate I felt like a voyeur. I tried to convince myself two people could make each other so miserable merely through a business deal.

Ruby turned toward me, managed a crooked smile. "Well, Tres. Your ranch is saved."

Garrett's face was murderously calm. "You said the plumbing's working?"

"Yes, dear heart. It is."

"Little bro, I'll be inside. You want to leave, come get me. Something about being in Ruby's place too long—I start feeling sick."

He wheeled himself toward the sliding glass door, spun inside.

The night got intensely quiet.

Ruby rubbed her face. She still had that naturally quizzical look, but the impishness had been replaced with sour dissatisfaction.

"Your brother is impossible," she said.

I imagined her looking like this as an older woman—in her sixties, handsome and stern, the red hair turned to steel, cut short, that eyebrow still raised in disapproval, her aged eyes like a falcon's, critically watching other people's grandchildren, thanking her stars that she didn't have any.

She fished something out of her pocket—a medication bottle. She popped out three pink pills and swallowed them dry.

I watched the pill bottle disappear back into Ruby's pocket.

She crossed her legs at the ankles, looked up at the stars. "Tonight at Scholz Garten, you almost killed Clyde."

"I wouldn't have killed him."

"The way you say that—like you could have killed him if you wanted to. Tres, why did you get involved?"

"I don't like uneven fights. Too many *Underdog* cartoons as a kid."

She laughed.

"What were you popping?"

She looked confused, then remembered the bottle. "Popping. God, that sounds so dirty. Just my attitude medicine, Tres. I'm a real nasty redheaded bitch without it, I'm afraid. I know that must be hard for you to imagine."

"Jimmy's autopsy report," I said. "He'd been taking tricyclic antidepressants."

She pushed her legs straight on the deck, pointed her toes toward me. "Jimmy and I were quite a compatible match. Both fucked-up rich kids. You want to know why I couldn't live with him? We were too much alike."

"You got along with Matthew Peña."

She stared at the sellout papers, still untouched at her feet. "Give Peña credit, Tres. He understands people. He understood how we'd overextended ourselves—how desperate Garrett must have been to mortgage that family ranch, for instance. He can sense immediately what's important to someone. He's the first person I ever met who really understood why I dive."

"And why is that?"

She came back to the railing, looked toward the water. "You have your ranch. Jimmy had that lakeside property—that damn shrine to his mother. I have this."

"The marina."

"Not just the marina, Tres. My family, the McBrides—we used to be big landowners out here on the Colorado River. This was in my grandfather's time, the 1930s, before that. When the state built Mansfield Dam, they bought out the farms, the orchards—every damn thing. Eminent domain. What you see here, this little point of land, is the one percent that wasn't flooded. That's my inheritance out there—under the lake. That's what I showed Peña, the day he wanted to take me diving. I said, 'Come see the property line.' Our orchards are still down there. Trees my great-grandfather planted. Pieces of the original barbed wire fence. Eventually, I intend to map the whole estate."

She stared out at the water as if peeling back the flood, trying to see the land that had been there seventy years ago.

"And Peña understood that," I said.

"He understood why I needed money to build this house, why I'd never had the courage to build before. It's hard to put down roots on land when you've spent your life hearing about a flood."

The lights began to go off at the marina, Clyde Simms shutting down for the night.

"Jimmy's property," I said. "You called it a shrine to his mother. Why?"

Ruby's eyes flicked uncomfortably across mine. "How much of the story do you know?"

"I know Clara had a falling-out with the Doebler family, lost custody of Jimmy when he was young. She reunited with Jimmy when he was an adult. I know she died about five years ago. I know she never thought much of Garrett."

"Jimmy never told you anything else?"

"We were never close."

She shook her head, fascinated. "No wonder you don't mind staying at the dome. Jimmy's family has a history of mental illness, Tres. Clara was diagnosed with severe depression as a young woman. After Jimmy's dad died, she really went off the deep end. She started disobeying the family's wishes, keeping company with men they didn't like. Believe me, I *know* what Clara went through. If I'd been born thirty years earlier, I would've *been* Clara. The Doeblers damn near owned the county justice system around here during the 1960s. The courts found Clara legally unfit to parent. I never met her, but from what Jimmy says, she was a very sad woman when they finally reunited. A broken woman."

"At least they reunited."

She studied my face. "Not happily. The Doebler family money covered it up well, Tres, but I figured you knew how she died. Jimmy's mom committed suicide."

"Suicide," I repeated. "How?"

But as soon as I asked, I had a pretty good idea what the answer would be.

"She parked her car by the water," Ruby told me. "Down at the shore of her property, just about where you found Jimmy. And then, Tres, she shot herself in the head."

I sat there for a long time, listening to the crickets. The meteors kept streaking above us—the beginnings of a full-fledged shower.

Ruby got up. "And now it's time I apologized to your brother, I suppose. If you'll excuse me."

She looked back over her shoulder and smiled at me on her way in.

At that moment, I could believe what my brother said. I could believe Ruby McBride was pretty fucking awesome at breaking things.

CHAPTER 15

When the alarm clock went off the next morning, I slapped at the sleep button and hit only pillow.

I opened my eyes, saw the curve of a white-domed ceiling, a black-light Beatles poster taped to it.

My apartment didn't have a curved ceiling. I was pretty sure it didn't have an overhead black-light Beatles poster.

I patted around. Flannel sheets, a mattress firmer and wider than my futon. In my sleep I'd gone almost spread-eagled, trying to find the edges of the bed.

The only thing familiar was Robert Johnson, curled around my head like a coonskin cap.

I sat up. Robert Johnson murred in protest as he slid off my scalp.

Sunlight sliced across the floor of Jimmy Doebler's loft. On the nightstand, the alarm clock was flashing 6:02 A.M.

Teaching class today, I remembered. UT Austin. The big time.

And on five hours' sleep, too. What more could a man want?

I got up, turned off the alarm, fumbled around for clothes. I'd unpacked my suitcase the night before, but couldn't remember where I'd stashed anything. I rummaged through the oak bureau, pulled on workout clothes before realizing they weren't mine. I looked down at Jimmy

Doebler's Coral Reefer tour shirt, decided against changing. Somehow, tai chi in a dead man's clothes seemed fitting this morning. I laid out slacks, a dress shirt, and a tie for later. Those I knew were mine. Jimmy wouldn't have owned any.

I climbed down the ladder to the ground floor. The dome was country quiet.

I made coffee, scrambled some eggs, and fried some corn tortilla strips for *migas*. I made a Friskies breakfast taco for Robert Johnson. We ate together at the counter, me standing up, reading the *Austin American-Statesman* on my laptop.

I scrolled down to tech news and there it was—the first story, posted only a few minutes before: *AccuShield of Cupertino to Acquire Techsan*. Ruby and Matthew Peña had wasted no time getting the sellout rolling.

The article chronicled Techsan's beta-test problems, the lawsuits, the bad press—all of which would now be handled directly by AccuShield. Matthew Peña promised his client would have Techsan's software problems fixed and an industry-standard encryption program to market by the end of summer.

"It's a matter of resources," Peña said. "AccuShield has them. Techsan didn't."

The article also quoted Ruby McBride. She said the deal would be good for all parties involved. Peña would pay four million in AccuShield stock, with a lock-in period of ninety days.

I copied the article, composed a quick e-mail to Lars Elder at the First Bank of Sabinal. I tried to sound upbeat, promised that Garrett could work out a new payment schedule for the ranch's mortgage soon. I didn't mention anything about possible murder charges.

I closed my laptop, drank some coffee, and stared at the pink cake box—the memorabilia Ruby McBride had almost pilfered the day before. Finally, either my breakfast or the photo of Clara Doebler had to go. I muttered an apology to Jimmy, then turned his dead mother facedown.

I needed to work out, then get ready for my morning

class. Instead, I found myself sorting through Jimmy's *Family* folder—the queries he'd been making into the Doebler past. There was one letter to a local hospital, requesting inpatient records of Clara Ann Doebler's stays for clinical depression. Jimmy had written the *American-Statesman* for information about obituary archives. He'd written the Travis County clerk for Clara's death certificate, her will, the original deed to the lake property. He'd also asked if it were possible to do a birth certificate search without knowing the baby's name. He was interested in births from 1966 to 1968—mother's name Clara DOEBLER, or possibly Clara LOWRY. Father's name LOWRY, or UNKNOWN.

I thought about what Ruby had said—how Clara had hung out with men her family didn't like. Given the years she'd been separated from her son, Jimmy, how little he must've known about her, the queries for a lost sibling struck me as sad. I could imagine the psychology—an only child, taken from his mother and overseen by relatives who primarily wanted him out of the way, raised in boarding schools. At a younger age, Jimmy probably fantasized about "real parents" somewhere else—parents who cared for him and would someday rescue him. At an older age, when the terrible reality set in that his mother was in fact for real, he could harbor a more mature fantasy—a sibling, someone out there who at least could share his misery, maybe someone who needed rescuing by *Jimmy*. And maybe, deep down, Jimmy had needed a reason for Clara stopping her journal to him in 1967. A baby would've been a less painful explanation than the idea that Clara just had stopped making the time.

I set the folder aside. I tried to remember Jimmy the way I'd always thought of him before—the permanently dazed beach bum, the well-meaning screwup, as impervious, rootless, and free from worries as a chunk of driftwood. I couldn't quite reconstruct the image.

The last thing I reviewed from yesterday was the list of phone numbers Jimmy had called in April—his cousin W.B., the Doebler Oil offices, Aunt Faye, Garrett.

I scanned it again, kept coming back to one number I

almost recognized—an Austin number, a two-minute call on April 16, sandwiched between two shorter calls to Garrett. On a lark, I picked up my cell phone and dialed.

The pickup was immediate. "Homicide. Lopez."

I hesitated.

"Hello?" Lopez's tone told me he was about to hang up.

"This is Navarre." Then I added, "Tres."

"Well. Aren't we the early birds?"

The only thing that *didn't* surprise me was that a homicide detective would be at his desk at 6:30 A.M. That was the only time they could catch up on paperwork.

I stared at Jimmy Doebler's phone bill. Two minutes, twelve seconds. April 16.

"Just got off the phone with Detective Angier in San Francisco," Lopez told me. "She sends her regards."

"The Selak drowning?"

"Angier said we're welcome to keep Peña and his attorney, the lovely Miss Lee, in Texas just as long as we want."

"She look at the in-house files for you?"

"Nothing earthshaking. Peña and his girlfriend were bickering at dinner. Boat had a few dozen people on it, mostly computer execs. It was one of those big commercial charters—room for several hundred, so when Peña and Selak went for a walk they didn't have to go far to get out of range of witnesses. There's general agreement that Adrienne Selak had had too much to drink. She was slurring her words, stumbling, was plenty pissed at her wonderful millionaire boyfriend. Peña's account, he took her aft to cool off and to sober up. She was embarrassing him. She wasn't rational, kept calling him names, trying to hit him. Anyway, the boat was cruising the north part of the Bay, due east of Sausalito. Peña and Selak left the stern bar around 11:00 P.M. Around 11:30, Peña's employee, guy named Hayes, got worried, decided to go aft. The way Hayes told it, he heard the couple arguing, turned a corner and there they were—Peña with his hands raised, trying to calm Selak down. She was throwing weak punches at him, crying. Then she turned like she was going to run away from him but she stumbled against the railing, hit one of those spots where it's a rubber-coated chain—where they put the stairs up for boarding, right? And she fell over the side. Hayes swears Peña lunged for her, caught her sleeve for a second, but over she went—about a twenty-foot drop from the deck. Hayes ran for help. Peña threw a life preserver, yelled for the boat to stop. But Selak never surfaced. Straight over and she was gone. Coast Guard helped with the search, but no body was recovered. Then your friend Maia Lee got involved in the case. That's it."

"Angier think Peña pushed Selak overboard?"

"You know how it is, Navarre. We detectives are totally objective. We go simply on the facts."

"Uh-huh. You think he pushed her?"

"I wouldn't doubt it. This guy Hayes—he either saw nothing, or he saw the push, and his boss bribed or forced him into silence. But can SFPD prove it? This happened in January. Mr. Peña is still a free man. What do you think?"

"Dwight Hayes ever treated as a suspect?"

"Not that I heard. The only thing Angier said about him, what troubled the investigators the most, is that they couldn't shake Hayes' story, no matter how they tried. They couldn't catch him in an inconsistency, and Hayes didn't strike them as the iron-willed type. He was shaking, sweating, terrified of the cops. If he'd been hiding a lie, they should've been able to get it out of him, you know? He was the best proof, the only real proof Peña was innocent."

"You filing charges on my brother?"

Half a minute of silence. "Navarre, there was something else the good folks at SFPD told me, about your friend Maia Lee."

"Such as?"

"I hear you two used to be together. Sorry if you don't want to hear this. Your ex-girlfriend apparently burned an awful lot of bridges in San Francisco defending Peña. A lot of people who used to respect her, they're in agreement that Miss Lee crossed the line on that case, sold her ethics. Happens to every defense lawyer eventually, Tres, even the decent ones."

"You sound like a homicide cop talking."

"Take it or leave it. What I'm saying, if that case bothers her—if she is down here trying to make some kind of moral amends—her motives are suspect. Her judgment might not be too clear. I'm not sure you should encourage her to represent your brother."

I looked down at my cold eggs, then the phone bill.

"Lopez, why did Jimmy Doebler call you in April?"

"What?"

"April 16. A short call, about five in the afternoon."

Lopez was silent, as if thinking back. "He wanted information—the files on the death of his mother."

"That didn't strike you as strange?"

"Jimmy said he'd been gathering information about his mom, wanted to understand her life. What makes a guy do that? I don't know. Jimmy's past with his mom ain't what you should be worried about, Navarre. It's Jimmy's past with your brother."

"Meaning?"

"The accident. Your brother blamed Jimmy for what happened to him."

I didn't respond.

"Come on, Tres. I've been doing my homework. Jimmy taught your brother how to jump trains. Then Jimmy didn't show up one night, left Garrett on his own, went up to see his mom. Your brother got maimed, didn't speak to Jimmy afterward for what—years, right?"

"That was a long time ago, Lopez."

"Soured him pretty bad on the Doeblers. Maybe Garrett didn't take out his hostilities at the time, but there's no telling how long somebody's fuse is, or what'll finally set it off. Ruby McBride, for instance. I suppose you know Garrett and she met at UT; they took some upper-division math courses together. I suppose you know they were an item before Garrett had his accident."

"Yeah," I lied. "So what?"

"If that was an old wound," Lopez continued, "if Garrett got into business with Ruby and Jimmy after all those years, thinking he was okay, and then Jimmy started to get romantic with Ruby—a lady Garrett used to love . . . You see how it could go?"

"I see where you could put it, Lopez."

"Just tell Garrett I'd welcome a phone call, okay? Be good if he came to me voluntarily. Maybe we could work something out."

Before I could respond, Lopez had hung up.

I checked my watch, found that my hands were trembling.

I grabbed my tai chi sword and went down the trail to the lake.

The morning was as cool as an oven door, just before the knob is turned to preheat.

I used Jimmy's concrete slab as my workout surface, started with basic stances, ten minutes each. It was therapeutic, getting the sting in my muscles, until I turned north and found myself staring at the unfinished kiln.

The remnants of the barbecue fire were still in the doorway. The little red kiln goddess grinned at me. She didn't seem to mind her left arm being shot off.

After ten years doing tai chi, I still rarely achieve a truly meditative state. This morning was no exception. All the way through the Yang long form, I tried to push thoughts out of my head, but they kept crowding back again.

I thought about Maia Lee, the way she'd looked on Windy Point with the sun in her hair. I thought about Matthew Peña and Victor Lopez, trying to decide who was more dangerous.

Mostly I thought about Garrett and Ruby on the deck in the meteor shower—the look of mutual recrimination they'd given each other. If Lopez was right, Garrett and Ruby had known each other as long as Garrett and Jimmy had—since college, at least. And yet, Garrett had never mentioned Ruby's name to me. There were only two explanations I could think of—that the relationship was not important enough to mention, or that the relationship was too important to mention. I wasn't betting on the first.

As I went into my sword set, the sun was coming up full force, turning the lake to metal. Heat stirred the air, moving through the branches of the cedars with a sound like a distant nest of rattlers.

When I finished, I'd thoroughly soaked the Coral Reefer T-shirt with sweat. The exertion had brought Jimmy Doebler's smell out of the fabric—his copal incense and deodorant, smells I associated with trips to the coast as a child. I promised myself I'd work out in my own damn shirt tomorrow morning.

I sheathed the sword and was about to head back up to the dome, but I found myself staring at the kiln.

I walked over.

The mortar had dried in the bucket, Garrett's trowel embedded in it. The stack of bricks sat nearby, the copper binding snapped and sproinging to four sides as if the bricks had landed on and squashed a metal spider.

Nearby, Jimmy's wooden pottery rack was draped in plastic tarp. Underneath, the shelves were stacked with unfired pots—some red clay, some white clay, all glazed but unfired. They looked ugly that way, like Easter eggs dipped in too many dye pans.

Maybe another day of masonry. Then the gas lines would have to be hooked up. The iron doors would have to be hung.

I shook my head. You're crazy, Navarre.

Then I started up the path.

I knew something was wrong when I saw Robert Johnson on the porch, the front door cracked open. I never leave a door open and I never let Robert Johnson outside.

He looked like he didn't quite know what to do with himself. He was sniffing something on the porch—something gray and glistening.

When I got closer I caught the smell.

I stepped up, moved around the thing, quickly scooped up Robert Johnson. "That's not for you," I chastened.

I went inside, did a quick scan of the room, went directly to the kitchen counter and retrieved Erainya's gun.

I remembered to look upstairs this time. There was no one in the house. I checked the back—the outhouse, the shed. Nobody there. I walked the circumference of the dome, looked at the driveway for new tire tracks, checked my truck. Nothing.

Nothing—except for what was on the porch. I went back and stared at the thing, tried to breathe through my mouth to keep the stench out of my nostrils. Robert Johnson kicked his hind claws into my stomach, trying to get down.

The catfish was nearly three feet long—as big as the hot-dog-fed monsters I'd seen at the bottom of Lake Travis. Its whiskers were limp gray whips. Judging by the smell, the fish had been allowed to rot overnight before being dumped here.

Its belly had only just been gutted, the rancid innards allowed to spill across Jimmy Doebler's porch. There were undigested pieces of hot dog in the milky fluid. Fish eyes usually strike me as expressionless, but this one's seemed terrified, amazed, like it still could not get over the fact that its demise had not come by fishhook.

The thing had been impaled—as if speared by a scuba diver.

Date: Mon 12 Jun 2000 02:36:40 -0000
From: charity@orphan.com
To: charity@orphan.com
Subject: the private eye

Ah, the private eye.

I remember a late afternoon in January, not long after my incident in the snow.

I'd gone home. It would've looked bad if I hadn't. And of course, once home—I found myself alone.

I was in a foul mood. My night in the country had left a bad taste in my mouth—hollow victory. I hadn't seen their faces, hadn't been able to let them know I was there.

Many nights thereafter, I'd found myself in the bathroom, the Old Man's straight razor pressed against my wrist. Or I would be standing at the medicine cabinet, staring at bottles. Never any shortage of prescription drugs around the old homestead.

I felt cheated. The only thing left worth destroying, I didn't have the courage for.

So when I answered the doorbell that afternoon, I pitied whoever it was—a nuisance. A policeman. A family friend.

Instead, I got a small balding man in a threadbare suit, his eyes blinking excessively. He held a briefcase in one hand, a business card ready in the other. The line on the card, right under his name, read: *Discreet Investigations.*

He hadn't come looking for me, but when he learned who I was, he asked to come in.

What could I say? He intrigued me with his card and his demeanor. I wondered if he were good at his work, simply because he was so small. So unimposing.

The private eye complimented the house, which seemed strange to me. I'd lived there so long I'd never thought of it as nice.

He sat on the sofa. I sat in a chair across the coffee table. I remember the curtains were drawn, not that it mattered. No one ever looked in those windows.

The little man showed me photos of people I did not recognize, dropped names I did not know.

And then, when he saw that I wasn't responding, he told me a story that spelled out the connections. He told me who he was looking for, and why.

It was as if a magnifying glass had been held up to my eyes. The world expanded twenty times, got fuzzy around the edges, perfectly focused in the center. I looked at the pictures again, realized what they had to do with me. I realized this small man had done something I could never have done on my own—he had crystallized my hatred into something coherent.

He must've read the change in my face. There was no way I could hide it. He said, very carefully, "You know the name, don't you?"

I admitted that is was familiar.

"There's money to be had," the private eye suggested.

It was the wrong thing to say, and I think he realized it.

He'd gotten too excited at the possibility of a lead.

The shabby private eye was an entrepreneur. He had gone beyond what he'd been paid to do. He'd found himself a tawdry secret, and he meant to exploit its market potential.

I told him I had some papers he might be interested in, asked if he would excuse me.

I could see his apprehension lift. He was thinking he'd finally caught a break. He would get home in time for dinner now. It was probably a long drive.

"Would you like a drink?" I offered. "Hot chocolate?"

He declined.

That negated my easiest option, but no matter. I smiled, said I would be right back.

I went into the study. The Old Man's things were there, his World War II trophies. My eyes fixed on one possibility, and I took the thing down from its display rack. I grabbed a box of papers—I don't remember what they were. It didn't matter.

I went back into the living room.

The anger inside me felt like a steel rod, as stiff and old as the blade in my hand. It was a horrible choice, but I hadn't had any time to think. I had to improvise.

The private eye looked at the sword curiously.

"You'll see the connection," I promised. "It's a family heirloom."

He put the box of papers on his knees, began flipping through them. "I don't—"

"Toward the bottom," I apologized. "I didn't sort them."

I drew the sword. It was a Japanese Imperial officer's weapon—ornamental, but functional. It said much about the Old Man that the metal was brown with age except the point, the blade. The ornamental dragon, the clouds and demons some craftsman had worked so hard to fashion down the spine of the blade—the Old Man had had no use for them. He had only maintained the punishing side.

The private eye looked up, uneasy, but still not alarmed. I was, after all, a kid. A kid who had been helpful, offered him hot chocolate. Perhaps, in the back of his mind, he suspected that I might be the one he was looking for. That would be valuable to him. Very valuable.

"Incredible workmanship," I told him. "The family connection is right here. There's an inscription near the point."

I was standing over him. I held the blade up, the tip resting flat against my left hand, the hilt raised high in my right. I held it close for the private eye to inspect. I moved my left hand, guided the point so it was just above his collarbone, not an inch above.

He said, "I don't see—"

I moved both hands to the hilt, used the weight of my entire upper body. The blade met surprisingly little resistance. The carapace of a beetle would've been much, much harder.

His little eyes opened wide, as if to overcompensate for a lifetime of blinking. He tried to rise, but I had leverage on my side. We held that position, nose to nose, his breath growing faint against my lips.

His briefcase alone was worth all the trouble. The files I found later in his office—just before I put the match to the kerosene rags—opened up the world.

CHAPTER 16

When I got to the University of Texas, Guadalupe Street was nearly deserted. A few homeless people were cocooned in sleeping bags in merchants' doorways. Two students were buying coffee at the sidewalk vendor. Pigeons practiced their serpentine maneuvers across the pavement.

I had about fifteen minutes, so I grabbed some iced tea at Texas French Bread, checked over my syllabus and my notes, and tried to convince myself that the shower had really removed the stench of rotting catfish.

My classroom turned out to be a miniature amphitheater with seats for fifty, but nowhere near that many had trickled in. Most were middle-aged—return students like the ones I was used to teaching at UT San Antonio. In the back row sat a few younger undergrads—hungover, sandy-haired guys in shorts and tees and hiking boots. As I was arranging my handouts, a man who must've been a septuagenarian wandered in—potbellied, frayed jeans and T-shirt, long ivory hair around a balding crown, a beard like Father Time. He smelled of patchouli, among other things.

He wheezed, "You the professor? Hell, I've got *socks* older than you."

I smiled, thinking he was probably wearing a pair of those right now.

Then Maia Lee made her entrance.

She wore a white cotton dress, sunglasses, espadrilles, black knit purse—the kind of outfit she preferred when visiting a potentially helpful witness. She looked like a young single woman on her way to breakfast with friends: casual, attractive, nonthreatening. At least she looked nonthreatening if you didn't know, as I did, that Maia's purse contained a gun and pepper spray and several other deadly toys. She had a notebook and pencil. She walked up to my desk with a piece of paper that looked like a class admit slip.

"You still have space, Professor?"

I murmured, "What are you doing here?"

"Can't I watch? I'll try not to mess up things for you too badly."

I probably blushed, damn her.

"I think there's a seat in the back, miss," I said. "Just for today."

Maia smiled, then climbed the steps to the back tier. The younger dudes all checked her out.

By 9:05 I had nineteen students, not including Maia.

I started with my standard jokes, my standard disclaimers. I told the class it was impossible to sardine the whole of British literature into six weeks, but we'd try to hit the really salacious bits. I warned them there would be dirty jokes in the Corpus Christi cycle, bigotry and torture in Marlowe's *Jew of Malta,* a needlessly high body count in *The Revenger's Tragedy.*

One of the younger dudes said, "Cool."

Father Time wheezed and grinned at me from the first row like nothing could surprise him. He'd probably seen *The Jew of Malta* opening night.

"Right," I said. "Might as well start at the beginning."

I launched into the story of *Beowulf.*

By the third or fourth minute, most of the students were hooked. I'd figured this was better than asking them to read *Beowulf* cold, on their own tonight. Two-thirds of the class would sink in the mire a long time before Grendel ever did.

Halfway through, a middle-aged lady in the back raised her hand apprehensively. She asked what I was doing.

I said, "Telling the story."

She frowned. "Isn't that—" She fumbled for the right word. "Cheating?"

One of the younger dudes said, "Cool."

I suggested that the Saxon warriors who'd first heard *Beowulf* had probably not sat around in rows of desks analyzing it.

"This is storytelling," I said. "Entertainment. You have to imagine a filthy-drunk audience on a cold winter night, demanding their skald give them a good rip-roarer or they'll cut his throat."

Inspired, one of the dudes raised his hand and asked if we could adjourn to the Hole in the Wall Saloon.

Father Time asked, "Can we kill you if we don't like it?"

I told them both regretfully, no. Group health and liability coverage had been significantly better for Saxon skalds than it was for part-time professors.

We got back to Heorot.

Maia listened dutifully in the back row.

At last we got the monsters slain and Beowulf home to the Geats.

Some of the students even clapped.

We discussed historical context for a few minutes, then the imagery and literary devices they should pay attention to when they read the text on their own. I distributed handouts of questions they should be prepared to discuss tomorrow.

Maia accepted the assignment along with everybody else. At the top of her sheet, I'd written: *Don't even think about it.*

We adjourned. I stayed behind to answer questions and was relieved—albeit confused—to see that Maia didn't wait around to harass me. She slipped out the door with a smile and a discreet thumbs-up.

After the last person was gone, I shut off the lights and stood in the doorway, looking at the dark tiers. I tried to reconcile the fact that I'd just put aside PI work for an hour and gotten paid to tell a story. Compared to what I was planning for the rest of the day, this was like being paid to show people the sunset.

I locked the classroom, walked through the campus' West Mall—down the flagstone paving, past twisted live oaks, bronze fountains, sign-up tables for student political organizations, kids pushing newspaper subscriptions.

I crossed Guadalupe. On the other end of the 24th Street parking lot, I saw Maia leaning against the side of my truck. The driver's-side door was open and the stereo was on, KGSR turned up very loud. Toni Price was jamming about her old man.

Maia said, "Can I drive?"

"Funny thing—I always lock my car."

"Must've forgotten," she sympathized. "Keys?"

"No."

If she weren't a grown woman, I would've called her expression a pout. She got in and scooted to the passenger's side. I started the AC before shutting the door. The joys of owning a black truck—all the heat in Texas gets sucked right into your cab.

Maia rubbed the dashboard. "I didn't ask yesterday about the new wheels."

She politely didn't add: *Because I was too pissed off at you.*

"Jess Makar's," I told her.

"What'd you do? Kill him?"

Jess Makar had been my mother's live-in boyfriend until a few months ago, when Jess dumped her.

I explained to Maia that I'd kept track of Jess through my PI contacts.

"The credit agencies," she guessed.

"Just out of concern, you understand."

"Oh. Sure."

I told her things hadn't gone financially well for Jess. My credit agency friends had helped a little bit with that. When it came time to repossess Jess' pride and joy, his black '97 Ford F-150, I'd been more than happy to do the honors. Strangest thing, I'd also gotten the high bid for the truck at the creditors' auction.

"I never considered you much of a pickup truck guy," Maia said.

"But you got to admit—" I gestured over my shoulder. "The tai chi swords rock."

She looked back, nodded. "Yes. They fit perfectly in the gun rack."

We pulled out of the parking lot, heading west toward Lamar.

"You going to tell me why you're here?" I asked.

"I can't seek higher education?"

"You've reconsidered. You're desperate for my help."

It was the first laugh I'd heard from her in over two years.

We drove past the Lamar playground, the rusted old bridge over Shoal Creek. I had no idea where I was going.

"I spoke with Garrett," Maia said. "He told me about the Techsan sale. Said you were very encouraging."

We reached the red light at 12th Street. I looked over. "You want to whip me?"

Her eyes were hidden behind sunglasses now, dark as solar panels. "Tempting, but no. It struck me as odd, though, how quickly Ruby and Matthew Peña were able to seal the deal."

"Almost like they had a hot line set up," I agreed.

A horn honked, letting me know I was sitting on a green light.

"By the way," I said. "Peña left me a housewarming present this morning."

I told Maia about the gutted catfish.

I might've been announcing another ninety-five-degree day with mosquitoes and rain, for all the surprise Maia showed.

"Goddamn him," she muttered.

"Last night," I said, "you were going to tell me how Peña had gotten under your skin."

"You assume I was going to tell you."

We drove a few blocks in silence.

Maia crossed her legs—a task that would've been impossible in my old car, the VW bug. She touched her sunglasses. "In February, after it was clear the SFPD wouldn't be pressing charges in the Selak case, Matthew invited me to dinner—a thank-you present, he said. I wasn't thrilled, but I saw no reason to be rude. I didn't realize that by accepting, I was opening a door. He began calling me. Sending e-mails—increasingly personal e-mails, as if he'd been doing research on my life. I mean, thorough research, Tres. Once . . ." She paused. "He came into my apartment."

I glanced over, but her face was impassive.

The idea of someone forcing his way into Maia's apartment seemed incredible. Not to mention insanely dangerous.

"You caught him?" I asked.

"No. I could just—tell. He was becoming a stalker. I should know. I've defended a few. Finally, I forced him into a meeting at a very public place—a café in North Beach. I gave him a cease-and-desist speech. I was rather forceful."

I couldn't help grinning. "And after that?"

"After that, things got better for a while. Then, when Garrett called me in March, asked my advice about Techsan, Peña became a problem again, as if he knew I'd been talking about him. Peña started calling my bosses, telling them I was being unprofessional, perhaps even breaking attorney-client confidences."

"April Goldman must've laughed in his face."

Maia stared out the window, watching shops go by, suntanned bikers braving the heat. "April's leaving the firm, Tres. I work for Ronald Terrence now—only."

In my darkest moments, when I had been the angriest with Maia, I never would've wished that on her.

Ronald Terrence was the archetypical conservative law partner, politically moderate by Texas standards; by San Francisco standards, a neo-Nazi. He didn't have much use for professional women, or liberals, and so had made the deliberate decision to hook up with April Goldman, a liberal woman partner, to soften his image and increase his clientele base. The result had been a surprisingly successful and long-lived firm. At least until now.

"April wouldn't take you with her?"

Maia's face got even darker. "No. She would not."

Her tone told me not to pursue that line of questioning.

"And Ronald Terrence is tight with Matthew Peña," I said.

She nodded. "Ron had words with me about this . . . vacation. He didn't threaten, but he let me infer that I might not be welcomed back. He's called twice since I got here, mentioned that Matthew Peña has been in touch with him."

"What did you tell Ron?"

"I haven't returned his calls."

This was so unlike Maia, I didn't know what to say.

She closed her fingers around her knees, took a breath.

"Forget all that," she said. "What I really came to tell you—Dwight Hayes called me this morning. The Techsan sale seems to be weighing on his conscience. He said you'd spoken with him last night, encouraged him to call me." She hesitated, steeling herself. "I guess I should thank you for that."

I tried to stop thinking about Maia's job—the junior partnership she'd worked so many years to get. "Dwight give you anything good?"

"He was still pretty cagey, but he said in a couple of days we could expect AccuShield to announce they'd fixed Techsan's software problem."

"A couple of *days*?"

"Dwight said they'd wait just long enough to make the announcement seem plausible."

"Then they've known what the problem was all along."

Maia moistened her lips. "Another little secret Dwight let slip—Peña has made a very sweet little deal with his client, AccuShield. Apparently they're a lot more impressed by Techsan's security product than they let on. If Peña manages to turn Techsan around, get the beta-testing back on track, get the investors lined up, AccuShield has promised to let him spin off the company as a separate IPO."

"Meaning what?"

"Money, Tres. Lots of it. AccuShield would keep seventy percent of the stock. Peña gets thirty percent. And Dwight thought the IPO—with the proper backing— could be *huge*."

"Huge like family size or economy pack?"

"Total valuation? Think billions, with a B."

My hands went numb on the steering wheel. "A company Peña paid four million for. Garrett's company."

Maia nodded. "I'd say this is the career-maker deal for Mr. Peña."

I pulled into the parking lot at Waterloo Records, stopped the truck. The neon cows were dancing above the Amy's Ice Cream sign. Even in the daytime, in the middle of June, Christmas lights blinked in the palm trees.

I replayed every word I'd said to Garrett the night before, about how he should sell his company. Now, despite the ranch, despite my best rationalizing, I felt like those words should be tattooed on my back with a hot needle. Billions.

I wondered if Ruby had known the real value of what she was signing away. I wondered if she'd made some inside deal with Peña. Or maybe that was just wishful thinking. It was easier to get mad at Ruby than at myself.

"Dwight won't go on record with this," I guessed.

"Even if he did," Maia said, "it's nothing we could take to the police. Dwight had nothing to say about Jimmy Doebler's murder. Or Adrienne Selak's drowning."

I told Maia about my morning phone call with Lopez, about the call Jimmy had made to homicide two months ago. I told her about the family research Jimmy had been starting.

Maia stared out the windshield. "The fact Lopez knew Jimmy, had talked to him recently, might be enough to taint his investigation. If I had to, I could use it. That and the fact he coerced you and Garrett into making initial statements without a lawyer."

"Coerced?"

"Sure. You remember. You said Jimmy was asking about his mother."

I started to tell her about Clara Doebler's suicide.

"I know," she interrupted. "You think the family history is important?"

Her tone told me it wasn't just a process-of-elimination question. She was testing, putting out a line. I wondered how she knew about Clara's death.

"His cousin W.B. runs the family company," I said. "He wouldn't tell me anything, but I got the feeling there might be something about Jimmy's death—something that makes the family nervous."

Maia watched the neon cows. "Garrett and Jimmy had a long history—a lot of bad blood between them. Lopez will use that for motive."

"I know."

"We have to be sure Lopez doesn't have a point."

I didn't like the silence between us—a heavy feeling, like the beginning of a landslide. I didn't like the fact that neither of us felt confident enough to leap to Garrett's defense.

"Jimmy has an aunt in town," I said. "On the phone, she seemed a little more pliable than W.B. We could go see her, try running the family angle."

Maia studied the palm trees.

"*We,*" she said, like she was testing the word, seeing how much weight it would hold.

I waited through a full rotation of the Sixth Street light, but Maia said nothing more. I figured I'd gotten as much of a *yes* as I could hope for.

I put the truck in drive and headed north again, toward Hyde Park.

CHAPTER 17

Faye Doebler-Ingram's house was a small folk Victorian on an unmarked residential half block, tucked behind a vegetarian restaurant and a lesbian gift shop. I drove past, U-turned, and parked across the street at the base of one of the city's moonlight towers.

The front porch was outlined with lacy white trim. The screen door was peach, the porch swing green. Her side-gabled roof had recently been sheeted in galvanized steel. Her yard was a quarter-acre garden—every square foot cultivated with herbs and wildflowers, pathways made from broken flagstones. A good deal of money had gone into making the house look quaint and rustic. It didn't look like the kind of place where the resident was accustomed to being rocked by tragedy.

Maia opened the passenger's side door, bringing in the scents of the neighborhood—cut grass and garden herbs.

"*Tú es pres?*" she asked.

"Just like old times."

Even a hint of her smile gave me more pleasure than I wanted to admit.

Maia led the way. The white cotton straps of her dress made an X across her shoulder blades. Her hair had grown longer than I'd realized. Gathered in a white scrunchie-tie, her glossy chocolate brown ponytail didn't look so much girlish as formidable—like the mane of a T'ang warrior.

The garden was hazy with the smells of catmint, thyme,

and sage. We climbed the front steps, ducked under a trellis of grapevines.

The lady of the house opened her screen door before we reached it. "May I help you?"

She was a slight woman in her sixties—stick arms, a pleasantly wrinkled face surrounded by enormous permed hair the bright color of new pennies. Her jeans and blouse were covered with a gardener's apron, but she wore full makeup and silver jewelry. She looked like a friendly earth gnome who'd just been to the beauty parlor.

Maia said, "Mrs. Doebler-Ingram?"

"Just Ms. Ingram," the woman replied gently. "Yes?"

She held a spade, a clod of mud stuck to the point.

I said, "We spoke on the phone. I'm Tres Navarre. This is Maia Lee, a friend."

Faye Ingram's eyes got smaller, more wary. "I don't . . . you mean about Jimmy's death?"

"Yes, ma'am," I said. "There've been some developments since we spoke, Ms. Ingram. We thought you'd want to be prepared if the police contact you. May we come in?"

She wavered, but refusal wasn't really an option, the way I'd phrased it. She let us in.

The house had the same wildly cultivated look as the front garden—clumps of floral-pattern sofas, sprigs of end tables blooming with houseplants, tall pedestals topped with artwork, even one of Jimmy's large ceramic pieces. The smell of fresh-baked cinnamon bread wafted from the kitchen. Somewhere in the back rooms, Dylan's *Blood on the Tracks* was playing. Faye Ingram may have looked nothing like her nephew, but being in her house, I could believe they were related.

Yet something struck me as out of character— something that told of fear. There was a blinking sensor by the door, discreet wires running up the sides of the windows, a keypad next to the light switch. Laid-back Ms. Ingram had one of the finest security systems money could buy.

She led us through a hallway, out into the backyard.

The sun was filtering through the branches of an enormous oak tree. On the sidewalk, a circle of five sun tea jars glowed like some weird, translucent Stonehenge. Lining the fence were tomato and pepper cages, man-sized sunflowers slouched in their last weeks of life—leaves curled brown and seed faces blasted from heat and the work of birds.

We sat in patio chairs under the oak.

"So," Ms. Ingram said uneasily. "You have something to tell me?"

"We wanted to ask about Clara's suicide," I said.

If I was expecting a strong reaction, I didn't get it. Ms. Ingram's smile stayed polite, colorless, wavering no more than her hairdo. "I'm sorry. I don't understand what this has to do with Jimmy."

"In the weeks before he got murdered," I said, "Jimmy was researching his mother's past. I know he called you and W.B. and several other relatives. He also called the police, asking for the files on Clara's death. I know Clara's relationship with the Doebler clan was . . . rocky. It may have nothing to do with Jimmy's death. It just strikes me—"

Ms. Ingram's eyes were watery, unfocused, courteous. I suddenly felt guilty, as if I were forcing something unpleasant into a fragile container.

"It unsettles us," Maia said. "The way Clara died, the place. Jimmy dying in the same spot, the same way."

Faye Ingram laced her fingers together, set them like a little igloo on the mint green patio table. "The police tell me they are close to an arrest."

"They are," I agreed. "And once they have a convincing possibility, they won't look elsewhere unless they have their arms twisted. The rest of the Doebler family isn't likely to twist, are they?"

"Your brother—he is the one they will arrest. Yes?"

"Yes."

"And would it surprise you greatly if I refused to help you?"

"No."

Ms. Ingram read my eyes, then looked toward her garden—the giant, ruined heads of sunflowers. Ms. Ingram nodded, as if she'd made a decision.

"Excuse me a moment," she murmured.

She rose, almost trancelike, and wandered inside.

Maia and I looked at each other.

I shook my head doubtfully, by no means sure Faye Ingram would be coming back without the police.

Inside the house, a Bob Dylan track played through. Faye Ingram reappeared. She carried a brown leather binder the size of an *Oxford English Dictionary* volume. Two sweaty glasses of tea sat on top.

"My manners need polishing," she apologized. "Except for the herb society, I don't entertain many guests."

We thanked her for the tea.

Ms. Ingram's smile started to re-form as she ran her fingers over the old brown binder, smearing the rings of condensation.

I finally realized why her face seemed familiar. She looked like the picture Jimmy had kept on his mantel—her sister Clara. The resemblance wasn't much—a faraway look in the eyes, frailness in the smile, features too delicate to maintain much emotion.

She opened the binder, carefully extracted a photograph.

"This is Clara and James—Jimmy's father."

The photograph paper was parchment-thick, the colors hand-tinted in late 1950s pastel. Clara Doebler wore a satin bride's dress. Her smile was perfunctory, her hair done in a beehive the same unnatural copper color as Faye's hair today. At Clara's side was the groom—a rough-cut man with unruly Elvis hair and a rakish face that reminded me pleasantly of Jimmy's.

"James died of tuberculosis when Jimmy was only three years old," Faye Ingram told us. "More than anything, that event fractured Clara. She'd always been . . . brittle. Prone to depression. She'd allowed the family to arrange her marriage with James, and then she blamed them for leaving her a widow. She refused to remarry, took back her maiden name for herself and her son—something you just didn't do in Travis County in 1960. She became extremely possessive of Jimmy, how he would be raised. She became . . . contrary. Erratic. The family was concerned enough to bring legal action to gain custody of Jimmy. It was W.B.'s father, William B. Senior, who pulled most of the reins of power back then. It was a horrible mess, but finally, of course, the Doebler money won. Clara couldn't compete."

From her tone, I couldn't tell if Faye admired her sister, or was simply expressing fascination, the way a child is fascinated by peeling off Band-Aids.

She pulled out a second photo, handed it across. "That is the man Clara called her second husband, although they were never actually married. His name was Ewin Lowry."

Lowry—the name Jimmy had specified as the father's name on his search for birth certificates.

Ewin Lowry was as different from James Doebler, Sr., as two men could be. Lowry was small, slightly potbellied, dark-complexioned. His hair and mustache were thick and black, his eyes predatory. The gypsy charmer. The man you watched carefully at poker, never introduced to your wife, and certainly never let marry one of your daughters. In the photo, Ewin and Clara stood together in front of a red '65 Mustang. The two of them looked happy.

"Ewin was charming," Faye continued. "Something of a poet. Affectionate when it suited him. Sometimes violent, though never with Clara. The rest of the family—our parents, our grandparents, the aunts and uncles on W.B.'s side of the family—they tolerated Ewin and Clara, but only barely, and only for a while. When Clara became pregnant for a second time—this was in '67—she announced her intentions to marry Lowry."

"Pregnant," I repeated.

Faye nodded. "The family went into war mode. To make a long story short, Clara lost. William B. Sr. drove Ewin Lowry away by a combination of threats and bribes.

Clara was convinced to have an abortion. She never recovered from that. She cut all ties with the family, did a lot of traveling to the West Coast and to Europe, but she couldn't bring herself to leave Austin for good. She and I kept in touch, but I'm ashamed to say—Clara scared me. She was so . . . intense, so sad and angry. When she killed herself, I wasn't surprised. Reuniting with Jimmy was her only comfort for all she'd lost, and in the end, even that wasn't enough."

Daylight filtered through the oak tree, the leaves a mesh of green and yellow. Looking up, I felt like I was under the weight of a giant gumball machine.

Maia said, "I'm sorry for your loss, Ms. Ingram."

The older woman smiled. "My loss is nothing, Miss—"

"Call me Maia."

"I'm used to being alone, Maia. I hope you have many happy years with your soul mate, dear, but that just doesn't happen for some women. I accepted that long ago. My sister never did. Compared to Clara, I lost nothing."

I concentrated on the heat vapor rising from the flagstones, the reflections of the sun tea jars.

"When Jimmy called," Faye murmured, "I told him I couldn't help him. He was so insistent."

"He didn't believe the abortion happened in '67," I said. "He thought Clara had the child."

Faye Ingram stiffened. "How did you know?"

I told her about the paperwork at Jimmy's house, the birth certificate search.

She folded her hands in her lap. "Jimmy was quite irrational about it. His mood reminded me—I hate to say this—he reminded me of Clara. He claimed someone had told him about her pregnancy, told him the child had been given away for adoption."

"Who told him?" Maia asked. "How recently?"

"Jimmy wouldn't say. But I was with Clara in 1967, dear. I know the abortion happened." Ms. Ingram turned a page in her binder. "It would've been better for Jimmy if he hadn't dug into all that," she said softly.

She brought out a yellowing document with a rusty

paper clip mark at the edge. She studied the paper, then looked up at Maia and me. "We kept Clara's suicide out of the press, but naturally I was curious. I asked for the police report. Take it. W.B. can hardly crucify me now."

Maia took the report, thanked her. "Ms. Ingram, would anyone want to kill Jimmy?"

"I didn't know my nephew very well, I'm afraid. Not since he was a child."

"Whatever happened to Ewin Lowry?"

She shook her head. "I don't know. There was a time, back in the mid-1980s, when Clara got a scare. She thought he'd resurfaced, but nothing ever came of it."

"A scare," I said.

"Ewin called her—1987, this would have been, the twentieth anniversary of the day he left her. It was a horrible call. He caught Clara at a vulnerable moment. Ewin threatened to kill her, demanded money. He said he would be coming to find her. It was the last time Clara ever came to me for help."

"You went to the police?"

"Clara didn't trust them to help. She said she needed money, wanted to hire a private investigator to find out where Ewin was. We tried that, had no success. A few weeks later, a letter from Ewin arrived in the mail. And that was the last we heard from him."

Ms. Ingram sighed, fished around in her binder again. "You'll think me a ghoul, but here it is, that letter."

Sure enough, it was postmarked May 1987 from Waco, Texas. It was typed—no signature, no return address. It said,

> Clara,
> Don't think I have forgotten you. Soon we'll discuss retribution.

Simultaneously, Maia and I said, "May we keep this?"

We glanced at each other.

Faye Ingram looked amused. "You may keep it. You two are an interesting pair."

"Ms. Ingram," Maia said, "is there anyone else in the Doebler family who might be willing to help us? Anyone who might've spoken with Jimmy about your family history?"

Faye reached toward her oak tree, plucked a brown pod from the creeper plant. The berries inside the pod were splitting out, fat and neon orange as jawbreakers. She cracked the pod, held up one orange orb.

"Coral bean," she said. "Can you imagine anything prettier? Hard to believe they use these as fish and rat poison, isn't it?"

"Ms. Ingram?" Maia asked.

"I don't know, dear. You could try to speak with W.B. He would merely refer you to his lawyers. I'm afraid that unlike Jimmy, unlike me for that matter, W.B.'s very much a Doebler. He's become just what the family wanted him to be."

There it was again, the undertone of fear I'd heard the first time we spoke on the phone.

Maia said, "How old would Ewin Lowry be now, Ms. Ingram?"

"I don't think Ewin is still in the world, dear. I can't imagine he would've lived to be this old, with his knack for causing trouble. The private eye we hired took our money and vanished, stopped returning our calls. He never told us a thing of importance, though he did seem a rather incompetent sort." She looked at me. "I'm sorry."

"Don't be," Maia assured her. "Most of them never complete a proper training."

We traded collegial smiles.

Faye Ingram said, "You two work well together, don't you? Despite the bantering."

Neither of us responded.

Faye closed her old leather binder. One hand still gripped her bean pod full of poison. "I have a sense for these things. You're very pleasant people. Thank you for having tea with me."

I looked at the tea glasses, which neither Maia nor I had touched.

We thanked Ms. Ingram for her time, left her sitting at her patio table, arranging coral beans into a loose necklace on its surface.

As we walked through Faye's house, *Blood on the Tracks* was winding down to the final, desolate chords of "Buckets of Rain."

Maia and I went out to my truck, Maia reading the police report as she walked. She got into the Ford. I got into the driver's side.

"Supposedly we work well together," I said.

"An amateur's deduction."

Maia flipped to the back page of the police report, scanned it, then handed it to me. "The first officer at the scene of Clara Doebler's death—how do you read that signature?"

I looked at the bottom of the paper. The signature stood out like a familiar spider—one I'd hoped I'd squashed. "Looks like Deputy Victor Lopez."

"That's what I thought," Maia said.

We sat there, watching dragonflies going giddy above Faye Ingram's sage plants.

CHAPTER 18

Detective Lopez wasn't answering his phone. Probably keeping his lines open for Garrett's confession.

After some deliberation, Maia and I decided to swing by Techsan's offices, see if we could find Garrett, maybe take a look around before Matthew Peña claimed his billion-dollar prize.

If you think of Austin as a Rorschach test, downtown would be a little blob in the center, framed above and below by enormous, mirror-image crescents of black—Research Boulevard to the north, Ben White to the south.

Both were former country roads transformed into multilevel highways. Both had superheated with development over the last two decades, and there seemed to be some unspoken rule that the two areas had to be developed at equal speed. If a new chain store went up in the north, an identical store had to open in the south, as if the developers were afraid lack of balance would tip over the city.

Construction spilled into valleys and over hills like a stucco-and-limestone fungus, leaving small islands of ranch land surrounded by apartment blocks, shopping centers, industrial parks. An occasional horse pasture gasped for life between a Starbucks and a Best Buy; turkey buzzards circled over ravines once full of coyotes, now crammed with office buildings.

Techsan Security Software had commandeered space in one such facility in the southern sprawl.

The building was a wedge of red brick and black-mirrored glass, rising from a hillside in the middle of ten wooded acres. The sign out front bore the name of a bankrupt software company.

Garrett's van sat at the curb in a red zone, the side door open.

I parked next to a Lexus with a SOUTH PARK bumper sticker and a Ren and Stimpy sucker-cup animal on the window. Give an adolescent screenhead $80,000 a year to start and you'll get cars like that.

A few gangly developer types who looked like they hadn't seen the sun in months were shooting hoops on the outdoor basketball court.

In the front lobby, the directory was an object lesson in Austin high tech. The building's original occupants had confidently engraved their names on brass plaques. All those names had since been covered with masking tape. For the replacement companies, a newer set of cheap, plastic plaques had been mounted. These in turn were taped over, replaced with printed cardboard signs of the third-generation businesses, and three of these were crossed out. One of the cross-outs was Techsan.

Matthew Peña had wasted no time moving in, and he hadn't opted for cardboard. A large red and gold canvas banner, pinned above the elevator, read *AccuShield, Austin Division, Top Floor.*

"He commissioned that back in March," I told Maia. "What do you bet?"

She nodded. "Probably got T-shirts made, too. Let's go see."

The fourth-floor hallway was L-shaped, with the reception office at the crook. Maia and I walked past the entrance, turned, went to the other end of the hallway. Restrooms, a stairwell, an employee door with a combination lock.

Under normal circumstances, Maia and I would've gone through the front, simply asked the receptionist if we could see Garrett. AccuShield's banner out front had changed that. Without any discussion, Maia and I both understood we did not want to enter these premises on Mr. Peña's terms.

I tried the employee entrance. It was locked.

Maia punched 1-2-3-4-5, turned the knob. No luck. We hung out at the stairwell for a minute, hoping somebody would come out the door. Nobody did.

"Plan B?" Maia asked.

I took off my tie, tossed it to her. "Be right back."

I walked down to the receptionist's office.

The receptionist had a novel propped on her desk like a shield between her and any potential interruptions. The cover said THROBBING EDEN in gold letters on a field of roses. Either a romance novel or a frightening new trend in inspirational literature.

There were two empty desks, an interior door with a deadbolt, and a corner table heaped with technical manuals and donut boxes and brochures. Draped over one of the empty desks was an extra red and gold AccuShield banner, just in case morale got so high somebody wanted to run down the hall waving it.

The receptionist's computer screen saver was bouncing around the words *Ms. Negley.*

I knocked on the open door. "Hey, Ms. Negley?"

She checked me out over the top of her book, smiled. She was brunette, mid-twenties, a hundred ten pounds with an extra fifteen in makeup and hair spray. Her fingernails were royal purple. She said, "Hey, yourself."

"I'm supposed to move out the rest of that old Techsan hardware and I can't remember what the hell they told me for the combination. Do you want me to just lug it through the front?"

Her eyes got very wide. "No, no. Mr. Peña would kill me. 55555. How could you forget that?"

I slapped my head. "And here I am trying to remember—jeez. Thanks . . ."

"Krystal," she offered.

Aha. The famous Krystal.

I pointed to my chest. "Tres. Guess this means I have to haul that stuff out after all."

"Guess so."

"Friday yet?" I asked.

She laughed.

I went back to the employee entrance, smiled at Maia, and let us in.

The door opened into the network center—a walk-in closet with a blinking hub, splays of cabling, backup units for the software.

The next door opened into the main work area.

It was big enough to play soccer in—cool, dark, nearly empty. Low ceilings, fluorescent lights, chocolate brown dividers breaking the room into cubicles. The fact that Garrett and his partners had leased such a large space told me a lot about their early optimism, and their acute lack of business acumen.

A young Latina was hunched over a glowing screen, quietly clacking at a keyboard. A few more cubicles down, two Anglo guys in their twenties were leaning over another guy, looking at something on his computer screen. All three of them had dyed purplish black hair, cut like half-eaten artichokes. They wore gold and red AccuShield T-shirts, oversized khakis, love beads. DVD players were clipped to their belts, headphones around their necks.

The only other people in the room were packing up their boxes—Techsan's dazed temporary employees, learning what temporary means.

On the far wall, shadows moved behind frosted glass windows of a conference room. Maia gestured in that direction. I was about to follow when my brother wheeled himself out from behind a cubicle at the far end of the room, dumped some books into a cardboard box.

"Garrett," I called.

He watched us approach as if each of our steps inflicted a small amount of pain in his right eye. "You trying to make things worse, little bro?"

His cubicle was a corner spot, the window behind him looking out over live oaks and the basketball court and rolling hills. Through the heavily tinted glass, the scene looked like a winter evening. Not an executive office, but a definite step up from Garrett's old box at RNI.

His bookshelf held a potted fern in an advanced stage of mummification, several tomes on C++ Visual Basic and Java, and a careful lineup of Chinese bronze warriors. He'd stuck his carving knife in the side of his cubicle wall, impaling this morning's news—*AccuShield to Buy Out Troubled Techsan*.

I pointed toward the conference room door. "Peña in there?"

"With the Securities and Exchange guys. Picking over my carcass."

A few cubicles down, the young dudes with the artichoke hairdos were laughing, trying different commands on the keyboard. One of the guys glanced toward Garrett, then back at the monitor.

"Screenheads," Garrett mumbled. "They should just upload themselves and get it over with."

Garrett went back to packing. He was sorting through computer manuals, throwing the keepers in his box. When he found one he didn't need, he took out a permanent Sharpie, wrote PEÑA SUCKS! on it, threw it back on the desk.

Maia pulled up a chair. "We need to go see Lopez today, Garrett. I know you don't want to, but we've got to make him think we're cooperating."

"That's me." Garrett tossed another manual into the box. "Mr. Cooperation."

"We have some leads." I appreciated Maia's *we*, appreciated that she was trying to put a positive spin on some pretty sketchy information.

She told him about our conversation with Faye Ingram, about the man from the past, Ewin Lowry, who had once threatened Clara. Maia mentioned that someone, possibly Peña himself, had dug into Jimmy's past, unsettled him by suggesting he had a missing sibling. She told him about the catfish on my doorstep.

"Mind games," she said. "But if nothing else, Lopez

will be obliged to investigate—spend his time focusing on alternatives other than you."

Garrett didn't look reassured.

Across the room, more soft laughter from the artichoke heads. They were making comments about the Techsan program—wondering what moron had designed it.

I didn't want to, but I filled in the rest of the story for Garrett. I brought him up to speed on what Dwight had told Maia—how the software problems would be fixed quickly, how the late great Techsan might turn overnight into a billion-dollar proposition.

Garrett picked one of his Chinese warriors, tossed it to me. "I told you it was a good program. You got what you wanted, little bro. Don't be so down."

His listlessness scared me more than any amount of anger. I almost wanted to hand him a Lorcin, tell him to start shooting. Almost.

"Ruby McBride," I said. "You've known her a lot longer than you let on. You two used to . . . date?"

"Ancient history," Garrett told me. "I never would've agreed to work with her otherwise."

"That serious, huh?"

A young woman in sweats came toward us, a box of plants and keyboards in her arms. One of the temps, probably, hoping to say goodbye. When she saw Garrett's expression, she hesitated, then did a quick retreat. Maybe she decided a final farewell wasn't so important after all.

"Lopez will use Ruby," Maia told Garrett. "If he can establish a motive for you killing Jimmy—jealousy, resentment, a jilted lover's revenge—he'll make the DA's day."

I'd had trouble looking at Garrett the last few days, with the weight he'd lost, the unhealthy color of his skin, the distant possibility that he recently killed someone . . . Now he seemed even less like himself. With his black shirt, his beard trimmed, his dour expression, he reminded me of a renegade Greek Orthodox priest.

"When I was in physical therapy the first time," he

said, "I had a nurse named Schöller. Hard-ass German woman. Used to scream at me."

Garrett didn't often talk about his accident, or the days immediately following. Now he spoke like he was building a bridge of ice, freezing section by section, seeing if it would hold his weight.

"Schöller made me do sit-ups," he said, "which was really hard for me. I mean it's *still* hard, because I've got no leverage. She would hold my hips and holler at me to work. I hated her. I could barely get out of bed. Once I was on the floor—anything would stop me. An electrical cord lying across the carpet was like the fucking Great Wall of China. And here was this German bitch, making me get over it, prodding me to get to the mat so she could force me to do my fifty sit-ups."

"But looking back," Maia guessed, "you appreciate her."

"Hell no. I still hate her guts. The thing is—the struggle never changed from that first couple of weeks in PT. Getting out of bed never got any easier. There are days when that electrical cord seems like the biggest damn thing in the world, and the only thing keeping me going is that voice screaming in the back of my head."

He stared at the Chinese warrior in my hands, grabbed it back.

"You want to know how serious Ruby and I were? What you live for after PT—you try to find reasons to get up in the morning that are better than Nurse Schöller. There was a time—early on—when I thought Ruby would be my reason. I found pretty quick it wasn't going to be that way. Ruby couldn't even look at me after I lost my legs."

"And you blamed Jimmy."

Garrett didn't answer. He turned the bronze warrior around, examining its tarnished spots. "The last few years, little bro, my reason for getting up has been this place. Ruby and Jimmy—they ruined that for me, too. Lopez wants to use that as a reason why I'd be resentful, there's nothing I can do about it. He's right."

I looked at the wooded hills outside, the expensive view-for-lease, feeling Garrett's sense of defeat fully for the first time.

Here we were in his office, in the company he'd labored years to build, and we were the intruders. The only difference was, I could leave anytime and it would mean nothing. When Garrett left, it meant the end of everything—his life's work, his dreams, his two oldest friendships.

I didn't want to feel responsible for that defeat, and I resented Garrett because I did anyway. He was the one who'd quit his secure day job. He was the one who'd mortgaged our family land. Why was I feeling guilty?

The frosted door of the conference room opened.

Matthew Peña stepped out, followed by two briefcase warriors in dark blue suits.

Peña zeroed in on us immediately, but was too busy shaking hands with the blue suits, telling them goodbye. As soon as the visitors were safely out the door to the reception area, Peña made a beeline toward us, walking leisurely, his expression no more confrontational than a tank about to roll over a bicycle.

"You don't work here," he told Maia and me. "You will leave."

His face was an even creepier albino hue in the fluorescent lights. The bruise on his jaw where Clyde had punched him looked like a smoke ring.

"They're helping me," Garrett growled. "Lay off."

Peña studied him. "I'm sure you can understand our security concerns, Mr. Navarre—not letting unauthorized visitors in. You remember the idea of security, don't you?"

Garrett yanked his knife out of the wall. The headline fell to the floor.

I put my hand on his forearm. "Let's talk, Peña."

"We have nothing to talk about."

"Come on, Tres," Maia Lee said. "We can catch up with the gentlemen from the SEC, have our conversation with them."

Peña's eyes narrowed.

He looked at the point of Garrett's knife, then back at Maia.

"I can give you five minutes," he decided.

Peña started walking toward the conference room.

I turned to Garrett. "Keep it cool, okay?"

"Sure," Garrett grumbled. "One homicide at a time."

I left him holding the knife in one hand, the Chinese warrior in the other like a grenade, and I followed Maia through the frosted glass door.

CHAPTER 19

Peña's newly acquired conference room had one wall that was all window, a rectangular table with six chairs, and a bare bookshelf. On the conference table was a box marked *Trash*. Inside was a Jimmy Doebler pot, a picture of Ruby and Jimmy's wedding, and a dried bouquet of pink roses.

Peña was looking out the window—his back to us, his hands folded behind his waist.

"Five minutes," he reminded us.

I sat down next to Maia, took advantage of Peña's dramatic pose to stick my bottle-cap-size digital recorder to the underside of the table. Maia raised her eyebrows at me.

Peña turned around.

"Well?"

"I'm sorry," I said. "I was savoring the moment."

He checked his watch—a stainless steel Tag Heuer, a diver's model. Three thousand dollars' worth of tick-tock. "Perhaps you have time to waste, Mr. Navarre."

"Speaking of wasting time," I said, "thanks for the fish guts. Must've eaten up a chunk of your morning—what with hostile takeovers, lives to ruin. I'm flattered."

His face told me nothing. One of Peña's computers couldn't have spit out data as non sequitur any more quickly than he did. "You now have three minutes."

Maia Lee ran her finger along her lips like the barrel of a gun. "We need to have our discussion again, Matthew—the one where we review the rules of polite society."

His eyes dimmed.

At least he wasn't a total fool. He'd learned to associate pain with Maia.

"You shouldn't have come here," he warned her. "Ron Terrence agrees with me—it isn't like you to be so unprofessional."

"You haven't seen unprofessional yet," she promised. "But keep talking. Tell me how your little high school lackeys out there—the ones who can't seem to find their way into the program—are going to solve Techsan's software problems in a couple of days."

It took Peña a good thirty seconds to remember to look condescending.

"Dwight Hayes has been talking to you," he decided. "No matter. Dwight's job was terminated last night, the moment he touched me. Whatever he says now can be dismissed as the rantings of a fired employee."

"I thought you two went way back," I said.

Peña stared at me, as if he didn't see my point. "Whatever Dwight told you, Mr. Navarre, Techsan self-destructed with no help from me. Like so many other start-ups, your brother and his friends didn't have the first clue how to bring their product to market. They should feel lucky I gave them as much as they got."

"They should grovel," I agreed. "And if they don't, they should be made to grovel."

"Your brother has enough troubles, Mr. Navarre. Let him pack his boxes. Wheel him home, plan your legal strategies. At least now he can pay his lawyer's bills once he sells his stock."

Maia leaned forward, picked a dried rose out of the *Trash* box. It crumpled in her fingers. "You've overextended this time, Matthew. Anticipation of the big money has made you sloppy. What did you tell me once?" she asked. "You like to find the fault lines, keep hammering in spikes until the target cracks apart? Maybe I'll try it with you, Matthew."

Peña's expression got close to real anger—almost as if he were human.

"Be careful how you talk, love," he said. "One phone call—your junior partnership at Terrence & Goldman goes into the shredder. Two phone calls, I can have you disbarred."

"Hard to use the phone, love," I said, "if the cord is wrapped around your neck."

Peña came around the table, slowly, and sat on the edge, leaning over me so our faces weren't more than two feet apart. His breath smelled of cardamom. I happened to see the depth gauge on his Tag Heuer, still logged to his last dive. Eighty-six feet.

"Don't make this about Maia," he said. "She's good, Navarre, but she's not worth it."

I tried to concentrate on the fact that the recorder I'd placed under the table was running. It calmed me down sufficiently to avoid escorting Matthew Peña out his fourth-floor window.

Peña leaned back, satisfied. "It's been nice talking with you. And, Maia— If you ever change your mind, ever feel that you don't want to go down with the ship . . ." He feigned an embarrassed smile. "But that's a bad metaphor. Still terrified of diving, aren't you? A shame. I'd love to get you under the water."

"Shut up, Peña," I warned.

He laughed. "Oh, but this Maia Lee. Inscrutable Maia who was put on earth to protect people like me. She never shows her fault lines, much as I'd like to see them. Where are they, Tres? I suspect you put a few in her yourself."

Maia Lee pushed her chair back, got up gracefully.

Her snap kick caught Matthew Peña in the mouth, sent him backward over the table.

Before I could do anything—assuming I'd wanted to—Maia had collected Peña from the carpet, put him in an armlock, and shoved him against the empty bookshelf.

"First rule of polite society," she said. "Never annoy Maia Lee."

She spun him around, slammed him against the corner of the table—his groin at just the wrong level.

"Second rule of polite society. Never. Annoy. Maia. Lee."

She pulled him off the table—Peña doubled over in pain—and bowled him into the bookshelf, which being empty, peeled away from the wall and fell, the top whamming against the table so it made Matthew a tidy little office furniture tent.

"Third rule," Maia said, catching her breath now. "Figure it out."

She collected her purse, tugged at my arm to bring me out of temporary paralysis, and we left Matthew Peña to his busy schedule.

In the main work area, people were standing up at their cubicles, all looking in our direction—like a prairie dog town on high alert.

"Thank you for your cooperation," I announced. "This safety drill is now concluded."

Garrett was waiting for us by the water cooler. "Did you kill him?"

"Maia calmed me down before I could," I assured him. "This building have a security detail?"

He grinned. "No. Ain't it great?"

"Nevertheless," Maia said, "perhaps Garrett and I should go visit the police now, before they find a reason to visit me."

Her white scrunchie had slipped down on her ponytail, and the third button of her dress had come undone, but something told me this was not the time to point out these details.

Maia escorted Garrett through a cluster of the gaping screenheads, back toward Garrett's cubicle to collect his things.

I went out through the reception area.

Krystal Negley was reading her romance novel. She smiled in surprise. "Hey. Didn't get that equipment?"

"Matthew Peña kicked me out. If he asks, you did *not* let me have the access code."

Her face paled. "You some kind of spy?"

"A private eye," I said. "Sorry I wasn't straight with you."

"A private eye. No shit?"

"Sorry if I caused you trouble."

She managed a laugh. "With Mr. Peña for a boss? I'm his fourth personal assistant since he got to Austin. I was ready to quit anyhow. But I figure you owe me a favor now, right?"

"I figure I do."

She slid open her drawer, pulled out a small leather binder. "Mr. Peña's appointment book for the year. My predecessors kept printing out hardcover backups from his computer. You figure you could find some annoying ways to use the information?"

I smiled at her. "I think I could, Krystal. And you're something else."

"The wrong men keep telling me that," she sighed, and went back to reading her romance novel.

X-MimeOLE: Produced By MimeOLE V5.00.2919.6700
Date: Mon 12 Jun 2000 14:36:40 -0000
From: EL <waynorth@ashield.com>
Reply-To: pub_index@ashield.com
To: <recipient list suppressed>
Subject: firearms

I found the house easily enough—a grimy little bunga-low in the shadow of I-35. The yard was dirt and crab-grass, the windows covered with silver insulation material. Just the sort of rat hole I'd imagined he would live in.

His back door latch was easy to jimmy.

Inside, the kitchen smelled of raw chicken left out too long. Television light glowed in the next room. I could hear something insipid playing—something with lots of canned laughter.

I remember being thankful for the checkered grip on the gun, because my palms were sweating. This time would be so different. I hadn't planned anything close-up before, nor with a gun. This time would count.

I crept forward, stood in the doorway.

He was slumped in a corduroy recliner, his eyes glued to the set. I was amazed at the way he had deteriorated, how little he looked like the photo in my pocket. His face was a war zone of melanomas and capillaries. His hair had thinned, grayed to the color of pencil lead, but that stupid mustache was still as black and bushy as ever. His belly was a hard little thing, like he'd swallowed grapeshot.

I watched him a long time, waiting to be noticed. Ten feet away, and he didn't even see me. I got so nervous I started to smile.

He sensed something was wrong. He looked over, locked eyes with me, and it wasn't funny anymore.

"What the hell . . . ?" His voice dragged itself out of his throat. "*Pinche* kids."

He started to get up, his eyebrows furrowing.

"Come into *my* house . . . ?" he grumbled.

I tried to say what I'd intended, but things weren't going as planned.

He was supposed to stay there, frozen by my gun, and give me time to talk. Instead, he was struggling to his feet, mumbling that he'd give me a thrashing, that I'd best run before he got his rifle.

He took a step toward me.

Someone had told me the pressure on the trigger would be the same as lifting a jug of milk with one finger. I'm telling you, it was easier than that.

My hand bucked from the recoil.

The arm of his corduroy chair ripped open, spitting out cotton filling. The Old Man's expression just turned angrier. He put a hand out to grab me. My second shot bit off part of his palm, left a bloody groove where his heart line ended.

It wasn't supposed to happen this way.

He started to scold me and the third shot caught him in the shoulder, tore it open like a paper package of meat.

The fourth found his chest, right below the sternum. He knelt painfully, as if entering a church pew. Then he fell forward, turned over, and looked straight up into my face.

The ringing in my ears faded. His eyes were going glassy. His throat made heavy wet noises, like gargling.

Four shots. Enough noise to wake every deaf retiree in the neighborhood.

And I stood there, stupidly, letting him die on me. My knuckles turned white, the checkered grip of the gun grafting its pattern into my palm.

Finally I remembered what to do. I knew the last sound I needed the Old Man to hear. I grabbed him by his hairy wrists and left blood streaks down the hall as I dragged him toward the bathroom.

The mess I left still amazes me.

But there again, it was Providence.

I learned how little the police really know, how easily they can be manipulated, how desperately they want to see the obvious.

Most importantly, I learned there is no grace to a gun, no intimacy. I panicked. Things got away from me. And I couldn't have a second chance.

That gnawed at me afterward: thinking about ways I could've done it differently, things I never got to say.

But I learned. I got better at prolonging my time, slowing things down.

And, of course, I got to be a much better shot.

The trick with guns is not practicing for greater and greater distance. That's for the firing-range jocks.

The trick is learning to get right up close.

CHAPTER 20

I spotted Dwight Hayes tailing me before we even left the Techsan parking lot.

He was driving the gray Honda I'd seen last night in his mother's driveway. The car was nondescript enough, but Dwight's blue and yellow Hawaiian shirt made up for it. He stuck out in traffic like a clown who was late for work. We drove up South Lamar, Dwight staying too close, changing lanes with me diligently.

I made the tail as easy for him as I could. I stayed on Lamar all the way to Riverside, then along the river, left on South Congress.

Midday joggers wended their way along the shoreline of Town Lake. Hookers waited on Fifth Street, hoping to sell somebody a memorable lunch break. A homeless guy in a bedsheet was lecturing Asian tourists outside a Mexican restaurant. Above it all, at the north end of South Congress, the red granite rotunda of the Texas capitol loomed like D.C.'s Apache stepchild.

I turned on Sixth and slowed to look for parking outside One Metropolitan Plaza. The garage was on the other side, but I wanted Dwight to see where I was heading in case we got separated. I thought about rolling down the window and pointing for his benefit, but decided it might spoil his fun.

I lost sight of him when I made the turn on San Gabriel.

The security guard in the lobby of One Metropolitan kept his eye on me as I walked toward the elevator. The light from his desk console shone up into his face like he was about to tell a ghost story.

I kept walking, tapping Matthew Peña's leather appointment book against my leg. I was an important part-time member of the UT extension faculty, damn it. I could pronounce Old English names like Hrothgar with a straight face. I was untouchable.

The corporate headquarters for Doebler Oil took up the tenth and eleventh floors. In contrast to the high-tech firms of South Austin, Doebler Oil was all stone and bronze and permanence. The reception area exuded wealth so deeply rooted and self-centered that I almost expected the polished marble walls not to bother giving back my reflection.

I spent half an hour getting the passive-aggressive run-around from several different receptionists, only to discover that the custodian down the hall had the information I needed. Two five-dollar bills and some talk about blues music bought me the fact that Mr. W.B. Doebler always takes a break at the Met Health Club on the thirteenth floor at this time of day.

Sure enough, I found W.B. in a plush maroon and green lounge, slouching on a fake Louis XIV sofa, French doors behind him leading out to a red granite patio and the kind of view of Austin you'd expect for private club prices.

He was wearing workout clothes. His face and neck were striped with sweat, his feet propped on a gold-embossed coffee table, and a tall yellow drink listed in his hands. He was chatting with an older, similarly outfitted gentleman—probably his racquetball partner.

The only other person in the room sat at the bar—a large Anglo man with a dark suit and a gun bulge under his right arm. He might as well have worn a placard that said BODYGUARD. His sunglasses zeroed in on me the instant I entered the room and stayed on me as I approached W.B.'s sofa.

The older gentleman didn't notice me. He was guffawing a lot, slurring his words as if he'd had a few yellow drinks already. He was telling W.B. about his last trip to the Caymans.

I cleared my throat.

"Call for you," I told the older man. "Something about your mutual fund folding."

His face looked like a boiling crab—that moment when the blue-white shell turns bright red. "Wh- what—?"

"Don't know," I apologized. "That's just what they said at the front desk. Better go ask."

The fact that he had a cell phone and a beeper attached to his tennis shorts didn't seem to occur to him. He sprinted out to find the club phone.

I took his seat on the sofa next to W.B. The cushions poofed with the smell of Polo cologne and old man sweat.

"Dangerous prank, Mr. Navarre," W.B. said. "You realize he's on blood pressure medicine."

"Who, Gramps?"

"*Gramps* is a retired broker. He could buy you with pocket change. He owns stock in my company."

"Your company. All the other Doeblers in Austin know it's your company?"

W.B. held up his glass, drained it to yellow ice cubes. "I suggest you leave. We have nothing to discuss."

His friend at the bar was still staring at me through the silver sunglasses. His face looked vaguely familiar.

I opened Matthew Peña's appointment book. "We have a lot to discuss, W.B."

I flipped to the page I'd marked and read: "*April 3, Lunch, 1:00, WBD, Met Club.*"

W.B. scowled at the book. "Where exactly—"

"It gets better." I flipped back in the book several pages. "*January 10, 7P on, Mr. Doebler, McCormick & Kuleto's.* Matthew Peña blocked off a whole evening for dinner with you in January, months before he ever decided to move in on your cousin Jimmy's start-up company. What's more, McCormick & Kuleto's is in San Francisco. You went to him. You still want me to leave?"

Doebler's cheeks flushed like handprints. He looked over at his friend with the silver shades. "Mr. Engels—advise me on the legality of stealing an executive's date-book. This is still a crime in the United States, is it not?"

I recognized Engels now. He'd been Detective Lopez's driver last Saturday—the deputy who'd taken us to Garrett's apartment.

"Part-time security work, Deputy?" I asked. "Or is the Met Club bar on your patrol route?"

The ceiling fan circled above the bar, making the light flicker in Engels' sunglasses. "Your call, Mr. Doebler," he said. "I can take him away."

The way he said it, I got the feeling Engels was receptive to more possibilities than simply driving me down to the station.

W.B. gave me an indulgent smile. "Mr. Engels is a valuable asset. He spent time in the SWAT unit, a few additional years as a firing range instructor. When he was returned to patrol—thanks to some unfortunate politics in the department—I was able to convince him to spend his off-hours working for me. I find his talents quite helpful."

"Don't blame you. If I met with Peña, I'd take a bodyguard, too."

W.B. rattled his ice cubes. A waiter appeared with a refill, then disappeared back into his little waiter cave behind the bar.

"I don't know what leverage you think that datebook buys you, Navarre," W.B. told me. "But it buys you nothing. I make a lot of trips. I have dinner with a lot of businessmen."

"You're telling me it's a coincidence. Peña met with you in January, than again in April, just before he tried to buy out your cousin's company, and it's a coincidence."

"Mr. Peña e-mailed me last Christmas, said he had a proposition. I was coming to San Francisco on business anyway. Peña had a solid reputation, so I agreed to meet with him. Only at dinner did I find out Peña was operating under a misconception. He'd come across an article about Techsan and assumed Doebler Oil was backing

Jimmy's start-up. He had hoped to deal with me on the idea of a buyout. I told him I couldn't help, that Jimmy had no support from Doebler Oil. Peña apologized for taking my time. We finished dinner. We shook hands. That was the end of it. When I invited him here to lunch in April, I was merely being courteous."

"If Doebler Oil was underwriting Jimmy," I said, "Techsan would've had plenty of financial help. They would've been difficult to take over. If you'd given Peña indications to that effect, he would've backed off, looked for an easier target. Instead, you gave Matthew Peña a green light to destroy your cousin."

W.B. slid his feet off the table, sat forward. "You sound like a man who's trying to find any theory to absolve his brother of murder. I understand that. But Jimmy didn't need my help to destroy himself, Mr. Navarre. He didn't need help antagonizing your brother, either."

"You could have called Peña, not the other way around."

"To what end?"

"Clara's branch of the family—they've always been an embarrassment."

W.B. put his drink down, pushed it away with one finger. "Mr. Navarre, the Doeblers have given endowments to half the charities in the county. We've been a cornerstone of Austin politics, business, law. The Doebler name means a great deal in this community. The family never desires to present a negative image. All our business dealings are strictly aboveboard."

"Straight from your company brochure," I guessed.

His face darkened. "When we have family problems, they are just that—family problems. We take care of them ourselves."

"Your father," I said. "When he was chairman, he took care of Clara very nicely—forced her to give up her first child, her lover, an unborn baby. He broke her spirit, shuffled her aside, and when she died, he bought her a nice obituary without that nasty word *suicide* in it. Talk about positive image."

W.B.'s nondescript handsomeness was coming undone. His cheeks were mottled with anger, his jaw muscles pulling his face out of symmetry. Strangely, he looked a lot more like Jimmy this way.

"My father took his duties seriously, and he did not tolerate disrespect. Aunt Clara flaunted her problems. She sought scandal. Jimmy wasn't any better—hopping trains like a bum, making pots, living in that ridiculous dome—"

"You're jealous."

"Don't be absurd."

"You resented your cousin. You would've resented him even more if, after all those years of squandering, Jimmy ended up a financial success. You wouldn't have been able to bear that, would you?"

W.B.'s eyes were every bit as cold and shiny as Engels' glasses.

"Isn't this your department, Deputy?" he said. "Removing pests?"

Engels slid off his stool, came to stand next to my shoulder.

"What were you trying to buy from the sheriff, W.B.?" I asked. "A cover-up—following in your father's footsteps?"

"If I see you again, Mr. Navarre, if you ever show your face, I will not be merciful."

Engels said, "Come on."

We left W.B. at the coffee table, studying its gold-embossed surface like it was a war map—one on which his forces held only the low ground.

Engels escorted me toward the elevator.

After nine or ten steps, I said, "How long in SWAT?" Engels kept walking. "Three years."

"And now back to patrol. Must be hard to swallow." The sunglasses told me nothing.

"Doebler's money can't make up for the demotion," I said. "What was it—you do something out of line? Fail the psych profiling?"

When we got to the elevator, Engels pressed the button. He watched the elevator numbers creep up.

"How much can he buy, Engels? Who else besides you?"

The elevator doors dinged, then opened.

"Right now," Engels said, "while we've been talking, I could've killed you five, maybe six times."

I stepped inside the elevator, smiled at Engels. "Missed opportunities. They suck, don't they?"

Those chrome lenses gave back my reflection as the doors slid shut.

CHAPTER 21

Dwight Hayes was a natural.

Not only had he found my truck in the Met garage, he had discreetly parked right next to it. I walked around behind his Honda and came up on the open passenger's-side window.

Dwight was occupied looking at the F-150, craning his neck, trying to see through the tinted glass of the back window.

"What are those?" he muttered. "Swords?"

"Yeah."

I guess he wasn't expecting an answer. He jumped so hard he bumped his head on the Honda's ceiling.

I said, "Hey."

He cut his eyes to either side, seemed to come to the conclusion he was cornered.

"I followed you here," he blurted.

"Really? You did that?"

He blushed. "When did you spot me?"

"About the time we left the entrance of the Techsan parking lot. Until then you were tailing me flawlessly."

He put his elbow on the window of the Honda, rubbed his forehead.

His face had the same slightly nauseated expression as yesterday. The colorfulness of his blue and yellow Hawaiian shirt didn't do anything to offset the morose poodle-eyes, the chevrons of Band-Aids patching cuts on his neck and forearms.

His floorboard was littered with cassette tapes—Lightnin' Hopkins, B.B. King, Fabulous Thunderbirds. Points for Dwight on the taste-o-meter.

On the passenger's seat was a yellow legal pad, a pen, half a pack of Hostess Sno-balls. From the rearview mirror hung a small plastic Jesus, its arms spread like the Rio de Janeiro model. It seemed to be making some kind of pathetic promise—*Some day, Dwight, you'll catch a fish this big.*

"Don't worry," I told him. "Any fired employee of Peña's is a friend of mine."

Dwight scowled. He gave his rearview mirror Jesus a tentative nudge. "I shouldn't have called Maia."

"Peña was so true to you. So loyal."

Dwight's scalp glistened under his fuzz-cap of brown hair. Sweat was trickling down my back. The summer midday parking garage was getting about as comfortable as the mouth of a Labrador retriever, but I waited while Dwight did his internal wrestling.

"He was my roommate at UT," Dwight said. "That's how far we go back. Freshman year. He kept track of me when he went out to California. When I was looking for work he sort of—adopted me. I owe Matthew a lot. Not just my job. I never expected to be as successful as him, but I've watched him. I've tried to learn some things about business."

It was almost verbatim what Dwight's mother had said. I decided not to point that out.

"Peña fired you, Dwight. You'd had enough, you argued with him, and he fired you."

"I shouldn't have pushed him."

"He used you like a dowsing rod for new victims. You saw the results."

Dwight thought about that. "I followed you—I don't know, I guess after I talked to Miss Lee this morning, I started thinking about all the things I'd left out, things I should've told her."

"I can take a message."

"If I tell you something about Techsan's software, what can you promise me? I mean, about confidentiality. Protection."

"I can promise that if you're desperate enough to talk to me, Dwight, it's going to come out anyway. You might as well tell me."

He blinked, then gave me that wobbly smile again, that same ill-fed sense of humor I'd seen at Windy Point when I'd borrowed his wet suit. "You always make your informants feel this good?"

"Wait until I get rolling. You got air-conditioning in this thing?"

I climbed inside and shut the door.

Dwight turned on his engine, let it idle. I slanted one of the little air vents my way, got a blast of cool that smelled like old Silly Putty.

Dwight said, "Jimmy Doebler called me about the software, about a week before he died."

Dwight was staring out the window, watching the concrete columns of the parking garage as if he expected them to move.

"Why you?" I asked.

"Jimmy and I met when Matthew first approached Techsan about a deal. We spent an afternoon going over the code so Jimmy could show me it was solid. He treated me really nice. Even after Techsan rejected Matthew's offer, Jimmy stayed cordial, told me I could come out to his place sometime for barbecue."

"When he called you two weeks ago, what did he say?"

"He thought Matthew was sabotaging their program. And he thought he knew how."

I felt like a hunter who'd just had a sixteen-point buck sit down next to him. I wanted to shoot the thing pretty bad, but I didn't dare move. I let Dwight take his time.

"Jimmy needed someone with access to Matthew's computer," he told me. "He wanted me to confirm his suspicions. He thought Matthew was using a back door in the program."

"A back door."

"Programmers call it that. It's a command that's not advertised—something that lets you inside the program. You hit your special access sequence, and you can get behind the program, go into God mode. The back door can give you unlimited access, let you change data at will."

"Or steal confidential files from beta-testers," I suggested.

Dwight didn't answer.

"This back door," I said. "Where'd it come from?"

"Jimmy didn't tell me. Probably one of the original programmers—Jimmy, Ruby, or Garrett. Maybe they forgot about it, or thought it so well hidden there was no reason to take it out. One of them could've even snuck it into the program maliciously."

"Dwight, we're only talking about three people, here—how would the others not know?"

"You have to trust your partners in a start-up—there's no time to check each other's work. A high-level encryption program has millions of lines of code—millions of places to stash a back door."

"If one of the principals, a malicious one, gave Peña access to that back door . . ."

"Matthew could destroy the beta-testing," Dwight finished. "The other principals might never know what hit them. Once Matthew bought Techsan, he could fix the back door quickly, document the problem, blame it on the original programmers, then turn around and make a huge profit. He could afford to bribe his informant several million and still come out ahead."

I thought about that. There were only three principals at Techsan. One was now dead.

"You told Jimmy you couldn't help him," I guessed.

Dwight nodded slowly. "I couldn't go behind Matthew's back. Jimmy couldn't give me any more specifics. The conversation came to an impasse."

"But now you think Jimmy was right."

Dwight stared at his little Jesus on the rearview mirror. "The way Matthew was talking yesterday, about how quickly he would fix the software, yes. I think Jimmy was right. But that's not what bothers me most, Tres—not *how* Matthew hurt your brother's company, but why."

I waited.

"I've seen Matthew do bad things," Dwight said. "Scary things. But this acquisition seems . . . special to him. I gave him a list of four or five possibilities in Austin. Not just Techsan. But he looked at the names of the principals and zeroed in on Techsan immediately. He's spent a lot of time on this project, more than anything else he's done."

"The money potential," I said. "You indicated it was huge."

"That's just it. He's *making* it huge. He could've made the same size IPO with any other company I showed him, probably with less work. But Matthew is pulling in all his markers with venture capitalists to make Techsan his biggest play. It's like he intentionally wants to hurt *these* principals, make them know they've been crushed. He's being worse about this than I've ever seen him. Almost like—"

"It's personal," I supplied.

He nodded.

"Why would it be?" I said. "Peña ever meet Jimmy before?"

"No."

"Ruby or Garrett?"

"Not that I know of."

"UT," I said. "That's where you and Peña met. That's where Jimmy and Garrett and Ruby met. No crossing of paths?"

"We must've graduated at least ten years after the Techsan folks."

He was right. There really wasn't much coincidence— a school with fifty thousand students. It was hard to find five people in Austin who *hadn't* gone there.

"What about before college—you know anything about Matthew's past?"

Dwight hesitated. "I know he was from a well-off family. I know he hated his parents."

"Because?"

"He said— I don't know why this would help you. His parents were doctors, lived in Marble Falls, did a lot of charity work in orphanages, homeless shelters, places like that. According to Matthew, he was like their trophy child. They gave him everything but never paid attention to him. When he turned eighteen, he pretty much severed all communication with them."

"Parents still alive?"

"No. They died while we were in college. Car accident."

I stared into the parking lot.

I wondered whether my urge to dig up Peña's past was really my investigative instinct, or just the desire to find a weak chink in Peña's armor, a place he could be hurt. I didn't trust myself to stop if I found the latter to be true.

"W.B. Doebler," I said. "How tight were he and Peña?"

Dwight shook his head. "An occasional meeting. I wouldn't describe them as tight. The only person Matthew spent any real time with in Austin besides me—"

He stopped himself.

"Dwight?"

He ran his knuckle along the windshield. "I was going to say, Ruby McBride."

I'd looked through Peña's appointment book and seen only one meeting scheduled with Ruby—the one Dwight had already mentioned in the spring, when Peña had first approached Techsan.

I decided against asking Dwight about this discrepancy. For one thing, I didn't want to admit having the datebook. For another, Peña might not have written down every meeting for his secretary to see.

Dwight apparently took my silence for disapproval.

"I wasn't implying anything," he assured me. "Miss

McBride . . . I mean, I never saw them talking business. Matthew just got along well with her socially. She was a lot like Miss Selak—same personality, same interests. It probably just made Matthew feel better, being with her."

Dwight's assurances about Ruby left me ten times more unsettled than I'd already been, but I didn't tell him that.

"Last question," I said. "Did you tell Peña about Jimmy's call?"

Dwight nodded slowly. "I told him that if Jimmy was right about the sabotage, I would go to the SEC. Matthew just laughed, told me I was crazy and I should stick to what I do best—finding him fresh blood."

"And a week later, Jimmy was murdered."

Dwight's eyes were small brown points of pain. "Why do you think I'm talking to you?"

CHAPTER 22

In daylight, Ruby's property looked much less romantic—a series of eroded limestone shelves, dotted with twisted live oaks, sloping down toward the shore.

I'd noticed the illuminated sign at the gates the night before—POINT LONE STAR, *docking services, day trips, eats.* Back from the road was a much older sign—deep block letters burned into a weathered square of wood. It was barely readable now, but the underbrush and tree branches had been carefully trimmed away from it. MCBRIDE FARMS—*pecans, peaches, in season.*

The giant padded forklift was bringing a yacht out of the warehouse. On the deck of the floating restaurant, couples were having lunch. Up the hill, construction workers were taking a soda break in the driveway of Ruby's tower.

I parked my truck in the marina lot, watched the boat jockeys, and pondered my next move.

I grabbed my backpack, got out of the truck, and took a stroll toward the pier.

It was easy enough to get past the boat jockeys. The security gate was open. When I asked one of the dockworkers where Ruby was, he told me she'd gone into town on business. I tried to look disappointed.

"Tell her Mr. White would like to see her on his yacht when she returns," I said. "Tell her it's about the purchase of the new sixty-footer."

The dockworker let me pass.

I walked down the pier, scanning names of boats without slowing down. Fortunately, Ruby's was conveniently named the *Ruby, Too*—a white Sea Ray with bright red trim, docked in wet slip 12-B.

I climbed aboard, dropped into a squat next to the main cabin door, out of sight unless another boat happened to come up from the stern. I put on surgical gloves and opened my backpack, spread out my leather roll of lock-picking implements. I chose the one for deadbolts—a thin metal rod curved like a W at the end.

In a few minutes, the lock clicked; the door slid open with a sigh.

At the bottom of the stairs was a large living room/workroom with a kitchenette in the back. One wall was devoted to computer equipment—two high-end Dell workstations, a portable power generator, a wireless modem setup, a color printer, and several backup tape units. The trash can was full of Pecan Street Ale bottles. An incense holder on top of one monitor was loaded with a half-burned stick of copal. Sticking out of a CD tray was Buffett's latest live recording. All the signs that Garrett and Jimmy Doebler had once worked here. This was the room where Techsan had been born.

I spent too much time booting up the computers, only to find I couldn't get past the first password.

I went down a narrow hall into the sleeping cabin. Open boxes were filled with winter clothes—sweaters, long-sleeve shirts, things Ruby wouldn't need for months. The bed was made, though there was an impression like a snow angel in the center, as if Ruby had lain there looking at the ceiling.

On the dresser were photographs. One showed a young Ruby in graduation robes, standing next to an older, rusty-haired man in a tuxedo—her father, I assumed. Ruby was smiling brilliantly, as if to make up for her father, who stared out at me with a slightly dazed expression. The next photo showed Ruby midair during a parachute jump. Another photo was Ruby in scuba gear, underwater, waving as she floated over a bank of coral. The final photo showed Ruby and Jimmy together, standing on a beach. I compared the photos, didn't like what I saw. In each, Ruby had the expression of a thrill-seeker. Her excitement seemed forced, her eyes too wild, as if her desire to have fun was almost desperate—as if she'd never yet caught fire with anything, and was beginning to fear that she couldn't.

What I liked least was my own imagined addition to her photo collection—Ruby standing next to Matthew Peña, signing away her company. *Garrett's* company.

I checked the nightstand drawer. It was locked. I picked it open. I found a .380 caliber automatic and a half-finished pint of Jack Daniel's.

I sat on the bed, deliberating whether to call Lopez about the gun. By breaking in, I'd rendered all potential evidence useless, of course. If it became *known* that I broke in. I wondered if Travis County would serve a search warrant based on an anonymous tip. I doubted it.

I turned my attention to the moving boxes, found that a few of them contained archived paperwork—more than I could possibly read. There were orders for boat repairs, personnel files on boat jockeys, maintenance records for numerous yachts. Letters from an accountant documented financial troubles the marina had been suffering from in the early 1990s.

From a box marked 1990 and prior, I pulled a stack of yellowing brochures that announced the opening of the marina in 1975. POINT LONE STAR, *Rouell McBride, Proprietor.* Behind these was a whole folderful of photographs that Ruby's father had apparently considered using for promotional materials. Many of them were ancient black and white shots showing the family orchards before they'd been flooded. In one, a large family sat under a pecan tree, rows of other pecans stretching out behind them, a split rail fence running along one side. Afternoon sunlight filtered through the branches. The dark-suited patriarch sat on a folding chair, his wife beside him in a white Edwardian dress. Children of various ages fanned out on either side, sitting cross-legged on quilts—the boys in coat and tie, the girls with bobbed hair and 1920s dresses.

It was obvious they were all McBrides. I could imagine the photo in color—so many green eyes, so much red hair.

A note paper-clipped to the back of the photo was written in what I assumed was Ruby's father's handwriting: *The McBride name has been an institution*—Here a few words were scratched out—*The McBrides have been landowners on Lake Travis*—more scratch outs—*No one knows the lake better than the McBrides. Trust us for all your boating needs.*

I looked at the brochure. Mr. McBride hadn't used the old photo. He'd opted instead for glossy color aerials of the marina.

A little more digging in the clothes boxes got me something I had not been anxious to find—a letter from Matthew Peña, folded into the pocket of Ruby's winter coat. It read: *Next weekend, then. I'll see about the Farallons. Fondly, Matthew.*

Hardly damning evidence of anything illegal, but it meant that sometime during the winter, very possibly before Matthew approached Techsan, he'd been corresponding with Ruby McBride. And while Ruby was still married to Jimmy, she'd been talking to Peña about a weekend trip to San Francisco—a boat ride out to the Farallon Islands.

I crumpled up the letter, made it into as small a ball as I could. I had an irrational impulse to overturn Ruby's nightstand, dump her boxes on the carpet.

The only thing that sobered me was thinking what Garrett would do if he'd found the letter instead of me. If he blamed Ruby for abandoning him, then watched her marry Jimmy Doebler, and then, on top of it all, suspected Ruby was spending time with Matthew Peña . . . betraying *both* of them. I thought about the night Jimmy had died—Garrett getting so angry upon hearing Ruby's name that he'd shot off the kiln goddess' arm.

While I was thinking about this, I found myself staring at a poster on Ruby's bedroom wall. It was a huge topographical map of the lake with longitude and latitude coordinates. Depths were noted. Boating hazards. I got up to take a closer look.

There was a green pushpin marking Point Lone Star, and out in the water, five red pins, making a curve from the shore to a point close to the boating channel. The pins were equidistant—about one hundred yards apart.

Her flooded family land, I guessed. I remembered what she'd said about mapping the old property lines, and about taking Matthew Peña down there.

And then a voice behind me said, "There is no Mr. White at this marina."

Clyde Simms stood in the doorway. His nose had a butterfly pattern of bruises around it from our encounter at Scholz Garten. There was a tire iron in his hand.

"Thank God," I said. "I must've taken a wrong turn. I was on my way to Jimmy's—"

"If I liked police," Simms snarled, "they'd be hauling your ass away right now."

"And since you don't?"

He lifted the tire iron, patted it against his palm. "You're walking with me over to my place. Nice and friendly, no scaring the customers. No joint locks. And then we'll see."

CHAPTER 23

Clyde's homestead was set back in the woods about fifty yards from the marina, just enough to be out of sight of the paying customers.

Along the gravel path, we passed two Chevrolet carcasses, three cow skulls nailed to mesquite trees, and a bikinied store mannikin who'd been given a lobotomy and an appendectomy by shotgun. The joys of simple country living.

The house itself was an overgrown portable shed with a plywood porch and a corrugated tin roof heaped with fuzzy brown cedar fur. Parked out front was a Harley-Davidson hog. On the front porch post, a sign read FEROCIOUS DOGS—NO UNANNOUNCED VISITORS.

"Come in," Clyde told me. "And don't think I won't kill you, you try any more of that kung fu shit on me. You know how much I snore when I get my nose broke?"

Clyde opened the screen door and the smell of burning pork and beans came wafting out.

He cursed, pushed past me toward the stove. Apparently he'd forgotten a culinary experiment in his haste to apprehend me.

I stepped into the dark kitchen area, and one of the advertised ferocious dogs appeared from the hallway.

It was a Doberman—sleek black, tan muzzle, little devil-horn ears. It took one look at me with its sad, milky eyes and squeaked the toy in its mouth—a pink rubber bunny. Then the Doberman plodded forward a few steps, collapsed on the rug as if it had been shot, and sighed.

"Vicious," I said. "Terrifying."

Clyde glowered at me. He picked up a spatula with baked bean crust on the edge, took his black, smoking pan of lunch off the electric stovetop.

"I had me two other ass-eating Dobes," he growled. "Mean ones—Harley and Davidson. Both died since Christmas. Now all I got left is Miata."

"Let me guess. Ruby named her after her car."

His ears turned bright red. "Fucking disgrace. You don't go out of here talking about this, you understand?"

I crossed my heart.

Clyde's living room was a cozy combination bike garage, poker den, and army surplus center. Tables overflowed with greasy wrenches, nuts and bolts, cartridge boxes, and pieces of disassembled weapons. Somebody had played 52-pickup across the rug. There was one sofa that looked like a piece of chewed gum.

Clyde told me to sit down. I chose the edge of a table. Clyde offered me a drink—raw egg shake, Gatorade, or beer. I declined.

He plopped himself onto the chewing gum couch, popped open a beer. "Before I kill you," he said, "what were you doing on Ruby's boat?"

"Just visiting. Finding out Ruby's a lot closer to Matthew Peña than she lets on."

Clyde sipped his beer, got some white foam on his mustache. "Ruby's a good woman. Don't judge her."

"She sold out her company, went behind Garrett's and Jimmy's backs—"

"If I thought Ruby had done something to hurt Garrett, I'd talk to her."

"You must have a pretty narrow definition of hurt."

Clyde studied me, the tape on his broken nose making him look slightly cross-eyed. "Your brother's a stand-up guy. The Buffett summer tour this year—he got tickets, swung some for me and some friends, too. You think I like this shit with the police? I want him free to go."

He said *free* the way a con says *free*—like it was a kind of weather.

Miata the ferocious dog was closing her eyes. She was just about to go to sleep when the weight of her snout closed her jaw around the pink bunny and made it squeak. She lifted her head, looking around sleepily for the intruder.

"There's a thing about Matthew Peña," I told Clyde. "People think they can work with him. They find out they're wrong."

Simms scratched the Doberman's muzzle with his toes. "Ruby knows enough to call her own shots."

"You care for her."

His eyes got dangerously hot. "She's a good boss."

"That's not what I meant."

He finished his beer, crumpled the can, tossed it somewhere behind the pink sofa. "I got discharged from the Marines in '82, Navarre. I spent a few years hanging with bikers, striking with the Diablos. Then I started bumming with dock rats at the lake. I met all kinds of people. You know what I figured out? Only friends worth having are the ones who can hurt you, man, hurt you worse than any random shithead in a barfight. I hang with Ruby because she stands by me; she tries to be good to me. Is she dangerous? Fuck, yes. Is she a little screwed up, all that shitty family history? Sure. But you want to boil it down to— hey, Clyde's got the hots for her, well you go ahead, man. That's how you think, you'd never understand anyway."

The Doberman was looking at me mournfully, chewing her pink bunny.

"I apologize," I told Clyde.

He grunted.

"You mentioned Ruby's family," I said. "You knew them?"

"Only stories. The grandfather was the one that sold out, left them with this little piece of land. He sat on the money he'd made from the sale, pretty much pissed it away on drink and gambling. What Ruby's dad inherited wasn't a third of the value. He tried a lot of things, ended up starting the marina, never made much of a go of it. Toward the end of his life, Ruby was running the place, trying to make it pay off for the sake of her old man. Ruby did it, too. Wasn't her dream to get rich, or to keep the land. But by the time her dad was gone, she couldn't get away from the place. Building that house up there on the hill—you don't understand what a big deal that is for her, Navarre. It's Ruby admitting she's here for keeps; she ain't going to get away."

The sound of a motorboat went by out on the lake. The smell of burnt pork and beans was slowly giving way to cedar from the open windows.

"Where is she now?" I asked. "Do you know?"

Clyde gave me a look I couldn't quite read. "Yeah, I know. She don't always let me tag along."

"Like when she goes to meet with Matthew Peña?"

Clyde shook his head. "I ain't your enemy, Navarre. I ain't Garrett's enemy. But you ask me, you're barking up the wrong pole. I seen Garrett around Ruby, how they dance around each other. I seen how Garrett looked when she told him she was marrying Jimmy Doebler. You want to help your brother—maybe you should start by thinking: Hell, yeah, he killed the guy. Go from there. You understand me?"

"This advice from you, who wanted to kill Matthew Peña months ago?"

But when I met Clyde's eyes, I understood what he was saying. Clyde could believe Peña deserved to die. He could also believe Garrett had murdered Jimmy Doebler. He could also believe that Garrett was a decent man who deserved to be free. These ideas were not mutually exclusive. For Clyde, murder was no more astonishing than chicken pox, certainly no reason to judge a man.

I stood. "I'll keep your advice in mind, Clyde."

"And I won't kill you," he decided. "But stay off Ruby's boat, hear?"

I left Clyde on his chewing gum couch, Miata the ferocious dog sleeping at his feet.

Outside, the lake spread out glittering and blue, but

for once I couldn't help seeing it the way Ruby must've seen it all her life—as a cool heavy funeral cloth over a million acres of land.

Date: Mon 12 Jun 2000 20:03:12 -0400
Reply-To: The Original Jimmy Buffett List
        <BUFFET@LISTSERV. MUOHIO.EDU>
Sender: The Original Jimmy Buffett List
        <BUFFET@LISTSERV. MUOHIO.EDU>
From: Automatic digest processor <LISTSERV@LIST-
        SERV. MUOHIO.EDU>
Subject: Clara/First Show of the Season

She was sitting by the water, on the tailgate of the truck, not twenty feet from me.

Her hair had gone almost steel gray. Her face was swollen, no longer delicate. Fifty years of crying will do that to you. She wore a white blouse and white shorts, so she fairly well glowed in the night.

She would write a word or two, then look up and talk for a while, but she would look through me—dazed. I couldn't be sure if I was still there to her; I could only hope. I hoped she heard me tell her that this was a reunion.

The fact that *she* had the gun made it all the more exciting. I wasn't quite sure what would happen, how long I had. My recipe was still pretty new.

She was apologizing. She was crying.

It wasn't everything I wanted, but it was close. I felt that painful sting in my mouth, the tension of waiting, like I'd bitten into a lime and couldn't yet swallow. I wanted to step out of the darkness. I wanted to close the distance between us, embrace her, kiss her forehead.

But then, the intrusion.

I'd timed things as best I could, tried to err on the side of caution, but here came company, much too early—boots cracking twigs.

"Ma'am?" he called. "You all right?"

She turned toward the voice.

She could've ended things for me right there. But in her mind, the deed was already done. She'd signed her name.

She raised the gun, and the intruder's voice got frantic. He ordered her to drop the weapon.

And then she turned the barrel, raised it to her mouth for a kiss.

A thousand tons of pressure, an entire miserable lifetime, escaped in one tremendous burst.

The intruder's face saved him then, it really did. I wanted to show myself. I wanted to destroy him. But his expression told me that Providence had spoken.

He was meant to see what he saw. I couldn't have hurt him any worse than that.

P.S. Sorry for the off-topic post.

It's going to be a great tour this summer.

First show tomorrow night, and I am *pumped*.

CHAPTER 24

Despite how close Jimmy's dome looked from the water, it took me half an hour to get back on the winding lake-shore roads.

I found no new presents on the front porch, no signs that anyone had tried to get past my newly installed lock. The minicam timer I'd placed on the door—set for motion-detection, three freeze-frame shots per hit—had not been triggered.

Then I looked down toward the water.

Docked at Jimmy's pier was a white and red Supra Conbrio—a two-seater racing boat, sleek and fast, a midlife crisis killer.

Ruby McBride was sitting on the pier, her back to the shore.

I thought for a few heartbeats, then went inside the dome and pulled two beers from the fridge. Robert Johnson circled my feet, sniffing, murring. He seemed to approve of my visit to Miata the Doberman. I took my two beers outside and made my way down to the water.

Ruby didn't turn when I walked up. She was sitting cross-legged, and in her lap was one of Jimmy's unfired pots—a large egg-shaped vase Ruby must've pulled from the storage shelf by the new kiln..

"We need to coordinate our plans better," I told her.

She glanced up, squinting into the sunlight. "How's that?"

"I just came from your place."

"I suppose I should've expected that."

Her tennis shoes were wet, her cotton pants rolled up mid-calf. She wore a one-piece bathing suit for a top, her bare back a tan expanse of freckles.

"Well," she said. "Despite our best efforts, we seem to have found one another. You wanted to tell me something?"

"At the risk of being old-fashioned, ladies first."

I offered her one of the beers.

"I shouldn't have alcohol," she mused. "Not good with my medication."

But she took the longneck.

"I phoned Garrett an hour ago," she said. "I tried to apologize for the sellout, the way things ended. Like most of my conversations with Garrett, it didn't work out the way I planned. Left me feeling like crap."

"Why apologize?"

She shot me an angry look. "You think I don't know how he felt about the company?"

"Five days ago, I didn't know you existed. Today I found out you and Garrett go back twenty years. I don't know what to think."

The wind picked up, carrying the smells of rotting wooden planks, crayfish, and cedar.

Ruby balanced her beer bottle on the wet toe of her shoe, turned it around in a pirouette. "I was a sophomore in college, Tres. Your brother was one of those people you meet and you think, 'He's going to be important. He's going to rise above.' Believe me, when you come from a family like mine, you appreciate potential. You don't see much of it. Garrett and I dated for six months. We talked about marriage the way stupid college kids talk—like you can pick out the rest of your life deli-style from the undergrad catalogue. Then Garrett had his accident."

She was silent, watching the water.

"I know it shouldn't have mattered. I know he was still Garrett. But physically, I couldn't deal with it. The next time I saw him was five years later, a chance meeting.

And Garrett was the decent one. He said he forgave me. I guess I believed what I needed to believe."

"You really thought you didn't hurt him?"

A turkey buzzard hovered above us, probably betting that two humans dumb enough to stand outside in this heat wouldn't last for long.

"When Jimmy and I got engaged," Ruby said, "Garrett pulled me aside, told me I was making a mistake. That was the first time I realized how hurt he was. When things started going bad between Jimmy and me, Garrett just got more dismal. It became impossible for the three of us to work together. Tres, I thought I was doing something good, getting Garrett involved in the start-up. I thought I was making amends."

This struck me as either the most brazen lie or the most pathetically sad truth I'd ever heard.

"You signed away the company," I told her. "If you were trying to make amends, you failed spectacularly."

She glared at me. "Yesterday we were in agreement. Now I'm a traitor?"

"Yesterday I didn't know you'd been cruising the Farallons with Matthew Peña. I didn't know about the back door in the software."

My words hit her like an Arctic front. She laced her fingers around her beer bottle, looked out at the lake long enough to count every buoy in the boating lane.

"You don't understand."

"You wanted to sell from the beginning. You said yourself—it was getting impossible for you to work with Garrett and Jimmy. When your partners wouldn't go along with the sale, you helped Peña force the situation. Maybe you didn't realize how zealous he would be."

"You're suggesting I would sabotage my own company?"

"How'd you work it, Ruby? What did Peña promise you—just extra money?"

Her eyes zigged their way down from my face to my chest. Her anger seemed to be collapsing from the inside. "*Just* extra money. That's good, Tres."

"Peña doesn't quit when he's won," I warned her. "He won't leave you alone. If you come clean, maybe I can help."

She shook her head. "You're cute, and all, Tres. But sorry—I don't do the damsel-in-distress routine. There's nothing going on I can't handle."

A speedboat went by, far out in the channel. I watched its line of wake roll toward us, hundreds of yards, until it broke against the shore, lifting Ruby's red racing boat in a gentle swell.

"If everything's so great," I said, "why are you here?"

Ruby absently swatted a mosquito from in front of her eyes. "I couldn't apologize to Garrett, so I thought I would apologize to you."

"Nice try."

Her smile was fragile, covering a world of fear.

The scary thing was that despite everything I suspected about her collaborating with Peña, despite the fact that her ex-husband had been murdered, despite the fact that she was quite possibly the worst thing that ever happened to my brother with the exception of the northbound train—I found myself wanting to help her.

In part, I wanted to undermine Peña, to prove to myself that his influence over people wasn't total. But my instinct to help Ruby went deeper than that.

I felt like out of the three people who'd created Techsan, I might relate to Ruby the best. The past weighed on her as heavily as it weighed on Garrett or Jimmy, and yet she'd done her best to get out from under the McBride legacy—to make her marina business pay off, to build her tower. I couldn't help admiring that, and I couldn't blame her for getting disillusioned with Jimmy and Garrett, either. I had a growing suspicion that if there were one person in the world I might be able to talk to honestly about my brother, it would be Ruby McBride.

"When you came here on Sunday," I said, "you were looking through Jimmy's things. You picked out Clara's picture, her journal."

"I wanted to understand the Other Woman."

"You wanted to know why Jimmy was obsessed with his mother's past."

Ruby lifted the unfired pot, cradled it in her lap. "With Jimmy—there was always something going on that he didn't share, always something else taking up his thoughts, even when he was working nineteen hours a day on Techsan. That's what attracted me to him. When you have ninety percent of someone's attention—I suppose it drove me crazy, not knowing where that other ten percent was focused."

"And did you find out?"

She shook her head. Her eyes were getting teary, red. "It's the goddamn Elavil, okay? It's not me. The alcohol . . ."

"Don't protect Matthew Peña, Ruby. He's not worth it."

She looked down at the vase—the smooth surface, muddy with unfired glaze, the ribbed interior made by Jimmy's fingers. "You still think he murdered Jimmy. You think I helped."

She waited for me to respond. I didn't.

I was thinking about leaving, heading back up to the dome for a bitter, silent supper with my cat, when Ruby said, "You really want to believe someone else killed Jimmy. Someone besides Garrett."

"Don't you?"

She looked at me defiantly. "Then where'd they go afterward?"

"You mean to get away."

"You came rushing down from the house, right? You would've heard a boat. Coming down here, so soon after the shots, you would've run smack into the killer if he'd tried to get away up the road. The only person you saw was Garrett."

"The shoreline," I said. And then, realizing it only as I said it: "There's an access road about two hundred yards south. I passed the entrance driving up."

"Wouldn't the police have scoured that entire area?"

"Probably not."

Ruby lifted her eyebrows in challenge. "I think you owe me a walk."

She gave me her hand. I pulled her up.

There wasn't a trail to speak of, but the terrain was fairly easy. We hiked through agarita bushes, pushed past live oak saplings. Limestone outcroppings made a ridge along the water, in one place high enough to be a diving spot. The remnants of a fraying rope swing hung from the branch of a massive water cypress. Instead of evoking childhood memories, it just reminded me of a lynching tree.

I wasn't sure what we were looking for, and nothing screamed "clue."

There was only the glint of water, the ground thickly littered with cedar needles and leaves.

By the time we got within sight of the access road, we were no wiser, no cooler, and I was down several quarts of blood from the chiggers and ticks and mosquitoes.

Ruby stopped in front of me, turned. "Nothing," she decided.

I was about to agree with her when I caught myself staring at the water. The ground at my feet was littered with something besides cedar needles—a large scatter of sunflower seed shells.

I crouched down.

"What?" Ruby asked.

I looked back toward Jimmy's house. The shore curved between here and there, with a clear line of sight along the cove. You could see the kiln, the dock, Ruby's sleek Conbrio. You could easily stand here in the woods at night, undisturbed, and munch sunflower seeds while you watched Jimmy's dock. Perhaps you could study a murder scene you'd just left, like a painter standing back from his canvas. And if you were so inclined, you could discard a piece of evidence without much worry that it would ever be found.

I looked over the edge of the limestone ridge. The

water rippled two feet below. It was shallow here, and one glint under the surface was a little brighter than the rest.

Sheer luck. It's scary how often it boils down to that. But there I was looking at it from the only right angle to see it—a .380 caliber brass casing in the water, flashing like a coin in a fountain.

CHAPTER 25

I met Vic Lopez the next morning after my UT class. I had never wanted to get through a discussion of *Gawain and the Green Knight* with more haste.

The state crime lab was an unassuming yellow brick box wedged between two warehouses at the back of the Department of Public Safety complex. Black and white state trooper units lined the street. In the visitors' lot, Lopez sat on a loading bay between two stacks of crates, waiting for me.

He slid down from his perch. "You have any idea how many markers this cost me? Putting my neck on the line to get evidence processed on a day's notice? It's goddamn irregular, man."

Lopez wore his normal smile, but his tone had an edge that told me joviality was not to be reciprocated.

"You drop the names I gave you?"

Lopez put his finger on my chest. "IR-RE-GU-LAR. Word gets around I'm running to DPS 'cause some private dick found a piece of brass in the lake—I'm going to be laughed out of the deputies' quilting club."

"But if I'm right . . ."

He sighed, checked his watch. "Ten minutes. And these people are serious about appointment times."

He leaned back against the loading bay, fished a pack of cigarettes out of his coat pocket.

"You interviewed Garrett yesterday?" I asked.

"We had a friendly conversation. Hard not to be friendly, with Miss Lee present. I heard Matthew Peña learned that lesson."

"You still haven't filed charges."

Lopez plucked out a cigarette, pointed it at me. "I only smoke when I'm pissed off. Just so you feel honored."

"You're waiting for ballistics on the casing."

He checked his watch again. "I told my sergeant to be here at 11:15. He wants to observe the test himself."

"You told me it was at eleven o'clock."

"I got to have time to look first, don't I?"

"And I'm irregular."

"And a bad influence. Did I mention that?" He sparked a flame from his lighter. "Your friend died early Friday A.M. This is Tuesday. Five days is a hell of a long time in homicide, you know that? They started throwing me new cases yesterday—a couple of drownings. A mom-and-pop shooting. You think my sergeant likes me churning a case from last week?"

"That piece of brass was over a hundred yards down the shore, Vic—down a rocky path."

"We've got your word for that."

"And Ruby McBride's. You're going to tell me Garrett rolled down the shoreline in his wheelchair?"

"As I remember, you were at the lake that night, too."

"If you really thought I'd planted evidence, we wouldn't be here now."

He tried his cigarette, didn't seem to like the flavor much. "What I think, Jimmy's killer met him at the water that night. The killer was able to drug him—maybe a laced beer, some kind of drink. That meant spending some time together, talking in the truck for more than a few minutes. Drugs start to kick in, Jimmy starts to fade. Killer took a .380, put the muzzle about two inches from Jimmy's head, and told him goodbye. It was intimate, Navarre. Like an old friend. You want to tell me Matthew Peña could pull that off, get *that* close to Jimmy Doebler?"

I looked at the lines of highway patrol cars.

The hell of it was, I agreed with Lopez. The setup of the crime was too personal.

I told Lopez about Jimmy's call to Dwight Hayes the week before he died. I told him about Ruby, the strong possibility that she'd help Matthew Peña sabotage her own company for a sellout.

Lopez slid his lighter into his pants pocket. "And she just happened to walk with you straight to the place where you just happened to find this casing."

"I wasn't implying—"

"Like hell you weren't," Lopez said. I could almost see the homicide detective gears turning in his head. "Sounds like I should pay another visit to Ms. McBride."

"The night Clara Doebler died," I said. "You were the reporting officer. You were there."

I told him about Maia and me visiting Faye Doebler-Ingram—how she'd treated us to tea and homicide reports.

Lopez looked less than ecstatic.

"I thought I told you, Navarre. You need a report, ask *me* for it."

"I'm asking. Jimmy was killed at the same spot his mother died. What happened with Clara Doebler?"

He pulled himself up on the ledge of the loading dock. "Five years ago, the Doebler property was a good place for patrol cops to hang out. Before Jimmy built on it, a lot of deputies used it. You could sit there in your car and catch up on paperwork and be within striking distance for most calls in the David Twenty sector. One night I was finishing B shift, pulled in at the Doebler property about 2100. My partner's unit was a few miles south, and he was on the way to rendezvous with me. I was sitting there doing paperwork when I heard a shot from down the hill. First I figured it was nothing—just a hunter, or some kid screwing around—but I called it in, got out to investigate. There was this pickup truck by the water, this woman sitting on the tailgate with her back to me, and she was playing with something, like she was rolling a joint. She was talking to herself, mumbling.

"I walked up around the side, called to her. She got

startled and turned. It was Clara Doebler. She wasn't at her property much, but she'd called patrol a few times—poachers, drunk drivers running down her fence, that kind of stuff. So I knew who she was. She had a pistol next to her on the tailgate, and what she was fiddling with was pen and paper in her lap. She looked at me, kind of frightened, then picked up the gun. I drew my weapon, told her to put it down. She gave me this kind of dazed look—could've shot me if she wanted, or forced me to shoot her—but instead she put the pistol in her mouth—"

Lopez made his hand into a gun, lowered his thumb. "My partner arrived six minutes later. I was not in good shape. The detectives told me the first shot was Ms. Doebler's test fire—getting up her nerve to do the real thing. When I walked up on her, she'd been writing her suicide note. The letter was to Jimmy. Said, *Dearest son, I'm sorry.* A few more lines, apologizing, what you could read through the blood."

I stayed quiet for a long minute. "Rough thing to see."

Lopez nodded. "I did my share of counseling."

"The Doebler family—W.B.'s father—covered up the suicide. He had it swept under the rug."

Vic made a popping sound with his lips. "I wasn't in homicide then. No one asked my opinion."

"But that's why Jimmy called you for information," I said. "You were there."

"Yes."

"That's why you want to find Jimmy's murderer so badly."

"Don't put too much stock in that, Navarre. You work patrol, you collect a lot of landmarks. You can't drive down the street anymore and see a row of houses. You see, 'that's where the kid was strangled,' 'that's where the drug deal went down.' Ms. Doebler's death—it was bad. But it was only one time."

I couldn't tell if he'd really been able to get past the suicide as much as he claimed, but I got the feeling there was something else about it he wasn't telling me—something that still burned in his gut.

"W.B. has a deputy working security for him—guy named Engels. You wouldn't know anything about that."

"Not unusual. Lot of the guys work off-hour jobs."

"You don't see a possible conflict of interest?"

Lopez reconstructed his usual smile. Whatever had been there, just below the surface, was submerged.

"Conflict of interest—you mean like a homicide detective doing a PI a favor? Naw, man—that shit never happens in this county. Come on, Navarre. Let's get your sorry ass inside. We've got a bullet to look at."

CHAPTER 26

The window on the crime lab door was covered with fake stick-on bullet holes. Ballistics humor.

The guy who buzzed us in was around forty-five, wearing jeans and a rumpled blue T-shirt, a laminated ID around his neck. He looked like he hadn't seen a disposable razor in eight weeks—his grizzled hair, beard, eyebrows, mustache, and sideburns all so copious it was impossible to tell where one crop of follicles stopped and the other started. I fancied you could peel one corner and rip the whole hair cover off in a single piece.

He chewed on something underneath the mustache, knit his eyebrows at Lopez. "Which are you?"

"Vic Lopez, Travis County homicide."

The hairy man looked at me. "Then you're Navarre?"

"Ben Quarles?"

Quarles shook my hand. "Gene Schaeffer at SAPD vouched for you. Said you kept them supplied with some of their more humorous work."

"That Gene," I said. "He's a sucker for knock-knock jokes."

Quarles looked at Lopez. "Told me Tres—T-R-E-S—I figured a Spanish guy."

Lopez patted my shoulder. "You know, we're trying. We keep feeding him *frijoles*. So far he ain't turned brown. Now if you don't mind, Ben—?"

Quarles' mouth twitched. "Come on in, gentlemen."

Our host walked as if someone had shot him in both feet. He led us down a narrow corridor, past a couple of offices to a big metal door. He swiped his security card across the lock.

The room inside looked like a Branch Davidian garage sale—pegboard walls hung floor to ceiling with weapons, all tagged, arranged by size from tiny .22s on the left to rocket launchers on the right. In the back corner was an umbrella stand full of swords and tire irons and baseball bats.

Quarles picked a small black and silver handgun off the wall. "Your suspect's Lorcin. Came in about an hour ago."

My stomach went cold just looking at it. I hated the thing—hated the fact Garrett had been stupid enough to buy it. I wanted it obliterated, melted down, ground into rebar.

Then I looked around the room at the two hundred, maybe three hundred other weapons—each the last stage prop in someone's life. Each had been cleaned, sanitized, impartially cross-referenced with a bright red tag. I was standing in a closetful of endings. Among them, Jimmy Doebler's murder was unremarkable.

Quarles turned to Lopez. "Projectile's in my office. You're saying it was fired from this, right?"

"Our man couldn't rule it out. You going to tell us different?"

Quarles' eyes crinkled. "Haven't test-fired yet. You want to come?"

He took the gun and a box of .380 ammo.

We followed him out of the lab, around the parking lot, to a building in back. The test range was a concrete hall with a lead-curtained trap at the far end, a paper target holder overhead on a motorized track. At the near end was a folding table with several sets of ear protectors and a staple gun.

I picked up the staple gun. "You test-fire a lot of these?"

Quarles handed us the headsets. "Gene Schaeffer also

said if you didn't amuse me, I could go ahead and shoot you."

I decided against the peppy comeback.

Lopez and I put on our ear protectors. Quarles didn't fire downrange. Instead he loaded the Lorcin and went to a large tin box on the side of the room. It looked like the industrial bait tanks they use to stock lakes—about a two-hundred-gallon model, with a hollow spout sticking up on one side, high enough so that Quarles had to stand on a stool to put the gun into the opening.

He fired six rounds—each a muffled boom and a flash of light in the tank's spout. He pointed at the floor. Lopez and I collected the ejected casings. Quarles dragged his stool around to the side of the water tank, opened the top, and fished around with a long piece of PVC pipe until he'd speared all the slugs.

"Get me a lobster while you're in there," I said.

I knew the comment amused him because he did not shoot me.

Quarles showed us six little mushrooms of copper and lead. The water had slowed them down so the shapes were almost uniform, the lower ends retaining perfect striations from the gun's barrel.

Lopez said, "They're just lovely. I figure we got about five more minutes before my sergeant gets here and makes us eat them."

We adjourned next door to Ben Quarles' office.

His window looked out on the asphalt parking lot, with a scenic side view of the DPS loading ramp. The walls were adorned with framed black and white photos of Geronimo and John Dillinger. A John Prine song was playing from the computer's speaker. On the shelf above Quarles' desk was a line of fired bullets, four Larry McMurtry novels, a red roll of evidence tape circled around a Play-Doh can.

Quarles picked up a Ziploc evidence bag from his desk, pulled out a slug. "This is the one from your victim's head. They cleaned the cooties off it."

He threw it to me before I could protest. I looked down at it—a little bit of metal, small as a gumdrop. Quarles plucked it back from my palm, then put the slug and a test slug from Garrett's Lorcin under his comparison microscope.

The machine looked like an old-fashioned ice-cream blender from a malt shop—same size, same turquoise and chrome finish. Quarles peered into the lens, turned some knobs, and said, "Yeah."

"Match?" Lopez asked.

"Come look."

Lopez did, then turned away, his face stony. "Go on, Navarre."

The image in the microscope was the left half of one bullet jutted up against the right half of another. You could turn a knob to move the dividing line, seeing less of one or the other bullet, comparing size, lines, markings. The bullets rotated slowly, and in the microscope light they were beautiful—gold and silver, like a piece of jewelry highlighted in a home-shopping ad.

I was no expert, but even I could see that the ridges—the lands and grooves—were fairly well aligned.

"You've got a right-six GRC on the projectile that killed your friend," Quarles said. "That's the pattern of the spin, and the number of lands and grooves. The projectile we just fired from the suspect's Lorcin is compatible. The damage to the projectile is bad enough that Lopez's man is right—I couldn't swear it's the same gun, but it's definitely from a similar .380."

I had expected that. It did not dampen my spirits too badly.

"The casing?" I asked, pushing my luck.

Quarles produced another Ziploc bag from his desk drawer, took out the brass I'd found in the lake. "It's a .380, all right. I put it in the microscope earlier—the crimp marks, where the projectile fits in the casing, line up beautifully. These marks are on the base of the projectile, you understand. Not as mangled as the top."

"Meaning?"

"The casing fits the projectile from the murder."

"A casing in the lake," I said, "maybe a hundred yards

from the scene. It was picked up by the killer, dropped in the water during his exit."

Proof. Goddamn, perfect proof that Garrett was innocent. I looked at Lopez for vindication, but Lopez was staring at Quarles, apparently realizing there was more.

"Ain't had the real test yet," Quarles said. "The BOB markings—breech or bolt face—on this here casing. Give me one of the casings we just fired."

Lopez handed one over, and again Quarles adjusted the comparison microscope.

"Royal flush," he told us.

When it was my turn to look, I saw a circle of brass, cratered in the middle. Nothing exciting.

"The firing pin impression can't always tell you much," Quarles said. "They're circular, pretty much featureless, all the same. One thing, though—look at the outer ring. Those score marks. Now look at the other casing."

I saw what he was talking about—tiny breaks in the circle around the crater. They were similar on both casings.

I pulled away from the microscope. "But you said BOB marks all look the same."

"Mostly," Quarles amended. "For the same type of gun. Usually the firing pin strikes the back of a bullet in a Lorcin, you get a pattern of concentric circles that isn't very distinctive. This casing here, though, has some gaps in those circles—three distinctive gaps, maybe from the gun being cleaned improperly, I don't know. The thing is, your suspect's gun leaves the same kind of marks."

My chest turned cold. "Meaning—"

"This is ballistics. You don't usually get one hundred percent. But the chances of two guns making that same BOB pattern on a casing—they're astronomical. Without that casing you found, I couldn't be very certain, if I had to testify in court. But with the casing—well, the projectile fits the casing, and the casing fits the gun. I'd say your suspect's gun just got pinned to that murder about as well as you can pin it. About ninety percent."

Quarles treated us to a coffee-stained grin. Then he noticed my expression. "I hope I helped. You ain't looking too happy for somebody just solved a case."

"He's ecstatic," Lopez promised. "You'll do a Drugfire search for matches on the casing?"

"Yeah," Quarles promised. "That'll take a few more days. Christ, Navarre, I thought I was repaying some favors. You look like I just stabbed you in the back."

John Prine started singing about flag decals on Mr. Quarles' computer.

Lopez looked out into the parking lot, where a maroon LeBaron was just pulling in. A large military-type African-American man in a coat and tie was getting out of the LeBaron, glowering.

"Come on, Mr. Navarre," Lopez told me. "Thanks for your time, Quarles."

In the hallway, Lopez said, "There's a back way through the CODIS office. Take it."

"A hundred yards away, Lopez. I showed you where I found the bullet. You know this is wrong."

His eyes were burning. "I know what ninety percent means, Tres. I know what it'll mean to my sergeant, who's about to walk through that door. And Tres—the bad things I said about Miss Lee? Forget them. Your brother is going to need all the help he can get."

CHAPTER 27

At sunset, the top windows of Ruby McBride's dream house glowed orange.

Most of the yachts were out enjoying an evening cruise. The restaurant was nearly empty. The boat jockeys had little to do except smoke cigarettes, recline on their massive forklift, play cards at the lakefront.

I sat in my truck, idling at the bottom of Ruby's private driveway, trying to decide if I really had enough courage to face another human being.

I'd spent the afternoon at Jimmy's dome, hiding from reporters' phone calls, hiding from the news reports, finishing Jimmy's kiln at the waterfront.

Because of me, because of one brass casing, the investigation had gained lethal momentum. At 2:00 P.M., my brother had been formally charged with murder.

I should've called our sister, Shelley, in Wisconsin, broken her long, self-imposed exile from the family to give her the news. I should've called my mom in Colorado, ruined her vacation. As of yet, I hadn't done either.

At the top of Ruby McBride's driveway, her blue Miata glistened—nose-out, ready for action. Up on Ruby's deck, I saw a flicker of red hair go past.

I put the F-150 into gear, rumbled up the drive, and skidded to a diagonal stop, blocking the Mazda.

I got out of the truck, walked up the stairs. I heard

two voices before I got to the top—Clyde Simms mumbling something, Ruby answering, "No!"

Clyde sat on the railing bench, looking about as happy as a fourth-string quarterback.

Ruby stood by the hot tub, running water over her hands with a garden hose. She'd been crying. Her hair hung in a stiff red mesh around her shoulders. She was barefoot, and an apron covered her T-shirt and shorts.

I could see why she wanted to wash off. Her apron and her hands were stained with blood.

"Damn you, Tres," she said. "Not now."

I pointed at the streaks of red on her apron. "What the hell—"

She dropped the hose, grabbed a bucket of pink water on the edge of the hot tub.

"We blew it," she told me. "We really *blew* it, didn't we?"

A big yellow sponge sloshed angrily around the bucket as she stormed off toward the kitchen area.

Clyde stared at me. "She's right, you know. You and that fucking brass casing."

A week's worth of anger surged inside me. I followed Ruby, yelling at her back, "I didn't sell out my own friends, Ruby. I didn't—"

And then I stepped inside and saw the problem.

Most of the room hadn't changed since I'd been here Sunday night. It was still a bare box of walls and windows, the floor littered with odd bits of lumber and power tools. The far wall, however, looked like a Jackson Pollock painting. The sheetrock was marred with swathes of dark, sticky red-brown—crusty and thick and splattered. It smelled like a rending plant.

Ruby dropped her bucket, tried to wring pink water out of the sponge.

"When did it happen?" I asked.

She ignored me, tried to scrub the blood off the wall. She only managed to turn more of the sheetrock pink.

Clyde came up behind me.

"Wee hours," he said. "Workers didn't go to the upper

level all day. They were doing wiring on the bottom floor. Ruby always goes up to the deck when she gets home in the afternoon."

"Somebody knew the workers' schedule," I said. "They wanted Ruby to be the one to find this."

Ruby kept working—rubbing at the stains, cursing, splattering herself with pink water.

"Found the deer about fifty yards downhill," Clyde told me, "gutted with a sharp knife. My Dobe Miata ain't good for much, but she's got a decent nose. Bastard who did this carried a bucket of blood all the way here. He spilled some on the steps."

"Did you call the police?" I asked.

"*The police*," Ruby spat. She crushed the sponge in her fists, lines of red leaking down her forearms. "Tres, the police are fitting your brother's neck for a noose. They'd explain how he did this, probably lugged his wheelchair all the way up the stairs."

She kicked the sheetrock, then kept swiping at the blood.

"That's not doing anything." Clyde said it gently.

"My—goddamn—house." Every word was more elbow grease with the sponge.

"Ruby," Clyde said. "I told you I'd deal with it."

She flung the sponge in the bucket. "You will not deal with anything, Clyde. GET. OUT."

I kept my eyes on Ruby. I didn't so much see Clyde leave as I felt it—his gravity suddenly missing from the doorway.

"Who did this?" I asked Ruby.

She wiped her hands on her apron. Her fingernails were scarlet crescents. "I don't know."

"Of course you don't. You don't know how Matthew Peña got inside Techsan's program. You don't know how Jimmy got shot. You don't know what that damn bullet casing was doing in the lake."

She closed the distance between us in two steps, then slapped me across the face. I didn't try to stop her. The sting was the first real sensation I'd had all day.

From somewhere out on the deck, Clyde called Ruby's name.

It wasn't an offer of help. More a warning.

Ruby stared back at her splattered wall, then at all the other places she'd managed to smear pink—the floor, the doorframe, the new kitchen counter.

"This is my house," she murmured. "No one can do this to my house."

"Someone did."

She closed her eyes. Her lips were trembling. "I'm all right. I just have to take care of things."

I tried to cup my hand around her elbow, but she yanked away, wrestled off her apron. She washed her hands again, gathered up her shoes and purse, held them against her stomach like a melting football.

"Ruby—"

She brushed past me. "I'll fix it. Goddamn if I won't."

Clyde stood motionless at the railing, letting Ruby go.

I followed her down the steps.

When she got to the drive and found my car blocking hers, she headed down the hill, cursing as she stumbled barefoot over sharp pieces of broken limestone.

I followed about fifteen steps behind.

"Ruby," I called.

"GO—AWAY!"

She'd made it to the marina parking lot now, started limping toward the docks. She dropped one of her shoes but kept walking—one parking space, two parking spaces.

"You think you can stop him, Ruby? You think he'll allow that?"

Three parking spaces.

"You told me Peña understood people," I called after her. "I guess you're right. He's sure got your number."

She whirled to face me.

The nearest boat jockeys had stood now, their poker game forgotten. One of them called, "Ms. McBride?"

"I'm all right!"

I picked up her Adidas, brought it to her.

"No one has my number, Tres," she told me. "No one."

"Peña wouldn't do something randomly. He'd pry into your past, look for weaknesses, pick something he knew would rattle you. Why deer blood, Ruby?"

"I didn't—" She choked, forced a shaky inhale. "No one destroys my property. That wasn't . . ."

"Part of the deal?"

She snatched the shoe, hobbled over to the nearest car, slid down against the bumper, and started fumbling with her laces. "I can make things right, Tres. At least I'm going to try."

It was the same thing Garrett had told me five days ago.

There was blood between two of Ruby's toes—her own blood now—but she didn't seem to notice.

One of the boat jockeys called, "Ms. McBride? You sure—"

"Leave me alone!" She tugged on a shoe, started picking at the laces of the other.

"You can't confront Peña," I told her. "Not by yourself. Don't be stupid."

"I'm not confronting Peña."

Her purse lay in the gravel. The black butt of a gun—probably the one I'd seen on her boat the day before—peeked out the top.

"I can fix this," she told me again. "But *I* have to do it. Carefully. You can't help me, Tres. Neither can Clyde. I'm not asking you to understand—"

She stopped, looked out toward the water. "Maybe I am asking you to understand. Jimmy is dead. Garrett doesn't have a clue what's really going on. I can fix this. But that can't happen if I don't go out tonight—by myself."

Ruby got her other shoe on, stood up. The setting sun turned her shadow into stilt person.

"Where are you going?" I asked.

"You could follow me, Tres. You could seriously screw this up. But I'm asking you—if it were the other way around, would you want me to stop you? Would you like it if I barged in, assumed I had the right to tell you what was safe, what you needed to do?"

The boat jockeys had gone back to their game and their cigarettes. Clyde hadn't moved from the top of the deck.

"I want to make amends," Ruby said. "I was serious about that, Tres. You were right. It's my fault—I opened the door."

"The back door."

She closed her hand into a fist. "All right. Yes. Now let me stop it."

She shouldered her purse.

She seemed to be part of the sunset—her entire form glowing red. I felt like I could touch her, and I would disappear into the glare.

"Be careful," I told her.

She let out a long, relieved exhale, came up and kissed me roughly on the cheek, exactly where she had slapped me. "I'll make it all right."

She turned and walked toward the docks—toward the *Ruby, Too.*

I watched her until she got to the pier, then I headed back up the drive, toward the tower where Clyde was still playing gargoyle.

I wouldn't say he was exactly waiting for me at the top of the stairs, but he was there—leaning against the redwood railing, looking over the tops of the live oaks toward Mansfield Dam.

Ruby's hot tub cover had been peeled off. I hadn't remembered it being like that a few minutes before. Water bubbled and rumbled and small objects bobbed in it—pecans, though where these would've come from in early June I had no idea.

"Where's she running off to?" I asked.

Clyde shook his head. "She wanted me to know, she'd tell me."

"So much for protection."

Clyde was silent. In the sunset, his eyes were so blue

they were translucent, like bottle glass. "You shook her up yesterday. There was no talking to her. I tried . . . I'd do anything for her."

"Same as you'd do for my brother."

He stared at the churning water in the hot tub, the dark little orbs of pecans bobbing in the foam. "Garrett might kill a guy who took his woman. He wouldn't do that—" He waved toward the open door of the kitchen.

"I ain't going to let nobody mess with my friends anymore," Clyde decided. "Not the cops, not Peña. I'm going to call a few of my buddies, have them come around tonight, just in case."

"In case what?"

No sound but the hum of the hot tub. The daylight was almost gone.

"I'm not going to trust the police, man," Clyde said. "That's all I'm saying."

"You going to form a human chain of bikers around Garrett?"

"You're not a biker—not a one-percenter. You don't know."

I felt like I was talking to my brother, which suddenly made me realize why Garrett got along with bikers so well. For both, conversation is like spinning wheels in gravel. It doesn't matter if you get anywhere, as long as you make noise and shoot out a bunch of rocks.

"Best of luck, Clyde," I said. "Have a good evening."

I started to leave.

He put a massive paw on my shoulder, pushed me back a step.

"I know you don't like your brother much. But you should respect him. The man says he'll be there for you, he will. The guys in my club know that."

"You're right, Clyde. Garrett's a regular Eagle Scout."

"He going to be out on bail for the Buffett concert tonight?"

"He got a quick hearing. The wheelchair helped, the

fact he's got no priors. Maia Lee took care of things the best she could. He'll be out."

Clyde looked somewhat mollified. "Buffett music—Buffett knows what it's all about, man. Renegades got to stick together."

He stepped out of my way. "I expect you to be there for Garrett, Tres. You got some makeup work to do."

Part of me wanted to slug Clyde because he assumed he knew what I needed to do, as if he knew the history—who had abandoned whom over the years. Part of me wanted to slug him because I thought he was probably right.

"Call me," I said. "Let us know Ruby got back safe."

He nodded. "End of the day, man, you better stand with your family. And guess what: the end of the day is here."

CHAPTER 28

Southpark Meadows was throbbing with canned music by the time we pulled in.

The parking lot smelled of hay and mown grass. Headlights cut across a haze of dust. A few late tailgaters hung out drinking beer—women in cutoffs and bikini tops, men in Hawaiian shirts and khaki shorts, humanoids of indeterminate gender dressed as Caribbean life forms. Even the lobsters had drinks in their hands.

Garrett pushed his wheelchair along between Maia and me, occasionally getting his wheels snagged on a rock or a tire rut. Dickhead the Parrot sat on his shoulder, flapping his wings helpfully whenever the chair got stuck.

When we got to the rise, we could see the stage two hundred yards downfield—a wired black box of Mecca, the pilgrims swirling around it a sea of drunk pirates and Key West outcasts. A huge rainbow beach ball bounced over a forest of hands. Caribbean music played from building-sized speakers. Stage lights pulsed. Around the perimeter, long lines snaked away from the beer booths.

We passed a guy in a foam shark suit, a couple making out in matching crustacean hats, a woman dressed as a tequila bottle.

"Like the Bay-to-Breakers race in San Francisco," I said to Maia.

She gave me an icy look. I'd been getting my share of those from her today.

"A little," she agreed, "except no one is naked."

"Give it an hour," Garrett promised.

We wove our way around the periphery of the crowd. The smell of ganja was everywhere, the field strewn with beach blankets and lawn chairs and coolers.

Every few yards somebody would recognize Garrett and we'd have to stop for introductions and compliments about the parrot and, invariably, a proffered swig from somebody's secret flask. If anybody knew about Garrett's newfound celebrity status as a murder suspect, no one mentioned it.

Maybe the murder charges didn't matter. At the rate we were going, I figured we'd be dead from alcohol poisoning by the time we found a place to sit anyway.

We finally settled on a knoll to one side of the stage, close enough so Garrett could park his chair and have a fair chance of seeing, far enough away so he wouldn't blast out the parrot's eardrums. Garrett settled back on his Persian cushion and proceeded to get out his joint-rolling kit.

Neither Maia nor I had come so prepared—no blanket, no provisions, no funny costumes.

A warm-up act came on stage and began an instrumental number to a spattering of applause.

Maia's eyes were fixed on the horizon, studying the stars above the oak trees.

"I've apologized," I told her. "I don't know what else to say."

"I don't blame you for bringing evidence to Lopez's attention. I blame you for not calling me. Not telling me. Not warning me."

Garrett glared up at us from his half-rolled joint. "Could we not talk about this anymore? I'm trying to get stoned. You want to plan my funeral, how about you two go up that way some?"

Then Garrett was besieged by a group of tropical-shirted fans who wanted to admire his bird. Flasks of liquor came out.

Maia and I exchanged looks, then moved up the hill.

We found an abandoned quilt kicked into a U—its owner either gone to get beer or gone toward the stage.

Metal drums trilled on stage. The lights surged.

What I'd taken for a warm-up band was actually Buffett's band.

Mr. Margaritaville himself was now coming on stage. The mega-screen TVs flashed online to either side of the stage, so that J.B. was either a small orange and red dot walking across the stage or a huge, grinning tan face with blond cropped hair.

The cheering started.

"At least Garrett's talking to you again," Maia said.

"Sure," I agreed. "What better punishment?"

She didn't try to make me feel better.

Buffett launched into something I didn't recognize, but the crowd did. A guy near us raised a beer can and did a pretty good approximation of a rebel yell.

Maia hugged her arms, as if the eighty-five-degree night warranted shivers. "I want you to know, I tried to convince Garrett to get another lawyer. The DA didn't contest my right to represent, but . . . I don't want a trial. That's not why I came to Texas. Garrett insisted. I guess he was too shaken to think about hiring someone he didn't know."

At the moment, Garrett didn't appear shaken. He and his friends were nodding their heads to the music, drinking, passing around the joint.

"You'll have to suggest a plea bargain," I told Maia.

"Unless something changes drastically. Manslaughter, maybe."

"He won't go for it."

"Of course not," she said bitterly. "Navarre stubbornness forebears."

A prickly silence formed between us.

"Tell me I'm not crazy," I said. "Peña could be responsible for Jimmy's murder. Or Ruby. Or W.B."

"Garrett's your brother. You don't need permission to take his side."

It wasn't the kind of answer I'd wanted, and I guess it showed.

"You've been acting guilty for days," Maia said. "It's not just finding that casing. What's bothering you?"

Buffett was still playing that song I didn't know. Pot smoke was so thick that every few seconds another wisp of it would cross the moon like a cloud.

"Listening to Ruby," I said, "how she abandoned Garrett after his accident. I guess I hadn't thought about that night in a long time."

Maia studied my face.

In all the years we'd been together, I'd never discussed my family with her much. She hadn't even known Garrett was disabled until she'd met him.

"We found him on the tracks," I told her. "My father, my sister, and I. I knew where Garrett went to hop trains. I waited almost two hours before I said anything to my dad."

"That was twenty years ago," she said. "You were how old, twelve?"

Garrett was up on the hill, having a great old time. A young blond girl, maybe twenty-three, had settled into his lap. She coaxed Dickhead the Parrot onto her wrist, then lifted her arm up and down to the beat, forcing Dickhead to hold his wings open for balance like a hang glider.

"Garrett's fine," Maia said gently. "Look at him, for God's sake."

I didn't answer.

I wasn't sure I could explain to Maia that she was giving me too much credit. What bothered me wasn't the idea I might've done more for Garrett, all those years ago. What bothered me was that I finally understood how Ruby McBride felt. She'd made me remember the revulsion, the horror of Garrett's condition, the desire to run away from him. She'd reminded me of my darkest, most contemptible wish when I was twelve years old—that perhaps it would have been better if I'd just gone to sleep that night, not said anything to my father.

Maia reached out, took my hand.

She was about to say something when her face went blank.

Matthew Peña was walking toward us.

He'd changed out of business clothes, into a sleeveless Gold's Gym T-shirt and workout pants. Unfortunately, he did not appear to have sustained any permanent injuries from Maia Lee tossing him into his bookshelf yesterday. His hair gleamed with gel and his eyes were brighter than I'd seen them before, almost animated. If dead things can be animated.

"A picnic," Peña said. "How cozy."

"Matthew." Maia's tone was steady and cold. "I didn't figure you for a Buffett fan."

He held up the laminated card around his neck. "Gift from a prospective client—backstage pass. How could I say no?"

For Peña, the event could've been ballet or baseball or an art opening. It didn't matter. The important thing was that he could walk around with that backstage pass on, prove to the diehard fans that he could do better than they could without half trying.

I looked back at Garrett. He saw us, all right. He made a finger gun, fired it at us, then he returned his attention to the young blonde dancing in his lap.

Peña crouched in front of me. "Had a busy day, Navarre? I heard your brother is in a little trouble. If there's anything I can do—"

"Like confess?" I asked.

Peña smiled. "By the way, I thought I'd return this to you."

He took the button recorder I'd left stuck under his desk, tossed it in my lap.

"Expensive piece of equipment," he said. "Shouldn't leave it sitting around. I had my people erase it for you. All it failed to pick up, I'm happy to tell you, is good news. We've isolated the problem in Techsan's software. Stupid mistake on the part of the original programmers, I'm afraid. Easily corrected."

"Surprise, surprise."

"Of course, there's the matter of those confidential documents being posted. I can't promise there won't be a criminal investigation against your brother and Ruby, maybe some more lawsuits, but hey—at least the program will be on track. Your brother's AccuShield stock should go up. By the time he gets out of jail, he'll be able to pay his debts, retire to the lower middle class."

"I think," Maia said, "that you should leave."

The Buffett song ended to deafening applause.

Peña checked his watch. "You're right. I'd better get back to my clients. We've got a night dive scheduled after the concert—going to check out an old observatory mirror and a few concrete sculptures sunk at eighty feet off Starnes Island. Sure you don't want to come along? Either of you?"

Before Maia could strangle him with our quilt, I said, "Treat Ruby well, Matthew. Listen to her."

He looked at me as if I'd just slipped into another language. "Whatever you say, Navarre. Enjoy the evening."

Then he melted back into the crowd, people around him fawning over his backstage pass.

Maia followed him with her eyes. Her face was pale, tightly controlled.

I asked the question I'd been trying to avoid for two days. "Did you tell him about Hawaii?"

Maia's eyes reproached me. "No."

"Then how?"

"How does a shark smell blood, Tres? I don't know."

Hawaii, four years ago, had been Maia's and my last vacation together as a couple. We'd spent a week on the west side of Oahu—drinking, walking on the beach, making love. And then I'd gotten the bright idea it would be fun to dive the Mahi shipwreck off Waianae.

I remember Maia forcing herself through the scuba class, coming up shaky after every practice dive, even the pool sessions, but successfully conning me into believing she was fine. She made it through the skills tests, even convinced our instructor, who was no slacker for safety, that she could handle open sea. We didn't know the kind of terror she'd been suppressing until she hit deep water—sixty-five feet under—and panicked. We fought to get her to breathe and not shoot to the surface. Through the mask, her eyes had been the size of silver dollars. As we made our emergency ascent, she'd purged the contents of her stomach through the air manifold, then clawed my regulator out of my mouth and breathed on it, forcing me to grope for my backup.

For another diver, the failure might not have been so personal, but Maia Lee never retreats, never surrenders. She was raised on stories of her great-grandfather who survived the Long March, her grandfather who survived reeducation during the Cultural Revolution. For Maia, admitting defeat to a phobia is unthinkable.

We'd flown back to San Francisco twenty-four hours later, Maia curled into her plane seat, intensely quiet, as if she were trying to compress the Mahi dive into her safe-box for darkest memories. For months afterward, whenever she looked at me, I saw a tinge of resentment—shame that I'd witnessed her moment of vulnerability.

The fact Matthew Peña had so quickly read that fear, had played up the part of his own life that would maximize her discomfort, filled me with dread. What worried me more was Maia—the fierce pride that had made her push through scuba lessons, deny the warning signs, get sixty-five feet under before realizing she couldn't handle it. I was worried what would happen if she handled Matthew Peña the same way she handled scuba.

The second song ended. The crowd yelled.

Jimmy Buffett told Austin hello. He wished us all a very merry piña colada, then began something I knew—"Coconut Telegraph."

There'd been a time in Maia's Potrero Hill apartment, cooking green pepper and ham omelets, coffee percolating, Maia barefoot, in linen white shorts and one of my T-shirts. This song had come on and she'd forced me to dance through the breakfast nook, ended up spraying me with the champagne she was using for mimosas.

The memory passed between us. Her expression softened.

"You want a drink?" I asked her.

"You don't know how much."

We joined the beer line, made uncomfortable small talk while we waited, listened to the Buffett set in progress. The band played "Little Miss Magic" while we tried very hard not to look at each other, not to give each other any cue that we remembered what this song had once been our sound track for.

We got our beers. By the time we made it back to our borrowed quilt, the song had ended and a new peal of excitement had broken out down by the stage. A couple was making their way toward the front in a spotlight. They wore full wedding regalia—the bride in a white silk dress that must've been a thousand degrees inside.

Off mike, the whole audience heard Jimmy Buffett saying, "When—just now?"

Then to the audience, his face grinning on the big screen, "Got a special dedication to the newlyweds, folks."

A big cheer, which got even more riotous as the audience realized the song he'd just begun was "Why Don't We Get Drunk (and Screw)." The bride disappeared below the audience. Maybe she fainted. Somebody knocked the groom's gray top hat off.

I had no special memories associated with this song, which was either reassuring or disappointing, depending on your perspective.

Maia caught me staring at her, tried to look annoyed. "Yes?"

"Nothing. I just—" Stop. Regroup. "What happens next for you—after you clear Garrett of all charges, get Peña sent to the asylum?"

She didn't look happy with the change of subjects. "My choices may be limited."

"Terrence call you again?"

"We've agreed to part company. My junior partnership is over. How amicable the split is, how it affects my chances at a job in another firm—Terrence claims that's up to me."

The "Get Drunk" song wound down. The cheering kept going. Jimmy Buffett yelled, *"Well what did you think I was going to play?"*

More cheering.

Maia looked at me like she was choosing her words carefully. "Tres, I may want to look outside the Bay Area."

My heart slowed. "Such as?"

She circled her arms around her knees. "I want to defend people who deserve defending for a while. Coming out here—I may have been trying to tell myself something. I can see why so many Bay Area people have moved to Austin."

I stayed quiet.

"Nothing is certain, Tres. And you are not to get any ideas about my motives."

"No. Of course not."

"You would not stay in San Francisco for me. I would definitely not move here for you."

"Understood."

Something hung in the air between us—fluttery and unformed as a new cobweb, vibrating with the breeze. I was afraid to speak for fear it would rip.

The band started their next song. Jimmy Buffett sang about boat drinks.

I looked down the hill for Garrett, whom I'd momentarily forgotten about. There was no longer a girl on his lap. Next to him stood a biker—a guy in his fifties, with an enormous belly, grizzled beard, and a greasy gray ponytail tied with leather strips. His arms were flabby and lobster red, bulging from a leather vest that had the word DIABLO and a cartoon devil face stitched above the breast. The biker was pointing, his eyebrows raised, his face grim, as if making sure Garrett had heard his point.

Now Garrett looked shaken.

I was on my feet, pushing past a couple of guys with

beers in their hands, not bothering to see if Maia was following me.

When I got to Garrett, the biker had vanished into the crowd. Garrett was staring into space, all his enthusiasm for the concert gone.

"You okay?" I demanded.

Garrett nodded, dazed. The parrot waddled back and forth on his shoulder, eyeing me accusingly.

Maia came up next to us.

"Who?" she asked. "And what did he want?"

"Nothing," Garrett said. "A friend of Clyde's. He was saying—he asked if I needed any help. That's all."

He was lying. I hadn't been brothers with him all my life and not learned to tell.

"Look," I said, "if there's a problem . . ."

Maia put her hand over mine.

She was right. It did no good to push.

Buffett kept singing about warm climates, but Garrett didn't seem able to focus. The little bit of spirit the concert had managed to instill in him had drained away.

After another verse, he mumbled, "God help me, but I think I need to leave early."

He asked if he could stay with me out at the dome for the night. I told him he could. I didn't ask why.

As we made our way back to the parking lot, the cheering and music getting farther and farther behind us, I tried not to think about what Garrett had said earlier—about coming here just to plan his funeral.

CHAPTER 29

When my eyes opened the next morning, it was already full light. John, Paul, George, and Ringo beamed down at me from the poster on Doebler's ceiling. *Cheers, mate. Feel like crap today, yeah?*

I crawled out of the bedsheets, which were conspicuous for the absence of a sleeping feline.

The last things I remembered from the night before were Maia and Garrett arguing defense strategies in the living room, Robert Johnson curled contentedly in his long-lost mommy's lap, the parrot scuttling along the railing of the sleeping loft, looking by no means certain about his new feline housemate. I didn't remember going to bed at all.

I found exercise clothes and snuck downstairs. Garrett's sleeping bag was empty. I didn't see Maia either, but there was a body-shaped impression in the other sofa, indicating she'd stayed the night. Robert Johnson was curled on the kitchen counter, a bowl of familiar tan liquid next to him.

I took a sniff. Sure enough—Maia's café au lait for kitties, Robert Johnson's favorite. I dipped in a finger. Still warm.

The parrot was sitting next to the cat. Apparently they'd come to some sort of truce.

"Mornin', boys," I said.

The parrot eyed me, then waddled over to Robert

Johnson, put his beak close to the cat's ear, and whispered, "Go away."

I blinked. I was afraid if I stayed there any longer, the three of us would start having an intelligent conversation, so I picked up my keys and went out the front door.

The sky was overcast with ugly clouds, the air heavy with humidity. It was going to be a killer of a day—storm or sauna.

I crunched my way down the path toward the lake. The water was teal, a weird reflection of the clouds, as if the world had turned upside-down.

At the concrete slab, Maia Lee had beaten me to the practice routines.

She was wearing Jimmy Doebler's clothes—his green Ocean Pacific swimsuit and a large white polo shirt. One dead man's wardrobe fits all.

Her hair had been brushed out and re-ponytailed. Her face was fresh, alert, no worse for her long evening. She practiced barefoot, her black espadrilles set neatly on the base of the kiln.

The morning was quiet except for the rustle of the plastic over Jimmy's pottery shelf, the sleepy drone of crickets.

Maia was in the middle of a Chen form—slow, fluid movements punctuated by bursts of speed. Tiger stance. Punch under palm. A quick attack sequence of fists and snap kicks, then back into slow motion with White Crane Spreads Its Wings.

I did my stretches, rolled my head around, and got a sound like sugarcane snapping. I ran through some stances to get the burn into my leg muscles.

Maia crouched into Snake Creeps Down—her front leg fully extended, her weight on the back, low to the ground. Her spine was perfectly straight, her back hand forming a bird's beak, front hand a palm-strike to the ground. She held that position, which was not easy to do.

I stood there admiring her until I realized she was inviting me to join.

I walked to the slab, sank into position. Maia unfroze. Together, we finished the form.

Maia's style was different from my usual routine, but I found it easy to follow—smooth and logical. For her, tai chi had been an afterthought, something she learned to augment the harder Shaolin style she preferred. Despite that, her execution was humbling—the flow of her movements, the graceful stances, the fire and spirit that can't be faked. She practiced as if her life depended on it, yet her face stayed perfectly serene, her eyes fixed at all times on an imaginary target.

We ended the form facing the water. I was drenched with sweat and a mosquito was floating around my eyes, but I felt good. I'd forgotten what it was like working with someone who was better than me, who made me push the limits.

We unfroze, but still didn't talk. I enjoyed the silence and *chi*—the feeling of breath and warmth and focus all concentrated in the center of my body.

Maia wiped her forehead with her wrist. Her face glowed from the workout, a tiny trickle of sweat ran down her neck behind her ear, but she looked neither tired nor winded.

"Good morning," she said.

"*Sifu.*"

She smirked, gently kicked my shin with her bare toes. "You don't want me as a teacher. You're overextending your knees. You need to keep your elbows down."

"Yes, master."

"Push hands with me," she said. "And stop with the *master* shit. I could grow to like it."

We faced each other in cat stance, right hand to right hand, touching at the back of the wrists. We began with small movements—circling our hands, pushing gently on each other's wrist, trying to feel where the other person was going to move. Once that was established, anything was fair game.

Maia advanced a step and I retreated. We reversed. She tried to push me off balance and I stepped back, forcing her to come forward. We corrected positions, kept going. I waited for the next attack, sensed it coming, then withdrew before Maia's push, twisting to the side as Maia committed her weight forward. I pushed. She lost her footing, went over sideways, and landed hard on her hip against the concrete.

A strand of black hair from her ponytail stuck to the side of her cheek with sweat. She brushed it away. There was white cement dust on her thigh.

"Okay?" I asked.

She nodded. "I was too aggressive."

"Shaolin will do that to you."

She stood, dusted herself off.

This time we circled longer. Her fingers were delicate curls, her wrist warm. I should've kept my head clear, used my *chi* to sense what she was up to, but I happened to catch her eyes and was instantly hooked by them—warm and bright and amber. She smiled just before she pushed me onto my butt.

My teeth clacked. My spine felt like it had been sunk into the cement with a pile driver.

"Not fair," I said.

"Oh," she said. "Now we'll talk about what's fair."

She offered me a hand. I smiled, took her by the wrist and somersaulted backward, pulling her over me.

Someone else I might've hurt, throwing her face-first toward the cement, but Maia turned the fall into an easy roll, took almost none of the impact, ended up facing me in a crouch.

"So that's the way you want to play?" she asked.

She came at me with a heel kick, which I ducked. I tried to sweep her leg off balance but she spun a 360 and got me in my gut with her other foot. I blocked a punch, then guarded for her next one. It was a feint. She caught me in the trap perfectly—grabbed my wrist as soon as I presented it and twisted herself under my arm, putting my wrist and elbow up between my shoulder blades in the same joint lock she'd used on Matthew Peña two days ago.

It hurt not a little bit.

"Okay," I told her. "You win this one."

She increased the pressure. "Say 'Maia kicked my ass.'"

"Maia kicked my ass."

"Say 'I was a dumb-shit to ever leave her.'"

"Go ahead," I grimaced. "Break it."

She let me go, came around front and tried to hit me in the stomach, but the punch was easy to catch.

"Bastard," she said.

I held her fist until it relaxed. Her fingers laced with mine.

A man's voice said, "Damn, I hate to interrupt a good workout."

I hadn't heard him approach, but fifteen feet up the path stood Detective Vic Lopez, smiling his normal diabolic smile.

"What can we do for you, Detective?" Maia asked. "You come to apologize for wrongful arrest?"

Lopez laughed, but there was an edge to it as sharp as a broken bottle. "Maybe later, counselor. In the meantime, you wouldn't happen to know where Garrett Navarre is this morning?"

Maia and I exchanged looks.

She said, "I assumed— He isn't inside?"

Then I realized Maia and I had both thought the same thing—that Garrett had simply gone to the outhouse. I looked up toward the house, noticed the obvious—that the Carmen Miranda wasn't parked there anymore.

"He's probably picking up breakfast tacos."

Lopez smiled. "I'm sure. You saw him last when?"

Maia told him about the concert. "We came back here, talked until maybe two A.M. He went to sleep on the sofa, right across from me. Why?"

"Two A.M." Lopez seemed to be calculating. "Oh, nothing, really. Just that we have a small problem I was hoping Garrett could help us with."

Lopez watched my face carefully—his nets trawling for any reaction.

"Okay," I relented. "What small problem?"

"We found Ms. McBride's boat moored on the lake this morning," he said. "There was nobody on it. I thought you folks would want to know. The Search and Recovery divers are going in the water just about now."

From: "McBride Marina" <Lake_2000@aol.com>
To: GN1@rni.com
Subject: Defeat Hollow
Date: Wed 14 Jun 2000 17:14:26 0700
Originator: Lake_2000@aol.com
X-Mailer: UnityMail
X-Mailer-Version: 3.1
X-UnityUser: guest1.com

Moonlight is beautiful around a boat, the way it points to you over the water, no matter which direction you approach from, like a compass needle.

My wet suit was uncomfortable, but that was nothing new. Defeat Hollow is a narrow inlet, its banks mostly wilderness. It would be a short trip, and no one would be watching.

I made silent progress—a dozen paddle strokes, drops of cool on my knees as I changed sides, back and forth. I wondered out of habit how deep the hollow was—forty feet, maybe?

Her Sea Ray blazed with light. She was standing on the forward deck, waiting with a wineglass in her hand.

It seemed impossible she wouldn't notice me, but she wasn't looking up-cove. She was expecting me to come from the main channel—the same boat as last time, the shining slick, red and white Conbrio. A friendly, well-lit approach.

Mahler was playing—the Fourth Symphony, one of the CDs I'd given her. I knew she hated the music, but she would be interested in setting my mood, making me at ease. The fact that it was the music of an abused son, a man who died of a diseased heart— these things were lost on her. She could not have chosen better, really. The music always makes me burn with pity, gives me the desire to wipe someone off the face of the earth.

The raft bumped into the aft of the boat with a satisfied hiss, right next to the ladder. No problem to tie on, even wearing neoprene gloves.

Three steps and I was aboard, bringing my pack. I left the air tank on the raft. And the gun. No need for them yet.

The hatch leading below deck was open, a square of buttery light.

She stood in the prow, hugging her arms. A sleeveless dress, her hair loose.

What was in her glass—red wine? I'd hoped it would be white. More convincing to make the switch to champagne.

I watched her over the top of the pilot's deck, and at any time she could've turned, seen me. But she didn't. The Mahler symphony kept playing.

I stripped my wet suit to the waist, left the diver's knife strapped to my thigh.

From my pack, I took the bottle of Moët, still cold from its insulation. I slipped the capped syringe into my shirt pocket. So much easier to put into the drink, but in case matters got less elegant, the syringe was there.

I went below deck.

The music was louder in the galley—set to a volume to be heard above deck. I found two glasses, prepared one for her.

I was already feeling nostalgic. Of all of them— even Adrienne—this one had been the most interesting. She seemed put together from shards of ice. You always had to avoid the points, the sharp edges. And she was sure of herself. I'll give her that.

The terms she'd offered on the phone—it was touching, how much she was willing to pay. Millions in stock, everything I'd offered her—as if that money would have ever been hers. She wanted to use it as a bargaining chip, give it all up, promise to keep a secret for me—the secret that mattered the least. All she wanted in exchange was a different victim to throw to the idiot wolves.

How could I refuse? She was so sure I could not. After all, she'd done everything I'd asked.

Everything.

She couldn't know how I'd practiced, how I'd stood over her friend in the dark, studying that wasted, grizzled face, thinking what an unlikely choice. What a *perfect* choice. She couldn't have seen me with my makeshift tools the night before—field stripping a weapon for practice, comparing the firing surfaces. Just a few nicks. So easy. She couldn't have known all the other pieces I'd laid out for the puzzle, not knowing whether they'd been found or not. I'd once heard George Lucas say in an interview that he wasn't afraid to spend four months on a scene that might be on screen for five seconds, or might not make the final cut at all. That's what made a man a genius.

I let her be optimistic on the phone. I soothed her. It had been easy to win back her faith, even easier than after the shooting. This time she was rational. She was desperate. The two things together made me certain she would operate under the delusion that I play by rules.

I poured champagne.

When I went above, she had just made the discovery. She was staring at my wet prints on the deck, my bag.

I called to her and her eyes widened. It took her a moment to decipher my shape, silhouetted in the light from below. She seemed surprised to find me smiling. To find me so close.

I couldn't help the warmth in my voice, the friendliness, the tone of absolute confidence that everything would now be all right.

"This is a celebration," I told her. "I have a plan to solve your problem."

CHAPTER 30

"If she's down there," the lieutenant said, "we'll find her."

I gave him credit for trying to drink coffee while standing on Mansfield Dam. The morning wind was strong enough to knock the breath out of us and make the lieutenant's hair do a Medusa number. But with every bout, he corrected his balance like an old ship's captain and kept drinking.

The clouds were laced with lightning on the eastern horizon. Vic Lopez, Maia, the lieutenant, and I stood on the two-lane pedestrian road that ran atop the mile-wide dam. We were about a third of the way out from the east end, where the cement railing turned to riveted steel.

On the west end, the slope to the water was a gentle mountain of gravel, but here it was a sheer drop two hundred feet. Below, the lake's surface rippled in wind-sheets of green and silver. Lower Colorado River Authority and Travis County Sheriff's boats made a dotted line from shore to shore. Marker buoys and diver-down flags bobbed in the wind.

I had a clear view of Point Lone Star—the marina, Ruby McBride's tower on the hill. The point would be a steep but short hike from here, down the hill through underbrush and woods.

"The *Ruby, Too* left from there," the lieutenant said. "We found it moored over yonder—Defeat Hollow."

He pointed toward a small wooded cove. "My men

dived the area around the boat, then moved down here and started working a compass pattern up-current."

"Too rough for a jackstay?" Lopez asked.

The lieutenant nodded.

"Can they search in the rain?" Maia asked him.

"Rain, yes. Not lightning. We've got about fifteen more minutes before I have to pull them out. But a storm is good. It brings bodies to the surface."

The observation failed to comfort me.

I thought about Ruby McBride in her blood-smeared clothes, barefoot, the small automatic pistol slipping from her purse. "She could be somewhere else. Not even on the lake."

Lopez and the lieutenant exchanged glances.

The lieutenant said, "You gentlemen excuse me? Miss Lee."

He walked back toward the east end of the dam, the wind flicking tiny brown waves off his coffee cup.

Lopez said, "Cheer up, Navarre. Maybe you're right."

He spoke with all the optimism of a Russian economist.

Down on the lake, the tiny black-hooded head of a diver came to the surface. Then another. I might've mistaken them for turtles or snakes. Neither diver made any sign that they'd discovered anything, but my stomach tightened anyway. I walked across the road to the opposite railing.

This was the Colorado River side. Here the hills were dotted with luxury homes, garlanded with power lines. A white-columned highway bridge spanned the river to the south.

Maia leaned next to me on the railing. "Don't beat yourself up."

"I let her go," I said. "I could've stopped her."

"That wasn't your job, Tres. It wasn't your decision to make—it was Ruby's."

The problem was, I didn't agree with her. Some guilty, chauvinistic part of me believed that maybe, this one time, the damsel really had needed a knight. And perhaps she'd run straight into the arms of the wrong one.

Lopez joined us. "I'll need to get a list of Garrett's friends. Also his hangouts."

"You're treating him as a fugitive?"

Lopez rubbed his chin. "Well, let's see. He's out on bail for murder. His own lawyer can't locate him."

"You don't believe your own case anymore," Maia told him. "You know Garrett didn't kill anyone."

"What I know is that the machinery is in motion. It's not about me anymore, counselor. I couldn't stop it if I wanted to."

The river was so clear I could see the bottom—a series of broken limestone sheets that looked like a submerged set of child's blocks. Against the base of the dam, a multicolored beach ball bobbed and dipped, stopped from its meanderings by three million tons of concrete.

"Ruby's boat," I said. "I want to see it."

Lopez looked over. "You want to say why?"

I didn't answer.

He sighed. "I'll see what I can do. They should be through processing it by this afternoon."

"What are the odds they'll find her, Vic?"

He planted his elbows on the cement wall. "The waterline is low. That works in the divers' favor. I don't know . . . the area they're searching, the current . . ."

"You used to dive recovery?" Maia asked.

"When I was a cadet. Sounded like a cool cop thing to do, right? Search and recovery. You think that before you run into your first body underwater. Most frightening thing I've ever done—a hundred and thirty feet deep in some places, down in the old river basin—"

"What?" I asked.

"Nothing."

"Another landmark?"

His expression hardened. "The reason I got out of recovery was a kid who drowned. Down that way—the public park, just before Point Lone Star."

"Kids must be the hardest," I said.

"Thirteen-year-old son went into the water after lunch—I mean, this is a small swimming area, marked with buoys and everything. He went in, and the family said it was like he was sucked underneath. Family was Asian. They kept trying to tell us about some Chinese superstition—a dragon got him, an evil spirit or something."

"That's an old belief." Maia's eyes were on the beach ball, trapped and still pushing against the dam. "Every body of water has its own spirit. You always run the risk that the spirit will take a liking to you, make you pay a visit to the bottom."

"Yeah, well, this was a thirty-day visit, this kid had. We had a dozen volunteer divers. The family would come down every day to watch, until it's like two weeks later and we had to tell them—there's nothing else we can do."

"But you found him?"

"*I* found him, Navarre. And trust me—you don't want to know about it. I don't work recovery anymore."

Lightning did a triple play across the horizon. The cicadas woke up with the storm, humming in the woods like electricity.

Maia didn't look well—as if Lopez's story had caused a tremor under her feet, somewhere down in the center of the dam. "I should get going, Tres. You'll get Lopez that list?"

I nodded. "Call me."

She brushed my sleeve with her fingertips, told Lopez goodbye. She walked down the dam road, leaning into the wind.

"Might be a bad time for a reunion," Lopez said, watching Maia. "You and her."

"Vic Lopez, advice columnist."

"If they find Ruby McBride in the water, Navarre, after what went down between Ruby and Garrett, the way she screwed him on that business deal—then God help your brother."

"Maia's right, isn't she? You don't believe in your own case anymore."

He laced his fingers. I noticed again the strange scars on his hands, like permanent blisters.

He saw me looking, rubbed the back of his hand with one finger. "When I was a kid—playing at this friend's house—I noticed this brown stain on his bathroom wall, like somebody had held a match close to the wallpaper. So I told his parents about it. They didn't pay any attention, told me not to worry. But I couldn't leave it alone. I went back and touched it, thinking maybe it would rub off, and my hand went straight through. It was winter. A nest of yellow jackets had eaten its way into the insulation of the house. The brown stain was them on the other side, thinning out the wall. I put my hand straight through the paper and into the center of their nest."

He flexed his fingers, showing me the pattern of scars. "Later the doctors told me I'd gotten over a hundred stings. I almost died. They told me the nest in the wall was the size of a washing machine. There's the lesson, Navarre—if you're the kind who likes to touch the dark spots, maybe you should think twice."

The beach ball bounced against the dam in the wind. Lightning flashed almost overhead now.

"Clara Doebler's death bothers you more than you let on," I told Lopez. "You don't want Jimmy's death mishandled the way hers was."

"Keep your assumptions."

"I've been there," I said. "I've seen a person killed right in front of me."

Lopez kept his eyes on the storm. "No, Navarre. You have *not* been where I have been. It's a place you do not want to go."

Down at the boats, horns were sounding. More divers were starting to come out of the water.

"I'll see you later," Lopez told me. "Go teach your class."

He met my eyes, and just for that moment I saw the anger behind his smile—the offense I'd done him by digging too deep.

And he was right. He was giving me fair warning. It was a dark spot I did not want to touch.

CHAPTER 31

I got to UT five minutes late for my class, soaked, but no one seemed to notice. My septuagenarian student, Father Time, was standing in front, regaling everyone with his last trip to Roswell.

As soon as I'd brushed the water out of my hair and sorted my lecture notes, Father Time yielded the floor with a yellow-dentured grin.

"Figured it wasn't any stranger than what you'd tell us," he explained.

Just what every professor needs—a warm-up act.

I did a quick roll check, realized with mixed emotions that not a single person had dropped. I hear stories from other instructors about fifty percent drop rates, classes of five or ten with an accordingly small number of papers to grade. No such luck for Navarre. Like buzzards, my students tend to stick around to the bitter end. A colleague once told me I wouldn't have that problem if I just stopped doing lesson plans, got boring, and did my part to uphold the reputation of American higher education.

Of course, that colleague never had to use teaching as an escape from PI work. He'd never had to help himself forget, at least temporarily, that his brother was a murder suspect and a woman he'd just met had disappeared.

The thunderstorm drummed on the roof while we talked about the background of the Corpus Christi plays.

I fielded the standard questions. No, we were not talking about Corpus Christi, Texas. The medieval English hadn't yet discovered the joys of Spring Break at Padre Island. No, the plays weren't actually stage plays, but parade-float shows, performed on traveling wagons as part of a street procession. Yes, they really were all Bible stories. Yes, we really would read them in Middle English. Yes, they might be fun anyway.

"Corpus Christi was like Fiesta," I explained. "The Battle of Flowers, except religious."

Blank stares reminded me I was not in San Antonio anymore. A few students nodded like they'd hit Fiesta before. Most did not.

"Mardi Gras?" I tried.

Better. Still no consensus.

I searched my memory for an Austin equivalent. "Aquafest? South by Southwest?"

A tentative voice in back said, "The Gourd Festival?"

"Exactly," I said. "Just like the Gourd Festival."

A collective "Ohh." Satisfied nodding. We had bonded.

Father Time grinned at the ceiling, as if he were getting signals of approval from his friends in Roswell.

"Think of a Gourd Festival put on by the Catholic Church," I suggested. "A religious holiday, and all the entertainment based on something from the Bible."

"Dude," said a guy in the back. "That would suck."

"But if it's all you had," I countered, "if that were the only festival you were allowed every year, you'd make it count, wouldn't you?"

With that we launched into the Gourd Festival rendition of the Wakefield *Noah*.

It took most of the class period just to get the students used to the language, but we were rolling along pretty well by the time Noah and his wife started arguing about getting on the ark.

"Why won't she get on?" a student asked.

I let another student answer. "Typical woman. She doesn't trust her husband."

The first woman looked incredulous. "She's going to drown? She'd rather sit there and nag him than get on the boat?"

"Yeah," a younger girl in the back said. "She's cool."

A few lines later, another question stopped us. "What's Noah calling her there? Ram-skit?"

"Ram shit!" Father Time interpreted, thoroughly delighted.

We read through the fistfight between Noah and wife, the kicking and screaming, the insults. Uxor, the wife, sat down to knit in the rain while the flood came up around her ankles. Once the pleading family finally herded the old matriarch on board, the class was almost sorry to see her lose the argument and live.

"She should've held out," one contended. "Noah's a bastard."

We got to the end. The wife sent out a raven to find land. Noah sent out two doves. The raven's hunger for carrion kept him from returning, but the dove's gentleness and true heart brought it back to the ship with the olive branch.

There was a moment of silence after we read the last line.

"So women send out ravens," the girl in back said. "Is that an insult?"

We could've talked for another hour just on that point, but we were out of time. I told them we'd continue to discuss *Noah* tomorrow, then asked them to read the next play, *The Crucifixion,* on their own.

Thirty minutes later, I was sitting in Texas French Bread on Guadalupe, the rain beating down outside. My Bevington *Medieval Drama* was open, a blank yellow pad and portable *Middle English Dictionary* on top. My cell phone, a cup of coffee, a ham and cheese croissant, and a bottle of extra-strength Tylenol filled up the rest of the tabletop. All the comforts of home.

I stared at the phone, then at the Bevington book.

Planning for tomorrow's class seemed a lot safer than the other things I needed to do today.

And then the phone chirped.

Maia Lee said, "Hey."

"We win the lottery?"

"Finding Garrett—no luck. And nothing on Ruby. The search divers aren't going back in until later in the day."

I wasn't sure whether to be relieved by no news, or not. "Where are you?"

Rain static hissed on the line. "Tres, I went back to Faye Doebler-Ingram's house. She's gone."

"Gone as in *gone?*"

Maia told me how she'd found the Hyde Park house locked up, dark, no car in the driveway. Maia had taken a discreet look around inside and found empty clothes hangers, missing toiletries, everything else clean and tidy, nothing perishable in the refrigerator.

"She left under her own steam," I said.

"Or it's been made to look that way."

I ran down the mental list—Jimmy, Jimmy's ex-wife, Jimmy's aunt. Five years ago, Jimmy's mother. Except for my good friend W.B., every Doebler I knew had been taken out of service. And even W.B. had hired a bodyguard.

"Jimmy's family history," I said. "That tip he got about a lost sibling. What are the odds, Maia?"

Maia was quiet so long I thought I'd lost her.

"I know what you're thinking," she said at last. "There was one case like that in North Carolina. A woman went to court to open her adoption files. Gave medical reasons, but really, she'd harbored years of resentment, felt she'd been abandoned to abusive foster care. When she found her birth family, she tracked them down—murdered her mother and two sisters. But she was caught immediately, Tres. The paper trail was clear. The consent of the birth family had to be given for her to track them."

"That assumes the paper trail is legitimate," I argued. "We're talking about South Texas in the 1960s. An unmarried society woman getting in trouble with the wrong man, going off to a 'resort,' paying a little money for the baby to vanish. Better on the family's conscience than abortion. That was anything but rare, Maia."

The rain was letting up outside, coming down in random cupfuls on the sidewalk. A street person shuffled by in a green parka made of Hefty bags.

I took Maia's silence for disapproval.

"All right," I relented. "So it was a long shot. What made you want to check back with Faye?"

"Listen, Tres. I've had a lead for a couple of days now, but I wasn't sure what to do with it. I was afraid you'd say I was crazy, grasping at anything. I know Lopez would accuse me of that. After going to Faye's, I decided to do a little paper-digging. I spent the last hour at the Travis County Courthouse."

"Jimmy's search," I said. "The birth certificates."

"As near as I can tell, that's a big blank. No birth certificates with Clara Doebler as the mother for the years in question. At least, nothing on file. Nothing legal."

"But?"

"Dwight's story," she said. "About Peña's parents."

"The car accident."

"I made some calls. It wasn't easy, but I found out the parents lived in Burnet County. I talked to a deputy out there who knew them, remembered the accident. According to this guy, there was nothing suspicious. The parents were coming back from a Christmas party late at night. The road was icy. They'd been drinking. They swerved off a sharp turn in a hill. End of story. The police did a thorough check on the car, and no tampering was found. The deputy said the Heismans were good people, said he never thought much of the son, but Matthew had been away at college at the time. Nobody seriously suspected him of any complicity."

"The *Heismans*?"

"That was their name. The search I did a couple of days ago, Tres, when I was trying to dig up dirt on Peña's past . . . I hit a brick wall—no records at all before he was eighteen. My deputy friend says Matthew took back his birth name, even changed his Social Security number the day he turned eighteen—a kind of 'screw you' present to the Heismans. It'll be a hard job to confirm that his birth name really was Peña."

I stared at the lines of Middle English in my book. "Peña is about as old as me."

"It may mean nothing," Maia cautioned.

"Sure."

"Might be worth talking to Dwight Hayes, see if he knows any more."

"Sure."

"But given Matthew Peña's age, we know one thing."

"Sometime after 1967," I supplied, "Matthew Peña was adopted."

CHAPTER 32

Mrs. Hayes was exactly where I'd left her, on her couch under the portrait of Jesus.

Her dress was pistachio green today, and she had no child to fan her. Otherwise she looked no different than she had Sunday night.

"Dwight went out for a moment, Mr. Navarre," she said. "But please sit down."

Grimy sunlight streaked through the windows. Jesus gazed toward the dead moths in the light cover on the ceiling. I could hear the two older kids, Chris and Amanda, playing full-tackle freeze-tag in the front yard.

"Only two little lambs today?" I asked.

Mrs. Hayes' makeup suggested a scowl, but there was no life to it—just paint.

"Matthew called me yesterday," she said. "He told me Dwight lost his job because of you."

I tried to remind myself she was just a frustrated mother looking out for her son. She didn't know all the things I had to deal with. And Jesus was looking at me, too. Despite that, I had the overwhelming urge to crack her rosy image of Matthew Peña over her head like a *cascarón*.

"Don't worry," I told her. "Losing that job might be the best thing for Dwight. Cutting the apron strings."

It took her a moment, but the metaphor sunk in. She

didn't seem to like it. "I don't appreciate your tone, young man. If you were one of my children . . ."

She looked out the window at a flash of metal. A gray Honda was turning into the driveway.

"But never mind," she said. "Matthew Peña was good to my boy."

"You ever deal with foster children, Mrs. Hayes?"

Her eyes traced an imaginary box around me. "Occasionally I help a child from Gardener-Bettes."

"Gardener-Bettes, the juvenile home."

"Yes. Why do you ask?"

"Just a case I was working on. A child I think was adopted. I think it might have been locally."

"How long ago?"

"Oh, years. Thirty-plus years."

There was an archipelago of tiny brown moles on her rounded shoulders. I imagined a laser burning them off, one by one, as I waited for her reply.

"I couldn't help you," she told me. "The life expectancy for adoption agencies is not good. The one you're looking for probably would not be around anymore."

"Probably not," I agreed. "A shame. This particular placement didn't work out too well. The adoptee in question turned into quite the little cold-blooded killer, Mrs. Hayes. Someone I'm sure you wouldn't admire. No one you'd want your son to work with."

Her eyes became small, amber points.

Dwight came up the sidewalk, his backpack on his shoulder. He stopped to chew out Chris and Amanda, who were throwing rocks at each other, then came inside.

He looked from me to his mother, read the tension immediately. "Goddamnit, Mother. Leave him alone."

He tossed a plastic drugstore bag onto the table.

Mrs. Hayes raised her eyebrows. "You will *not* speak in that way, Dwight. Not while you're in this house."

"I'll arrange for a hotel tonight, then. I'll give you a check for the month's utilities." He glared at me. "Come on, Tres. Don't sit with her. You'll never get up again."

He wheeled around and headed for the stairs.

I smiled apologetically at Mrs. Hayes. "Nice seeing you again, ma'am."

I could feel her eyes on my back as I left, like ice cubes pressing into my shirt.

Halfway up the stairs, one of the smaller children was blocking my path. It was Clem, Mrs. Hayes' fan-wielder, watching me with feral brown eyes under a mess of brown hair. He had a shoebox pinched between his knees.

"She doesn't like you," he confided.

I looked in his box. Brown and green things moved, glistening in the bottom—things about the size of almonds. My skin crawled.

Not that I hadn't seen cicadas before, but Clem had tried a new experiment. He'd put them back into their former skins—liberally Scotch-taping their desiccated shells to their bodies. He'd left some of the legs free, so the suffocating cicadas could crawl in helpless paths, going nowhere, waiting to die.

"It's a race," he confided.

I hugged the wall as I stepped around him.

Dwight's bedroom was on the left. He sat in the dark on a trundle bed, his backpack between his knees, staring dejectedly at a dumped-over bucket of toy cars on the carpet.

A bookshelf dominated the south wall—comic books in protective plastic sleeves, science fiction paperbacks, hot rod magazines, computer programming manuals, Clive Cussler novels. There was a window on the right, light filtering through the upper branches of a redbud in the backyard. Posters were thumbtacked to the wall: Nolan Ryan, Stevie Ray Vaughan, the Dallas Cowboys Cheerleaders. If the room had been any more Average Texan Boyhood it would've cracked the meter.

I started to reach for the light switch.

"Don't," Dwight said. "She doesn't like the lights on. Wastes energy."

I wondered how Dwight had gotten so tan growing up in a dark house. The answer immediately presented itself: Dwight would've left as soon and as often as possible.

"You okay?" I asked.

"The kids. It's like having a Little League team invited to trample over your childhood."

I went to the window, looked out at the yard. "At least they limit a Little League team to nine."

Dwight nodded sourly. He fished something out of his pack, threw it to me. "Good news. What I did this morning."

A handwritten label on the tape said TECHSAN. It looked no different from the eight-tracks Garrett used to keep in his car when I was a kid—certainly nothing worth dying for.

"What did you find?"

Dwight zipped his bag. "What Peña will announce today. There's a sequence in the code that shouldn't be there. He'll blame it on the original programmers."

"The back door."

Dwight lay back on his bed, stared at the ceiling. "It's a beautiful subroutine. Elegant, really. And until it's closed, nothing is safe—not a single file on a client's server, as long as they're running Techsan's product."

I looked out the window. The yard below was balding crabgrass, lined by a wooden fence with missing planks. A barbecue pit squatted between a toolshed and scraggly hibiscus bushes.

"You said you had good news."

"It depends on whether you find Garrett," Dwight replied. "Whether he'll help. I heard—I heard about Ms. McBride. I'm sorry."

"How can Garrett help?"

"I think it would be possible to track where the stolen files were diverted to. I'm not sure. This isn't my area of expertise. But if Garrett got into the source code, if he retraced the steps of the original sender, identified the packet sniffer and the PGP key involved—he might be able to triangulate an IP address."

"In English?"

"Find the saboteur."

"Before, Garrett couldn't even find the problem in his own code."

Dwight's ears turned red. Apparently, the idea that he'd found something Garrett had missed embarrassed him.

In the backyard, one of the smaller boys—John, maybe—ducked under a loose board in the fence. He was carrying a VCR that was much too big for him. It was partially wrapped in a blue towel. He saw me watching from the window and froze. He slid the VCR behind the nearest hibiscus bush and walked toward the house, trying not to run.

The scene made me feel sad down to my bones. I'd seen my share of disturbed children in eight years of PI work, but never so many in one place. The hell of it was, I wasn't going to talk to the kid about it. I wasn't even going to turn him in. I wondered how many days fanning the Leviathan you'd get for stealing a VCR.

"I talked to Maia this morning," I told Dwight. "She had some information about Peña."

I told him about Maia's conversation with her new pal, the deputy in Burnet County.

Dwight stared at his comic book collection, shook his head. "That doesn't mean anything."

"You knew he was adopted?"

"Of course I knew. What difference does it make?"

"The harassment of the software developers, the disappearance of Adrienne Selak—I think that's just a small sample of what Matthew's capable of. His main agenda with Techsan isn't about money. It's personal—retribution."

Dwight opened the trundle bed cabinet at his feet, yanked out an empty duffel bag. "I told you—there's no reason the deal would be personal. He never met the Techsan principals before."

"Matthew's age," I said. "Born around '67. Clara Doebler, Jimmy's mother—she supposedly had an abortion around then, but just before Jimmy died he was searching birth certificates, asking questions—looking for that lost child. He was told that the child had been born—and I think Peña was the one who told him."

"And you think . . ." Dwight's throat seemed to be closing up. He shoved underwear into his bag. "That's nuts."

"Clara had already lost custody of one child," I said. "She couldn't bear to lose another one—not completely. She never had the abortion. She gave the child up instead. You said it yourself: Peña is treating this takeover differently. He's making it the centerpiece of his career. What better way to get revenge on your birth family than building on their ashes?"

"I've known Matthew almost fifteen years. He's never given any indication. He would never—"

His voice faltered.

"The night Adrienne drowned," I said. "You weren't with Peña, were you?"

Dwight yanked a Hawaiian shirt from the drawer— the blue one with the yellow lotus designs.

"All right," he admitted. "I lied. I lied to protect a guy who's helped me ever since college. When I walked aft that night, I ran into Matthew. I didn't see Adrienne go over. I just saw Matthew, frantic—coming my way, looking for help. We roused the whole damn ship together, didn't have time to talk about exactly what had happened. Later, when people started questioning us, I saw a kind of fear sink into Matthew's eyes, like he was suddenly realizing what they'd accuse him of. He said that I'd been with him when Adrienne fell. He told what had happened, only as if I'd arrived a few moments earlier. I had to make a split-second decision. I went along with it. I didn't know what else to do. But he didn't kill her, Tres."

I'd spent years listening to people's stories, learning to separate out the lies. There wasn't anything suspicious in Dwight's voice. The night of Adrienne's drowning, some cop had merely committed the cardinal sin of interrogation— not isolating the witnesses prior to questioning. Somebody had done that, given Peña the chance to shape Dwight's testimony before he made it.

"You're chasing ghosts," he told me. "If you want me to, I'll go to the police, change what I said about that night on the boat. I'll help in any way I can. But if you go to them, say this is about some long-lost child—"

"They'll think what the police have thought all along. That the obvious answer is the right answer. And all along, they've been wrong."

He threw his duffel bag on the bed. He went to the bookshelf, pulled out a drawer, and began tossing papers and pictures. There were photos from Dwight's childhood, report cards, Christmas cards, college transcripts.

"You want to save your brother," he said.

"Of course."

"But you don't want the truth."

My face turned hot. "What are you *not* telling me, Dwight? What's got you so upset?"

He shoved the drawer closed, stared at the documentation of his childhood on the shabby carpet. He kicked an old report card. "I was trying to get up the nerve, Tres. Now, I'm not sure it's a good idea."

"*What?*"

"You said Garrett couldn't find the back door in the software. I don't think that was his problem at all. I'm wondering if you already knew that."

He stared at me, waiting for some kind of confession.

"I'm sorry, Dwight. I'm lost here."

He picked up a leather belt from the shelf. "The way the back door was written, the way it's embedded in the program. Not many people could do that, Tres. Not many programmers are that good, at Techsan or anywhere else."

Only then did I see where he was going.

The walls of the little dark bedroom seemed to be closing in. I wanted to open the window, turn on the lights.

Dwight curled his belt into a limp snake, shoved it into his bag. "Your brother wrote that damn back door, Tres. I'm positive."

CHAPTER 33

This time, I didn't fail to inform Maia.

On our way to the marina, I told her and Detective Lopez what Dwight had said about the back door in the software—how Garrett might've been responsible. My only consolation was that Maia and Lopez didn't know what to do with the information any more than I did. Lopez said he'd call the High Tech Unit, bat the problem over to them.

When we got to Point Lone Star, Clyde Simms was waiting at the gate, and he did not look delighted to see us.

He removed the giant chain with the CLOSED sign, then followed us down to the water on his motorcycle. He unlocked the security gate at the pier, walked us down to where the *Ruby, Too* was docked.

"What's the matter?" he growled at Lopez. "Six hours' questioning, and you didn't get enough out of me?"

"Thanks, Mr. Simms," Lopez said courteously. "You can wait here."

Clyde glared at me, like he wanted to have a very long conversation over beer and brass knuckles, but he said nothing.

On board Ruby's yacht, aluminum fingerprint powder covered the hatches and railings like pixie dust. Some evidence tech had left a surgical glove and a Ziploc bag on the pilot's deck. I could see Maia Lee taking mental notes, her defense lawyer's mind assessing the trial potential—

sloppy handling of evidence, amateur crime scene processing.

We went below. The Dell workstations were gone. There was nothing but dustless squares on the tables.

"Machines were impounded by High Tech," Lopez told us. "Early reports—they'd been wiped clean. Nothing to trace without a deep recovery method—very expensive, very time-consuming. Kind of like my machine."

Maia had been lifting pages on Ruby's wall calendar. She stopped on November, turned her attention to Lopez. "*Your* machine?"

"Yeah, counselor." Lopez mimed a strike on a keyboard. "I got mail. Message came in when I got back to the office this morning. I read it, hit the print command, froze my system to hell. You should've seen the look on our tech guy's face when he rebooted and got a screenful of static."

"The killer," I said, understanding. "The killer e-mailed you."

Lopez looked like he was trying to swallow a foul taste out of his mouth. "Anything's possible, Navarre, once you get some local press. The Techsan buyout, Jimmy Doebler's murder—both have been in the news the last few days. We got our share of hackers in Austin. Could be some seventeen-year-old looking for something to do on his summer vacation. But this e-mailer—he claimed he shot Jimmy Doebler. He knew the caliber of the weapon. He also said something interesting—said it was a hide-and-seek game now. He thanked me for closing my eyes and counting to ten while he slipped off."

The boat rose and fell gently under my feet.

"Someone's toying with you," I said. "It isn't Garrett."

"Of course not, Navarre. It's never Garrett. I got an APB out for the killer and that's the first line of the description—*It's not Garrett*. Now if you don't mind, maybe you could tell me what you expected to find here?"

Maia brushed past him, went into the sleeping cabin. We followed.

Nothing had changed in the bedroom as far as I could

see. Maia studied the photos, the Lake Travis wall map with its green and red pushpins. The nightstand drawer was open. There was no gun inside.

"Scuba equipment?" Maia asked.

Lopez shook his head. "We don't know what was normally aboard, and Mr. Simms wasn't much help. He said Ruby often stored a dive tank or two on board. There weren't any when we got here. That doesn't necessarily mean anything."

Out the small porthole window, the lake was hazy. A momentary slice of sun made its way through the rain clouds. Smoke rose from a barbecue at the public park. A hawk circled the woods.

Lopez's cell phone rang. He answered, listened for a long time.

Maia came over to me.

"The e-mail," she said. "Peña."

"If it's wiped off the hard drive, there's no proof."

"In the spring, I got several messages like that, Tres. I'm sure."

Lopez was looking at the ceiling. He said into the phone, "Yeah. You're probably right about that."

More listening, then his face paled. He looked at me, offered me the cell phone. "For you. Just thought I'd screen it for you first."

I took the call.

"Navarre?" a man's voice said. "Ben Quarles. Firearms."

"Quarles." I forced myself to sound upbeat. "Miss me already?"

His next exhale was a strong wheeze, maybe what passed for riotous laughter down in the ballistics lab.

"I wanted to follow up," Quarles said. "I got the full picture after you left—well, shit. Listen, that was a tough break about your brother."

"Not your fault."

"Yeah, well. I did a little digging—ran a Drugfire search on the casing. We keep a database of casing images from all over the state, goes back two, three years. It's hit or miss, depending on what individual departments choose to enter into the system, but I ran a check for similar firing pin impressions on spent brass, just to see if I got any hits."

"And?"

"And I got one. Maybe. Scored a cold hit on a case from Waco, robbery-murder back in 1987. It's an old damn case. Waco PD just put all their unsolved homicides on the network last month. Sheer luck—"

"The case," I interrupted.

"Robbery gone bad. Perp broke in the back door, surprised the occupant, shot this old guy four times. The victim's stuff was rifled through—boxes of papers, a file cabinet overturned, all his IDs and money taken. Perp wasn't too bright. Dragged the body all the way into the bathroom, dumped it in the tub, ran water over it. Who knows, maybe he was shaken up, got some stupid idea he could scrub the scene clean, then realized it was no good. Despite that, he got away—no leads, no prints. The murder weapon was never found, but Waco PD did recover the four casings—all with distinctive BOB markings. Almost an exact match to the one from Jimmy Doebler's murder."

"You're saying Garrett's gun was involved in a crime in 1987?"

"No. That model wasn't even made back then. What I'm saying is that a gun was used in Waco in 1987 that left an almost identical BOB marking to the casing you found in the lake. And the Waco gun was never recovered."

"Hell of a coincidence."

"Don't use the C word with me, Navarre. Another thing I found out, chatting with people up in Waco—police weren't careful with their information. They publicized that they were working an anomaly in the shell casing, put a quote to that effect in the local paper. Either they were desperate for leads, or maybe they wanted to sound like they were making progress. Maybe they just didn't see the case as important enough for tight security. Whatever, it wasn't any secret."

"I still don't—"

"What I'm saying, Navarre—if I were that killer, and I heard the police talking about my gun that way, I could have some fun with that information. I could examine my own casings, then deface another gun's firing pin area. I'm saying *I* could do this, a master gunsmith, somebody who knew what they were doing. In a couple of minutes, I could make another gun have the same BOB markings as mine— as long as it was a similar caliber and make. Potentially, you could play hell with ballistics—modify somebody's gun, commit a crime with your gun, and then frame the other guy. The BOB markings would be so rare, your frame-up victim would seem like a dead ringer. I'm not saying it's likely, but it's sure as hell possible."

I looked at my friendly neighborhood homicide detective, who was stone-faced, tapping his fingers against his sidearm. "Quarles, you share this information yet?"

"Yeah. And look, Lopez will tell you it's a far-fetched idea. He's right. I'm just trying to give you something you could use. You get a good lawyer, maybe he could use this Waco case to cast some doubt on the evidence, point out that ballistics aren't exact. Shit."

"What?"

"I can't believe I'm giving you advice to help a defense lawyer. God forgive me."

"Waco. What was the victim's name?"

I could hear Quarles shuffling papers. "Lowry."

Out the window of the sleeping cabin, the white barbecue smoke was streaking the tops of the trees. My chest felt like it was turning into something just as insubstantial. "Ewin Lowry?"

"You know the case?"

I thought about the picture I'd seen in Faye Ingram's garden—the rakish gypsy gambler next to Clara Doebler, both of them smiling. I thought about the letter Clara had received from Waco in 1987, the letter she'd thought was from Ewin Lowry, promising retribution.

"Navarre?" Quarles asked.

"I've got to go, Quarles. Thanks."

I hung up, handed Lopez back his phone.

"Forget it, Navarre," Lopez said. "It's the longest of long shots."

I told Maia about the Waco case. Then I told Lopez who Ewin Lowry was, and about Matthew Peña's parentage.

It's hard to shake up a homicide detective, but Lopez's face completely deconstructed. For once, he was without a reply.

"The bathtub," said Maia. "Water. Adrienne Selak drowned. Jimmy's truck was half submerged. Clara was shot by the lake. This man—Lowry—intentionally dragged into a bathtub. The girlfriend, the brother, the mother, the father . . ."

"And Ruby," I said. "Disappeared off a boat."

Lopez snapped his phone shut, clipped it to his belt. "I like criminal psych profiles as much as anybody, counselor. But what you're suggesting . . ."

He stared at the photos on the nightstand—the smiling pictures of Ruby McBride.

"All right," he relented. "What are you saying—the water has meaning?"

"The killer submerges his victims," Maia said. "At least, he tries to. Water could mean cleansing. Absolution. My guess—he *cares* for the people he's killing."

"Cares for them," Lopez repeated.

"He's a sick individual. He wants to be close to these people. Maybe he even picks special places—Doebler's lakefront property, for instance. He killed Jimmy just where his mom died."

"Kills his victims and then washes them," Lopez said. "Tries to cover them in water. A purification ritual."

Maia nodded.

"Shit." Lopez scowled. "Now you got me doing it. Okay. So you've got a crazy theory. Now what?"

"The killer has contacted you," Maia said. "Made himself known to the investigator in charge. Usually, that means one thing. He's preparing for the endgame."

I studied the Lake Travis wall map—the white topographic lines etched into the blue.

"There," I said.

Maia and Lopez turned. I went to the map, counted up the arc of red pins, the submerged property line that Ruby had been mapping. I put my finger on the sixth pin—the one farthest out from the shore.

"A special place," I said. "A submersion. Call your recovery unit. Tell them to dive there."

"In the middle of nowhere," Lopez said. "*Upstream* from where we found the boat. You want me to call Search and Recovery and tell them that?"

"Tres," Maia said. "Why there—why that pin?"

"Because," I said, "when I broke into this boat, two nights ago, that pin wasn't there."

X-eGroups-Return: sentto-375227-171-958727973
returns@shell_list.com
Mailing-List: Murder@shell_list.com
Delivered-To: <mailing list>
List-Unsubscribe: mailto:Murder
    unsubscribe@shell_list.com
Date: 14 June 2000 09:19:32 -0000
From: host@shell_list
To: guest_subscription@shell_list
Subject: dinosaurs

I was in the backyard. This is my earliest memory.

My friend and I were playing. We'd taken an old card table and covered it with mud, stuck some plastic dinosaurs in it.

I don't remember what my friend looked like back then, which is funny, because he is such a presence for me now. Later images have superimposed themselves on that first memory—years of hating and wishing.

He must've been a cute little guy—talkative, funny, always the one who made up our games. I remember he ran to get something I'd thrown in the

---

bush—another plastic dinosaur, maybe—and I heard car sounds in the alley.

Then there was a woman at the back gate, and she asked me to come with her, quickly.

I wasn't really startled. I was too young to understand that strange women weren't supposed to sneak into your backyard. Her face was tight with emotions I didn't even know the words for.

She asked me again, more desperately, to come with her. This was all happening in a few seconds.

And now, God knows, I wish I'd taken her hand.

But then she looked over my shoulder—at my friend, coming out of the bushes, grinning with a blue triceratops in his hand—and she realized her mistake. She told my friend, "Come on. Come with me." She said a whole bunch of other soothing things. Her voice was so kind, so loving, that it hurt. I wanted to go.

Her back was to me. My friend gave me one confused grin. And then they were gone together, through the gate, and the car sounds disappeared down the alley.

I don't remember the rest of the afternoon. I think I went back to playing. I must have caught hell when I was finally called for dinner, when I was found alone. I must have been punished.

But here's the strange thing.

I remember the seats of the woman's car, her lavender smell, the kindness in her voice. I can close my eyes and see trees going by, neighborhoods of tidy houses and blooming honeysuckle fences. I can see the house she took me to, a big swing in an old oak tree, lemonade on the porch. I can close my eyes and be in that place again, a long way from the mud table and the chewed plastic dinosaurs.

There are times I can't remember which child I was.

CHAPTER 34

Lopez cut the engine, let the boat drift into the swell.

Two in the afternoon, and another thunderstorm was threatening. The temperature had risen into the steamy high nineties. Boat traffic was almost nonexistent. There was nobody to admire our forty-six-foot party pontoon, which was probably just as well.

Lopez had impressed Clyde Simms into service, and Clyde had reluctantly agreed to furnish dive gear and a boat. But in passive-aggressive revenge, Clyde had given us top-of-the-line in big, slow, and clunky, insisting that the *Flagship of Fun* was the only thing in working order. The two-level pontoon normally rented for $120 an hour, he assured us. Ninety horsepower engine, bench-sofa seating for fifty people. We had a barbecue grill, a rest room, a ten-disc CD changer, a 150-quart cooler, and a water slide that went from the top deck into the lake. I'd pushed for a mirror disco ball, but Maia Lee told me to shut up.

Lopez came out from behind the wheel.

He wore only a swimsuit. With his dark, muscular build, he looked like a Polynesian fire dancer. All he needed were some tiki torches, and I was pretty sure we could find those somewhere aboard the *Flagship of Fun*.

He picked up a net bag stuffed with yellow polypropylene line, dug out one end and looped it through the eyehook of a small anchor that looked like a lopsided dumbbell. Despite the scanty clothes, Lopez somehow looked more serious and professional doing this task than he ever had in coat and tie.

Clyde stood at the wet bar at the stern. He wore a five-millimeter suit peeled to the waist, and was loading a revolver. Lopez had been none too happy about Clyde bringing the gun, but Clyde had started quoting the Second Amendment at him, calling him a fascist, and Lopez had given up.

As for Maia, she sat on the center couch, as far from the water as she could get. Given the options of not coming along at all, going into the water, or going out on the boat, she'd chosen the least of three evils.

So far she'd done a good job not getting sick, despite being surrounded by scuba gear.

Lopez crouched next to his regulator, checked his hand console—a top-of-the-line dive computer, complete with GPS locator.

He said, "We're here."

I looked across the water. We were only about fifty yards out from the marina.

Upstream I could see Jimmy's cove—his old boat dock, his dome. A quarter mile farther up, the limestone cliffs of Windy Point. Downstream was Defeat Hollow, where Ruby's boat had been moored. Then Mansfield Dam, a concrete curtain across the lake. Everything seemed so close together.

Clyde finished loading his revolver, clicked it shut.

I said, "You expecting aggressive catfish?"

"I expect you to fuck up, man. One way or the other." He looked at Lopez. "Let me go down with you."

"Thanks all the same, Mr. Simms. But if Navarre is right, I don't want you down there to see what we find. And I need an experienced person up top as safety diver."

"You don't trust me," he said.

Lopez busied himself with his gear, tested the polypropylene line.

Maia made one last pitch. "Let me call in the dive team."

"And tell them what, counselor? Lopez is running leads from *Magnum, P.I.,* now? Lopez thinks corpses float upstream?" He shook his head. "No thank you. I'll check it out first myself."

He turned to me. "You've done this before, you said."

"Diving, yes. Recovery, no."

"Tell me again—when and where and how deep?"

"Recreationally, as a kid. Salt water in the Caribbean. Once as an adult in Hawaii, down to sixty-five feet."

Lopez and Clyde exchanged looks.

"Oh good," Lopez said. "A blackwater expert. Lake Travis is the clearest lake in Texas, Navarre, which means your visibility here will be three to ten feet rather than zero. Unless you stir up the bottom, in which case you're blind."

"Stop the scare tactics," Maia snapped. "Tres can handle it."

Lopez turned, the muscles in his neck tensing. "That's good to know, counselor. 'Cause he and I, we're dive buddies now. If he freaks out down there and gets me killed, he's going to need a damn good defense attorney."

The boat bobbed. Lopez grabbed a Body Glove shortie, threw it to me, then another wet suit—a Farmer John style. "You'll need both," he said. "Layer them. We'll probably hit three thermocline layers on the way down. Even in June, the bottom is going to feel like an icebox."

"What's underneath us?" I asked.

Clyde and Lopez exchanged another look, but neither responded. Clyde started unlatching a med kit.

I said to Lopez, "You've been down there before, haven't you? This spot in particular."

Lopez picked up a mask. "There's about a hundred and ten feet of water under us, Navarre. We're floating on top of a pecan grove."

"The McBride farm."

Lopez spit in his mask, rubbed the glass. "It's an eerie place, Navarre. It's a fucking forest at the bottom of the lake. It's so deep, we'd bust the charts if we went down with the regular pressure gauges, the SPGs. We'll go on computer—more accurate nitrogen allowance. Even then, we've only got about ten minutes at the bottom. Probably less."

He put the mask down, took the dumbbell anchor to the side of the boat, and dropped it over with a sploosh. The line fed out.

"What we'll do," Lopez said, "is a modified circular search. You're going to be anchorman, Navarre. All you got to do, you follow the line down, float just above the bottom. Not on the bottom. Don't touch that. It's about three feet of silt and muck, and you put so much as a fin in it—poof. We'll be in a blackout."

The line went slack.

"Snag." Lopez tugged at it, moved down the boat a few feet, then kept lowering it. "There. That should be the bottom. Looks like a hundred five feet. We'll let the silt settle for a few minutes."

Lopez cut the top end of the rope, tied it to a yellow inflatable buoy the size of a bike tire. It had a diver-down flag fastened to the top. Lopez made the line taut and set the buoy over the side.

"I go down with you," he said. "I take a second line out from the anchor—a tender line. I do a quick sweep of the area, as much as the trees will let me. The signals are like this. One tug from you or me means stop. Two tugs, take up the slack. Three tugs from you means come here. From me, it means let out some slack. Four tugs, pull me in slowly. Five tugs, I'm in trouble and can't get back. You get five tugs, pass that signal along to the surface by pulling hard on the main line, and Clyde comes in. He'll be fifty percent ready to dive the whole time we're down. Counselor, you know enough to help Simms suit up?"

Maia nodded.

Lopez stared at me intently. "You got all that?"

"I think so."

"Give it back to me," he ordered. "All the signals."

I did.

"Now the basic dive signals," Lopez said. "Let's make sure we're using the same ones."

I ran through the ones I remembered. I needed a little prompting, but in the end, Lopez seemed satisfied.

"We wear a minimum of gear," he told me. "It's easy to get snagged down there. You get caught, don't panic. You might get in a zero-visibility situation. You might not even be able to see the rope. In that case, you find east on your computer compass. The console is illuminated—stick it against your mask if you need to. Then you swim east. You'll hit the shore that way no matter what, and you just follow it up. How fast do you ascend?"

"No more than thirty feet a minute," I said. "Safety stop twenty feet from the surface for at least fifteen minutes."

"All right," he said. "You know what nitrogen narcosis feels like?"

"One margarita for every thirty feet. Sort of like walking through the Texas Folklife Festival."

Lopez did not look amused. "You start feeling like you want to offer your regulator to the fish, the mud starts looking beautiful—you ascend to a higher level. Got it?"

"Got it."

He exhaled. "Now let's hope we don't need any of that. Suit up."

Lopez walked over to Clyde, who was getting the tanks ready.

I sat next to Maia, started pulling on the legs of the shortie suit. "You okay?"

"Just get down there and get back up," she said. "Quickly."

She wouldn't meet my eyes. Her hair was tied back loosely, wisps of it trailing down in front of her ears like brown silk thread. She wore white shorts, an oversized blue T-shirt, flip-flops. I could see the crescent scar on her calf that I'd traced with my finger many times, the single tiny mole on her forearm, the perfect diamond-shaped corners of her eyes that had always reminded me of comet tails.

Maia caught me looking, gently pushed my face away. "I think you've got somewhere to go."

"Come on, Navarre," Lopez growled. "Get to it."

Two layers of five-millimeter neoprene later, I understood why he was impatient. Standing on the boat deck in the June heat, I felt like I was being microwaved in Saran Wrap. I pulled on the hood, attached the regulator to the tank, slipped a knife in one leg-holster and lineman's pliers in the other. I pulled on orange Day-Glo gloves and wondered if they would blind the fish. Clyde hefted a steel tank for me while I got buckled into my BC.

Clyde said, "You watch it down there. You pay attention."

"Thanks."

Then he gave my straps a violent tug, made sure everything was too tight for comfort, and went back to his own equipment.

I double-checked my gauges, reset the computer.

Clyde laid out a first-aid box, an emergency oxygen tank, and mask. I wished he'd waited until we were over the side.

"Right." In his hooded suit, all black except for blue stripes, Lopez looked like a buff, high-tech sea lion. "Time to party."

"You want to use the water slide?" I asked.

"Shut up, Navarre."

Lopez checked my equipment. I checked his. There was an entry bench on the party boat, of course. Lopez looped his fin straps around his wrist. He sat on the bench, facing the deck, scooted his butt to the end, put one hand on his mask and the other on his weight belt, and did a backward somersault into the water.

Next it was my turn.

The splash imploded around me in a haze of cold, white foam. I was surprised at how fast I was sinking, then realized I hadn't inflated my BC. I groped for the button, kicked without the benefit of my fins, which still hung around my wrist. I had a moment of panic, then remembered that I could in fact breathe. I got under control, sent a burst of air into the vest, floated upward, and met Lopez on the surface.

He kept his regulator in his mouth, which spared me several scathing remarks, gave me the okay sign. I responded. We pulled on our fins.

Lopez went to the buoy, pulled the rope taut, retied it. We gave the okay signal to Clyde and Maia. I thought about the last time Maia had watched me descend, at Windy Point, going down to meet Matthew Peña.

Lopez gave me the thumbs-down sign. I reciprocated.

We held up our inflator hoses, released air, and began to sink.

We faced each other as we went down, following the yellow line. Almost fully covered in neoprene, my body felt unreal, only the area around my mouth feeling the full effect of the cold.

Bubbles trickled up my fingers. Lopez was a dark, multilimbed thing across from me, vaguely outlined in spears of light from the surface. Below, a chasm—black and green brush strokes of water, shifting.

Lopez unclipped the flashlight from his belt, tapped it. I got out mine. We switched them on and continued descending fins-first.

About every ten feet I had to pinch my nose to equalize the pressure in my ears. Soon, the light in the world was reduced to our two yellow flashlight beams—like a cockeyed car driving through green Jell-O. Occasionally the ghostly form of a catfish or Guadalupe river perch would flit into our light, then turn as if scorched and vanish.

We hit a thermocline at thirty feet. The temperature line was as sharp as a razor—cold above, frigid below. Just when I'd gotten used to it, when I thought I'd gotten as cold as I could get, we hit the second thermocline layer at seventy feet. And we kept descending, following the yellow rope that was no longer yellow at this depth, but pale gray. Even the blue stripes in Lopez's suit were starting to seep away. I decided the rope couldn't have been this long, raveled in its net bag on the surface.

Slowly, the darkness below us intensified. I swept across it with my flashlight. One moment, nothing but water. The next moment, there they were—black Ys and Xs of wood;

branches; twigs doing aimless somersaults. It was a huge, skeletal landscape of lines and cracks, as if a whole sphere of the water had been frozen, then shattered. I was looking from above at the bare branches of an enormous tree—a bird's-eye view. It was a goddamn pecan tree at the bottom of the lake.

I heard an omnipresent *plink, plink:* Lopez, getting my attention by knocking the butt of his knife against his air tank. I could barely see him, two feet away from me, until I shone the flashlight on him. He was waving one palm horizontally over the knife—the sign to level out.

I was descending too fast, getting too close to the tree. I kicked up, added a little air to the BC, and my fin brushed against a branch. An ancient, open pecan pod snapped away from the top of the tree and went spinning into the void, its petals like a black claw.

Another two seconds and I would've been ensnared in branches.

I flashed my light around and momentarily lost the rope, and Lopez. Then, just as suddenly, there he was. I could see the danger—how easy it would be to get disoriented, tangled, panicked.

We floated, suspended above the tree, shining our lights on each other. I felt colder than I'd ever felt. My whole body was tight, like I'd been shoehorned into a much smaller man's wet suit.

Lopez signed, *Okay?*

I should've made the *so-so* gesture, but I responded *Okay.*

Lopez tapped his computer. I checked mine. My air supply read 2,700 psi. Depth: ninety-eight feet. Lopez pointed to the rope, then down to the tree, then used more gestures to indicate that since the rope had gone straight through the branches, we'd have to navigate around the circumference of the tree and underneath. Was I okay with that? I made the *Okay* sign.

He tapped his watch, held up ten fingers. Ten minutes. The clock had started running.

We turned horizontal, angled ourselves down, then carefully descended around the periphery of the pecan tree.

It must've been a monstrous specimen when alive, and down here in the murk it seemed even bigger. We tried to keep a safe distance, but the tree kept surprising us. We kept getting brushed and snagged, clawed at, almost impaled on branches that were worn to silty pikes from the decades underwater.

Then, at last, we were below the lowest boughs, shining our lights on a trunk so large our hands might just have met had we tried to hug its diameter.

Lopez *plinked* to get my attention again, gestured with his flashlight. He was warning me not to get too close to the bottom. It wasn't really solid below me—just a fuzzy layer of silt, lumpy and pitch black, like the remains at the bottom of a barbecue pit. Our line from the surface went straight down into the stuff, the anchor completely submerged.

Lopez gestured for me to come over and stay by the rope. He produced a second line from his supply bag—the tender line. He made a loose shepherd's knot, and slipped it around my wrist. He checked his computer, apparently calculating our GPS, then pointed off in one direction, pointed to himself.

I nodded.

Lopez measured out two yards of line the way they do in fabric stores—running the line from his nose to extended thumb. He handed me the slack. Six feet seemed a ridiculously small distance to start with, given how little time we had, but then Lopez moved away, and within a few feet he was gone.

There was no logic to it, what you could see and what you couldn't. In one direction, through a clearer patch of water, I could almost make out the trunk of the next tree in the row, but I couldn't see Lopez six feet away. If I shone my flashlight directly on him, I could just barely make out a smudge of black.

He gave me two quick tugs on the rope. I fed him

another six feet of line, and then he was gone completely. I was alone.

I shone my light up through the branches of the ancient pecan. It must've been frozen in winter, fifty-plus years ago, but it looked like it might've been submerged yesterday. There were still hardened knobs of pecans clinging to a few branches, more delicate black claws of open pods—things you would not think could withstand the flooding of an entire valley. The texture of the bark was still discernible. I wondered if the McBrides had picnicked here once, looked up at the sun through the branches, been grateful for the shade back on a Texas summer day before they'd had air-conditioning, when Austin had still been a small town a day's wagon ride away.

I reminded myself, a little dreamily, that I'd come down here to do a job. I checked my console—one hundred two feet below. The timer read 12:04 minutes, total dive time. My breathing had almost slowed to normal. I was relaxed. I started smiling for no particular reason, staring up into the branches of the tree.

Then I was brought back to reality by one sharp tug on the tender line. It meant more than just stop. We hadn't discussed it, but I was afraid that kind of tug must mean, *I found something*.

I waited. The cold enveloped me.

I calculated that Lopez was fifteen feet away now, but I couldn't see anything except the faintest bleached spot in the dark, perhaps his flashlight.

He gave three tugs, the signal that I was to come to him.

Not quite sure what to do with the line, I tied my end to the lead line, then, slowly, kicked my way into the gloom, my hand cupped loosely around the tender as I followed it out. Ahead was a tall streak of darkness—the trunk of the next tree. There was a smaller shape, too, with a tiny shimmer above it—Lopez and his bubble stream.

I got close enough to see him. He was floating right in

front of the tree trunk as if examining it, his back to me. I kept my flashlight beam on him.

The beam of my light must've caught his attention, because he turned.

And that is when I realized I was going to die one hundred feet underwater.

Lopez's eyes were wide inside his mask, hardly human. One orange-gloved hand held his dive knife, the point level to my nose, the thin blade toward me, serrated edge out. Just beyond him, in front of the tree's trunk, was the thing.

It wore a wet suit, its limbs floating loosely in the current. A cord was wrapped around its legs, tying it to the same anchor that had sunk it into the muck. There was a severed regulator rope floating like a dead vein, and a metal dive knife impaled to the hilt just under the thing's sternum. The face had lost all definition, and the hair was a billowy, colorless mass until the beam of my flashlight touched it; then it flared orange-red. And the eyes turned to glass. The mouth opened, and I was sure those white hands reached out to me.

I screamed an explosion of bubbles, kicked, flailed away, and suddenly found that I wasn't moving. I couldn't see the dead face anymore, just endless crosses and hooks of black wood, and something was holding me fast from behind. I lost my mouthpiece, clamped my teeth, panicking, ready to inhale lake water, then somehow managed to find the regulator again and breathe.

My flashlight beam crossed with Lopez's. He emerged not three feet away, still holding the knife pointed toward me, a look in his eyes that I could not mistake.

I kicked, swiped at him with my fins, heard a crack that came from everywhere, and then I kicked again and found I was free. The world exploded in an ink cloud. My flashlight slipped out of my hand.

There was no sight, no sound except my own exhale bubbles and the steady suck of air into my lungs from the regulator, dry and steady.

I tried to breathe normally. I'd stirred up the bottom. What had Lopez said about that? *Swim east.* Could I trust him? I'd seen the shore. It was east.

I groped along the top of my tank until I found the pressure gauge that led to my computer console. I brought it in front of my face, pressed buttons on the side until I found the one that made the console illuminate.

Suddenly I wasn't alone. I had faint, green dials to keep me company. I turned until the compass said I was pointing east. Then I started kicking slowly in that direction, still completely blind.

I heard the *plink-plink-plink* of Lopez's knife on his tank. Was he in front of me? Or behind? The plinking sounded more urgent than it had before. I slid my own knife out of the sheath on my leg, but my hand was so cold even through the glove that I couldn't feel the handle, much less see it. I let it go in the darkness.

I kept kicking—three cycles of left-right. Twelve cycles. I checked the console and found I had about nineteen minutes of air left. I'd been underwater for only sixteen.

I began to see again—the gentle slope of the lake bottom under me. Rocks the size of sofas rose out of the silt, and moving among them, catfish as big as I was. The black was turning to green. I could see the lower spectrum of colors.

I checked my depth and found that I'd risen to sixty-two feet. I stopped, and had no idea where I was. I was supposed to do something—*Go up. Go up slowly.* I followed the rocky slope.

At thirty feet I stopped, sat on a furry, silted ledge that had probably once looked over the river valley. It now offered a view of a dark green void. I forced myself to time ten more minutes, which according to the computer left me fourteen minutes of air. I knew the math wasn't right, somehow. Then I remembered that I was using less compressed air as I ascended.

Another ten feet of gradual ascent and I could see the surface—a flashing sheet of silver and yellow. The fish were now clear. I loved every speckle on every trout, every whisker on every catfish. If I'd had a package of hot dogs, those fish would've eaten like kings.

I forced myself to wait ten more minutes to expend the extra nitrogen. I stared into the green, tried to remain calm, tried to sort out the reality from the fantasy. What had happened down there?

Finally, I kicked up and broke the surface in the late afternoon light. I almost sunk below the surface again, then inflated my BC. I ripped the mask off my face, spit out the regulator. The air burned from the summer heat. It was charged with the smell of approaching storm and cedars. I promised myself I would never complain about cedars again, no matter how bad the pollen fever season got.

The *Flagship of Fun* was floating not thirty yards away—so impossibly close it made me angry, given the odyssey I'd just completed.

There was no place I wanted to go less, just then, than the *Flagship of Fun*. But I could hear the voices clearly over the water—Clyde, Lopez, and most frantic of all, Maia.

I yelled, "Hey!" with more anger than I knew I had, letting out twenty-two minutes of terror in a single word.

Lopez and Maia rushed to my side of the boat.

Maia spotted me and her whole body seemed to sag under the weight of an extra G force. "Oh God. Oh thank God."

Lopez yelled, "You son of a bitch!"

He'd stripped off his gear except for his mask, which was still stuck to his forehead—the sign of a diver in distress. I don't think, at that moment, Lopez cared what signals he sent.

His face was livid, but the look in his eyes was not what it had been at one hundred feet. It was not wild. He yelled: "You could've killed us both!"

I bit back comment, kicked over to the ladder on the boat.

Clyde was there, too, talking on a cell phone, giving the Lower Colorado River Authority our position. His expression could've been carved out of slate.

Lopez helped me aboard, Maia taking my other arm. I let them help me get my gear off.

Then I turned to Lopez just as he was starting to cuss me out and I slammed a right uppercut into his jaw.

His teeth clacked shut and his head did a little snap. He staggered back, looking momentarily stunned. That was all. I must've been even weaker than I felt.

Lopez's face hardened, got very calm. Then he charged me. He knocked me to the deck, began throwing sloppy punches into my ribs and face, kicking, kneeing. Clyde was above Lopez, trying to pull him off, either because he wanted to break it up or because he wanted his own shot at one or both of us.

A gun roared.

Lopez rolled off me instantly, stood. Clyde backed away. I rose to my elbows, wiped a trail of blood off my upper lip, and looked up at Maia, who was holding Clyde's revolver, the barrel pointed out over the lake.

"That's it, gentlemen," she told us. "You are now above water. Above water, I am the queen almighty. And the queen says no fighting. Any questions?"

I shook my head.

Lopez rubbed his jaw, stepped carefully to the bar and grabbed a bottle of vodka.

"What the hell do you mean hitting me, Navarre? Me, who just tried to save your sorry-ass life."

"Fucking fascist cop," Clyde growled.

Maia said, "Drink something, Clyde. Gin?"

"I hate gin."

She tossed him the bottle anyway. He caught it, uncapped it and drank.

She didn't even ask what I wanted. She tossed me a fifth of Cuervo Gold.

We all drank, except for Maia. The gun was enough for her.

I glowered at Lopez. "You were saving me, huh?"

"Yeah. Not that it was worth it."

"That what you were doing with the knife, Vic? Saving me?"

Maia watched for signs of new trouble, but Lopez just shook his head in disgust.

He stormed over to where my gear lay and yanked a broken branch as thick as a golf club out of my BC strap.

"Actually yes, Navarre. You stupid son of a bitch. I was trying to cut you free. And three tugs—that's *your* signal to call me in, not the other way around. You *never* leave the main line. *Never.* I was asking you for more slack so I could cut the corpse free, put a loop around it. Now Search and Recovery's going to have to do it, and you and I just royally fucked up an underwater crime scene."

Maia watched both of us, unsure what to do. Clyde looked like his only uncertainty was deciding which of us to kill first.

I said, "Lopez, I'm—"

I couldn't make myself say it.

Clyde spat a mouthful of gin over the side. "Somebody's going to pay, Lopez. Somebody's going to pay for Ruby, and his name ain't going to be Navarre."

"Shut up," Maia decided. "Let's just shut up."

And we did.

We paced around the deck in hostile silence, Maia holding the gun, the rest of us drinking liquor from the *Flagship of Fun*'s premium-stocked bar while the sirens of the LCRA and Sheriff's Department boats got closer and closer over the water.

CHAPTER 35

The *Flagship of Fun* was tame compared to the party the media was throwing.

We made shore at Windy Point around four o'clock, hoping to evade the bulk of spectators and reporters. No such luck. The Point's foot-traffic-only road was lined with news vans from Austin, Waco, San Antonio—all the network affiliates and several cable stations.

The usual contingent of scuba-campers looked bewildered by the invasion. Cameramen clambered around, knocking over air tanks and pup tents, setting up portable generators and satellite dishes and tripod lights. Reporters fussed with their makeup, lamented their wind-destroyed hairdos, and force-fed microphones to anyone and everyone coming up the ladder from the water.

Maia and I got through the gauntlet only because Vic Lopez was right behind us.

"Detective!"

And the feeding frenzy began. The reporters' questions told me that every important fact had already leaked out. A woman's body had been recovered from one hundred feet of water. She had been stabbed, weighted down. Had she been dumped overboard? Had the body been positively identified as Ruby McBride, ex-wife of the recently murdered Jimmy Doebler? Was it true her former business partner Garrett Navarre, already a suspect in Doebler's murder, was still at large?

As Maia and I were leaving, the PR director for the Sheriff's Department was trying to organize the chaos into a formal news conference. He got a lieutenant and a couple of sergeants to line up on one side of him, Lopez on the other side.

From the expressions of the brass, I got the feeling Lopez would've gotten chewed into catfish bait had the press not been present. But the press was present, so Lopez was the star of the moment.

I gave Maia the keys to my truck. The rain started to fall.

While Maia drove, we listened to the news conference live on an AM station. The police refused to release the identity of the victim. They refused to speculate on suspects, though they promised they were "actively pursuing leads." I tried to focus on the hills, the trees, the arc of rain outside the sweep of the windshield wipers—anything but what had happened at the bottom of the lake.

The anger had left me. Nitrogen was venting from my system, sapping every bit of energy my body had left. I drifted in and out of sleep.

When Maia and I got back to Jimmy's dome, my need for a scuba nap overrode all other concerns. I crawled up the ladder to the sleeping loft and passed out.

I'm not sure how long I was unconscious. When I opened my eyes the daylight was gone. Rain pounded steadily on the roof of the dome.

Maia's voice said, "I was about to put a spoon under your nose, check if you were still breathing."

I looked toward my feet. She was sitting on the corner of the bed, Robert Johnson pacing back and forth on her knees, purring smugly.

I grabbed an extra pillow, stuffed it behind my head. "News?"

"Not much. Lopez called, said he was taking a lot of heat. Said he should have the ME's report by morning."

"Garrett?"

"I'm sorry. Nothing."

I studied the Beatles poster on the ceiling. The Fab Four looked mad at me.

"It isn't your fault," Maia said. "If nothing else, it got Lopez on your side."

"Yeah, the minute I punched him."

"He knows Garrett couldn't do . . . what you saw down there. There's no way. Lopez got a revised statement from Dwight about Adrienne Selak's drowning. He's talking to SFPD. Momentum is starting to shift."

The rain kept drumming on the roof. The only one comfortable in the loft seemed to be Robert Johnson, now snugly nestled in Maia's lap, getting his ears scratched.

"Ruby wanted to fix things," I said. "She met with Peña, tried to reverse her deal with him. But she wasn't any use to him anymore. So he killed her. Just like Adrienne."

Maia picked at a fold in the bedspread. "We don't even know it's her yet, Tres. The condition of the body—"

"Yes, we do."

"We'll bring Peña down."

"You were right. It would have been better if I'd stayed out of this, let you handle it."

"No," she said. "That was my bitterness talking."

She slid Robert Johnson out of her lap, scooted onto the bed, lay down next to me. She put her arm across my chest, her chin resting on my shoulder.

We lay like that, the fan at the top of the dome pinwheeling shadows across the ceiling, for a long time. I thought about dark green water through the branches of frozen pecan trees.

She kissed my neck. "Stop, okay?"

"Stop what?"

"Thinking."

She slid the sheet down, away from my chest.

"You're running up a bill at the Driskill," I said. "For a room you aren't using."

"Mm-hmm."

She put a finger on my chest, ran it up to my collarbone, traced the starburst of pink scar tissue just below my right clavicle. "What's that?"

"Gunshot."

"I can see that." Three fingers now, tracing the skin. "But it's new. How?"

"An old friend. He gave it to me last spring."

She exhaled a laugh against my shoulder. "Figures."

I kissed her and she didn't object. Then another kiss—longer, more earnest.

I looked in her eyes—amber, bright, defying me to stop.

"I'm pretty sure this is a reaction to trauma, here," I warned her.

"So react," she said.

She shifted her weight onto me.

I crossed my arms around her neck, pulled her face down to mine.

Robert Johnson murred, protesting an obvious error in the direction of our affections. I nudged him with my foot, as gently as I could, to the edge of the bed, and then *thump*.

After that I didn't care much what the cat did all night. And he extended us the same courtesy.

CHAPTER 36

I awoke in full daylight. The house was silent. The two notes I found pinned to my covers made me feel like a piece of transfer luggage.

The first note said, *Gone to chase Garrett. No regrets. Call you later.*—M.

The second note said, *P.S. Aren't you late for class?*

I looked at my watch, then practiced my Middle English expletives as I disentangled myself from the sheets, got dressed, and ran to my truck to make the forty-five-minute drive to UT in half an hour.

I walked in so late Father Time had already done one warm-up story and was now starting the second. I thanked him, apologized to the class, then ad-libbed a lecture on the Wakefield *Crucifixion*. We skimmed through the Croxton *Play of the Sacrament*—just enough to introduce the Jewish communion-wafer-trampling villains who would prefigure Barabbas in Marlowe's *The Jew of Malta*. We spent the rest of our time talking about anti-Semitism. Your basic uplifting English lit session.

By the time we adjourned, West Mall foot traffic was starting to pick up outside. The air smelled of clove cigarettes and the eggroll vending carts on Guadalupe. The cute Asian girl with the Henry James novel had staked out a bench in the shade by the entrance to the Student Union.

Down at the crosswalk, Vic Lopez was talking to a street musician.

Lopez was dressed in fatigue pants, combat boots, tight blue shirt. His face was pasty and grim, his sunglasses reflecting the sidewalk.

The musician wore a poncho instead of a shirt, pants the color of bread mold. He had one Birkenstock planted on a small amp, a harmonica holder and a Gibson acoustic strapped around his neck. Written in black across the face of the guitar was *Australia or Bust*.

As I walked up, the musician was telling Lopez, "Yeah. It's really nice down there this time of year."

"Barrier Reef?" Lopez asked.

"Dude!" To emphasize his excitement, the musician sucked a few notes out of his harmonica. "I'm telling you, this friend of mine—his first night-dive and shit, they told him to watch for green eyes. And he gets down there and this Great White glides past him not five feet away. Oh, man. A little more spare change, and I'm there!"

I thought of green eyes underwater, tried not to shudder.

Lopez patted the musician on the shoulder. Dust poofed from the poncho. "You take it easy. Professor Navarre and I—we got to talk, now."

The musician wagged all his fingers at me. "Yeah, you're that new dude. Yeah. My friend said your class is fucking awesome."

"Fucking Awesome 301," I said. "That's me."

"Teach it again next summer so I can audit, okay?"

"You promise you will?"

"Hey, man, right after Australia, I'm there."

Lopez grabbed my shoulder. "Let's talk."

We followed a herd of pigeons toward a table under a live oak.

"Nice fatigues," I told Lopez. "Expecting a war?"

He leaned back in his chair, picked his sunglasses off, hung them from the collar of his T-shirt. "In one already. I've been put on paid leave."

"For finding Ruby?"

Seeing Lopez without his usual smile, I realized how big he was. I felt like I was back in high school varsity, looking across the scrimmage line at a full-tackle behe-moth patiently waiting for the signal to pulverize me.

"We don't have a positive ID, Navarre. I want you to hear that. The brass—they're willing to assume it's Ruby McBride, but things were done . . . I don't know how much you noticed underwater, but things were intention-ally done to the body to make the ID hard. It'll be days be-fore we get enough medical records together, call in the forensic anthropologists to be sure."

"You can't have any doubt," I said. "You saw the way she was. Right at the base of that tree. She was . . . placed. Displayed. And you know Garrett didn't do that."

"Which is why I'm on leave," Lopez said. "I told my bosses we were chasing the wrong guy."

"You told the truth."

Lopez laughed without humor. "Good old truth. Ain't what the brass wants, especially when they've got a fugitive suspect with no alibis, solid ballistics work to place him at at least one homicide. Good motives for both homicides. A friend that works the docks for McBride, could give him access. The DA likes all that just fine. His point of view—it doesn't take much to dump a woman's body overboard. Even a guy in a wheelchair could do it. Especially with the drugs in her system. It would look very bad on the Channel 4 news if the department backed down, reconsidered press-ing charges."

"Drugs."

Lopez brought out a sheaf of papers.

"I wasn't even supposed to get these. A guy I know in Toxicology, he ran me a copy." He flipped a few pages, handed me one. "Check the spike graphs."

I couldn't tell much about the chemical names, the ab-breviations, the numbers, but one thing was clear. "They're the same."

Lopez nodded. "The one on the left shows the levels of the alcohol and tricyclic antidepressants in Jimmy Doebler's blood. The one on the right shows the levels in the female victim. They match. Now check the next page."

Another match. The date on this one was much older—
May 1995.

"Clara?"

"I had my friend pull that out of the archived records.
That's her tox report."

"Three people," I said. "Virtually identical graphs."

Lopez nodded. "Taken separately, they can be explained. Jimmy and Clara both were on medication. If victim three is Ruby, she was on the same stuff. But taken
together—we've got a poisoner. He's doing an extraction
process with the amitriptyline, dissolving it down to lethal
concentration, mixing it with alcohol for quick dissemi-
nation. These three people were poisoned with the same
recipe. Ninety-nine to one—by the same person."

I looked across the plaza. The musician was playing
Pete Seeger. Even the pigeons made a wide arc around him.

"Jimmy's past," I said. "Clara's missing child."

Lopez stared at the pigeons. "I don't know, Navarre.
I still don't like it. But let's say the killer uses drugs to make
the victims pliable. They get sleepy, almost comatose—
they follow simple instructions. He can manipulate them.
My bosses would tell you this explains a lot about how
your brother could do this. Me, I'd agree with your friend,
Miss Lee. I think this bastard wants to talk with his victims. He wants to get intimate before he kills them. I think
the old guy in Waco, Ewin Lowry, I think that was our
boy's first attempt. It left a bad taste in his mouth, didn't
satisfy his urges. So he refined his strategy."

"He started drugging them."

The musician kept playing his harmonica music.

"W.B. Doebler," I said. "Has anyone interviewed him
since Jimmy's death?"

"No need," Lopez said. "W.B. calls the sheriff every
other day for updates. I don't know what gets said. I know
Sheriff's an honorable person."

He didn't need to say more. We both knew the
reality—a rich family, heavy political connections. Getting
the Sheriff's Department to expand a criminal investigation to include W.B. Doebler would take incontrovertible

proof and signatures in triplicate from God, Jesus Christ, and the Holy Ghost.

"Something else, though," Lopez said. "Peña's girlfriend, the night she drowned. We know now that his alibi is for shit. One thing the witness statements all agreed on: Adrienne Selak had had too much to drink. She kept slurring her words, losing her balance. Peña himself stated that he had to support her several times to keep her from falling over. She got very drunk very fast."

"As if Adrienne Selak had been given an amitriptyline cocktail."

Lopez nodded.

"But it's all still speculation," I said. "Garrett's been missing over twenty-four hours. I have to find him before your colleagues do. If he could trace the Techsan sabotage to Peña—it's a long shot, but it might be some leverage."

Lopez picked at the knee of his camouflage pants. "Which brings me to my last point. I put out feelers on Garrett's whereabouts early yesterday. This morning a CI of mine, local biker—he gave me a tip where your brother might be. Of course, he didn't know I'd been pulled off the case. Ethically, I should hand the information over to my superiors."

"Ethically."

Lopez's eyes glittered like a crocodile's. "My CI tells me your brother's hiding out with the Diablos. They got a whole network of safe houses. As of this morning, they moved him into a place where they figured nobody will look for him—the marina."

"You must have that place under surveillance."

"Boats go in. Boats go out. You know the guy who runs the docks, it would be pretty easy to come and go unseen. We can't search every boat, not without cause. I should tell my sergeant what I know, let him make the call."

I thought about what Travis County would do, how they would proceed against a suspected murderer hiding out with a motorcycle gang. They would activate SWAT. They would go in hard and fast. They would be quick to shoot and they'd cry no tears if there was any resistance.

"I'll go to the marina with you," I told Lopez. "But you forgot one thing."

The cords of his neck muscles stood out like bridge cables. "Yeah?"

"Clara Doebler supposedly killed herself," I said. "Unless you saw something that night you didn't put in the report."

Something in Lopez's demeanor changed, like a tide reversing, drawing back in.

"Heard," Lopez murmured. "I heard something. And yes, Navarre, I reported it. Every day for five years, I've tried to convince myself that my superiors were right—that I was imagining things. I went along with what the brass told me. I went along with my shrink, telling me it was just frayed nerves. But when I walked up to Clara Doebler that night, while she was writing her suicide note, I could hear her talking—whimpering, almost. There was nobody with her. If there had been, for me not to see them, they would've had to have been in the trees—ten, fifteen feet away, standing in total darkness. But just for a second, as I was coming up, I could swear I heard a second voice. A man's voice. Real gentle."

The tide was still pulling in Lopez's direction, washing out the patio stones under my feet.

"What did the voice say?" I managed.

Lopez shifted, pulled the sunglasses off his shirt collar.

"It wasn't a conversation, Navarre. More like the voice was instructing Clara Doebler, telling her what to write."

Date: Thurs 15 Jun 2000 03:17:54 -0500
From: RubyToo@ixnet.net
Reply-To: none
X-Mailer: Mozilla 4.7 (Macintosh; I; PPC)
X-Accept-Language: en
To: VLopez@travis.co.tx.state
Subject: search patterns

What was the hardest part, Detective?

Talking to the family? Those pinched faces. The old grandmother crying, cupping her hands over a grimace. They are chattering at you in Chinese, and the ones who can translate, the adolescents, are telling you with embarrassment that the family believes in evil spirits, that something down there took a liking to their child.

The victim's family always wants so much from you. You arrive on the scene and they have knives and forks ready to dig in—taking whatever they can from you. They want reassurance. They want answers. They want you to bring their little boy back to life.

And so you dive, day after day—such a small area on the surface, one little cove in one public park. You could throw a football across it and hit the opposite bank. But you dive the entire area and find nothing. You comfort yourself with formulas, buoyancy charts, DPS manuals that tell you where the body should be, what it should look like, how the currents might have moved it. But you find nothing.

Every evening you come up from your third, maybe fourth dive that day, and the family is still there, holding vigil on the shore, looking for any sign— anything in your face, any gesture.

You have to be a wall, completely impassive. You wish somebody would tell the family, "You don't want to be here. You don't want to see the thing when we finally find it." You wish you could tell them that the real find will be quiet. When it happens, the diver will say nothing. He will quietly direct the boat around, place it between the spectators and the surface site. They will bag the body underwater. They will do everything they can to keep it hidden.

You can't tell the family that. The only thing they want to hear is the one thing you can't tell them— that their kid is okay.

But that's not the hardest part, is it? The job isn't so bad. It's a community project. You're never alone, never more than a few inches from the neon gloves of the next diver on the line. You can think of the lake in grids, tidily partitioned by weights and yellow strings, flags and GPS coordinates. It's impersonal. Scientific. And when the time comes to call it quits, to face the facts that enough taxpayer money has gone toward finding one little Chinese boy, that eventually he'll surface anyway—the decision isn't yours. You don't have to tell the family. You just roll up your line, fold the unused body bag.

Afterward, you sit on the rocks at sunset, thinking about the boy, what he must have felt like that Saturday—a sunny picnic, the cool water such a welcome relief after lunch, no one worried about that extra hot dog he ate. Maybe he heard his mom calling to him—"Be careful." And he looked down the shore, way out past the bend where the rich yachters were eating lunch on the decks of the restaurant, and he thought how fun it would be to go there. It didn't look far.

That moment comes when you realize what the kid was doing, what he felt like when he ate water, then found he couldn't surface.

And for all your mapping, your talks with the parents, your days of searching—it all comes down to one horrible realization. You're alone, and you decide to do one more dive.

You find him there, the glint of his gold necklace in your flashlight. The rest of him is fuzzy, white, unhuman—a child turning into a cloud.

And rationally, you realize what happened. He dove under the deck, thinking of the novelty of swimming beneath a building. He didn't realize the old spools of wire were down there, bricks, fishnets, hooks, crayfish traps. And then he became tangled, and realized that the sounds above him were the last he would ever hear—people walking, the voices of diners, the clink of dropped plates, all amplified through the aluminum pontoon floats and the water. He drowned in the dark, and stayed there for days while above him, rich folk toasted the sunset with Chardonnay. Yacht purchases were discussed. Engagement rings were unveiled over crabcakes and microbrewery beer. Businesses were planned, incorporation papers signed. And nosy spectators watched the divers at the public access beach down the shoreline, wondering what the fuss was about, complaining how it affected their speed boating.

Rationally, you understand how it happened. You understand that this is just one more bad memory to associate with a place—another policeman's marker.

The worst part is, you can't help thinking that the old Chinese grandmother was right—some spirit, some dark thing in the water, took a liking to that boy. And it bothers you that you were the one who knew where to look.

CHAPTER 37

"I don't know any Clyde," the boat jockey insisted.

He couldn't have been over nineteen, but he appeared to be the man in charge. He was frantically filling out paperwork while two even younger jockeys worked the docks—using the forklift to lower a Fountain 32 Lightning into the water.

Several affluent-looking couples stood behind us, waiting their turn.

"Clyde Simms," Lopez said. "You know—big ugly white guy. Runs the place."

The boat jockey shook his head. There were two twenty-dollar bills folded in his fingers, a tip from the previous customer.

"Yes, sir," he said. "If the manager's name is Clyde, I'll take your word for it. I don't know him. He isn't around."

"That the office?" I asked.

I pointed to a set of stairs on the side of the warehouse, leading up to a second-story door. Parked below the stairs were two Harley-Davidson V-Twin hogs—both FLSTF models, black and chrome. Leather cones jutted up behind each seat—perfect for holding either long-stem bouquets or shotguns. I was betting that the owners, wherever they were, were not florists at heart.

The boat jockey said, "I'm sorry, you can't—"

Another customer shouldered his way to the counter

and put his elbow between the boat jockey and me. He brandished a claim ticket.

"My boat," he said. "It's three o'clock and my boat isn't in the water."

"No, by all means," I said. "You go right ahead."

The newcomer gave Lopez and me the briefest sideways glance, just long enough to determine we weren't members of his country club, then turned his attention back to the boat jockey. "Well?"

The jockey looked up and just about had a paperwork-shuffling coronary. "Mr. McMurray."

"That's right," Mr. McMurray said, with more than a little satisfaction. "Now where's my boat?"

The jockey launched into some explanation about how the bottom paint wasn't dry yet and Mr. McMurray started smiling, no doubt anticipating a really good ass-chewing on the hired help.

Lopez said, "We'll just help ourselves, thanks."

We made a beeline for the outer stairs of the warehouse. When we got to the top, I glanced back. The boat jockey was watching us nervously, trying to get our attention, but he didn't dare yell or leave the not-to-be-pissed-off Mr. McMurray.

Lopez opened the door and we went inside.

The room was a fifteen-foot square—one interior door, one chair, one metal patio table. There was a pile of boat-cleaning supplies in the corner. The old grizzled biker who'd been talking to Garrett at the Jimmy Buffett concert was sitting at the table playing solitaire, which struck me as weirder than anything else I'd seen that day.

Lopez got a twinkle in his eye. "Well look who's here. If it ain't Armand."

Armand studied us from head to toe, then slowly got up. His beard reminded me of Garrett's, except it was longer, braided with lug nuts.

He nodded toward Lopez. "Who the fuck you?"

His Cajun accent was as grimy as the Café du Monde's dumpster.

"How quickly they forget," Lopez lamented. "You don't remember Del Valley, Armand? Our little talk about that double knifing? Man, I'm hurt."

Armand's eyes narrowed. "Ain't no cop, you."

I couldn't tell whether Armand was being obtuse or stubborn or what, but he was pressing Lopez to pull a badge Lopez didn't have. He'd intentionally not brought it—wanted no accusations later that he'd been here under color of law.

"Listen," Lopez said. "No need to get any more gray hairs. My friend here just wants to see his brother."

Armand studied me again, did not seem overcome with compassion. "S'pose to know your brother?"

"Garrett," I said. "Just tell him I'm here."

The lug nuts gleamed when he shook his head. "I see anybody named Garrett, I tell him."

Lopez sighed. He pulled over a folding chair, propped his foot on it. "I could call your name in, Armand. I'm sure I could find some warrants. But that's not the way we're trying to play it. Why don't you just take us downstairs, we'll talk to Clyde, see if he doesn't see things our way. Otherwise, I guarantee you, you're going to have half the Sheriff's Department around this place faster than you can kick-start a hog."

Armand scratched his beard.

"*D'accord,*" he decided, pointing his thumb toward the interior door. "But you still an asshole, Lopez, hear?"

Lopez grinned at me. "See? I knew he remembered me."

Armand led us downstairs into the warehouse. Boats were stacked in three-story-high tiers, with an open space in the middle the size of a basketball court.

The forklift was in the warehouse now, its engine rumbling like the world's largest lawn mower. It had a twenty-foot Stingray balanced on its prongs, probably Mr. McMurray's plaything, and the jockey was desperately trying to get it out the door, but there were two uniformed deputies blocking his path.

Armand froze when he saw the cops. He glared at Lopez, who spread his hands, tried to look mystified.

"They ain't with us, man," Lopez vowed. *"Je ne sais rien."*

Armand let out a string of Cajun curses, but apparently didn't see much choice except to keep going down the stairs.

The kid on the forklift was shouting at the deputies over the noise of the motor, asking them to please move. The uniforms ignored him.

I recognized one of them now—Engels, the one who worked part-time security for W.B. Doebler. That did not reassure me. The other guy I didn't recognize, but both had obviously ordered their facial expressions from the same online catalogue.

We got to the bottom of the steps.

"You can't be in here!" the kid on the forklift was saying, exasperated.

"Deputy Geiger," Lopez said, trying for a grin. "Deputy Engels. What brings you two here?"

Deputy Engels took his eyes off me long enough to say, "Detective. I heard you were on leave."

"I am," Lopez assured him pleasantly. "That's why I'm at a marina. Y'all want to split the cost of a day cruise?"

Geiger and Engels did not look tempted.

"I'm telling you—" the kid on the forklift started to shout.

Geiger said, "Cut your engine."

The kid opened his mouth to protest, but Geiger's expression shut him up.

He cut the engine.

"Now get off," Geiger said. "And get out."

The kid did both.

Outside, the other boat jockeys converged on him and started asking what the hell was going on. The kid said, *"You* talk to them!" In the background, Mr. McMurray was screaming how important he was.

Engels nodded to his compatriot, Geiger.

Geiger walked to the warehouse doors and rolled them shut, to the renewed protests of the boat jockeys outside.

"Chain it," Engels said.

Geiger took a length of chain off a hook, ran it through the door handles.

Engels pulled out his asp, extended it with a rapid flick of the wrist. He looked at Lopez and me. "There's the staircase, Detective. I suggest you and your friend use it. Leave the piece of shit here."

I hoped that the *friend* reference was for me, but I wasn't sure.

"This is dumb, gentlemen," Lopez said. "You got a warrant?"

"No need," Geiger said. "Possible officer in trouble. I just called it in, based on a witness I talked to outside. I came in. My partner Engels was here. The backup unit will be here in about ten minutes, I'd guess. Plenty of time."

"Mr. Doebler know you're here, Engels?" I asked. "You getting a bonus for this?"

Engels ignored me. He stepped up to Armand. "Give us Garrett Navarre, everything's fine. Don't give us Navarre, then you are about to assault an officer. It's going to get a little rough when I have to subdue you."

From the back of the warehouse, Clyde Simms' voice said, "Engels, you prick."

Clyde appeared from between two motorboats, wearing white shorts and white T-shirt and flip-flops—like an overweight, Aryan Jesus coming out of the tomb. He was holding his weapon of choice—the Bizon-2—down by his side. Garrett was with him, a few steps behind, wheeling along in his chair. Garrett looked okay, better actually than I'd seen him in quite some time.

Clyde said, "You know I ain't letting you near any friend of mine."

Engels smiled thinly. Geiger, slowly, drew his gun.

I locked eyes with Garrett, trying to implore him not to do anything stupid. He lifted a hand to reassure me, defeat in his eyes. He was a man about to give up, even if Clyde didn't know it yet.

Lopez said, "Hey, Clyde. Garrett. Under the circumstances, guys, I'd go with the flow. Come on out here and surrender. We'll work it out."

"Do what the detective says," Geiger urged.

"Then we can file a report on these assholes together," Lopez added. "Get them suspended the right way."

The deputies looked at Lopez, and Armand chose that moment to charge.

He went for Geiger, the man with the gun.

Engels swung the asp and Armand's shoulder caught a glancing blow, but Armand had his momentum. He slammed into Geiger and the two went down hard on the cement. Geiger's gun went flying.

Clyde fired off a burst from the Bizon-2 that punched a downward arc of holes in the warehouse door, the last and lowest shot snicking Engels' head—his ear flowered in blood. Lopez dove for the cover of the forklift. I rolled the other way and hugged the nearest boat hull.

Clyde had disappeared behind a rack of boats. Garrett, wisely, had wheeled himself back at top speed, out of sight.

Geiger and Armand were still rolling on the ground.

Engels was on the asphalt, screaming, his hand clamped around his ear and blood seeping between his fingers.

Lopez scrambled over to him, examined the wound, decided it was not fatal, drew the deputy's pistol, and went into a police crouch.

He glanced at Geiger, seemed to be deliberating how best to help him with Armand, when Clyde shot off another burst from somewhere in the back of the warehouse—bullets pinging like pinballs against the metal scaffolding. Lopez quickly retreated around the far side of the forklift, going into stalk mode for Clyde.

Geiger got the upper hand on Armand, started strangling the biker, but that just gave Armand new spirit. He rolled on top and smacked the deputy's head into the asphalt once, twice, three times. Geiger loosened his grip.

More gunshots sparked off the forklift.

Armand staggered to his feet, leaving Deputy Geiger curling on the cement like a stepped-on spider. Engels was still yelling, bleeding from the side of his head. He would not be getting up soon.

I could see Lopez's feet on the opposite side of the forklift, sneaking around, but he couldn't see Armand, who mumbled, "Fucking cops!" and headed for the forklift.

Armand climbed aboard, cranked the engine to life, then swung the machine around. Lopez fired once, ineffectually, then had to scramble to get out of the way.

Armand's turn was too tight. The forklift slammed into the lowest rack of boats and its Stingray payload keeled sideways, slipping off the prongs. Mr. McMurray's pride and joy hit the warehouse floor with a sound like a forty-ton Tupperware bowl. It slid to a stop right next to the unconscious Deputy Geiger.

Lopez spilled onto the ground behind the forklift. He'd lost his borrowed gun. He was trying to get to his feet, but it looked like he'd broken something.

Armand slammed the forklift in reverse, trying to free it from its tangle in the racks.

Another spray of shots came from the back of the warehouse—probably meant for Lopez—but one of them hit Armand's thigh in a burst of red mist.

Armand bellowed, lost control of the machine. The forklift was now backing up toward Lopez, who was scrambling to crawl out of the way, much too slow.

I cursed, ran to the forklift.

I jumped aboard and Armand paid me no attention. He was clutching his thigh, rocking, screaming more Cajun obscenities. I tried to hold on to him and keep us both on the forklift while figuring out the controls fast. I did it, sort of. I managed to slam the thing out of reverse and back into full forward, which sent us away from Lopez but on an unfortunate collision course with Deputies Geiger and Engels.

I tried for a turn, slammed full steam into Mr. McMurray's Stingray—pushing it toward the warehouse doors with an immense fiberglass GRRRRRINNNND. We hit the doors; the corrugated tin bowed, gave way. Then we were in the open, pushing the boat along the asphalt.

When I finally got the forklift stopped, the boat jockeys were staring at us in horror. The rich Mr. McMurray was gaping at his boat, which had just been delivered the hard way. Armand was still yelling, his blood soaking his pants.

Out of the warehouse came Lopez—rearmed with Clyde's Bizon-2, limping, leading Clyde Simms at gunpoint. Garrett wheeled along behind. Garrett looked okay, but Clyde sported a large new welt on his temple.

Sirens were wailing far off in the hills.

I exhaled for the first time in several minutes, then looked at our audience.

"Mr. McMurray," I said, "your boat is ready now."

CHAPTER 38

The front of the Travis County Jail is a severe concrete triangle, jutting toward West 11th Street like the prow of a battleship.

Vic Lopez led Maia and me inside the tiny foyer. He deposited his gun in a police locker, then signaled the security guard behind the bulletproof glass. We were buzzed through the double airlock door.

The guard on duty was busy explaining parole forms to a guy in a threadbare suit.

I looked at Lopez. "Do we sign in?"

"Yeah," he said. "Take a tag—doesn't matter what color."

It's not often I get to be someone's attorney. I took a red tag.

"Bad enough you don't invite me to your parties," Maia murmured. "Now you want to replace me."

Her mood had not been sunny since she received word of our expedition to the marina. Lopez had, amazingly, gotten off with only a mild censure, thanks again to his prominent attention in the press for bringing in three dangerous men. Deputies Engels and Geiger had been taken to the hospital, where they, too, were receiving accolades from the press.

I'd been released after questioning, with no punishment but cold stares. Lopez had vouched that I'd saved his life by stopping the forklift, but I wasn't sure that had won me any points with Lopez's superiors. The marina had been closed until further notice. Clyde Simms and Garrett had both been taken here—the county's maximum security facility for violent offenders.

Strangely enough, Armand, who'd started the whole thing, was the only one who got out on bail. Perhaps that was part of his plea bargain for copping to assault charges—something Clyde had not been willing to do. Perhaps the police simply failed to provide a Cajun interpreter when they read Armand his rights.

As for Garrett, his bail had been revoked. The fact that he hadn't directly resisted arrest was ignored. Maia's best speeches and tirades didn't help. Wheelchair or not, Garrett had now graduated to hard-core incarceration.

The prison corridors smelled like day-old meat loaf. The walls were brown and beige, in keeping with Travis County's Hershey Bar patrol colors. We walked past the med ward—the psych patients, the newbies waiting for their TB tests to pass. Guards in white lab coats did their rounds, slipping food and drugs through the little slots in the cell doors. All the deputies knew Vic. They high-fived him, asked him what was up, gave Maia Lee appreciative glances.

We waited for the elevator with four inmates in blue-green scrubs who were helping a deputy transport a supply cart.

Lopez looked at one of the inmates, a young Anglo guy with starch-white hair and a pasty face and a nervous smile. Vic said, "How you doing, Hans?"

The jail deputy grinned, as if pleased by some inside joke.

Hans said, "Fine, sir. I'm fine."

"These boys treating you okay?" Lopez asked.

I looked down at Hans' feet. He was the only one of the inmates without shoes.

"They're treating me fine," he said.

Two of the other guys—both Latinos with hair nets—grinned at each other.

Hans mumbled, "I got hope. My boss knows he ain't going to get his deposits in the bank next Friday without me. I got hope."

"You got to have hope," the other deputy said.

"That's right, brother," Lopez said.

At the top floor, the inmates let us get out of the elevator first. One held the door for us. Everybody called Maia "ma'am."

Lopez and I walked up to the guard station. The sentry, a Weeble-esque woman, was talking on the phone.

We waited.

The deputy from the elevator led his four charges to their cell block and told them it was time to declare contraband items. The inmates started patting down their clothes.

There were no bars anywhere, just plexiglass walls and big brown metal doors. Inside the block, I could see a metal picnic bench with welded seats, like at a highway rest stop. A little TV was mounted from the ceiling. Along the back wall was a row of ten-by-ten cells, each with its own brown metal door, each crammed with books and magazines. The whole block was intensely quiet. Much quieter than any jail I'd ever been in.

Three of the inmates showed the deputy their empty hands. One of the Latinos, almost bashfully, offered up a spoon and a comb—two potentially deadly weapons.

The deputy looked satisfied. He took the spoon and the comb and buzzed the cell block door open.

"You bust Hans?" I asked Lopez.

"It isn't Hans, Navarre—it's Hands. Only been in here a couple of days. Killed a guy he owed money to—dumped the body in the woods and thought we'd never be able to track the victim's identity if he cut off the hands and threw them in the Colorado River. Absolute stupidity. Local fishermen found the left hand. Catfish probably ate the right."

"And he's really getting out of here?" Maia asked.

Lopez laughed. "Not a chance. His boss wouldn't touch him. But that's how easy it is, getting suckered into the logic of losers. Other guys you shared an elevator with are real sweethearts, too—that was a drug dealer, a hit man, and the Barton Creek rapist. But you talk to them for a minute, you can almost buy that they're rational, nice human beings. Scary."

The inmates filed into their cell block. Hands looked reluctant to go. The deputy gave him an encouraging pat on the shoulder, turned him around, then gently pushed him into the block. The door slid closed.

The sentry behind the glass finally ended her call. She said, "Sorry, gentlemen. Ma'am."

"Hey, Peg." Lopez grinned. "How's your fun factor today?"

"Oh, real high, Vic. Real high."

"We need to see Garrett Navarre."

Deputy Peg barked a laugh. "It just got higher. What room you want?"

Lopez looked at us. "I hate those interview rooms. You want to put your mouth on one of those greasy phones? Look, Peg—how about you bring him upstairs to the rec area. Can you do that?"

She shrugged. "You know the way."

The outdoor rec area was on the top floor—a caged-in basketball court that looked out over the city. The panorama was obstructed by a ten-story Justice Department building to the left, but we could still see the wooded hills of Clarksville, clusters of apartments at the edge of UT, the green ribbons of undeveloped land that marked Shoal Creek and Barton Creek.

"Nice," I said.

"Oh yeah," Lopez agreed. "This was an apartment, you'd have to pay big bucks for a view like this. You kill somebody, you get it for free."

The door opened behind us. A guard came out with Garrett.

His blue-green prisoner scrubs were way too big for him, the pant legs tucked under him in neat blue squares. His beard had been trimmed severely, his ponytail cut off.

He had a shiner for a left eye. He hadn't had that this morning.

"If it isn't my brother," he said. "Captain of the Good Ship Forklift."

"Your eye," Maia said. "What happened?"

Garrett touched the bruised skin. "Don't worry about it. Clyde's in the cell block with me—we've got things under control."

The jail guard smiled amiably, moved off to one side, picked up a basketball. He started twirling it on his finger.

"Don't suppose you've come to get me out," Garrett said.

"You decided the odds on that," Lopez told him. "Soon as you eloped with Clyde Simms."

Garrett grunted. "Yeah, Lopez. I should've stayed and taken the rap for another murder—with my kid brother finding all the evidence against me, my counselor telling me to plea-bargain, your deputy friends treating me to some of that county-style justice. At least with Clyde, I know whose side he's on."

The jail guard yelled, "Heads up, Navarre."

He threw Garrett the ball.

Garrett caught it without much enthusiasm, dribbled it a couple of times in front of his wheelchair.

"Lopez was pulled off your case," I told him, "mostly because he stopped believing you're guilty. He wants to help."

"He wants to help," Garrett repeated. "He'll have to queue up, won't he? Whole fucking world wants to help me."

Maia told him about the tox reports, the ties between the murders of Clara Doebler, Jimmy, and the woman in the lake, the woman we assumed was Ruby.

Garrett's face reminded me of a wall I'd been trying to repair at the family ranch—crumbling stone washed over with plaster so many times I was afraid to scrape away the outer layer, for fear the whole structure would collapse. "It wasn't Ruby down there."

"We should know in a few days," Lopez said.

"It wasn't her. Clyde and I—we've had time to talk. Ruby wouldn't let her guard down like that. She can't be dead."

For a moment, his eyes softened with the same sad, broken hopefulness I'd seen downstairs, in the face of a polite young inmate who severed body parts.

"Garrett," I said, "the murders are connected. There's a poisoner at work. Adrienne Selak, Peña's girlfriend—she was probably drugged the same way as the others."

"If that's true," Garrett said, "why am I still in here?"

"Because," said Maia, "the DA can still make his strongest case, his only case, against you. You might be ruled out of Selak's murder, but the link between her and the other murders is the most speculative. To satisfy the public, give the press a good story, the DA's simply got to get you out of circulation—convict you on one murder, Jimmy Doebler's. The DA had a strong hand to begin with. When you ran, his hand got even stronger."

Garrett gripped the basketball tight enough to squeeze juice out of it. "You come here to tell me I should plea-bargain?"

"I don't think that's possible anymore," she answered. "But there might be something you can do, assuming you give us some straight answers. Have you been getting e-mail from the killer?"

He hesitated. "I've been getting—e-mails."

"From Peña," she said.

"They come from different addresses, different X-mailers. They're embedded with some kind of text-based virus—damnedest thing I've ever seen. Freezes the computer if you try to print it, save it, screen-capture it—anything."

"What did they say?"

Garrett shook his head at me. "I'd rather not— Look, it was just sick shit. Most of it was about me. Some about the company. The only one that really bothered me, the one I didn't understand—the bastard talked about some kid who almost got drowned in a tub."

Lopez stared out the chain link fence. "A kid?"

"Like I said. Sick shit."

"Second confession," Maia said. "You wrote the back door in Techsan's security program."

Garrett's eyes darkened. He looked past me, toward the prison doors.

"Dwight Hayes found the glitch," I told him. "It took him a while, but he's sure you wrote it."

"I don't have anything to say about that," Garrett told us. "With or without my lawyer."

"Look," Lopez said. "This could be real bad news for you, Navarre. Or it could be a break. If you wrote this back door in the program, I want to call a friend in the High Tech Unit, get him over here to talk with you. You know the program better than anybody. Maybe if you two get together, you can trace the leaks. If you can tie the sabotage to Matthew Peña—well, it may not pin him to a murder. But it might be enough to sweat him, maybe even get a search warrant issued for his computer. That would be a very good start."

Garrett kept digging his fingertips into the black lines of the basketball.

Behind him, on the court, the jail guard did air three-pointers.

"Get me out of here first," Garrett said.

"Can't do that," Lopez said. "We got to clear you before you go anywhere."

"You'll screw me around," Garrett said. "You can't help it. You're a cop."

"You want to talk alone?" I asked.

Garrett hesitated, then nodded.

"Buckley," Lopez called to the jail deputy. "I'll be inside."

"One on one?" Buckley offered.

Lopez dismissed the offer with a wave, then went through the door.

Garrett said, "You, too, Maia."

She started to protest; the look in his eyes stopped her. She followed Lopez inside.

Garrett held my eyes long enough to count to twenty.

"I wrote the back door," he said. "It was a diagnostic tool. I used it to check the integrity of files."

A gust of wind smacked the side of the Justice Department building and reverberated across the jail roof.

"When the leaks started," I said, "you didn't suspect that was the problem?"

"The back door was *buried,* Tres. Nobody had the pass code except me, Jimmy, and Ruby. A saboteur would have to get help from one of us, and even then he'd have to be a technical whiz. I couldn't believe my partners would sabotage their own company. I thought it was much more likely Peña was bribing employees at the beta-test sites."

"You should've taken the thing out."

"I tried, little bro. As things got worse, I went in and pulled the original subroutine, but it was too late. The damage was done. The beta-testers were pulling the program off their machines, shutting us out of their systems. I couldn't fix all the old copies of the program. I was never even sure the back door had been the problem."

"Then you should've gone to the police."

"I couldn't."

"Because?"

Garrett turned toward the hoop, dribbled twice, shot. The ball whanged high off the backboard and bounced clean away.

"Because I'd used the damn thing myself," he said. "Illegally."

He looked at me, his eyes wet green, like windshield wiper fluid.

I braced myself. "Okay. What did you do?"

"Our beta-test customers—one of them was Ticket Time."

"The concert ticket company," I said. And then it hit me in the face. "You're not telling me . . ."

"I didn't get anything for free, little bro. I paid. I just . . . put my requests into their computer first. Went to the head of the line. It was a dream, with the summer season about to open up."

"You used the back door for Buffett tickets."

"Don't make it sound so goddamn trivial. I got tickets for the whole summer, almost every show—front row, center aisle, me and Jimmy and Clyde, a couple of other buddies. Starting next week, we were going on a road trip. It seemed harmless enough. It was just that one time, little bro. Never again."

The jail guard had retrieved the ball. He called, "Hey, Navarre, you going to play on the prisoners' team this year? Guards might just win, you shoot that bad all the time."

The deputy threw from the three-point line, made a basket.

I thought about shoving the ball down his throat.

"You didn't want to get arrested for scamming Buffett tickets," I said. "And now here you are, for murder."

Garrett looked toward the windows of the justice building.

I wanted to be furious with my brother. I wanted to strangle him. But what he'd done was so ridiculous, so damn . . . Garrett-like, I couldn't muster much more than exasperation.

"If I do what Lopez wants," Garrett said, "if I help the High Tech Unit, chances are pretty good we won't find anything solid enough to bust Peña. On the other hand, I'll be going on record for using my own security program for personal gain. If there were any chance I'd ever work programming again, this would nail the coffin. My career would be over."

"I can't tell you what to do," I said. "Not somebody as logical as you."

The wind kicked up again, knocking me a few inches sideways. Over in the far corner of the court, the jail guard kept dribbling a steady, slow beat.

"Last day or so," Garrett said, "I've had a lot of time to think. I've been listening to Clyde and Armand talking about this place they know in the Yucatán—guy can live like a king, never go back to the States. They say they could set me up. Extradition is a joke. I could screw all this, cut my losses, spend my days drinking *cerveza* by the beach."

He looked down at his hands. They were trembling slightly.

"And then I realized—I'm feeling the same way I felt that first night Ruby McBride bought me a drink at Point Lone Star, told me she had ideas for a new start-up. I feel the same way I felt when Jimmy taught me to jump trains. I start thinking—I've been a sucker my entire goddamn life."

There had been times I'd longed to hear Garrett criticize himself that harshly—to admit he didn't have a reality-check bone in his body. Now, it brought me no satisfaction.

"You believe in possibilities," I told him. "That's not all bad."

Garrett shook his head. "I keep getting punished for it."

He looked worse than I had ever seen him—the black eye, the chopped hair, the prison scrubs. But at that moment I realized I admired Garrett for the same reasons I resented him—his absolute faith in his friends, his unshakable belief that you could dream something and then go right out and do it. And he kept believing that, no matter how much the world kicked the crap out of him.

The more unsettling realization was that, just for a moment, I saw Garrett the way my dad must've seen him. For all their fights, their harsh words, their years of not speaking to each other—I suddenly understood why Dad, in the end, had left my brother everything. Garrett needed it more than I did. He was living without a net.

Garrett took hold of his armrests, bracing himself as if he were about to get up. "I spent most of my adult life hoping you didn't turn out like me, little bro. That's why I'm impatient when you try to help me. You can't get pulled into my shit. You got to do better. You got to get your own shit together."

I couldn't respond.

"You getting back together with Maia?" he asked.

"I don't know."

Garrett glowered at me, letting me know he would not accept indecision.

"You think I should help Lopez?" he asked me. "You figure he's on the level?"

"Yeah. I think you should."

He called to the guard, who tried to pass him the ball. Garrett caught it, threw it away. "Tres— Tell Lopez it's a go."

He winked at me with his good eye, then let the guard escort him inside.

I met Lopez by the guard station. He was using their phone, and didn't seem very happy about the conversation he was having. When he saw me coming, he lowered the receiver to the cradle without saying goodbye.

"Well?" he asked.

I filled him in.

Lopez shook his head. "I guess I got to get out my old LPs, take a listen to *Son of a Son of a Sailor*. I must've missed something."

"That call anything important?"

Lopez glanced at the phone, as if to make sure he'd hung it up properly. "Nothing you need to worry about."

We went down the elevator, now empty. At every locked door on our way out, some unseen guard on an unseen monitor noted our approach and buzzed us through.

When we got out into the foyer, Lopez reclaimed his gun. I gave back my red lawyer's tag.

Maia Lee was waiting for us at the main entrance.

I told her what Garrett had said.

She ran a finger across the glass. "We need to see Peña, try to break the bastard. I'm not sure Garrett can survive in here long enough to help the High Tech Unit."

"Any objections?" I asked Lopez.

Lopez straightened his gun belt. He stared out the window at the convict transport vans.

"Detective?" I asked again.

Lopez reached into his back pocket and pulled out a writing pad, flipped through pages of messy notes.

"Think I might take some flowers to the hospital," he said. "Deputy Engels has a few things to tell me about W.B. Doebler. He just doesn't know it yet."

"You sure that's wise?" I asked. "You know how tight W.B. is with the sheriff. And you're still supposed to be on leave."

Lopez put away his notebook, met my eyes. His expression told me he was past the point of caring about wise choices.

"You two go on ahead," he said. "Don't worry about me."

"You'll keep in touch?"

A small, thin smile. "Navarre. Counselor."

Then he slipped out the tinted glasses and headed for his car.

Maybe it was just the fact that I'd said too many goodbyes that had turned permanent in the course of the week—to Jimmy, to Ruby, almost to Garrett. But I had to fight back a chill as Victor Lopez pulled away—a strange premonition that I wouldn't be seeing him again.

CHAPTER 39

Happy hour was under way on Sixth Street. Early evening revelers roamed from pub to pub, bands were setting up, the smells of Mexican food and mesquite barbecue filled the street.

Inside the Driskill lobby, lights glowed on the marble floors. At the baby grand, a lounge singer was doing Sinatra. I had to hold Maia's hand as we walked past, just to make sure she didn't draw her weapon.

We punched the elevator call button.

When the gold mirror doors slid open, we found ourselves face-to-face with Matthew Peña, holding a suitcase.

His eyes got very small. "What—"

I pushed him back into the elevator.

"Not leaving us yet, Peña," I said. "Not by a long shot."

Maia came in behind me, closed the door, punched fifteen. "How are you, Matthew?"

"You—" He looked like he was swallowing something spiky. "You, Maia—should be gone. Fired and gone. Ronald Te—"

I punched him in the mouth.

The suitcase clattered to the floor. Peña sank into a crouch.

My hand hurt. I'd cut a knuckle on his incisors.

Maia shook her head. "Gut, Tres. Always the gut."

"I know."

Peña pinched his jaw. His teeth were stained with blood. "What the hell are you thinking, Navarre? You call this private?"

Before I could ask what he meant, the door binged open. Wrong floor. The tenth.

A woman started to come in, did a hasty back step.

"We're going up," I told her. "Can't you tell?"

Maia pushed the button. The door slid shut.

When we reached the fifteenth floor, I pulled Peña to his feet. Maia got the suitcase. Together we escorted Mr. Peña back into his luxury accommodations.

I wasn't even going to guess how much Peña was paying for the Cattle Baron Suite. The decor was cedar and bronze and granite, Lone Star motifs, plush furniture, eighteen-foot ceilings, and massive curtained windows overlooking the nighttime skyline of Austin.

Two steps inside, Peña yanked away from me and landed a haymaker on the side of my face. There wasn't much force behind it. He tried for a second punch, but I slapped his hand down, kicked his feet out from under him. He landed on the maroon carpet.

"Knock it off," I told him.

Maia put the suitcase on the bed. She opened the snaps, pulled out several bricks of cash, Peña's portable computer, and a semiautomatic pistol.

She held up the gun by two fingers. "New hard-sell tactics, Peña?"

"Get up," I told him.

He did, slowly, rubbing his hip. "I was about to ransom your brother's worthless life, Navarre."

"Really," I said. "How uncharacteristically noble. You want to explain?"

His eyes were dark and full of motion, not unlike snake pits.

Maia ejected the magazine from the pistol. "I'm disappointed, Matthew. There's no more than fifty grand here. I would've thought you paid better."

He put his thumb to his mouth, pulled it back, and looked at the blood. "The computer, Maia. The cash was the smallest demand—just an appetizer. The real price is an electronic stock transfer."

"And who's doing the demanding?" she asked.

Peña picked up an empty bottle from his champagne bucket, regarded it with disgust, dropped it again. "You need to ask? He just hit me in the mouth."

Maia and I exchanged looks.

"Um," I said. "Not that I have any aversion to bilking you of your stock portfolio, but what the hell are you talking about?"

Peña glared at me. His upper lip was starting to puff up and the blood looked like lipstick. "The e-mail, Navarre."

I shook my head. "Sorry, *amigo.*"

Peña started to respond, then stopped himself.

Maia picked up a silk sock, wiped her prints off the gun and the magazine, threw everything back into the suitcase. "Maybe you should start from the beginning, Matthew. What was this e-mail?"

"Maybe I shouldn't start at all," he said. "The package you put together—extremely impressive. And don't tell me it wasn't one or both of you."

"I'm glad you liked it," I said. "Tell us again what we said."

Eye level to us, out the window, a helicopter ruttered by—a police spotlight unit, probably seeking a fled-on-foot suspect. The spotlight made Matthew's white shirt glow.

"The Heismans," Peña said. "The fact I was adopted, the paperwork on my birth parents is a total blank."

When he saw we were not surprised, he seemed to interpret it as guilt.

"Goddamn you," he said. "You went to a lot of work. The Doebler child—the one born in '67. The fact that the father died when I was in college, the mother five years ago at a time I happened to be in Austin. Then Jimmy Doebler, and Ruby. The toxicology, the ballistics."

He looked at Maia. "Worst of all, Adrienne. How could you imply that? You *know* I didn't kill her."

Looking at him now, I could understand why so many people had been destroyed by him. If you weren't careful, you could read anything in his demeanor—concern, caring, mournfulness, vulnerability. You might even think he could be trusted.

"Adrienne was drugged," Maia told him. "Just like the others. Dwight changed his statement, took away your alibi. The only common denominator in all the murders is you."

He shook his head. "The traces on the beta-testing. How did you do that?"

I tried to choose my words carefully. "You admit you sabotaged the program?"

Peña laughed. "Well, I don't have much choice. It's all right there—every single time, every session logged. How the hell did you get into my system? Even the e-mails—those goddamn, hateful e-mails. Somehow you managed to pin them to my machine. You know I didn't send anything like that."

Maia walked to the window, looked out at the Austin skyline. "You're saying you never sent *me* any e-mails, Matthew?"

"I called you a few times. I'll admit I was a little . . . aggressive. But I never sent you anything like—those. I never crashed your system. The rest of the shit you accused me of—breaking into your apartment, all of that—I never *did* that. It's just like I told you last year—the crap they claimed I did to that guy in Menlo Park. I *didn't* do it."

It bothered me that I almost believed him. It bothered me more that the package he'd described—the case against Matthew Peña—was exactly what Maia and I had come here to pressure him with, except someone had beat us to it, someone a lot better prepared.

"Matthew," I said, "I'll suspend disbelief for a moment if you'll do the same. Let's say you really did get an e-mail like this—let's say you're not luring us into something, and you have been framed up about as well as anybody can be framed. I didn't send you any e-mail. Neither did Maia."

The color drained from his face. "Who the hell else would demand I help clear your brother?"

"What did they want, exactly?"

"He—"

"You're sure it's a he?" I asked.

Peña looked impatient. "He, she, it—take your pick. He threatened to hand me to the police on a skewer. The level of documentation he'd provide would clear Garrett, make me look like a multiple killer."

"With what you described," Maia agreed, "he's probably right."

"He wanted twenty million in stock, fifty thousand cash. The stock he wanted transferred to an anonymous account. In exchange, he wouldn't use me. He'd make somebody else the scapegoat."

"Who?" I asked.

"I don't know. I didn't care. I was supposed to meet you—him—tonight. At the restaurant marina, Ruby's place."

"And you trusted him?"

Peña smiled thinly. "No, Navarre. You'll notice the gun. I intended to kill you."

For once, I believed him. Little statements like that really build trust.

I looked at Maia. She read my thoughts, nodded acquiescence.

"Matthew," I said, "for fifty thousand dollars, you've just bought yourself some company."

Date: Thur 15 Jun 2000 18:40:26 -0400
From: list-owner@marina.com
To: list-digest@marina.com
Subject: digest for 15 Jun 2000

There is one message in this issue.

Topics:
        I. reunion

{#} Replies to this digest are directed to
list@marina.com

Date: Thur 15 Jun 2000 18:52:26 -0100
From: little brother <lilbro@marina.com>
Subject: reunion

My last story—the way he found me. And I must be brief, because he requires attention.

He came in the backyard, through the old fence, which I found more than a little ironic. Nevertheless, I was grateful he'd parked in the alley. That would make it so much easier, later.

He stood under the tree, stared up at the house through the branches.

And from my window, I could see the truth finally dawning on him. He walked to the back door.

I waited. I never had any doubts that he would come, and when he did, he would come alone. He had no one left to trust.

I heard his voice inside. Then his feet on the steps.

I stood to one side, in the dark little alcove that had never made any architectural sense to me, but I smiled—remembering that this was where I'd hidden so many times as a child, ready to jump out and seize my playmate.

He got to the top and froze, staring at the room ahead of him. He held a gun, but that didn't matter. I knew he would hesitate here. There was no avoiding that moment of horrified revelation.

I stepped out of the alcove, my blackjack already in motion. He didn't even have time to register the threat before the heavy end of the sap caught his skull, crumpled him to the floor.

"Tag," I said.

And I took the syringe from my pocket.

It's just a matter of waiting, now. Hoping the air lasts. Hoping his heart lasts. Hoping you join the reunion in time.

But as I told you, I'm not worried. Drowning is a patient art.

CHAPTER 40

Maia, Peña, and I sat in the cab of my truck.

There were no signs of life at the marina—just moonlight on the lake, the flicker of moths across the parking lot lights. The warehouse was closed, the two Harley-Davidson hogs still parked under the stairwell. The marina gate was locked, only a few boats left in the slips. Mexican doves roosted on the tines of the forklift.

I looked at Maia. "I could go first, scout it out."

Maia leaned forward so she could stare at me around Matthew.

"I didn't think so." I looked at Peña. "You ready, Matthew?"

"Do I have a choice?"

"Not really."

"Do I get my gun back?"

Maia said, "Ha."

Peña moistened his fat lip. "Then I'm ready."

I pulled out Erainya's Taurus 9 mm. from under the seat, loaded a clip.

Maia raised an eyebrow.

"Don't get excited," I said. "You're the one who can shoot worth a damn. Let's go."

Gravel crunched underfoot as we walked toward the water. I watched the restaurant for signs of movement.

Two different planks led from shore. Beer bottles floated in the scummy water between.

Maia drew her Sig Sauer and gestured that she would take the left plank. Matthew and I took the right.

I stepped across the gangplank, pushed on the heavy wooden door. The sign NO ONE UNDER 18 ADMITTED crinkled under my palm.

A dove flitted out of the exposed rafters and I nearly shot at it.

Matthew and I made our way through a barroom that smelled like lemon ammonia and dried whiskey. I brought out my pencil flashlight and shone it into dark corners—a plastic spoon, a napkin, a forgotten handbag. It was so quiet we could hear the lake gurgle and plunk against the aluminum pontoon floats beneath the floor.

I thought, just for a moment, that I heard a man's voice—a murmured question.

I stopped Peña. We listened.

Nothing.

We rendezvoused with Maia in the main dining room—a forest of upside-down chairs stacked on tables. The deck doors were open, letting in the smell of the water and the entire panorama of the lake.

Mansfield Dam rose up immediately on the left—an enormous slab of charcoal.

Peña started to whisper, "This was a waste—"

And then someone else spoke, directly in front of us. There was a human form out on the deck.

Peña and I moved toward it, Maia a few steps behind, bringing up the rear.

The man glistened—the glint of wet suit material. Victor Lopez was sitting on the railing of the deck.

"Vic?" I called.

We were at the open doorway now, Lopez only ten feet away.

As my eyes adjusted, I noticed his gear—the air tank, the regulator, the mask around his neck. He wore two weight belts that were solid with squares of lead, another two belts crossing his chest like bandoliers. No BC to counteract the lead. No fins.

If Lopez went over the side like that, he would sink fast and have a hell of a time coming back up. He was also holding a gun at his thigh—not a service pistol. Something smaller. An old-style Raven from back in the 1980s. A .380 automatic.

Lopez was staring out over the water, as if in a reverie.

I glanced back at Maia, who shook her head slightly— *I don't know.*

Then Vic mumbled something. "Here. Right here, I think."

"Lopez?" I called.

He looked over, said nothing.

There was more scuba equipment at his feet—another air tank, fastened to a BC. On a nearby table was a mask. Next to that, a computer disk.

I shone my pencil flashlight in Lopez's face.

His pupils stayed fully dilated. His expression didn't change—as if there were no circulation in his face.

"Is this—" he droned. "Is this . . . okay?"

"We should leave," Peña murmured. "Now."

Then the deck boards creaked behind us. I spun.

A second figure had separated from the darkness right next to Maia. The only thing that wasn't pure black was the gun. It was pressed against Maia's temple.

"Yes," said the voice I didn't recognize at all. "That's fine, Vic. Put your mask on."

Metal thudded against wood—Maia's gun dropping.

"That's good, dear heart," the voice crooned, the face still in the shadows. "Now your friend's—gun and the flashlight in the water, please."

Maia said, "Don't, Tres."

"Ah," the voice said. "But Tres can't shoot, can he? He doesn't trust his aim. He doesn't trust guns. And certainly, he knows I'll kill you if he doesn't cooperate."

Next to me, Peña stayed still.

I tossed my gun and flashlight over the railing, heard two tiny *plooshes* in the water.

The figure stepped forward, pushing Maia ahead.

A black baseball cap. A wet suit. A face painted black, eyes intense as a raptor's. The gun slid down, pressed tightly into Maia's jugular vein.

"My hero." Dwight Hayes gave me a pleasant smile. "Thanks for coming, Tres."

CHAPTER 41

"You son of a bitch," Peña said.

"You don't know how appropriate your comment is, Matthew." Dwight's wrist rested on Maia's shoulder. The neoprene of the wet suit was soaking the top of her shirt. He moved his free hand around her waist, spreading his fingers caressingly across her abdomen.

"You smell good," Dwight told her. "I've never been close enough—except for your apartment, looking through your things. I'm glad you decided to pursue us, Maia."

She swallowed. Her throat muscles pushed against Dwight's gun and made it look like she was nodding.

I watched her fingers, waited for our old sign—a three-finger countdown, which would mean she was about to risk a move.

"All right, Victor," Dwight said.

Lopez had raised his gun. He was pointing it at Dwight Hayes, but his arm was bent, the gun turned sideways, as if some invisible arm-wrestling opponent was forcing his hand back at the wrong angle.

"You won't need that," Dwight assured Lopez. His voice was calm, deep. "Don't you remember?"

"You're drugged, Lopez," I said. "Fight it. Shoot the bastard."

Lopez's arm trembled. His chest had begun to cave in like an old man's under the weight and heat of the scuba gear.

"Don't remember," he mumbled.

"The little boy," Dwight told him. "The little Asian child. He was right under the deck, wasn't he?"

"The boy."

"Right about where you're sitting."

Peña said, "Jesus Christ, Dwight."

Peña started to move forward, but Dwight pressed the gun into Maia's throat, made her gag. "Tsk, tsk, old friend. First things first."

Lopez mumbled, "Right here."

"Good," Dwight said, nodding pleasantly. "What should you do?"

"Search."

"That's an excellent idea. You can leave the gun, I think. Your prints are on it now. That should be sufficient."

Lopez's hand lowered. The Raven clunked on the floor. "I can't— No."

"You need your mask on," Dwight suggested. "And you'll have to keep looking. Even if it gets cold, even if you can't get out, you can't leave a little boy alone down there. Can't let that happen again."

Dwight's voice had taken on a cadence that wasn't quite human—more like a drum, hit by a small, angry windup machine. "You'll just need to keep searching, Vic. That little boy is down there somewhere. Drowning in the dark."

Lopez fumbled with his mask.

"No, Vic," I said.

But I was just part of the nightmare. His heart must have been slowing, his mind turning to thick sap, flowing over Dwight's words, hardening wherever they stuck.

He bit the regulator's mouthpiece, groping for a pressure gauge.

"Oh, there isn't one, Victor," Dwight reassured him. "Time is the diver's enemy. This dive, you won't have any limits. No charts. Just your task. Now over you go—it'll feel so good to get into the cold water, won't it?"

Lopez had trouble getting his leg over the railing. He

slid off awkwardly, his tank hitting the rail as he fell, and then he was gone.

The sound in my ears compressed into a roar. I looked at Dwight. "How much time, you sick fuck?"

He cocked his head. "Air consumption is unpredictable when their metabolism slows down. It's a race, really, whether his heart fails from the drugs before the air gives out."

Next to me, Peña made his hands into fists. "You killed her. You drugged Adrienne. You followed us—waited for me to leave. You goddamn—"

Dwight made *shh-shh-shh* sounds, the way you would for a restless infant. "Adrienne was getting too close to you, Matthew. She was softening you. I couldn't allow that. You made too good of a shadow to stand in, allowed me to get away with so much. I couldn't give up all the years I'd cultivated you."

"You pointed Peña toward Techsan," I said. "You made the pact with Ruby, killed her when she started having regrets. It was all your idea—you intended to destroy Jimmy."

He rubbed his hand across Maia's belly. "Lopez needs help. I'll tell you what, Maia—there's my equipment. I'll let you go in. Only you."

If it was possible for Maia to look any more tense than she already did, with a gun at her throat, Dwight's comment did the trick.

"It's only about twenty feet there," Dwight told her. "Pitch black. And of course, you'd have to feel around—not knowing when you'll touch human flesh, and if he'll still be alive when you do. What do you say, honey? It would be worth it, letting you save Lopez's life, just to see you face that."

Peña said, "I'll destroy you."

Dwight raised his eyebrows. "Don't lose your only admirable quality now, Matthew. You've got to be strong. You've got to cut those ties, stand alone. That's what you always wanted. That was why I visited your parents that Christmas. I granted your wish."

Peña was deadly still for half a second, and then, foolishly, he charged. It might have been an opportunity, but before I could even think of using it, Dwight fired.

The bullet caught Peña in the gut. He contracted like he was catching a football, slammed down on his knees.

After the shot, the silence was intense.

"I've learned a lot of lessons from you, Matthew," Dwight told him. "I was hoping to spare you. But it's only right you're here to help me end this."

Matthew hugged his middle, made small sounds of pain.

A sheen of sweat had formed on Dwight's blackened face, but I got the feeling it had nothing to do with the insulation of the wet suit. Dwight Hayes was overheating from the inside.

"You remember, Matthew? How many times we lay awake at night in the dorm room talking, that first semester? Don't you remember when you gave me the idea? You told me about changing your name, how you wished your parents were dead for ignoring you all those years? You were my inspiration."

"No," Peña managed.

There was a wet stain on the wood, blood spreading around his knees.

"Oh, yes, you were," Dwight insisted. "You gave me the courage to live. You gave me a purpose."

I met Maia's eyes, saw what she was thinking. *Distract him.*

"You're Jimmy's brother," I told him. "Clara and Ewin's son."

Dwight's smile became disdainful. "You don't see the resemblance, Tres? Don't worry—the disk there on the table, I take the blame for it all. When they find your bodies, they'll understand. All the roots will be pulled—all the pieces of my family, Jimmy's family, will be gone. I'm sorry Garrett couldn't be here, but he'll have enough charges against him to destroy him. After tonight, Clara's younger son can rest in peace."

The way he spoke of himself in the third person chilled me even more than his threat.

"Kill him, Tres," Peña moaned. "You have to kill him."

Maia's first finger went down.

I'd have to tackle him. But the way Dwight shot, the speed with which he moved—I was pretty sure Maia and I were both going to die.

Maia's second finger went down.

A floorboard creaked in the main dining room, and a voice grumbled, "Eh! What the fucking gunshot about?"

Armand the biker. I had never been happier to hear a Cajun accent in my life.

Dwight's eyes turned heavy-lidded. He readjusted the muzzle of his gun against Maia's neck, then turned her, walked her backward toward the railing where he would have a clear view of the doorway. I stepped back, too, slowly, moving around Peña, now crumpled on his side, his breath a faint rattle. The gun Lopez had dropped—the .380 Raven—was three feet from my boot.

"Eh!" Armand called again, irritably.

"On the deck," Dwight called, his voice completely altered, like a teenager's, feigning fright and surprise. "It's okay, man. We were just screwing around."

Armand appeared in the doorway, the lug nuts in his beard glinting, a sawed-off shotgun in his hands. But the shotgun was down, not ready to fire.

I met Maia's eyes one last time. Her third finger went down. Then things happened quickly.

Dwight said, "Hey, man," and shot over Maia's shoulder, hitting Armand in the chest.

Maia fell sideways out of Dwight's grasp and went into a prone sidekick, slamming her foot into Hayes' rib cage.

She knocked Dwight off balance but he spun as he fell, firing wildly behind him.

I lost a precious second trying to find the Raven, which had disappeared in the dark. Then I gave up and charged toward Dwight.

He fired again, and Maia rolled.

I slammed him into the railing with my best varsity

tackle. The railing creaked. Dwight clubbed me in the face with his pistol, but I grabbed his waist, slammed him backward again, and this time the rail cracked under our combined weight. One moment air, then we were consumed by water.

I clamped my teeth against the instant cold and black. There was no light, just the sound of churning bubbles and the fists and knees of Dwight Hayes. There was no weight to my punches, no air to breathe. Nothing but clawing and kicking in liquid.

My foot slammed into something hard—one of the aluminum pontoons under the building, maybe. The pain was enough to make me slacken my grip on Dwight's wrist. I clawed at him once more and got wet suit, grabbed again, got nothing.

The need for air overrode everything else. I let myself float up, felt cool on my face and gasped in a breath that tasted like gasoline. My eyes burned in the darkness.

There was tromping above me. Maia's voice. A man screaming—Armand. I was under the deck.

I took a breath, submerged, felt my way beneath the aluminum pontoon, kicked up in open water, the railing of the deck above me.

I yelled for Maia, then grabbed the deck floor. It took a supreme effort to haul myself up out of the lake.

Maia was tying a strip of white table linen around Armand's shoulder. Something was wrong with her foot— it was wrapped in cloth, too, and blood had already soaked it. She finished with Armand, then limped toward Peña, who was not moving.

"Hayes?" I yelled.

"I don't know." She examined Peña's gut wound. "Christ. I used Peña's cell phone, called 911. We've got to get Lopez out of the water. It could still be a ten-minute response time."

I wheeled around, scanning the horizon—saw nothing but darkness, glittering water. Then a faint reflection— moonlight on wet neoprene—and I saw Hayes. He was on the shoreline, running uphill.

"There," I said. "He's heading for the dam."

Maia had blood on the side of her face, and I wasn't sure if it was hers.

"Hayes will get away," she said. "And Lopez doesn't have ten minutes."

I looked at her foot, then at the scuba equipment. We both knew Maia would not be running up any hills.

"Go!" she said.

"Lopez will have to hold out," I said. "Don't try it, Maia."

Her face was utterly white, but she staggered over to the air tank, stared at it like it was a bomb. She picked up the .380 Raven, tossed it to me. "Just go, Tres. Now."

I ran—out of the restaurant, stumbling over the gravel in the parking lot, following Dwight Hayes uphill. My shirt felt like fifty extra pounds of water so I stripped it off. It was a hard trail through agarita and whitebrush and cactus, over limestone rubble at a thirty-five-degree angle. Dwight didn't seem to have any problem with it, even in a wet suit. He was far ahead, and he kept gaining.

When he got to the top, I shot at him. Instead of turning toward the parking lot, as I'd thought he would, he turned toward the dam, started running across. By the time I was at the top, on the dam access road, Dwight was fifty yards out and I could hear the first police sirens in the distance.

A Travis County patrol car was racing up the road on the far end of the dam, a mile away. His lights were flashing. He would be there, inadvertently cutting off Hayes' escape, before Hayes could ever reach the far side.

The wind that always buffeted the dam seemed to be blowing Dwight back in my direction, ripping at his short brown hair, making it dance in spikes. He stopped at the halfway mark. I slowed. On the other side, the police car braked, its headlamps pointed straight at us. A deputy's flashlight cut a wavering beam in the night as he ran in our direction.

Dwight looked at me, then looked over the railing on the north side of the dam—at the lake two hundred feet below, visible only because of the nickel streaks on the surface.

I kept walking toward Dwight, slowly, my hand tracing the rivets on the metal railing.

When I was about twenty feet away, Dwight took hold of one of the metal cables and stepped up onto the railing. He looked down, seemed gratified by what he saw, then looked back at me.

"One favor," he said.

"Don't do this, Dwight."

The cop on the other side of the dam kept coming.

Dwight's eyes were ferocious and clear, but there was nothing insane in them. I realized that the Dwight Hayes I'd befriended had not been a facade—not simply a mask covering a monster. Dwight Hayes was right there, standing on the ledge, imploring me.

"One thing left undone," he confided. The wind tore at him. "The most important. Don't let her do it again. You understand?"

"Come down," I said. "You can explain it to me."

Dwight smiled. "You have to improvise. Remember that, Tres. Improvise."

Then Dwight turned and faced the water.

The silence of his fall was terrible, the smallness of the impact on the water.

I stood with the wind ripping at my wet clothes, my hands on the metal railing, still gritty from the soles of Dwight's dive boots.

The deputy ran up next to me, cursed, then called on his field unit for a helicopter, LCRA boats. He shone his light down into the darkness, but there was nothing except the glitter of the black water, a small, shimmering template of lake, that had swallowed Dwight Hayes whole.

MAIA LEE

Maia wasn't sure her napkin bandage would stay on in the water, but she didn't have time to re-dress the wound. She didn't want to think about the diagonal groove Dwight Hayes' bullet had carved across the sole of her foot, straight through her shoe, making it look as if she'd stepped awkwardly onto a red-hot metal bar.

She fumbled with the air tank—dragged it onto a table, backed up to it, tried to wrestle on the BC vest. The damn thing was not meant to go over a silk blouse. It was a man's extra large, kept slipping around her shoulders.

Calm down, she thought. *You've done worse. Remember Hawaii. You've done twenty feet.*

The small voice responded—the voice that always scolded her, always spoke Mandarin, the language in which she could not lie to herself. *Never in the dark. Never alone.*

She tugged at straps, Velcro that wouldn't go through the rings. It was an eternity before she had her equipment in place, and still she heard no sirens—only the wounded cursing of Armand in the corner. Matthew Peña had stopped making noise a long time ago.

She stood, feeling as if she'd just offered a piggyback ride to a ten-gallon jug of Evian. Lake water from the BC trickled out the purge valve, leaking into her clothes. She limped toward the railing, trying to keep the weight off the wad of napkins that passed for her left foot.

She heard a gunshot far up the hill toward the dam, and she thought, *Tres. Was Dwight armed? Shit.*

Momentarily she thought about trying to get to the truck, maybe finding a road up there, but she knew that was just her cowardice talking.

You never get away once you back down. The fear is always there, waiting for a rematch.

She managed to get her bad foot over the railing, then the other.

Only then did she remember to check the air gauge.

The tank registered just above the red—perhaps six minutes of air, perhaps less. *Thank you, Dwight Hayes.*

She found the regulator, slipped it in her mouth. The mask was too tight, but she didn't take time to loosen it. She breathed in that cold oxygen mixture, like dry ice vapor, scooted as close as she could to the exact location Vic Lopez had jumped, and she went over the side.

The cold stopped her breath. She'd never thought she would miss wearing a wet suit. Her wounded foot was the only part of her that felt warm, and *that* hurt like hell.

She kicked uselessly. Her head was still above water, and she realized she had no weights to compensate for the BC. She'd have to let all the air out of her vest, hope the steel of the tank was enough to sink her.

She groped for the inflator hose, pushed the button, let the air hiss out. The BC got looser, impossibly big on her. As she tugged at the straps, trying to correct the problem, she started to sink.

Underwater, there was a brief layer of dark brown light, like beef bouillon, and then complete black.

She felt herself starting to hyperventilate, her breathing turning to gasps. She tried to remember what to do. Exhale fully—get the air out, let the carbon dioxide kick in, make her body realize she needed a deeper inhale.

She counted, tried to do chi kung breathing. She told herself this was no different than above-water meditation, an idea that had almost worked for her in Hawaii. Almost. It was like standing up on a galloping horse—telling yourself it was no different than on steady ground.

She couldn't tell if she was still sinking.

She used her arms, swept them up. Finally, her right leg crumpled against something hard, pain flared, and her knee stopped her descent on what must've been a shelf of rock. She felt it with her hands—a mossy surface, furry and cold.

All right, she thought. *I'm at the bottom. Now what?*

She felt along the rock, completely blind. Nothing.

She moved down, toward a lower place—mud. She put her hands into the stuff and felt a soda can, a slimy branch, rocks.

What the hell was she doing? Which way was the shore?

She half crawled, half swam along the bottom.

Something brushed against her face; she flinched. Something nipped the top of her ear.

Fish, she told herself. *Just fish.*

She swept one hand in front of her in an arc, used the other to pull herself along.

And then she brushed neoprene—a gloved human hand. She lurched backward, almost lost the regulator out of her mouth. She clamped down hard with her teeth, forced herself back toward Lopez.

She felt his fingers again, his wrist, and pulled herself toward him.

She felt along his face for the regulator manifold, panicked for a moment until she felt the weak trickle of bubbles that marked his exhale. How could anyone breathe that slowly?

Now what? The weights. She'd never get him to the surface unless those came off. She started groping around his chest—feeling the cold squares of lead, looking for a catch. There seemed to be a million damn weights, and none of them seemed connected. Just when she'd found the first buckle, Lopez began to put his hands on her, feeling her as if she were a rock or a sculpture for the blind.

Men, Maia thought. *You'd better be drugged out of your mind, Detective.*

She loosened the first belt, got it off his chest, heard the underwater *plink plink* as it hit rock at the bottom. She started looking for the second catch when Lopez's hands groped up her shoulders and found her neck. He started to squeeze.

Maia pushed herself away, fought to control her panic.

She breathed several times very slowly, listening to the exhales explode around her.

All right. So now he's trying to kill me. He's weak. Ignore it.

She got next to him again, and again he started working his hands up her body toward her neck.

She founded the second catch, lost it, found it again. It was stuck on something—the strap of the air tank maybe. She tugged.

Lopez's fingers found her throat, started to choke her. His grip was light, palsied, but his thumbs still found her trachea, made her want to gag. She pushed his hands away, went back to work.

The second belt was off his chest. Now just the ones around his waist. These are supposed to be easy latches, she remembered, for quick removal. Yeah, right.

Lopez kept strangling her. She wrestled the third belt off, groped for the final one, tried not to gag.

She imagined her grandmother in China, learning the news of Maia's death—strangled underwater by a drugged man who was feeling her body. Drowned in the beer-can-polluted muck under an American restaurant. Maia tried to think how she could translate that into Mandarin and make it sound dignified—something that would save face for the family. She couldn't think of a way.

The last belt came loose.

She tugged at Lopez, trying to get him to move.

Then she realized it was no use. She would have to let the BC do the work.

Could she ascend straight up? She didn't know. Had no clue how deep she was. But then she felt her own air starting to thin—the first sign that she had a few breaths left at most. She had no choice. She wrapped one arm around Lopez's waist, used her other hand to hit the BC inflator and let it inflate all the way.

Suddenly she felt as if her whole chest was in one big blood-pressure tester. The vest tightened, expanded with a rush of sound, and she and Lopez were rising, too slowly.

Lopez's hand touched her regulator, yanked it out of her mouth.

She clenched her teeth—tried to find the backup one-handed. No luck.

She inhaled a mouthful of water just as she broke the surface, coughing up half the lake.

Her entire body was shaking. She kicked and paddled with her one free hand, cursing at Lopez.

Sirens everywhere. She was at the corner of the restaurant. There were smeary lights on the shore—blinking red and blue.

She yelled for help.

Then two men in uniforms were coming for her—paramedics, splashing into the water, wading out to meet her.

And when she collapsed on the shore, staring up at the stars, more men moved around her, pulling at her straps, trying to loosen her equipment, and she tried not to tremble.

She pushed back the sensations of the water—the cold brown light, the mossy shelves of rock, the hiss of her own breath through the regulator.

As the lump formed in her throat, she spoke to herself silently, thinking the words in Mandarin so that she might believe them: *They will not see me cry. They will not see me cry.*

CHAPTER 42

Mrs. Hayes was a mountain of grief—black slippers, black sweat pants, black T-shirt advertising a tent revival. Her face was pasty from weeping, the skin under her eyes as dark as apple bruises.

"Excuse us, children," she said.

The younger ones continued to throw blocks. The two older kids, Amanda and Clem, stabbed each other with Tinkertoy swords.

Mrs. Hayes looked over at Chris, who was sitting next to her on the couch. He was scowling, copying verses from a King James Bible onto a yellow legal pad.

"Chris?" she said. "Take the children in the other room, please. There's a video loaded."

Chris' face brightened. He shoved the Bible and pad aside and herded the troops into the living room, leaving me alone with Mrs. Hayes and the portrait of Jesus.

She studied me, gave me plenty of opportunity to see the misery in her eyes. "You have nerve coming here, Mr. Navarre. After the lies you've told about my boy."

"Your boy," I said.

She closed her eyes. Her lips trembled.

"I've told the police all I need to," she said. "Dwight was my son. I did nothing wrong."

"The police have already gotten a warrant to search your bank records. William B. Doebler, Sr., made a payment to you and your husband in 1967—$30,000—plus smaller payments over the next five years—1,000 here, 500 there. You probably told Doebler the baby that Clara was giving up would go to a good home. The Doeblers didn't care enough to check—as long as you made their problem go away. So the boy stayed right here. You and your husband raised him, collected the money."

"Dwight was not that child."

"The computer disk Dwight left, explaining why he killed. Among other things, he admitted he was Clara's child, talked about a private investigator who unwittingly handed him the information. Dwight also wrote about growing up in this house. Your husband was a strict disciplinarian—used to enjoy submerging children in the bathtub until they nearly drowned. And you let it happen."

Her eyes opened, focused on me steady and hot. I knew how Chris must've felt, the moment Mrs. Hayes assigned him those Bible verses. I knew how Clem had felt getting caught with Mrs. Hayes' wallet, how Dwight must have felt his entire life.

"You use children," I said. "You raised Dwight to become what he was, stood by while your husband punished him, taught him to believe in a God that drowns. When the Doeblers stopped making payments—maybe because you tried to blackmail them, maybe because they decided you'd bled them enough—you began raising Dwight to hate his birth family. You told him—stories. Poisoned him. You knew what he would do, someday. You let children steal for you, lie for you. When they grow up, they might even kill."

"I parent them," she said coldly. "These children *need* a real parent. They get nothing at home, if they have a home. They need what I give them. They needed what my husband gave them."

"Pain. Fear. Hate."

"They get what they need."

The curtains ballooned in with a limp breeze. In the den, *Star Wars* lasers blasted away.

"The last thing Dwight told me," I said. "He said he'd

left the most important thing undone. He loved and feared you as much as he hated you, Mrs. Hayes, and so he could only kill your reflection. The others died in your place."

Mrs. Hayes put her hand on her knee, scraped her fingernails against the black cotton of her sweat pants. "My son is dead. He *was* my son. I've told the police everything."

"And the others who have died?"

"It was God's will."

"No, Mrs. Hayes. No, no, no."

The front door opened. Maia Lee came in, walking stiffly from the orthopedic hard-shoe she now wore on her left foot. She was followed by two uniformed APD officers, then a business-suited woman named Reyes from Child Protective Services.

"Dwight's last request," I told Mrs. Hayes. "To shut you down. It's amazing how helpful CPS can be when you bring them documentation on an unlicensed day care, run by a woman who raised a psychopath."

In the next room, Reyes started talking with the children, explaining that she was here to help. Maia Lee came up next to me. One of the officers stood impassively by the door while the other came into the living room and dropped a search warrant on Mrs. Hayes' King James Bible, then a cease-and-desist order from the State Attorney's office.

"They'll want a statement, Mrs. Hayes," Maia said, her voice cold. "Mrs. Reyes will want these officers to escort you to her office."

Mrs. Hayes looked at Maia, then the officer, then me. She gave me a meager smile. "You're so sure of yourself, aren't you? You think you know what is right."

In the next room, Reyes was talking to the children— recording their names and ages, where they lived.

"It's over, Mrs. Hayes," I said. "You won't raise any more children."

"Ask the police, Tres. They're so intent on paperwork, bending the facts to fit, ask them to check his blood."

"Dwight's body hasn't been found, Mrs. Hayes."

"Yes," she agreed easily. "But that's not what I meant. And you don't understand that simple fact."

Then she rose and let the deputy lead her out. On the couch where she'd been sitting, the dent of her form was embedded in the cushions as deep as foot-valleys on cathedral steps.

Maia put her hand on my shoulder. "She's just trying to hurt you. Trying to shake you up."

I listened to the voices of the children in the other room. *Two weeks—Every night—She's mostly nice—Only sometimes she gets mad—Bible readings—And one time I stole something—She calls me son.*

"They'll be all right," Maia told me. "Reyes knows her work."

She started toward the door, but I couldn't move.

Dim light filtered through the windows of Mrs. Hayes' living room, but I felt I might as well have been back in Ruby McBride's pecan orchard, one hundred feet underwater; or at Jimmy Doebler's waterfront; or even at the train crossing near my father's house in Olmos Park. I realized, as Dwight must have realized, that the cold dark weight of those places was no different, no less horrible. It would be easy to lose one's strength to ascend. And then the will. And finally even the desire.

I stared at the shaggy green staircase that led to the second floor. Then, half in a trance, I walked upstairs.

"Tres?" Maia called.

I looked in the doorway of Dwight Hayes' room. His car magazines and books had been scattered on the floor, the football posters taken down, the boy-sized mattress overturned.

In the bathroom opposite the stairs, I flipped the light switch and saw only myself in the medicine cabinet mirror. I looked at the bathtub—a small porcelain model, nothing special. Chrome fixtures, a permanent grime ring, faded 1970s flower decals on the bottom. The drain was wet.

The walls of the bathroom were avocado tile from waist down, yam-colored wallpaper from the waist up. I imagined how high a small boy could reach, ran my hand along the wall. I hit the soft spot just in the middle of the right wall—an area no bigger than a doorknob, where the wallpaper felt like membrane.

I punched through, ripped away the edges. There was a layer of lighter-colored wallpaper underneath, and a dark void eaten into the wall behind.

I stared at it for a long time, until Maia came up behind me.

"What?" she asked.

I said, "A hole somebody never filled in."

CHAPTER 43

The rains had been good for Faye Doebler-Ingram's front garden. Patches of wild rosemary had shot up to four feet. The bees were going nuts around her red and white hibiscus. Whitebrush was blooming, permeating the air with a scent like Christmas trees.

Maia Lee picked a black-eyed Susan. I got the morning paper off the porch, shook the dew off the plastic sleeve.

For an abandoned house, Faye's place looked pretty lively. An old yellow Honda and a brown sedan were parked in the driveway. Light shone through the living room window, flickering from the blades of a ceiling fan. The screen door was latched, but I could smell coffee inside, baking cinnamon bread. The stereo was playing an acoustic instrumental.

We knocked on the screen door, got no answer, called hello. Still no reply.

Maia kindly offered her key chain knife, which I used to unlatch the door.

The living room was bright with morning sun. Pothos and ivy crowded the windows. I put the newspaper down on the sideboard.

A suitcase lay open and empty on the sofa. On the coffee table was the large brown binder Faye had shown Maia and me the week before.

Maia went to the stereo, checked out the case on the

CD player. She might've been waiting in a doctor's office, for all the anxiety she showed.

I sat next to the suitcase, opened the memory book. The picture of Ewin Lowry and Clara Doebler stared up at me—Clara smiling, her hand resting on the hood of the '65 Mustang as if it were a favorite horse. Ewin Lowry's smile was more devilish, his teeth perfectly white. Small build, dark skin—not really olive, as I'd speculated before, but the hue of cinnamon.

Something shattered.

I looked up. Faye Ingram was standing in her kitchen doorway, shards of a Jimmy Doebler coffee cup at her feet.

Her fingers were flaked with mud. She wiped them absently on her gardening apron, then touched her face as if to make sure her mascara and jewelry and penny-red hairdo were still in place.

"Mr. Navarre," she said. "Miss Lee. What are you doing in my house?"

"You haven't disappeared," Maia said. "I'm glad to see that."

Faye glanced behind her, into the kitchen. "I'm fine, thank you. I think you should leave."

"He's here," I said. "Isn't he?"

She knelt down, began picking up pieces of the cup, using her apron as a collection pouch. "I'm afraid—I'm not quite awake yet, Mr. Navarre. I haven't had my second cup of coffee, haven't had my thirty minutes in the garden. I'm afraid I'm not following you."

I slipped the picture of Ewin and Clara out of its plastic pocket. "The resemblance is there, isn't it, if you blend the two of them together? I just wasn't looking for the right connection."

"You shouldn't be here."

She stood, the pottery shards in her apron. Plucking up the ends of the fabric, she looked as if she were about to curtsy.

"Twenty-five years ago," I said. "You saved your sister's child."

"Please don't ask me this."

"Clara had her second son, but it was another battle she couldn't win against the family, wasn't it? They forced her to give the baby away. W.B.'s father made the arrangements—no paperwork, no embarrassment, just discreet payments to a family that would keep the secret and ask no questions as long as the money kept coming. The Doeblers either didn't know or didn't care what kind of operation the Hayeses were running—what kind of hell they inflicted on their charges. But you found out. You'd watched Clara unravel—you knew that she was unfit to take care of herself, much less a child, but you also knew her misery. You resented the family for what they'd done to her."

Faye pressed her lips tight, turned her face toward the doorjamb. "I never married, Tres, never had children. I saw how the family's expectations destroyed my sister—how she kept giving them more rope to strangle her with."

"But you found a way to save something of your sister. You found a way to have a family, too. By the time your nephew was six, it was clear to you what kind of monsters the Hayeses were. Their own son Dwight was being twisted, misshaped by an abusive father and a dangerously unstable mother. Your nephew was not faring much better. In one incident, he almost died. That decided you. You rescued the child, kidnapped him. You placed him in a home of *your* choosing, supported by *your* money, and you made sure he was treated well. He became your son more than Clara's, and as he grew, you were not about to tell your sister—to see the one good deed of your life be tainted by the Doeblers. They would find a way to interfere again. Clara would insist on raising the child, and she would screw it up, the way she'd screwed up everything in her life. The child was yours now. That's why the payments to the Hayeses stopped. Because the child was no longer there."

In the kitchen, a coffee machine gurgled and steamed as it let out the last of its water into the filter. Faye clutched her apron. One tear was making its way down her cheek. Her mascara streaked like a smear of ashes.

"He warned me. He said the best we could hope for was a few more quiet days. I so hoped—Oh, Tres. You don't understand. Until Clara's death, we had so many good years. Even after, when he was worried for my safety, when he was so busy guarding our lives and our secret that he could barely enjoy my company—even then, every day was a gift. I would give anything to protect him. Everything else failed to matter long ago."

I could barely speak. The unequivocal love in her voice was humbling. "We need to see him, Ms. Ingram."

She hesitated, then nodded, resigned to the inevitable. She led us through the kitchen and into the yard.

The grass was dappled with light through the oak tree. A new jar of sun tea glowed on the sidewalk. Another Jimmy Doebler coffee cup and two plates of cinnamon toast sat on the patio table.

He was working near the tomato cages, cutting dead sunflower stalks with a machete. Nearby on the grass, a flat of lantana waited, ready to be planted in the sunflowers' place.

He wore swim trunks, flip-flops, a plain white T-shirt smeared with dirt and sweat and plant pigments. When he turned, expecting to see only Faye, his face was the most content I'd ever seen it—calm, happy, at peace with his morning's work.

Then his expression went absolutely blank.

"Hello, Vic," I said.

Vic Lopez raised his machete hand, used the back of his glove to wipe a sweat droplet off his chin. He studied us, the blade of the machete hovering over his left shoulder like an insect wing.

"Navarre. Maia. I was just giving Ms. Ingram a hand. Amazing the things you can do once you quit the day job."

"He knows," Faye told him.

Lopez met her eyes, had a silent conversation, looked back at us.

"Dwight's revenge," I said. "It wasn't against his family—it was against yours."

Faye moved to the patio table, sank into one of the chairs. She began putting the shards of the broken cup on the table.

"You're the friend Dwight lost," I said. "You were snatched out of the Hayes house when you and he were only six. You were rescued, and Dwight was left behind. He never forgot."

Lopez lowered his machete.

"I didn't know," he said. "Until very recently, I didn't understand who was doing the killing. I was too young when I—when I got free of that place. Thankfully, I don't remember much. The name Hayes meant nothing to me. He was just another interviewee."

Faye said, "He never told me about Dwight. If he had, perhaps I would've made the connection. But perhaps not . . . it was so long ago. It was something we put behind us."

"But it shaped Dwight's life," I said. "*He* never forgot. You were his personal quest, Vic. He resented you, hated you, but somewhere in the back of his mind he also loved you, identified with you the way he identified with Matthew Peña. Dwight thought he *was* you. He wanted to do for you what he wished someone could do for him— kill the family who had let him down."

Lopez turned the blade of his machete, watching it reflect the sunlight. "I never knew my father."

"Ewin Lowry was Hispanic," I said. "That was part of the reason the Doebler family didn't want him around. His name—"

"Was changed to something nice and Anglo when he was young," Lopez interrupted. "His surname was originally Lopez, which is the name Faye decided to give back to me. That's really all I know about him. When Dwight found Lowry in Waco, he killed a man who meant nothing to me. Clara—my mother—that was different, but mostly her death hurt me because she was Faye's sister, because I watched her die. I don't mean to be cold, Navarre, but you've got to understand—Faye has always been my mother. I never knew Clara well, or any of the other

Doeblers. I never wanted to. I know now that Dwight meant for me to be there the night he killed Clara."

"He'd studied you, knew your patrol schedule. You realized Clara's death was more than a suicide. You went into homicide because of what you saw that night."

"I knew there was something wrong."

"And after Jimmy was murdered—"

"I went off in completely the wrong direction—exactly the way Dwight wanted me to go. It's only when Ruby died, when I realized the connection to Ewin Lowry—it did look like Clara's son might be involved. But *I* was Clara's son. I thought maybe Peña was responsible, playing mind games with *me*. I didn't know what to believe." He gestured at Faye. "I insisted that Faye leave town for a while, until I could figure things out."

"Dwight's plan," I said. "Those unsigned files on the disk. He wasn't claiming to be Clara's son; he was leaving that as *your* suicide note. He meant to get away, leave you the blame—a dead man at the bottom of the lake, killing yourself the same way you'd killed your victims, your family."

"Except Maia saved me."

Maia said nothing—exactly what she'd said about her trip underwater for the past three days.

Victor tugged off his leather gardening gloves, threw them on the dirt. "So what now?"

Faye had arranged the pieces of broken cup into a line, the same way she'd done with the poisonous coral beans on my last visit. I wondered if Faye always tried to organize things into straight lines.

"No one will charge you with a crime," Maia said. "The police can't fire you for misrepresenting your identity if you've already quit. But the tabloids will have a field day. It's only a matter of time before the reporters find out the truth."

Vic nodded. "When it happens I'll deal with that. Until then, I plan on spending my time here."

The summer heat had started to burn through the morning.

Soon the garden would be a hundred degrees, fit only for cicadas and dragonflies and herbs. But I could picture Faye and Victor out here again this evening—drinking freshly brewed sun tea, enjoying the catmint and sage that had infused the air during the afternoon, watching the blue glow of the moonlight tower take over from the sunset.

Like all Texans, they had learned to make the most of the edges of the day.

"There is a lot I regret," Lopez said. "But the important things had to survive. Do you understand?"

I told him I did. I shook his hand and said good-bye.

But as we left him to his gardening, as we accepted Faye Doebler-Ingram's hugs and then headed back into her house, I wasn't at ease with my own jealousy.

Faye and Victor had salvaged a family from the ruins of a clan.

Maia laced her fingers in mine.

I looked at her.

Something about her smile made it easier to go down the front porch steps.

CHAPTER 44

I was spoiling the guys in English 301. This was the second time in two weeks I'd brought Maia Lee to class.

All through my lecture on Coleridge, the flip-flop dudes checked her out.

I thought about ways to recapture their interest—maybe get a dead bird and a rope and use Father Time as a visual aid for the Ancient Mariner. But in the end, I decided just to let them be distracted. They had a test next week. I had a red pen.

At the end of class, the students filed out. Maia Lee stepped down from the back of the room.

"All right," she said. "I must admit you do this rather well. I haven't fallen asleep either time."

She'd succumbed to the Texas summer—abandoning her business attire in favor of walking shorts, tank top, sandals. Her hair fell loose around her shoulders.

"The teaching career that might have been," I lamented. "Had I not been stolen out of the warm bosom of Academia by a certain lawyer."

"You were in the warm bosom of a bartending job," Maia reminded me.

"Technicalities."

"You ready?" she asked.

"Do I have to be?"

She held my eyes.

"Yeah," I said. "I suppose I'm ready."

We walked across campus together—under the shadow of the clock tower, through the South Mall. The distribution boxes for the *Daily Texan* and the *Austin Chronicle* had been filled with new issues, both carrying lead stories about the family scandal that had recently rocked Doebler Oil—the discovery of an heir the family had shuffled aside, apparently because they didn't like his Latino father. The *Chronicle*'s cover featured a huge close-cropped photo of W.B. Doebler's face, with the title: "Oil or Slime?" I promised myself I'd stop by the Met Club later, get W.B. to autograph a copy for me.

Maia and I walked down the red granite steps that rounded the side of the Poseidon fountain.

Matthew Peña was waiting for us at the bottom.

He was in a wheelchair, his lower half swathed in a crinkly black blanket. His face looked sunburned, as if he'd fallen asleep under a heat lamp. His mustache and goatee had started to spread into a full beard. It looked like he'd actually gained weight from his week in the hospital.

Behind him, at the curb, a milky green Lexus was idling. A young Asian chauffeur was talking into a cell phone.

Matthew and I shook hands unenthusiastically. Then Maia offered hers and Matthew clasped it. Maia sat on the granite lip of the fountain, her knees a few inches from the wheels of Peña's chair.

"I leave at one o'clock," Matthew said. "You have an answer for me?"

"The doctor give you a prognosis?" Maia asked.

Peña rubbed his fingers against the chrome of his armrests. "Does it matter for your decision?"

"No."

"Then it's too soon to tell. I still have no feeling in my right leg. This morning I had a slight tingle in my left. The doctors say that's a good sign, but they don't know. I'll start physical therapy as soon as I get back."

He did a pretty good job suppressing the fear in his voice.

"Encouraging," Maia said. "But my answer is no, Matthew. I can't work for you."

His face paled in a slow wash, like wet sand around a footprint. "I have leverage with Ron Terrence. If you won't work for me directly, I can get you your old job back."

"No, Matthew. Thank you."

"You could do very well as my lawyer. You could make millions in a very short time."

"Yes, I could. The answer is still no."

He nodded. "I thought as much."

"Good luck, though, Matthew. I wish you well."

He pursed his lips. "I'm sure you do."

Across 24th Street, the church bells of University Christian started clanging. A line of startled pigeons rose in a blue-gray arc, only to settle again half a block down by the eggroll vendor.

Peña gave me a sour smile. "This must be satisfying, Navarre—seeing me in a chair. Hearing Maia tell me no."

"Not at all."

"I should apologize to you. Part of me wants to. Unfortunately, most of me wants you to rot in hell."

"That's okay," I said. "I'm not sure which part of you I like better."

He looked satisfied with that reply.

Next to us, water cascaded down the front of Poseidon's patinaed team of horses. Across the street, the doors of the church opened and wedding-goers in tuxedos and dresses poured out. I realized it was the third wedding I'd seen since coming to Austin. And then I remembered it was June. This was supposed to be a month for weddings.

People threw rice. The bride and groom looked so young I felt like I must've missed an entire generation of people getting married.

A shaving-cream-decorated limo pulled up, and Matthew's driver looked across the street with distaste. Probably done his share of wedding gigs. Probably was a whole lot easier driving around one bitter paraplegic in a wheelchair. He called, "Mr. Peña? Plane time."

Peña stared at me. "Don't screw up with Maia twice, Navarre. You understand me? Every other insult I can live with, even being in this chair, but I could not live with that."

The water kept galooshing into the pool. The wedding couple got into their limo and drove off in a blizzard of rice and displaced pigeons. Matthew Peña turned and wheeled himself toward the Lexus. The driver helped him from the chair to the backseat, folded the chair, put it in the trunk. The last I saw of Matthew, he was staring at me with those cold dead eyes, giving me a warning. Then the black glass shut on him like a microwave door.

Maia pressed her fingertips together. Sprinkles of water from the fountain were freckling her blouse.

"You okay?" I asked.

She looked at me, managed a smile. "Just hoping he gets better."

"The scary thing is, he probably will."

And then we heard the rumble of motorcycles, looked toward Guadalupe and saw six Harley hogs coming up 24th, disrupting the wedding guests and pigeons alike.

Armand was riding left flank, his shoulder heavily padded but apparently not affecting his biking ability. Four other black leather warriors fanned out to his right, all of them overweight and slightly grizzled. The Metamucil Diablos.

Clyde Simms rode lead, his bike fixed with a brand-new flame-emblazoned sidecar in which my brother Garrett rode like some World War II general.

He had dark shades on, his rainbow shirt, his leather helmet straps flapping loosely around his beard.

"Hey!" he yelled. "Knew if we circled the campus enough times we'd catch you!"

He gave me that crooked piranha grin I hadn't seen in a long time.

The bikes pulled over. I shook hands with Clyde, Armand, got introductions with the others. Maia gave Garrett a kiss.

"Off to see the lizard?" Maia asked.

"Man," Garrett said, "I have never appreciated freedom so much. We are *off,* and we ain't stopping for anything but concerts and liquor till we hit Key West. You sure you don't want to ditch your real lives and come along?"

Maia and I smiled, shook our heads, though I thought—maybe—Maia was a little tempted.

"Speaking of real life . . ." I said.

"Hey, man. The check cleared. A little negotiating with Peña, he was able to see his way clear to a cash payment in exchange for dropping a lawsuit. He's already in enough trouble with the SEC."

Garrett's work with the High Tech Unit had indeed managed to trace the leaked security files to Peña's computer. In fact, the High Tech guys had been sufficiently impressed with Garrett's work to offer him some contract gigs.

"You going to be working law enforcement?" I asked. "What would Dad say about that?"

Garrett shrugged. "I got time to think about that now. Oh, and by the way, I got something for you."

He dug a manila folder out of his seat, tossed it to me. "Maybe I caught the Christmas spirit. Ruby's will—she left the whole damn marina to Clyde, did you know that? We damn near had to peel him off the ceiling when he heard. I figured Ruby was good enough to do that, I'd better make her proud of me."

I looked at the documents inside the folder, saw Lars Elder's name, First Bank of Sabinal. I saw yellow highlighted places, red Xs where I was supposed to sign.

I looked at Garrett. He was grinning.

"Garrett," I said. "This isn't right."

"Just sign that puppy, Tres. Make it official. I'm giving the ranch to you."

"This isn't what Dad wanted."

Garrett laughed. "Come here, ugly."

I took his hand and he pulled me into a sloppy hug, then pushed me back with equal force. "It's what *I* want."

I looked at Maia. She was smiling like she'd known this was coming.

Garrett told her, "Try to keep him from getting shot while I'm gone, okay?"

Maia said, "No promises. Take care of yourself, Garrett."

Clyde Simms said, "Concert in Houston ain't going to wait, man."

Garrett put down his shades, gave the thumbs-up, and the caravan moved out in a roar of exhaust and black leather and tie-dye.

Maia looked at me, looked at the deed, and had to laugh.

Then she kissed me, and everything went digital—sound, color, all of it super-real.

She pulled away, said, "What if I told you I was staying in Austin for a while?"

I tried to concentrate on the man selling eggrolls across the street. His vending cart, at least, I could think about without raising my blood pressure.

"Are you telling me that?"

She pushed a strand of hair behind her ear. "I need to get some things out of my system. I was thinking a few months of extreme heat might do the trick."

"Really. What things out of your system?"

She looked straight at me. "Mostly you, Tres. I don't know if I've quite gotten you out of my system, you bastard."

The wedding guests had all drifted away. Students walked around us, the water fountain churned, the eggrolls' smell wafted across the street.

Maia's smile made me remember a night in Berkeley a dozen years ago, when she'd left her business card on the bar next to the last round of margaritas I'd ever mixed for money.

"I have some calls to make," she said, "some apartments to look at. See you tonight?"

And as I watched her walk away down 24th, I thought

what I'd thought so many years ago in Berkeley—that this was a woman who would either change my life or get me killed.

"Come on, tonight," I murmured hopefully. Then I went to talk to the vendor across the street. His eggrolls smelled awfully good.

ABOUT THE AUTHOR

RICK RIORDAN is the author of three previous Tres Navarre novels—*Big Red Tequila,* winner of the Shamus and Anthony Awards; *The Widower's Two-Step,* winner of the Edgar Award; and *The Last King of Texas.* A middle-school English teacher by day, Riordan lives with his wife and family in San Antonio, Texas, where he is at work on his fifth novel of suspense.

Visit his website at rickriordan.com

If you enjoyed Rick Riordan's
THE DEVIL WENT DOWN TO AUSTIN,
you won't want to miss any of his novels!

Look for

BIG RED TEQUILA
THE WIDOWER'S TWO-STEP
THE LAST KING OF TEXAS
COLD SPRINGS
and
SOUTHTOWN
coming soon in hardcover

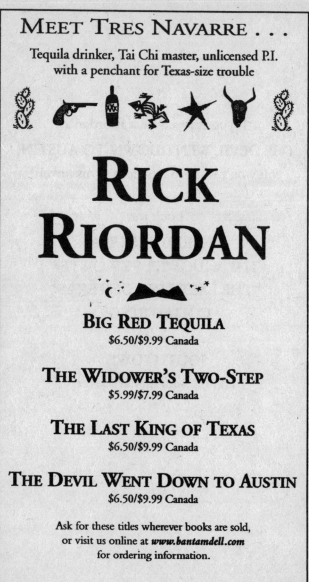